LESS THAN DEAD

OTHER NOVELS BY TIM DOWNS

First the Dead
Head Game
Plague Maker
Chop Shop
Shoofly Pie

LESS
THAN
DEAD

TIM DOWNS

THOMAS NELSON
Since 1798

NASHVILLE DALLAS MEXICO CITY RIO DE JANEIRO BEIJING

Published in Nashville, Tennessee, by Thomas Nelson. Thomas Nelson is a registered trademark of Thomas Nelson, Inc.

Author is represented by the literary agency of Alive Communications, Inc., 7680 Goddard Street, Suite 200, Colorado Springs, CO 80920, www.alivecommunications.com.

Thomas Nelson books may be purchased in bulk for educational, business, fund-raising, or sales promotional use. For information, please e-mail SpecialMarkets@ThomasNelson.com.

Publisher's Note: This novel is a work of fiction. Names, characters, places, and incidents are either products of the author's imagination or used fictitiously. All characters are fictional, and any similarity to people living or dead is purely coincidental.

Scripture quotations are taken from the *Holy Bible*, New Living Translation, © 1996, 2004. Used by permission of Tyndale House Publishers, Inc., Wheaton, Illinois 60189. All rights reserved.

ISBN 978-1-59554-577-0 (trade paper)

Library of Congress Cataloging-in-Publication Data

Downs, Tim.
    Less than dead / Tim Downs.
      p. cm.
    ISBN 978-1-59554-307-3 (hardcover)
    1. Polchak, Nick (Fictitious character)—Fiction. 2. Forensic entomology—Fiction. 3. Entomologists—Fiction. 4. Murder—Investigation—Fiction. 5. Virginia—Fiction. I. Title.
    PS3604.O954L47 2008
    813'.6—dc22

2008019840

Printed in the United States of America
09 10 11 12 13 RRD 6 5 4 3 2 1

For my beautiful Joy,
My sunrise, my sunset, my shining light each day

When Saul saw the vast Philistine army, he became frantic with fear. He asked the Lord what he should do, but the Lord refused to answer him, either by dreams or by sacred lots or by the prophets. Saul then said to his advisers, "Find a woman who is a medium, so I can go and ask her what to do."

His advisers replied, "There is a medium at Endor." (1 Samuel 28:5–7)

1

The sheriff looked out over the crowded backyard. People were frantically searching everywhere: sheriff's deputies, crime scene technicians, even file clerks and secretaries from the Warren County Sheriff's Department whose hearts had been touched by the news. Everyone wanted to help: friends, neighbors, church members, even total strangers from as far away as Front Royal who had heard about the missing three-year-old boy and had driven over to lend a hand with the search.

But there was no sign of the boy anywhere.

It was late now, well after midnight, and the sheriff was privately beginning to lose hope. He kept up a bold front for the sake of the frantic mother, but he had worked kidnappings and child abductions before, and he knew that the first twenty-four hours were critical. Unfortunately, this was the second day of the search, and the boy's odds of survival were diminishing fast.

"Is there anything new you can tell me? Anything at all?"

The sheriff turned to the woman; her face was contorted by fear and exhaustion, and her panic-stricken eyes stared up at him from sunken gray pools. "I told you I'd tell you the minute we know anything."

"That was an hour ago."

"That was ten minutes ago. We'll find your boy, Mrs. Coleman—it just takes time."

"It seems to be taking longer than it should."

"Not at all," the sheriff lied. "Look at all these people pitching in—if your boy's anywhere around here, they'll find him."

"What if he's not around here? Has Mark told you anything else?"

"I'm afraid your husband has decided not to cooperate."

"Maybe I should try talking to him again."

"I don't think that will help, and it'll only make you feel worse. Right now you need to keep your hopes up and let us do our work. I'll keep you posted—I promise."

"Then I'll help search."

"You'll only slow us down, Mrs. Coleman—people keep stopping to take care of you instead of searching. If you want something to do, go back and pitch in at the refreshment table."

"That's a good idea," she mumbled. "Everyone's working so hard—they'll be hungry . . ." Her voice trailed off as she turned away.

Just then a sheriff's deputy approached and nodded a greeting.

"Where have you been, Elgin?" the sheriff asked. "You've been gone for hours."

"I went to find her, just like you told me. She lives way up on top of the mountain above Endor, y'know—thought I'd like to never find her."

"Well, did you?"

"Eventually. It's like a prison up there—she's got the whole place surrounded by a chain-link fence and she keeps the gate chained shut. She don't have no phone—I had to just sit there and lay on the horn until she finally came to the gate. Any news here?"

"Nothing. We've looked everywhere we can think of."

"The crawl space?"

"Checked it twice. Checked the attic too, but he wasn't there, thank the Lord—the boy wouldn't have lasted an hour up there in this heat. I had the city engineers bring maps of all the storm drains and culverts—nothing. We searched the woods over there—been over it twice, but we're looking again. A bunch of the neighbors walked that cornfield hand in hand but they didn't find him there. Did you fetch her down?"

"She wouldn't come with me—insisted on drivin' herself. Creepiest thing I ever saw, Gus; I'm layin' on the horn and three big dogs come walkin' up to the gate. Biggest mutts I ever saw—they just stood there and looked me over—I swear I thought they were black bears at first. Then the woman comes walkin' up nice and slow, wearin' a long white robe with her black hair hangin' all around. And there's another dog walkin' beside her—a mangy old gray mongrel—and the thing's only got three legs. Three legs! What about the husband—has he said anything more?"

"Nothing. He took the boy, no doubt about it—but he's not about to tell us where he put him."

"Just to spite his ex-wife?"

"He's got a knife in her heart and he's just gonna twist it—a woman he used to be married to. We've tried all we can—threatened him with everything from hell to high water, but he's not talking. The fool's willing to let his own boy die just to cause the woman pain. You know, people can be mean as snakes sometimes. You say she wouldn't come with you—but she is coming, right?"

"She's already here. Get this, Gus: She walks right up to the gate and looks at me with one eye—then she snaps her fingers like this and all four dogs sit down at the same time. Never said a word to 'em—it's like the dogs could read her mind. I don't mind tellin' you, it made my skin crawl."

The sheriff shook his head. "She's as weird as her old man was."

"I don't mind 'weird'—hey, *I'm* weird—but this is somethin' else. Know what she said to me? 'Who dares to invade my privacy?' I'm tellin' you, Gus, it's true what people say about her: The woman is a witch."

"I don't care if she's the Ghost of Christmas Past, as long as she can help us find that boy. Where is she now?"

"Right over there—you can't miss her."

The sheriff looked; standing on a small berm at the far edge of the property was a woman in her midtwenties dressed in a flowing white gown. Her hair was long and straight, and she kept her head down so that the hair hung in front of her face. Beside her was a dog: mottled gray, lean and angular—and it had only three legs. Standing atop the berm, the two of them were almost silhouetted against the new moon—and the sheriff had to admit, the image was definitely eerie.

3

He walked over to her. She did not look up as he approached.

"Are you Alena Savard?" he asked.

The woman cocked her head to one side and slowly raised it until her hair parted slightly, exposing a pale sliver of flesh and one emerald eye that glared up at the sheriff. "I am."

"Can you help us, Ms. Savard?"

"What is it you require?"

"We've got a missing boy here, about three years old. It's a domestic dispute. There was an ugly divorce and a custody battle, and the husband lost. First he threatened to take the boy away, then he threatened to harm him—it looks like he might have done both."

"Why didn't you stop him?"

"Because you can't arrest a man for a crime he hasn't committed yet. I don't like it either, but that's the law. The wife got a restraining order, but it didn't much matter—a man who's willing to let his own boy die won't be stopped by a piece of paper."

"You people," she said. "My dogs are more human than you."

"Right now I'm inclined to agree with you. We've got the husband in custody, but he refuses to talk to us; the boy's been missing for almost two days now, and we're hoping we can find him before—"

"I find the dead."

"Well, we're hoping he's still alive."

"I find the dead—only the dead."

"Keep your voice down, will you? The mother is right over there, and she's about out of her mind already."

"Why did you send for me?"

"I've heard about your father—I thought maybe you could help."

"If the boy is alive, I'll be of no use to you. You think the boy is dead, or you wouldn't have sent for me."

"I think he *might* be dead—it's an option we have to consider. We need to know if we should keep looking, and you might be able to tell us. Will you help?"

Alena paused. "I will help—under the following conditions: No one is to speak to me or come near; the moment I finish I will leave—I will answer no further questions; and if anyone attempts to approach my dog in any way I will leave immediately. Do you agree to these conditions?"

"Agreed. What do you need me to do?"

"Nothing. Just leave me alone."

"One thing," the sheriff said. "That woman over there is the boy's mother. Try to stay clear of her; it's best if she doesn't know you're here."

He walked back to the house and turned to watch.

The woman seemed to do nothing at first—then she slowly raised both arms and looked up into the night sky. She lowered her head again and swung it slowly from side to side, as if she were mopping a table with her long black hair. She shook both arms loosely, like a pitcher limbering up, then began to walk around in small circles.

Everyone in the yard stopped and stared.

She knelt down in front of her dog and took a brightly colored bandanna from around her neck. She showed it to the dog as if she were asking for its approval; then she slipped the bandanna around the dog's neck and straightened it.

The entire yard fell silent.

She stood up again and snapped her fingers; the dog immediately circled her once and sat down at her side. She snapped her fingers a second time and made a tossing motion with her right hand; the dog jumped to its feet and began to zigzag across the yard with its nose quivering just above the ground.

The mother approached the sheriff from behind and tugged on his sleeve. "Who is that woman?" she asked.

"Never you mind," the sheriff said. "She's here to help us find your boy."

"How can she help?"

"We can use all the help we can get right now, Mrs. Coleman."

"But—what is she doing? It looks so strange."

"I don't know, exactly."

"You already tried a search-and-rescue dog—it couldn't find him."

"This is a different kind of dog. We're hoping it'll have better luck."

The dog quickly worked its way across the berm and around the backyard with the woman following close behind; she made no eye contact with anyone as they worked, and the other volunteers all nervously stepped back and gave them a wide berth wherever they turned.

When they reached the edge of the woods the dog suddenly stopped; it swung its head back and forth over an area no larger than a frying pan—and then it lay down. The woman knelt down in front of the dog and looked into its eyes; she made a shrugging motion and looked again. The dog just lay still and stared up at her.

The woman stood up and looked across the yard at the sheriff. She pointed to the ground near the trunk of an old beech tree.

The mother grabbed the sheriff's arm. "Why is she doing that? Why is she pointing at the ground?"

The sheriff didn't answer.

"What does that mean? Tell me!"

"Keep her here," the sheriff said to Elgin, then started toward the woman and the dog.

He called out to Alena as he approached. "Are you sure?"

She nodded.

The sheriff tested the spot with the toe of his shoe; the soil was loose. He turned to one of his deputies and called back, "Bring me a shovel."

The mother let out a shriek and twisted out of Elgin's hands.

Alena knelt down in front of her dog again and flashed it a beaming grin, then rolled onto her back as the two of them began to wrestle together in the grass.

The mother ran to the beech tree and threw herself in front of it. "It's not him!" she shouted. "He isn't dead!"

"We'll know in a minute," the sheriff said, readying the shovel above the ground—but the mother grabbed the handle with both hands and stopped him.

"Don't!" she screamed. "If you find him here, they'll stop looking for him!"

"Mrs. Coleman—please."

The mother released the shovel and turned on Alena. "Who are you?" she demanded.

Alena scrambled awkwardly to her feet.

"Who told you to come here anyway? I didn't ask you to! I don't want you here!"

Alena lowered her head until her black hair covered her eyes.

"I know who you are—you're the witch, come to take my boy! He was alive until you came here! He was—"

Her voice failed midsentence, and she collapsed to the ground sobbing.

Alena turned without a word and hurried away.

Northern Virginia, June 2008

Donovan approached the fluttering yellow crime scene tape and held up his FBI credentials to the officer, a sheriff's deputy from the Warren County Sheriff's Department. The deputy took the leather folder from his hand and began to read it carefully.

"We don't get many of you FBI fellas out here in Warren County," the deputy said.

"No kidding." Donovan took his credentials from the deputy's hand, and the man flashed a disappointed look, as though Donovan had taken away a book before he had finished reading it.

"My name's Elgin Tate," he said, and then added almost as an afterthought, "*Deputy* Elgin Tate." He grinned and extended his hand and Donovan took it.

"Special Agent Nathan Donovan."

The deputy let out a low, "Hoooo-ee!"

Donovan pointed to the tape. "Mind if I come in and take a look around?"

"Why ask me?"

"Weren't you guys the first ones on the scene?"

"Yes, sir. We got the call from the medical examiner's office yesterday afternoon."

"Then this is your crime scene, Deputy—you've got jurisdiction here, and I can't enter the crime scene until you give me permission."

The deputy took on a look of renewed importance. "Come right on in, Mr. Donovan."

Donovan swung one leg over the tape just as the deputy hoisted it high overhead and held it there. Donovan turned and looked at him. "I already flossed this morning."

"Sorry." The deputy released the tape and took a step back.

"Thank you."

"Gonna be a hot one," the deputy observed.

"It's getting there."

"Too hot for June. Too hot for this time of morning."

"Right on both counts."

"They tell me you boys are gonna be in charge here."

"That depends on what we find. Where are these graves?"

"Right over there."

Donovan looked across the field but saw nothing. Until a month ago this area of rural Virginia had been thick virgin woodland—but now the area had been scraped clean for two hundred yards on all sides, leaving nothing but featureless brown loam littered with gray-green rock as far as the eye could see. Masses of bulldozed trees lay in twisted piles, awaiting an endless caravan of trucks that would haul them off to paper mills farther to the south; red flags fluttered atop pillars of soil that stood like castle parapets, marking the level of the original surface before excavation had begun.

"Want me to show you?" the deputy offered.

"Just point. If you don't mind, I like to get my own first impressions."

Fifty yards ahead Donovan came to a ridge where four rectangular holes lay side by side in the earth, each just a few yards from the next. There were no headstones, but a crude wooden cross made of two-by-fours had been hammered into the ground to mark the head of each grave. The land around the crosses had not yet been disturbed by the excavators and bulldozers, but at the foot of each grave the ground suddenly dropped off, forming a short vertical cliff that exposed the end of each grave as if a four-toothed giant had taken a bite from the hillside.

Donovan could see at a glance what had happened: Some hapless construction worker had sunk the teeth of his backhoe into the rocky Virginia hillside, unaware that he was about to discover the location of a long-forgotten graveyard. It was a fairly common occurrence these days, especially in areas like rural Virginia where people had been living and dying for four hundred years. Survivors moved westward, towns expanded in unpredictable directions, and old graveyards like this one were gradually covered over and forgotten, awaiting the day—sometimes centuries later—when some unfortunate builder would stick a shovel in the ground and find a skull staring back at him. It was just bad luck, that's all, hard on the nerves and even harder on the checkbook—because every time it happened, the builder was required by law to stop construction until every single grave was identified and carefully moved to a new location. Heaven help you if the graveyard turned out to be sizable, and even heaven couldn't help you if somebody famous turned out to be buried there—because then the historic preservation people got involved, and that's when things really got expensive.

But that's the law, Donovan thought, and it didn't matter to the law whether your intended building project was just a new backyard septic tank or a project the size of this one—a thousand-acre super-regional mall and entertainment complex that would eventually include hotels, a water park, office condominiums, and a million and a half square feet of prime retail space predicted to attract "destination shoppers" from everywhere east of the Mississippi.

It doesn't matter who you are either—whether you're just a lowly Virginia homeowner with backed-up toilets or the guy who's bankrolling this place—a man who, just five months from now, would probably become the next president of the United States. The law doesn't care; no matter who you are or what you're building, you're going to stop everything until those graves are relocated, no matter how long it takes and no matter what it costs—and you're going to pick up the check.

But that's not why Donovan was there; the FBI wasn't in the grave relocation business. There was something different about this graveyard. The construction workers here had found something else—something much more serious.

He approached the first grave and carefully placed one foot beside the opening, easing his 220-pound frame forward to make sure the edge would support his weight without crumbling. He leaned over the opening and peered down.

There, at the bottom, was the body of Nick Polchak.

Donovan cocked his head to the left to view the body right side up. Nick was dressed the way he always was, the only way Donovan had ever seen him—in baggy cargo shorts that always exaggerated the leanness of his long legs. He wore a collared short-sleeved shirt that looked as if he had selected it blindfolded from a rack at Goodwill— which he might very well have done. The shirt draped away from his body like a cape, and underneath it he wore a gray Penn State T-shirt; the top of the logo was just visible above his large hands, which were folded across his chest with the fingers interlocked, causing his knuckles to blanch like knots in a rope. His feet were shoved sockless into a pair of well-worn Nikes, and his legs were incongruously crossed at the ankles as if he were lounging on a beach chair instead of lying at the bottom of a grave.

Donovan looked at his face. There they were, as always—Nick's enormous spectacles. Without those glasses Nick was legally blind, but with them he possessed extraordinary close-up vision, almost as if he had two microscopes straddling his nose—a valuable asset for a man who had spent his life studying the microscopic features of blowflies and maggots. After all these years the glasses had become a permanent fixture of his face; Donovan had sometimes wondered if he would even recognize Nick without them.

But Nick's face looked different this time; this time his eyes were closed—something Donovan had never seen before. His huge brown eyes no longer floated like two chestnuts, distorted and magnified by the thick lenses. His eyes were closed now, and the lenses looked like a pair of empty TV screens.

Donovan shook his head. "I knew I'd find you like this someday. It was only a matter of time."

He bent down and picked up a pebble from the ground. He held it out over the open grave, aimed carefully, and released it. It bounced off the center of Nick's forehead.

Two soft brown orbs suddenly blinked open. "Hey, watch it—you could kill a guy that way."

"What are you doing down there?"

"I was taking a nap—until somebody tried to bury me."

"You were taking a nap in a grave?"

"It's the coolest place I could find. It was empty—nobody was using it."

"I'm not paying you to take naps," Donovan said.

Nick's eyes widened. "You're *paying* me this time? Maybe I am dead."

"It was just an expression."

"I figured."

Nick climbed to his feet and began to dust himself off. The grave was shallow, no more than three feet deep, and the lip of the opening was even with Nick's waist. He extended his hand up to Donovan, who braced himself and hoisted Nick out of the hole with a single powerful tug. The two men stood face-to-face now; Nick was slightly taller than Donovan, but the FBI agent outweighed him by at least thirty pounds.

Donovan looked at Nick's face and smiled.

Nick shook his head. "You do that every time, you know."

"Do what?"

"Grin like a gargoyle the first time you look at my glasses."

"It's either that or scream and run."

"Look who's talking. I have to look at you *through* these glasses."

Donovan glanced down at Nick's legs. "Man, don't you *ever* get any sun?"

"I'm a college professor," Nick said, "not a field agent with the Federal Bureau of I-travel-to-exotic-hot-spots-and-save-the-world."

"Is that my job? I wish somebody had told me."

"How's Macy doing?"

"She's good, Nick. She's pregnant—did I tell you?"

Nick paused. "Is that a good thing?"

"It's the best."

"Then I'm happy for you both. Tell Macy that for me—and tell her I'm still available if she ever decides to stop polluting the gene pool through inferior mate selection."

"Yeah, I'll be sure and tell her that. When did you get up here?"

"About an hour ago. I drove up from NC State this morning."

"Just in time for your afternoon nap."

"An FBI agent told me he'd be here to meet me. Like most government officials, he lied."

"Then you got my message."

"You were lucky. We're in summer sessions right now—I don't have any classes."

"Would it have mattered?"

"No—but I like to play hard to get."

"Any trouble finding the place?"

"It's hard to miss."

"Have you had a look around yet?"

Nick motioned for Donovan to follow him; he led him around to the bottom of the ridge where the foot of each grave lay exposed like a row of open ovens. "It's pretty obvious what happened," he said.

"Tell me."

"The builders were excavating this hillside—you can tell from the surveyor's markers that this entire area is scheduled to be removed. They brought in a thirty-ton Komatsu excavator with a backhoe attached to the front."

"How do you know that?"

Nick pointed over his shoulder, and Donovan turned and looked: Twenty yards behind them sat a thirty-ton Komatsu excavator with a backhoe attached to the front.

"Are you sure you're an FBI agent?" Nick asked.

"Keep going."

"The bucket of the backhoe looks about three feet wide. I figure the operator made about six passes through the hillside before he finally noticed something; by that time he had exposed the ends of these four graves. He probably figured there might be more, so he stopped." Nick pointed to the openings and traced an imaginary line from left to right. "You can see that the caskets are buried at varying depths—that's typical of an older graveyard. I'd say the average depth is about four or five feet." He stepped up to the grave on the left and pried a crumbling splinter of wood from the edge of the hole. "The casket is almost completely decayed. It's definitely old; a forensic anthropologist might be able to give us a date—possibly even an identification if they're lucky enough to find any artifacts among the remains."

He pointed to a thin layer of stones stacked across the top of the casket. "You find this sometimes in older graves," Nick said. "The stones were put there to keep predators from digging their way in. It also keeps the ground from settling once the casket rots away." Above the layer of rock was an inch or two of compacted soil, and above that was the open space where Nick had been lying.

"You can see that they started to excavate each of the graves. The workers probably figured, 'Hey, they'll have to be moved anyway—might as well get started.' They got pretty far on the first one there—but the second grave was different. They stopped digging when they found this."

Nick pointed to a foot-thick layer of soil that remained above the second casket. Long thin strips of grayish-white bone peeked out from beneath the dark soil.

"That's the humerus up there. You can see the ball of the shoulder joint and a little bit of the clavicle underneath. The crest of the pelvis is just visible there, and down here—" He pointed to the soil at the end of the grave; the jagged stumps of four small bones projected from the earth like tree roots where the backhoe had cleanly severed them. "This is a tibia and fibula," Nick said. "Here's the other pair right beside them. You can see that the legs were pressed close together; my guess is that the body was buried on its side, most likely in a fetal position."

"Why?"

"When you fold a body up, it requires a smaller hole. It's a real time-saver when you have to dig the hole yourself."

Donovan looked at him. "You worry me sometimes."

"Two bodies in the same grave," Nick said, "the owner downstairs and a renter in the apartment above. It's pretty clever if you think about it. What better place to hide a body than a graveyard?"

"Then you think the renter was murdered."

"So do you—you wouldn't have called me if you didn't. This is a rural area, Donovan, there are plenty of places to bury a body—nobody has to double up. In older cities when the graveyards got overcrowded they used to bury people on top of each other, but always in a casket and always in ceremonial fashion—laid out on their backs nice and comfy so they could all 'rest in peace.' Nobody buried people like this—tucked up in a ball without even a wooden box to call home. This guy was murdered all right—a forensic anthropologist can probably verify that by looking for bullet fragments or cut marks on the bone. The question is, 'Who is this guy? And who killed him—and why?' What you need is a postmortem interval—you need to establish time of death so you can begin to assemble a list of suspects. I suppose that's why you sent for a bug man—that's why you need me. What I can't figure out is why you're here."

"What do you mean?"

"Why is the FBI involved in this? Why do you guys care?"

Donovan nodded to the remaining graves. "The third grave is just like the first one," he said. "One grave, one body. But the fourth grave is just like this one—there's a second body buried on top of the original casket. That strongly suggests the same person committed both murders."

"So?"

"There's a lot of land still to be excavated here—there's no telling how many more graves they might find. They've already found two of these double graves; there could be more. You know how the FBI classifies these things: three or more murders with the same modus constitute a serial killer—that's when we get involved."

"Okay—but why are *you* here? If I remember correctly, aren't you a counterterrorism agent?"

"That's right."

"Does the FBI suspect that this has something to do with terrorism?"

"No."

Nick waited.

"It's a little . . . complicated."

"I'm listening."

Donovan paused. "Remember the last time we worked together?"

"In New York, in TriBeCa, a couple of years ago. I remember clearly—you didn't pay me that time either."

"Well, that turned out to be a big case for me. It seems I stopped a guy who was planning to attack the city with bubonic plague."

"I remember reading about that—on the cover of the *New York Times*, in fact. Not bad—that must have been a shot in the arm for your career."

"To say the least. The Bureau takes a lot of heat these days; we get so many complaints and criticisms that when something actually goes right we want to make sure everybody knows about it."

"So they want everybody to know about *you*."

"I guess so. They pulled me off the field and brought me down to Washington. The camera seems to be following me right now, and I suppose they want to take advantage of it. It's kind of a PR job, really. I go to a lot of parties; I do a lot of interviews."

"They pulled you off the field? Is that what you wanted?"

"They didn't ask."

"I'm asking."

"Some days I could slash my wrists," Donovan said, "but that's another story. To answer your question, I'm standing here with you because this is where they want me right now."

"Here? Why?"

Donovan nodded to the massive excavation site that surrounded them. "*The Patriot Center*—that's what they're planning to call this place. It'll be the largest mall in the eastern U.S., situated right off I-66, the main east-west corridor out of Washington, D.C., just an hour from the city. A thousand acres of Virginia countryside—and one man owns the whole shebang."

"Who?"

"John Henry Braden."

"*Senator* Braden?"

"In five months it'll be *President* Braden, according to the buzz in Washington. This is all his land, Nick—not just the Patriot Center, but as far as the eye can see—most of it belongs to him."

"That was a pretty good investment."

"Can you imagine what will happen to the value of his land once the Patriot Center is completed? And not just around here—all along the I-66 corridor. Braden owns land all along the way."

"How can one man afford to buy so much land?"

"He didn't buy it; he inherited it. It's been in his family for decades—centuries, from what I hear. Braden is one of those old Virginia blue bloods. The man has deep roots, and deep roots make deep pockets."

"I suppose his people all came over on the *Mayflower*."

"Are you kidding? Braden can trace his family tree all the way back to Jamestown—he looks down his nose at the stragglers who came over on the *Mayflower*."

"I still don't get it," Nick said. "What if Braden does have a lot of money on the line here? Why does the FBI care?"

"Politics. Braden sits on some very influential committees—the sort of committees that decide the annual budget for the Department of Justice, which determines the annual budget for the FBI. Get the idea? If Braden wants something from the FBI, all he has to do is ask."

"And you think he asked for you?"

"That's what I hear."

"Why you? The FBI has all kinds of people who could handle this. If Braden wants you here, he probably wants the camera that's following you."

"I agree."

"But why would Braden want this kind of publicity?"

"Because he's running for president of the United States, and every presidential candidate needs to appear tough on crime. He's got a horse farm in Middleburg—about half an hour east of here. John Henry Braden can't have a serial killer operating in his own backyard; whatever develops here, he wants the American public to see that he's on top of it."

"Sounds like a risky move to me. What if it turns out worse than he thought? This could backfire on him."

"It could—but he's betting it won't, and in the meantime he looks like a man of courage and conviction. That's important; Braden wants voters to know that he won't put up with crime in his own state, and he won't put up with it when he's in the Oval Office."

"You mean *if*."

"Not from what I hear."

"So your role here is largely symbolic?"

"Thanks for the kick in the groin. Yes, my role is largely symbolic. I symbolize the full attention and complete resources of the FBI—and John Henry Braden."

"Impressive," Nick said. "The Department of Entomology won't even post my photo on their Web site."

"There might be a reason for that."

"Thanks. So—how do you want to proceed here?"

"I want us to work it from both sides. I want you here; like you said, I need a postmortem interval—an estimate of how long those two bodies have been dead. I mean, are we talking decades or centuries here? Is this an active serial killer we're talking about, or just ancient history?"

"I'm not sure I can help you," Nick said. "These bones look pretty old to me. You know how it works, Donovan—the older the body, the less an entomologist will find."

"Don't be so modest. I've seen you do magic."

"It all depends on what we find. *Calliphorids* are generally the first insects to colonize a body—the blowflies—sometimes within minutes of death. Suppose a murderer kills a victim, then sets the body aside while he digs a hole; even if he only takes a few minutes, female blowflies have already found the body and laid their eggs on it. So when the killer buries the body, he buries the blowfly eggs along with it. The eggs hatch underground, the maggots mature and pupate, adult flies emerge—but a lot of them can't make it back to the surface again. I might find their bodies left behind."

"What would that tell us?"

"It depends on the specific species. Suppose I find *Cochliomyia macellaria*, the secondary screwworm fly. The secondary screwworm fly doesn't like fresh bodies—it prefers to wait a day or two until things dry out a little. That would tell us the victim was left aboveground for a day or two before he was buried. And *Cochliomyia macellaria* is rarely found in buildings, so that would mean the victim was probably killed outdoors. *Macellaria* is a warm-weather fly—but suppose I find *Phormia regina*, the black blowfly—they prefer cold weather. In that case we might be able to narrow the time of death to a specific season. And if we're really lucky, we might even find a species that doesn't belong here—a species that isn't native to this area—and that would tell us the body was transported here from somewhere else. Like I said: It depends on what we find."

"Fair enough. See what you can find."

"If you ask me, what you really need here is a forensic anthropologist. He can give you a better PMI than I can—he can test the nitrogen levels in the bone."

"There could be other bodies buried here, Nick, and they might not be as old as these two. If we find one, I'll have to send for you anyway. I'd rather have you in on this from the beginning; you're good at puzzles, and this looks like a big one to me. You know how to work a crime scene and you get things done—in your own manic, self-destructive way."

"Well, I'll see what I can do—but until we find a fresher body I could use that anthropologist."

"You'll have one by tomorrow. You should have everything you need within twenty-four hours; if you don't, call me. Where do you want them to set up the tent?"

Nick looked over the area. "On top of the ridge, near the graves—but tell them not to put it too close. I don't want the shade late in the afternoon—I'll need the sunlight."

"Anything else?"

"I'd like to know a few details, like—where am I staying?"

"There's a little town called Endor in the foothills just a couple of miles from here. They've got a nice little place up there."

"Describe it for me."

"Nice. Little."

"I passed a Hyatt on the way out."

"So far away. So inconvenient."

"This 'nice little place' has cockroaches, doesn't it?"

"I wanted you to feel at home."

"Thanks. How do I find it?"

"Ask the sheriff's deputy. I think he's a local."

"Yes, I deduced that."

"Anything else?"

"I'd like to know something: While I'm collecting desiccated insects from corpses and camping out at the No-Tell Motel in Endor, what exactly will you be doing—attending extra parties?"

"No, I'll be checking with the FBI's National Crime Information Center to see if there are any old missing persons reports from this area that might help us identify those two bodies. I'll check the local law enforcement records too—though I expect that to take longer. Between the two of us, I'm hoping we can figure this thing out."

"And what if there are more than two bodies?"

Donovan shrugged. "We'll worry about that when the time comes."

The two men started back toward the sheriff's deputy.

"How long do you think they'll keep you in Washington?" Nick asked.

"Just until the spotlight fades, I suppose. I hope it's soon—we miss New York."

"You should screw up all the time the way I do. They let me go wherever I want."

"Thanks for the career tip." He stopped and turned to Nick. "One more thing: Stay away from the camera, okay? Don't talk to the press. No interviews. We'll have a public liaison officer here and everything will go through him. Got it?"

"Don't you trust me?"

"If I didn't trust you, you wouldn't be here. There's a lot riding on this, Nick. A lot of important people will be watching—the sort of people who care a lot about what other people think."

"Including a certain U.S. senator?"

"Yeah—especially him."

Nick knelt on two wooden planks he had placed on either side of the skeleton to keep his weight from compacting the soil further and possibly damaging artifacts that might be recovered below. *A fat lot of good it'll do now*, he thought. The construction worker who discovered this skeleton probably stomped all over it in hobnailed boots. But you couldn't really blame him—all the poor guy was expecting to find was the grave's rightful owner resting peacefully in a pine box; he sure wasn't expecting to find a second resident sleeping in the top bunk.

Still, the construction worker hadn't made Nick's job any easier. The hide beetles and rove beetles that are attracted to buried remains prefer to dig down through the freshly loosened soil directly above the body; by removing the earth above the skeleton, the worker had inadvertently removed most of the insect evidence that might help Nick determine a postmortem interval. Most of the pupal cases and insect body fragments would be gone; a few might still remain, but finding them wouldn't be easy.

He knew the job would be even tougher for the forensic anthropologist Donovan promised to send. Nick gently swept away the soil from the humerus with a soft bristle brush, gradually exposing more of the bone; sure enough, he found the bone shattered twice before it even connected with the radius and ulna, probably because the nose of a shovel had chopped it in half. He crawled forward on the boards and brushed the dirt away from the side of the skull; he found it crushed flat like an eggshell, forming a delicate mosaic in the shape of a human head. *Good luck determining cause of death with this guy*, Nick thought.

The FA would pull his hair out attempting to recover any reliable forensic evidence from this mess.

Nick hoped he'd have better luck with the body in the fourth grave—maybe it would be in better shape. But even if it wasn't, it might not be his last opportunity. There was no telling how many graves they would find in this old graveyard—and how many double occupants might be among them. Somebody had come up with the clever idea of disposing of a body by burying it on top of an existing grave, and whoever it was had used the technique at least twice. Who knows? Maybe the killer had used it three times—or four, or five. With each additional victim there would be more evidence—and more of a chance to find out who the killer was.

"Excuse me, I'm going to need you to leave."

Nick rocked back onto his heels and straightened; his eyes were now level with the surface of the ground. He cupped his hand over his eyes and looked up to see an imperious-looking woman glaring down at him from the side of the grave. She stood like a pyramid with her trousered legs spread wide and her fists planted firmly on her hips. The image triggered an old memory of the Jolly Green Giant standing astride a valley of Golden Niblets—but there was nothing jolly about this woman. She was dressed in green khaki from head to foot, with a hunter-orange vest draped over her work shirt. Both shoulders were emblazoned with official-looking insignia embroidered in gold and blue, though from his vantage point Nick couldn't read either one of them. Her hands were protected by white surgical gloves, making her long fingers look like a pair of cow's udders after a good milking. Her narrow waist was girded by some sort of combination of fanny pack and accessory holder, and around her neck she wore a gleaming silver whistle dangling from a black lanyard. Her head and face were enveloped by a billow of dark mosquito netting that draped down from a baseball-style cap, completely obscuring her features and expression—except for a condescending scowl, which somehow still managed to show through.

Nick looked up at her. "I beg your pardon?"

"I said, 'I'm going to need you to leave.'"

"Who are you?"

She twisted and pointed to the shoulder patch on one arm; Nick squinted but still couldn't make out the words. With an impatient huff she twisted farther and bent down a little more.

"We could save a lot of time if you'd just tell me," Nick said. "Unless you need me to read it to you."

She straightened. "My name is Marjory Claire Anderson-Forsyth."

Nick waited. "Is this multiple choice, or do I have to remember the whole thing?"

She didn't smile. "I am principal owner and chief trainer of the Virginia chapter of Fidelis Search and Rescue Dogs—*that* is what it says on my insignia. I have been contracted by the Federal Bureau of Investigation to locate the graves in this cemetery."

"I already found this one," Nick said. "You'll have to look someplace else."

She didn't reply.

Nick got up from his knees and dusted them off; he was almost even with the woman's waist now and the view was not improving. Twenty yards to his right he spotted a large black-and-tan dog darting back and forth, nervously sniffing at the ground. The dog was wearing a hunter-orange vest exactly like the woman's.

"Is that a cadaver dog?" Nick asked.

"That is a *forensic detection* dog," she corrected, "and I'm afraid your scent is distracting."

"The label said I'd be irresistible. I'm getting my money back."

Still no response.

It was quickly becoming apparent that the woman lacked a sense of humor—a human personality defect that Nick found particularly annoying. He hoisted himself out of the hole and stood up beside her. She was even taller than she appeared to be from below, flat-chested, and thin as a wire. She lifted the front of the mosquito netting and pulled it back over her head, exposing her face. *You may now kiss the bride*

24

was the thought that flashed through Nick's mind—and it was not a pleasant thought. Her face matched the rest of her: It was long and thin with high cheekbones that ran down into sinewy sunken hollows like wax dripping over a ledge. Her hair was pulled back from her face in a bundle of tight curls of black and gray, and her dark eyes seemed to be frozen in a permanent glare—and right now they were glaring at Nick.

"Who *are* you?" she asked in exactly the same tone of voice Nick used when he came across an unfamiliar species of dung beetle.

He wiped his hands on his cargo shorts and extended one. "Nick Polchak," he said. "I'm a forensic entomologist from NC State."

She raised her gloved hands in front of her like a surgeon. "I need you to leave the area immediately."

Nick paused. "I'm afraid that's a bit of a problem. See, the FBI hired me too, and my job is to collect insect evidence from the—"

"Mr. Polchak, do you understand how a forensic detection dog operates?"

"I'm an entomologist," Nick said, "but I imagine it's similar to the way an insect operates. As the human body decomposes, it emits a series of chemical compounds as by-products; so far, about four hundred of these substances have been identified. These chemicals work their way to the surface of the soil where insects can detect them. I suppose a cadaver dog works the same way: Because it possesses far more sensitive olfactory abilities than a human being, the dog is able to detect the same chemical indicators that insects do."

"That is essentially correct."

"Some of these graves might date back to colonial times. Can a dog find a body that old?"

"A border collie in the Czech Republic once detected a grave that was two *thousand* years old."

"Impressive."

"It's a very delicate process—so I'm sure you can understand that there must be no distracting odors when the detection dog is attempting to do its work."

"And I'm a distracting odor."

"How clever of you."

"Let me get this straight. 'Bosco' is over there trying to sniff out a grave—"

"His name is *not* Bosco," she said through clenched teeth. "His pedigree name is Augusta's King Edward of Stanroph. I address him simply as 'King.'"

"He's got a longer pedigree than you do," Nick said. "You'd better get yourself a couple more names or pretty soon he'll be tossing biscuits to you."

Nothing.

Nick was losing patience. "Look. Your dog is over there trying to sniff out a grave, but he's apparently not having any luck—so you think I must be distracting him. Tell me something: Isn't your dog able to distinguish between a living being and a decomposing body? Or is there something you're trying to tell me? Because a friend would let me know."

She took a slow, deep breath. "Mr. Polchak, I am trying to be patient with you, despite your adolescent attempts at humor. A forensic detection dog is a highly trained, highly sensitive animal, and you are posing a distraction to my dog. I'm sure you will agree that the first priority here is to identify the location of all remaining graves in this graveyard—a task which I will happily undertake just as soon as you—"

"Hey!" Nick shouted. He pointed at the dog, who was raising one leg and urinating on a small clump of grass.

The woman put her whistle to her lips and made two shrill blasts; the dog stopped and hung its head in apparent shame—but not before emptying its bladder.

"Tell your highly trained animal to stop peeing on my crime scene!" Nick said.

She waved off the comment like an annoying gnat. "That is an instinctive canine behavior. He probably detects the scent of a predator and he's 'overmarking' the spot. It's a normal territorial response."

"You tell him this is *my* territory," Nick said, "and that if he doesn't stop, I'm going to 'overmark' *him*. I'm interested in predators too, lady. Some of them scavenge for human remains—they disarticulate bodies and carry off bones and other body parts. They sometimes leave markings behind—markings that might tell us what kind of predator it was and which season it would have been present here. That information might lead us to the time of year the victim died—unless your dog destroys the evidence first."

"Mr. Polchak—" she began, but Nick cut her off.

"Look, Marge, I'm going to cut you some slack here—not because you deserve it, but because I'm a really nice guy once you get past my distracting scent. I'm going to back off and give you and Bosco a little space, because even though I hate to admit it I happen to agree with you on one point: The priority here is to locate all the remaining graves. So why don't you and Mr. Sensitive there get started and I'll just move off to the side?"

"Downwind," she added.

Nick bit his lip. "Of course. We wouldn't want Bosco to get distracted—he might wet his leg."

Nick turned without further comment and headed back toward the spot where the deputy stood guard—downwind. He sat down and stretched out on a patch of remaining grass and took out his cell phone. He dialed a number from memory.

"Donovan here," a voice said. "What's up, Nick?"

"There are three bodies in one of the graves," Nick said.

"Really? Which grave?"

"I haven't decided yet. I have to kill her first."

A pause. "Okay, what's the problem?"

"Who hired the cadaver-dog lady?"

"Beats me. I requested a dog team through the Bureau. She must be on somebody's Approved Vendor list. Why?"

"I need to know something: Whose crime scene is this?"

"Mine."

"Okay, what about when you're not here? Whose crime scene is it then?"

"Mine. Would you like to put your sister on the phone so I can tell her that the ball belongs to you?"

"Would you?"

"No. You kids will just have to work this out between the two of you—it's a part of growing up. Now if you don't mind, Dad has some work to do."

Nick closed the phone.

Three hours later he was still sitting in the same spot. Elgin was sitting beside him now; he had meandered over and taken a seat beside Nick, and the two men were leaning back on their elbows and watching "Marge" and "Bosco" work. Marge carried a bundle of small wire flags in her left hand, each one topped by a rectangle of bright red plastic; Nick assumed that their purpose was to mark the location of each grave as it was identified—but after three hours no red flags were visible on the ground.

"Not makin' much headway," Elgin observed.

"Not a whole lot," Nick replied. "Are you a betting man, Deputy?"

"At times. I play the lottery when the numbers get high enough."

"How many graves would you bet there are in this graveyard?"

The deputy considered. "No way to tell."

"If you had to bet."

The deputy looked over the area. "Well—I see four in a row right there. I suppose that could be the end of it, but most likely not—I figure they's at least another one or two on either side. But it don't make sense they'd plant 'em all in one row like peas or pole beans, so I figure they's another row or two behind 'em—maybe more."

"That's good figuring," Nick said. "So what's your guess?"

"If I had to bet? I'd say thirty—thereabouts."

"And how many of those thirty has Bosco found so far?"

"Maybe he's just warmin' up."

Nick looked at his watch. "What is he, a Crock-Pot?"

The dog wandered back and forth across the open area with its nose to the ground; from time to time Marge would call the dog back, reaching into a pouch at her waist and handing the dog some kind of tasty reward—for what, Nick had no idea. Then she would send the dog off again, sniffing and pawing in his brilliant orange vest. Throughout the whole process the woman would issue piercing commands with the silver whistle, causing the dog to constantly stop and shoot off in a different direction like a fur-covered bumper car.

"Any idea what she's doin'?" the deputy asked.

"I'm picking up a little of it," Nick said. "When she wants the dog to come, she blows the whistle; when she wants the dog to change direction, she blows the whistle; when she wants to give the dog a reward, she blows the whistle. I think I understand: After years of constant training, the dog has taught her to blow the whistle."

The whistle shrieked again and Elgin winced. "Sure wish she'd stop blowin' that thing."

"Me too," Nick said. "If I were the dog I'd go for her throat."

They watched a while longer. The dog constantly stopped and sniffed but never seemed to show any more interest in one spot than another.

"Nice-lookin' animal," Elgin offered.

"So am I," Nick said. "I can't find graves either."

He took out his cell phone and dialed again. There was a click and then a pause at the other end.

"Now what?" Donovan sighed.

"The wonder of caller ID," Nick said. "We've got a problem."

"What problem?"

"The dog—it's got a nose like a brick."

Another pause. "You know what I've always admired about you, Nick?"

"Nothing that I know of."

"You're not a whiner. I was just saying to Macy the other day, 'You know, Nick Polchak is weird and he wears big funny glasses, but he's no whiner.'"

"Flatterer."

"Whenever there's a problem, you always find a way around it. That's a great quality, Nick—I'd sure hate to see it stop now."

"I'm telling you, the dog can't smell. How am I supposed to analyze insect evidence from graves that we can't find?"

"How long has this dog been searching?" Donovan asked.

"An eternity," Nick said.

"Three hours—that's when you called to annoy me last. Has it occurred to you that this dog is trying to pick up the scent from bones that could be two or three hundred years old?"

"What about the bodies buried on top?" Nick said. "They could be a lot more recent—possibly only a few years old."

"And the dog has to pick up the scent through a couple of feet of compacted soil."

"I'm not expecting him to replace the headstones and plant flowers," Nick said, "but it's been three hours and he hasn't found a single grave."

"Give the dog some time. You've got two graves to get started on; do your work and let the dog do his."

"I can't," Nick said. "Apparently I'm a 'distracting scent.'"

"The dog told you that?"

"No, the woman did."

"So who are you distracting—the dog or the woman?"

"I'm not calling you anymore," Nick grumbled.

"Good. That Nick—he's no whiner."

Nick closed the phone and tossed it over his shoulder.

Elgin looked at him. "What'd the boss have to say?"

"FBI agents don't always think clearly," Nick said. "Too much time at the shooting range."

Another thirty minutes passed.

The sun was just beginning to dip behind the foothills of the Blue Ridge Mountains now; the woman, taking note of the shadows stretching toward her, attached a leash to her dog's collar and began to walk back toward the parking lot.

"Nice work today," Nick called out as she passed. "One suggestion:

You might tell the dog to search for graves instead of all the places where there aren't any. That might save time—it's a big planet."

The woman sniffed. "It's the temperature."

"Excuse me?"

"The warmer the temperature, the more difficult it is for the dog to pick up the scent."

"It gets cooler here in the fall," Nick said. "Why don't you come back then?"

"We will be back in the cool of the morning," she said.

Nick and Elgin watched her as she turned and led the dog away.

"An entire day wasted," Nick groaned.

"I take it you're not one for sittin' around."

"I'd rather be driving in the wrong direction than waiting at a stoplight."

"Felt that way myself at times."

"I can't just sit here and wait for Bosco to grow a nose. Somebody else around here must have a cadaver dog. What about the sheriff's department—don't you guys have any contacts in the area?"

"None that I know of—not much need. Y'know, if you really want to find those graves, you ought to ask the witch."

Nick turned and looked at him. "Who?"

"The witch—the Witch of Endor."

"There's a witch in Endor?"

"Not in Endor exactly—she lives in the mountains up above the town. Her people have lived up there as long as anyone can remember. She's the only one left now. She practically owns the whole mountain-top—got a big fence around the whole thing. I seen it myself."

"Does she ever come into town?"

"Oh, no, sir—witches don't associate. They only come out at night, and generally by a full moon. She only associates with animals."

"Animals?"

"Witches have power over animals, y'know. She can speak their language—make 'em do anything she wants."

"Uh-huh. And what makes people think she's a witch?"

"Well, she dresses the part—that's for sure. She wanders the woods at night with a three-legged dog—people catch a glimpse of her sometimes under a full moon. She does weird things with her hands—she makes these signs, puts the hex on people that get on her bad side."

"Your average witch stuff," Nick said.

"Pretty much—except for one thing."

"What's that?"

"She can raise the dead."

4

"Pizza for *Polchak*," Nick said.

A moonfaced boy in a grease-stained apron nodded and headed for the kitchen.

Nick leaned back against the counter and looked around the restaurant. The Endor Tavern & Grille was the only eating establishment in the town of Endor—not exactly a surprise, since the entire downtown consisted of nothing more than a single intersection. On the southwest corner stood the Skyline Motel, where Nick had checked in just a few minutes ago. He fished his room key from his pocket and held it up: It was a football-shaped disk of green plastic attached by an S-hook to a shiny brass key. Nick shook his head; he hadn't seen a keychain like this in years. The only places that used them anymore were truck stops and gas stations, to keep forgetful patrons from driving off with the restroom key. He wondered how long it would be before the Skyline Motel made the leap into the twenty-first century. *Probably never*, he thought. The twenty-first century could drive right past on I-66 and the little town of Endor wouldn't miss it one bit.

Across from the Skyline and up the hill was the Endor Regional Library. *An odd location for a regional collection*, Nick thought, but then again reading might be a very popular activity in a boring little town like this. Catty-corner to the Skyline was Endor Resurrection Lutheran Church—a mountain-style hamlet with a tall, sloping slate roof. The entire church was constructed of the local stone, making it look as if the building were just one huge outcropping jutting from the mountainside.

On Nick's left there was a long bar with a mahogany railing and six

padded barstools—evidently the Tavern portion of the Tavern & Grille.
It was "Grille" with an *e*, he noticed—probably somebody's idea of a
way to add a little class to an establishment that otherwise had none.
Across from the bar the room opened into a spacious eating area—the
Grille. In the center of the room was a canoe-sized salad bar, currently
vacant, with a well-buffed Plexiglas sneeze guard suspended like a tent
above it. The room was dotted with round four-tops and eight-tops
draped in red-and-white vinyl checkered tablecloths with draperies to
match, and there was a single row of red vinyl booths along the far
wall. The walls themselves were made of brick with dark wood trim,
and little yellow lanterns gave the room a dingy hue. *Lovely décor*, Nick
thought—sort of a Tudor/Swiss/Shakey's Pizza motif. Part watering
hole, part gathering place, part do-it-yourself, part sit-and-serve—a little
something for everybody, because everybody in Endor had no place else
to go—and neither did Nick.

It seemed to be a quiet night in Endor. Only one table was occupied—a table in the far corner surrounded by a group of teenagers.
Nick watched them for a few minutes.

"Pizza for Kojak," a voice behind him announced.

Nick turned. "Polchak," he corrected, and handed the boy a twenty-
dollar bill. "Do you know those kids over there?"

The boy looked over Nick's shoulder. "Sure."

"What high school?"

"Endor."

That figures. "What's their mascot?"

"Mountaineers."

That figures too. "Thanks. Keep the change—your government sends
its greetings."

Nick took the pizza and walked over to the table. As he approached,
conversations began to drop off and heads turned to look at him one by
one. Without a word he leaned out over the table and set the pizza in
the center, then pulled up a chair and sat down—then he opened the
box, took out a slice, and began to eat.

The group stared at him in silence.

"Help yourself," Nick said through a mouthful. "I ordered 'the works,' so just pick off anything you don't like."

No one moved.

"So how did the Mountaineers do this year?"

There was a long silence before one of the boys ventured to ask, "Football or basketball?"

Nick cocked his head and looked at him. "Now what do you think?"

One of the girls covered her mouth and giggled. "Yeah—we suck at basketball."

They all laughed—Nick could sense the release of tension.

"Did you go to Endor?" one of them asked.

"I'm from out of town," Nick said. "I'm staying across the street at the Skyline. I ordered this pizza, but when I got the thing I realized it was too big for me—so I thought maybe you guys could help me eat it. Hope you don't mind me barging in like this."

The girl closest to Nick squinted hard and said, "You've got really huge glasses."

"And you're a very observant young woman," Nick replied.

"Why do you wear them?"

"To keep insects out of my eyes at high speeds."

She blinked.

"So I can see," Nick said.

The girl leaned closer and studied the soft brown orbs that floated behind the lenses. "How big *are* your eyes?" she asked.

"They're the size of Frisbees," Nick said. "The glasses make them look smaller."

She still didn't change expressions, but some of the others laughed.

Nick lifted his glasses and showed the girl his eyes, then gave her a wink.

"You've got pretty eyes," she said.

"Thanks. I wish I could say the same for you, but I'm afraid you're just a big blur right now." He turned to the rest of the group and said,

"What are you guys waiting for? It's lousy pizza anyway—it won't taste any better cold."

They were on the pizza like jackals on a gazelle.

Nick listened to the group as they talked; his eyes darted behind his glasses like a pair of rebounding basketballs. These kids were like a collection of insects to Nick, each with its own rituals and pairing behavior. The girl on his right was holding hands with the boy next to her, but she kept looking at a taller boy across the table. The shorter boy beside her kept clinging to the girl's hand, but it was too late—a more suitable potential mate had already caught her attention. The boy directly across from Nick kept his arms folded with his fists tucked behind his biceps to make them appear larger than they really were, exaggerating his size and status. One girl wore more makeup than all the others combined; she kept touching it up with a pocket mirror, seeking to distinguish herself from the drabber females in the colony.

But the focus of Nick's attention was the boy seated to his left. He was the largest in the group, with a tousle of brown hair and a splatter of pimples across his fair skin. He was athletic and obviously proud of it—he wore a wool letter jacket with leather sleeves, even though the temperature outside was well over eighty degrees. He spoke with more volume and more self-assurance than the others, and other members of the group quickly deferred to him. This boy was the dominant male in the colony; he was the one Nick was looking for.

Nick turned and looked at him. "How's the fall look for you guys? Tough schedule?"

"We're gonna kick butt this year," the boy said. "We've got our whole front line and half the backfield returning."

"Who's your big rival?"

"Front Royal," the boy growled, and the whole group sneered with contempt. "We're gonna kill them this year."

"Front Royal," Nick said. "I've heard of them—I heard a guy mention them just this morning. He said Front Royal is gonna jerk your jocks up over your heads this year."

They all stared at Nick while he took another bite of his pizza.

"Who told you that?" the boy demanded.

"Like I said—I'm from out of town." Nick pointed to the '09 on the boy's jacket sleeve. "Senior year coming up—any college prospects?"

The boy shrugged. "I've had some calls."

"Think you're big enough?"

"You bet I'm big enough—strong enough too."

"College football is a whole new ball game," Nick said. "Size is important but what really matters is toughness—courage—*guts*."

"I've got plenty of that." The boy glanced around the group for confirmation, and his friends dutifully nodded. "We're gonna *destroy* Front Royal this season, and you can tell that guy I said so. Better yet, you tell him to come say that to my face, and I'll straighten him out personally."

Nick did his best to look impressed. He turned to the rest of the group. "So what's it like living in a town the size of Endor?"

"Boring," they groaned in unison.

"You must know everybody in a town this size."

"Everybody."

"What about the kid who sold me this pizza?"

"That's Donny," one of them said. "He's a dork."

"What about the old guy who runs the Skyline Motel—the one with the hair sticking out of his ears?"

"Mr. Denardo," someone said. "He's got artificial knees—both of 'em."

Nick let a beat pass before he asked, "What about the witch?"

No one answered.

Nick looked around the group. "C'mon—somebody here must know the witch."

There was a pause. "We know *about* her," someone said quietly.

"You mean nobody's actually met her? Nobody's talked to her?"

They shook their heads in astonishment. "Nobody talks to the witch. She lives up on the mountain, and she never comes down."

"Never? What does she do for food?"

"She eats dogs."

"She eats *dogs*?"

"It's true," one of the girls said. "My friend Keisha saw her—at the animal shelter over in Cedarville. She was opening all the cages and feeling all the puppies—she was looking for the fattest ones to take back with her."

"What does the witch look like?"

"They say she's a hundred years old, but she looks no older than you do. Keisha says she has long black hair that comes down to her waist. She was wearing dark sunglasses so she wouldn't give anybody the evil eye unless she wanted to. Keisha just stared at her—but then all of a sudden the witch turned and looked right at her and then she made a quick sign—sort of like this," she said, waving her hands in front of her in a mystic-looking gesture. "And you know what? One week later Keisha had to have her appendix out. She almost died—I swear, no kidding."

"That was a close call," Nick said. "You know, if your friend saw the witch at an animal shelter, then she must come down from the mountain from time to time."

They all looked at one another and slowly nodded, as though the thought was occurring to them for the first time.

"What's the best way to contact her?"

They looked at Nick in amazement. "You want to *meet* the witch? Why?"

"I'd like to talk to her," Nick said. "Sort of a project I'm working on." No one responded.

"She must have a phone."

One of the boys stared at Nick as if he had just said, "Pigs must have wings." "The witch don't have a phone," he said. "The witch only talks to animals, and animals don't have phones."

"Yes, I've noticed that—it's probably because they don't have pockets." Nick slowly leaned forward on the table and looked at each of them one by one. "Come on—do you mean to tell me that not one of you has ever snuck up there and climbed that fence just to take a look around? Just so you could come back and tell your buddies you did it? Just to feel the hair stand up on the back of your neck—to feel like you're *alive?*"

No one answered.

Nick turned to the football player and quickly glanced down at the name embroidered on his letter jacket: *Biff*. Nick almost winced—no wonder the kid was overcompensating.

Nick looked him directly in the eye. "Not even you, Biff?"

"Me? Why me?"

"Toughness—courage—*guts*."

"This is different," Biff said.

"Why, Biff—I believe you're *afraid*."

Biff glared back. "I'm not afraid of anything."

"Then take me up there," Nick said.

"What?"

"Take me up there. We'll climb that fence and we'll find that witch and we'll talk to her. We'll do something that nobody else in this whole town has the guts to do—and when we get back, you'll be a legend."

Biff sat frozen with his eyes as wide as saucers—and then he shook his head. "I'm not going looking for any witch," he said. "That's just plain crazy—that's askin' for trouble."

Nick shrugged and slowly rose from his chair. "It was worth a try," he said, "but if you won't do it, you won't do it. Thanks for the help with the pizza, everybody; nice to meet you, and good luck with your fall season. Oh, that reminds me—can somebody tell me how to get to Front Royal?"

"Why do you want to go to Front Royal?"

"I want to meet their football team," Nick said, looking back at Biff again. "Maybe somebody in Front Royal has got more guts than you do."

Nick stared at Biff and waited—and so did everyone else.

The boy stood up with clenched fists. "Okay," he said. "I'll take you up there, but only to show you that I'm not afraid."

"I'll meet you outside in five minutes," Nick said, and started for the door.

"What if we can't find her?" Biff called after him.

Nick turned and smiled. "We'll find her—there's a full moon."

5

Nick and Biff stood in front of an eight-foot chain-link fence, illuminated by the headlights of Biff's Ford F-150. The pavement had turned to gravel half a mile back down the road; it disappeared here behind a double gate wrapped with a thick chain and sealed with a rusted padlock. Nick jerked hard on the padlock, but it held. He put his fingers through the links of the fence and shook it. There was a sign on the gate that warned in large red letters: POSTED: NO HUNTING, NO TRESPASSING. VIOLATORS WILL BE PROSECUTED.

"So this is it?" Nick said, glancing over at Biff.

The boy's eyes looked as wide as the headlights. "This is her lair," he whispered.

"Well, we can't open this gate. Shut off your headlights—let's see if we can find another way in."

Biff looked at him. "Shut off the lights? Do we have to?"

"If you want to have a battery left when we get back. C'mon, it's a clear night—we should have plenty of light."

"I told you I'd bring you up here—that's all I said I'd do."

"You said you'd take me to see the witch. I don't see any witch, do you?"

"I don't see what you need me for."

"Look—I'm a total stranger here, but you're a local. You said it yourself: Everybody knows everybody in a town this size. Even if you don't know the witch, the witch might recognize you. I figure I might get a warmer reception if I bring a familiar face along—okay?"

Biff reluctantly switched off his headlights, and the entire area went black. As Nick's eyes slowly adjusted, shapes and forms began to emerge from a sea of deep shadows. The moon was a brilliant silver disk on the far horizon, glowing through the tops of the trees and silhouetting dead limbs like streaks of black lightning. The woods were dominated by towering old beech trees, with their bark stripped down from the tops until they resembled craggy old hands with the skin flayed back to the knuckles.

Nick walked along the fence, unconsciously running his hand along the links as he went. Suddenly his hand hit something soft and furry; he stopped abruptly and Biff bumped into him from behind.

"What's the matter?"

"There's something on the fence."

"What is it?"

Nick adjusted his glasses and took a closer look. It was a dead squirrel, stretched out and tied to the fence with long strands of field grass twisted into bundles. "It's nothing."

"Don't lie to me. That's a sign from the witch—it means 'Keep out! Go back!'"

"Maybe she just doesn't like squirrels."

"Stop kidding around, mister."

"Lighten up, will you? It's just a dead squirrel. Let's keep going."

Twenty yards farther on Nick felt another soft lump. This time it was a blackbird, tied to the fence by the neck and tail, with a strip of scarlet ribbon wound around its beak.

"I'm telling you, that's a sign," Biff said.

"I think you're right," Nick said. "It means 'Are you two coming in or not?' Let's climb over here—give me a lift."

"Climb over? You still want to go in? Are you nuts?"

Nick let out an impatient groan. "Look, we didn't come all the way up here just to look at a fence. What are you going to do, go back to Endor and tell all your friends that you went up to see the witch but a *squirrel* scared you off?"

"They don't have to know," Biff grumbled.

"Yes they do, because I'll tell them. Now we're going to climb this fence and we're going to find that witch, and tomorrow you're going to tell all your friends that you're the biggest stud in the whole Shenandoah Valley—and I'm going to back you up. Now are you coming or not?"

Biff scowled and formed a stirrup with his hands. Nick slipped his right foot into the stirrup and pushed upward, grabbing the top of the fence and pulling himself up. He swung one leg over the top, then the other; he lowered himself until he hung by his arms, then dropped to the ground on the other side. Biff followed close behind.

They started forward through the woods, walking in the direction of the moon.

"How do we know where we're going?" Biff asked.

"We don't—but we're walking parallel to that road, so sooner or later we have to run into something."

After a few minutes the woods closed up behind them. Biff kept looking back nervously in the direction of the fence. "We're lost. We'll never find our way back."

"There's a full moon," Nick said. "How big a night-light do you need?"

They walked on for several minutes, but there was no sign of a house or building of any kind—no warm glow from a kitchen window, no welcoming flicker of firelight, not even the stark blue glare of a utility light on a pole or an outbuilding. The woods were thick and it was dark all around them, except for the tops of tall brush and trees tipped silver by the moon.

Nick was beginning to wonder if this was such a good idea after all. If the witch really did own the whole top of the mountain, her house could be set back miles from the gate. But there was no sense thinking about it now; they'd come this far, and they might as well go on.

"What was that?" Biff said suddenly.

"What?"

"Listen—I heard something—over there!"

Nick turned to his left and listened; now he heard it too—footsteps, padding softly somewhere in the darkness.

"Something's following us!" Biff whispered.

"Relax," Nick said. "Footsteps always sound louder in the woods. It's probably just a . . . a . . ."

"A what?"

"How should I know? I'm an entomologist. It's probably just something small that sounds big."

"Why didn't you bring a flashlight?"

Why didn't I bring a kid with a backbone? "Take it easy—let's just keep moving."

But the footsteps kept getting closer and louder.

Then Nick noticed something else: There were two more sets of footsteps following them—one on their right, and one directly behind.

"Do you hear that?" Biff whispered.

"I hear it," Nick said. "Probably just three small things that sound big."

"You think so?"

"No—but it sounds reassuring right about now."

Nick caught a glimpse of movement on his left. He turned and stared hard into the darkness. He could see it now—he could make out the form of some large animal stalking them with its head slung low.

"Uh-oh," Nick said. "It's a big thing that sounds big."

"What *is* that thing?"

"I'm not sure, but it looks like some kind of dog—a very large one."

The creature drew steadily closer until it was finally in full view. It was the largest dog Nick had ever seen—not tall and lean like a Great Dane, but thick and solid with paws the size of toilet plungers and shoulders that shifted like a lion's as it walked. Its fur was black or very dark brown—it was impossible to tell in the deep shadows. Its ears were plastered back along its head and its tail hung down like a whip about to lash. But the most impressive thing about the animal was its head: It was enormous, boxlike, with great drooping jowls and a sagging brow that almost covered its eyes. The dog did not look directly at them; it seemed to stare slightly to the side and toward the ground, but Nick had no doubt that the dog was watching every move they made.

"It's the witch's hellhound!" Biff whimpered.

"Well, whoever he is, he brought friends."

To the right and behind them were two more dogs, just as large and formidable looking as the first, with dark shaggy fur and thick, sinewy limbs. But these dogs were different: One had more of a pointed snout, with slender ears that tapered at the tips; one had a shock of bright white fur down its chest and belly that made it look like an enormous stuffed animal with its seam ripped open; one had a long, bushy tail, and the other had no tail at all—just a rounded nub that jutted out from its haunches like the handle of an ax.

Biff pointed at the dog behind them. "Would you look at *that!*"

The dog's eyes were glowing pale green in the moonlight.

"I told you they were hellhounds!"

"Calm down," Nick said. "That's just the light reflecting off a layer of cells behind its retinas. It's just like the red-eye effect you get when you have your picture taken—only his eyes glow green."

"What do we do now?"

"Let's try something," Nick said. "Stay beside me—do what I do." He slowly started forward again, watching the dogs carefully; the dogs started forward when he did, gradually closing the distance between them. When Nick stopped, they stopped; when he turned and tried to retrace his footsteps the dog behind him stood its ground and made a low warning growl. When he turned and attempted to move forward again, the two lead dogs moved closer together and blocked his way. They were surrounded now, completely boxed in by three glaring dogs less than twenty feet away.

Nick nodded. "Very good. Very impressive."

"They're going to kill us," Biff choked.

"They don't want to kill us. If they did they could have done it before now."

The panic in Biff's voice was rising. "I'm getting out of here!"

"Don't be stupid—any one of these dogs could be on top of you in two strides."

"You said they wouldn't kill us!"

"I said they don't *want* to—I didn't say you couldn't talk them into it."

"Then what do we do?"

"We wait."

They didn't have to wait long.

Soon they heard the sound of softly crunching footsteps in the distance. Two figures were slowly approaching, walking side by side, silhouetted against the moon; one was tall and one was short; one was a human form, and one was animal.

Biff swallowed hard. "The witch."

"It's about time."

Nick adjusted his glasses and watched her as she approached. She was of medium height, with straight black hair that came almost to her waist, ending in a ragged razor cut at the ends. She kept her head down as she walked, causing her hair to hang in front of her like a veil, concealing her face. It was difficult to estimate her build; she wore loose-fitting clothing that draped over her like a white shroud, with billowy sleeves that covered the tips of her fingers and a long flowing skirt that came just to the tops of her bare feet.

Beside her was a fourth dog. It was smaller and more slender than the other dogs, but still of considerable size. It was a mottled gray color, with long tufts of fur on its chest and head and along the ridge of its back. It walked with an obvious limp, and as it came closer Nick could see why: The dog had only three legs. Its right foreleg had been severed cleanly at the shoulder, and though the dog had learned to compensate impressively, the rhythm of its stride was slightly broken.

The witch and her dog stopped in front of Nick without a word. She snapped her fingers and barely lifted one hand palm down; all four dogs immediately sat, never taking their eyes from Nick and Biff. The witch tipped her head to the left and raised it slowly; when she did, her hair parted slightly and one eye peered out at them from behind the silky black curtain. She looked Nick over carefully, then slowly lowered her head again, causing the eye to retreat back into the darkness.

Nick cleared his throat. "Look, I can explain all this—"

The witch snapped her fingers and lifted one thumb—all four dogs barked simultaneously, then stopped.

Nick got the message.

Now the witch stepped directly in front of the boy. She tipped her head to the right this time and raised it; an eye slowly appeared again, like a bottle floating up in the ocean at night. She looked him over from head to foot—at his youthful face, at his high school letter jacket emblazoned with the letter *E*, at his denim-covered legs that were trembling like the tines of a tuning fork.

Nick looked at Biff too; he was panting like one of the dogs. Nick hoped that the boy wouldn't hyperventilate and suddenly pass out; he had no idea what the dogs might do if he did. The animals seemed to be trained to respond to motion—for all he knew, suddenly dropping to the ground could be the command for "dinner."

The witch spoke to the boy in a deep voice: "Who dares to invade my privacy?"

Biff tried to speak but nothing came out.

"I asked him to bring me up here," Nick explained.

She didn't take her eye off the boy. "Did you climb my fence, boy?"

He managed a nod.

"Did you not see my warnings? Did you dare to cross my hex on the night of a full moon? You foolish boy—whatever befalls you next is on your own head." With that, she raised one finger and slashed an *X* across her chest, then wiggled her fingers in an ominous mystic sign. When she did, all four dogs rose up on their hind legs and began to slowly turn in circles, baying at the moon.

That was more than Biff could handle. He turned on his heels and bolted back through the woods toward the fence, crashing through the underbrush like a wounded water buffalo.

The witch snapped her fingers and made a sweeping gesture with both arms; the three black dogs took off silently after him through the woods.

Nick watched until the last of the dogs disappeared into the brush, then turned and looked at the witch. "When you said, 'Whatever befalls you,' I'm hoping that didn't include being eaten by dogs."

"They won't harm him—unless I tell them to." She stepped in front of Nick again. "So who are you—the high school science teacher, come to prove to his star pupil that witches don't really exist? He'll need some convincing now."

"I don't think Biff is anybody's 'star pupil,'" Nick said. "Too many head tackles." He paused. "You know, you're a hard person to get ahold of."

"I like it that way."

"In Endor they told me you only talk to animals."

"That's because animals listen. They're even capable of understanding simple commands, like 'Do not trespass.'"

"Animals can read?"

"As well as you seem to. Why are you on my land?"

"I need your help."

"You've got a funny way of asking for it."

"Can you suggest a better way? They told me you don't have a phone."

"That's right."

"What was I supposed to do, mail a postcard to 'Witch's Lair, Endor, USA'?"

"This is not Endor—this is my land. The people of Endor have never lifted a finger to help me, and I have no desire to help them."

"I'm not from Endor."

"Good—at least you have something going for you."

"Look," Nick said, "if you'll just give me a minute to explain—" But as he said this he made the mistake of taking a step toward her. The instant he did, the three-legged dog seated peacefully beside her looked as if a surge of electric current had jolted its body awake. It widened its stance and lowered its head, barking and snarling and baring its teeth at Nick.

The witch snapped her fingers and the dog fell silent again. "Do not underestimate this dog," she said. "She can do things with three legs that most dogs can't do with four."

Nick took a careful step back again. "I didn't mean any harm."

"I believe you—she isn't so sure. I think you need to go now."

"You know, I went to a lot of trouble to come up here."

"You mean climbing my fence and trespassing through my woods? Sorry for all your trouble." She raised her hands over her head and clapped twice.

Nick turned and looked in the direction of the fence; a few moments later he could hear the sound of the three huge dogs bounding back toward them. "I knew we should have taken my car. Now how am I supposed to get back?"

"That isn't my problem. I didn't ask you to come."

"Yes, you've made that clear."

The dogs returned now, panting like the bellows of a furnace. The witch turned without a word and started back into the woods with the four dogs accompanying her.

"I'm looking for a cadaver dog," Nick called after her.

She didn't reply.

"I wish you'd let me explain."

She had almost disappeared into the shadows again.

"Hey! Hold on a minute!"

She turned and looked at him.

"I feel a little cheated. Aren't you going to put a curse on me too?"

"If you wish," she said, and once again made a slashing X across her chest, followed by a mystical flourish of fingers. "Satisfied?"

"What does it mean? I'm not very good at interpreting curses."

She held up one finger.

Nick nodded. "Okay—that one I understand."

6

"Morning, Deputy," Nick said, ducking under the yellow barrier tape.

"Hi there, Nick. Sleep all right?"

"It was a short night but an interesting one."

"Endor's a nice little town."

"Yeah, there's no end to the fun. I see several cars in the parking lot this morning—who's here?"

"Your people, mostly. A whole crew showed up first thing this morning."

"Good. What about Marge and Bosco?"

"Yep—they're here too."

"Are they having better luck?"

"Can't say. They been here since the crack of dawn, though. I sure hope they do better than yesterday."

"Yeah, me too."

Nick took his equipment box and headed for the graveyard. When he crossed the small rise he saw a long canvas tent set up at the foot of the four open graves, with the tent flaps pulled back and tied off at the poles. Black power cords ran along the ground like licorice whips, connected to a gas-powered generator a safe distance away. The tent was lined with folding tables covered with digging tools and forensic equipment, but no one seemed to be using them—and Nick knew why. By now he had hoped to find half a dozen forensic technicians scattered over the search area busy at work, but instead he found half a dozen forensic technicians leaning against the tables in the shade of the tent, staring stone-faced at a woman and a dog darting back and forth across an empty field.

"This is ridiculous," Nick groaned. His instinct was to head directly for Marge and Bosco the Wonder Dog to ask if the temperature wasn't quite cool enough for them or if Bosco might need anything else—like a nose transplant. But Nick knew that would only slow things down even more, so he headed instead for the tech tent, where he found a familiar face.

"Hey, Kegan—how's it going?"

"Nick. Nice to see you again."

"How's Charlottesville?"

"Beautiful, as always. How's NC State?"

"Raleigh, as always. So you're the forensic anthropologist—I was hoping they'd grab you since you're just down the road."

Kegan Alexander was a petite woman, no more than five feet in height, with smooth, fair skin and eyes that were too large for her face, giving her a kind of elfish appearance. She was an endurance runner—a triathlete—and there wasn't an extra ounce of fat anywhere on her body. *Mostly bone*, Nick thought, and it seemed somehow appropriate for a woman who spent her time reassembling skeletons and uncovering their secrets. Her hair was brown and straight, cut off just above the shoulders and always pulled back behind her ears, and on the job she always wore a white painter's cap. Nick had never asked her why; he assumed it was because of all the brushing anthropologists tend to do. Kegan was a professor of anthropology at the University of Virginia, just an hour and a half to the south. Nick had worked with her at least twice before, and he wasn't surprised to see her here; she was not only good at what she did, she was from Virginia—and knowledge of the local soil is crucial to dating human remains.

Kegan squinted at the trainer and her dog. "I can't figure out what she's doing out there."

"Neither can she."

"She does this little skipping thing. Watch, she'll do it again. See, she calls the dog over, and then she hands it some kind of treat. Now she'll send it off again, and when she does—there! Did you see it? She sort of skips along beside the dog for a few steps—like those people at the dog shows do when they run around in circles with the dogs."

"This isn't a dog show," Nick said.

"It is right now." Kegan pointed to her feet; Nick looked under the table and saw a technician curled up taking a nap.

"What time did you guys get here?" Nick asked.

"Seven, seven thirty—she was already here."

"She ran you off?"

"After about thirty minutes. She said we were a 'distracting scent.'"

"That's what she told me yesterday."

"I can understand it with you—me, I bathe."

"Did you get a chance to look at anything?"

"I got a quick look at the first grave."

"And?"

"The skeleton's in pretty bad shape—somebody stomped all over it. The victim was a male, judging by the head of the femur and the coarseness of the eyebrow ridge. I couldn't measure the skull—it was smashed flat—but I found the external occipital protuberance, the place where the neck muscles attach. It was large with heavy muscle markings—another male characteristic."

"What about age?"

"The wisdom teeth are fully formed, so it's definitely an adult. I found a piece of the cranial vault intact; the sutures are mostly fused but still clearly visible—that puts him in his thirties or forties. I'm not sure about his height yet—I'll know more when I can pull the femur and put it on an osteometric board—but I took a quick measurement. I'd guess he was about six foot, maybe a little less—but that's just a guess."

"Race?"

"The nasal opening is narrow and there's a horizontal dam at the base—plus the tops of the molars are smooth. Those are characteristics of a Caucasoid skull."

"Any chance of getting an ID from the teeth?"

"It's possible, but like I said, the skull was crushed flat. That means we've lost the tooth alignment and jaw structure. We've got the individual teeth, but it'll take time to put Humpty Dumpty back together again. We'll need an odontologist for that—and even then we might have a problem."

"What's that?"

"Time. If this skeleton is as old as I think it is, there won't be any dental records to match it with."

"How old do you think it is?"

She frowned. "This may come as a surprise to you, but it takes more than thirty minutes to figure that out. I need more time, Nick—and I want to take a look at that second skeleton. There's probably more we can learn from the first one, but I doubt it's going to be a slam dunk. These are old bones—there's only so much we're going to get from them. The second skeleton might tell us more—and so would any others that are out there. Every one we can find will give us a little more to work with."

"Agreed. I want to get a look at that other skeleton too. The first one's pretty much a write-off for me—they removed all the dirt from around the body. I want to set up a sieve next to the second grave and sift the dirt a layer at a time."

"What are you looking for?"

"Insect parts and puparia—the little casings that maturing insects leave behind."

"Tell me the truth: Can you really tell one fly from another?"

"Can you really tell a male skull from a female skull?"

"Of course—male skulls are solid."

"Funny."

Nick looked out at the dog and its trainer again, scurrying back and forth across the field in their matching orange vests; there were now two small red flags planted in the ground and fluttering in the breeze. "We've got to get back to work," he said, "and neither one of us can do that until Marge and Bosco wrap things up out there. Look at that—two lousy flags—that's all they've got to show for a whole day's sniffing around—and I'll bet you twenty bucks that when we excavate those sites there's nothing down there."

"I'm beginning to think you don't like that dog," Kegan said.

"I dislike animals that dress better than I do."

"Well, I feel sorry for them both."

"I beg your pardon?"

"It reminds me of the World Trade Center. Remember? You were there—there were dog teams everywhere. They were the kind that search for survivors—only there weren't any survivors. By the end the dogs were all getting depressed, so the firemen started hiding in the rubble just so the dogs had someone to find."

Nick looked at her. "How do women do that?"

"Do what?"

"Manage to feel sympathy for someone who doesn't deserve it. I just can't do that."

"Really? I feel sorry for you."

Fifteen minutes went by.

Kegan looked at Nick and smiled. "This makes you crazy, doesn't it?"

"It drives me absolutely bonkers."

"I think it's good for you—you could use more patience."

"That's another thing women do," Nick said.

"What?"

"Take pleasure in a man's pain because it's 'for his own good.'"

"That's not true," she said. "We just like to see men suffer."

They watched for another half hour—then Nick saw the trainer remove one of the two red flags from the ground.

"That's it," he said. "I've had it."

He took out his cell phone and dialed.

"Whiners Anonymous," Donovan said. "What's wrong now?"

"Send me another dog," Nick said. "A bloodhound, a poodle, one of those little Taco Bell dogs that talks with a Spanish accent—I don't care, as long as it has all five senses."

"Look—I checked this woman out after the last time you called. The

Bureau uses her all the time. This is a FEMA-certified cadaver dog team—you should see their credentials."

"You should see mine," Nick said. "I can't smell either."

"Nick—"

"I'm telling you, Donovan, this just isn't working out. Maybe it's the dog or maybe it's the trainer; all I know is, I'm standing here with six forensic specialists on your payroll who can't do their jobs because some dog has a sinus condition."

"C'mon, she can't be that slow."

"Two graves," Nick said. "In twenty-four hours this woman has managed to find two graves—and she just changed her mind about one of them."

"Maybe there aren't any more—maybe that's what the dog is telling us."

"Then I can go home and you can call the backhoe boys and tell them to dig in—but I guarantee they'll find more graves when they do, and I'll be back a day later—and we'll still need a new dog."

"Is the dog really that bad?"

"I'm standing here with Dr. Kegan Alexander, forensic anthropologist and professor of physical anthropology at the University of Virginia. If you like, I'll put her on the phone and she can give you a second opinion."

"Okay, I believe you," Donovan said. "I'll see what I can do—but cadaver dog teams are hard to find, and it won't be easy to find one with better credentials than hers. I'll put in another request, but it could take a couple of days."

"A couple of *days?*"

"It's the best I can do, Nick. Look, I gotta go—I've got an appointment with Senator Braden in about two minutes, and these people don't like to be kept waiting."

"Neither do I."

"Then get yourself fifty million bucks and call me back—that's what Braden did. Money talks, Nick—the rest of us have to listen."

"Tell the senator something for me, will you?"

"What's that?"

"Tell him his entire construction project has ground to a halt because of one dog—see what he has to say about that."

"Yeah, I'll do that. In the meantime I suggest you let this woman keep working."

"Why?"

"Because it might just take a little longer than you think. Face it, Nick, you're a bug man, and you don't know squat about dogs—now do you?"

"I'll be waiting," Nick said. "There's not much else I can do."

Nick dropped the phone into his shirt pocket and looked at Kegan. "Did you hear all that?"

"Most of it."

"Can you believe it? A couple of *days*."

"He's right, you know."

Nick frowned at her. "What happened to all that sympathy?"

"Entomologists are always in a hurry," she said. "I suppose it makes sense, since you people work with things that hatch and grow up and die in just a week or two. But anthropologists work with bones, so we tend to take a longer view. Relax, Nick. These graves have been here for a long time—they'll be here for a couple more days."

"You can be really annoying sometimes."

She grinned. "Something else that women do?"

Nick glared at Marge and Bosco. They were taking a break now under the shade of a nylon lean-to set up on the opposite side of the field; the dog was lapping water from its trainer's hand. "I *hate* to wait," Nick grumbled.

"Sorry. Looks to me like you're out of options."

"There are always options," he said. "It just depends on how far you're willing to go."

7

"Mr. Donovan, the senator will see you now." The woman made a come-with-me gesture with two fingers, flashing a brilliant and orthodontically perfect smile.

Donovan rose from his leather chair and followed her down the corridor. She looked to be in her early twenties, probably just out of college, like most of the aides and legislative assistants who worked on the Hill. She was probably a political science major, pre-law, trying for one more impressive entry on her résumé before she sent off her application to Georgetown or UVA. Not Harvard—definitely not Harvard—at least that's what she probably told the guy who hired her, since this was the office of the senior senator from Virginia, and a man with the deep roots of John Henry Braden wouldn't want a Virginia malcontent on his staff. She was probably grossly underpaid too, like most of the bright young men and women who took these staff positions. But money was beside the point here; the point was just to get a leg up—either on the Hill or someplace else.

The corridor was lined with black-framed photographs showcasing the beautiful state of Virginia: a determined-looking man in breeches and a red hunting coat gliding across a hedge on a chestnut mare; the mist-covered Shenandoah Valley in summertime as seen from Skyline Drive; a sprawling antebellum plantation along the James River; and, of course, the glittering jewel in Virginia's crown—Monticello and its famous west front. *They're not making it up,* Donovan thought, *Virginia is one beautiful place.* Whoever selected these photos could have chosen from a hundred other scenic wonders; Donovan wondered if the Patriot Center would ever be considered one of them.

The hallway widened into a large foyer, with five separate offices that opened off of it. The walls were covered in raised panels of matched-grain cherry, giving the room an incredibly rich and aristocratic feel—like the cigar room of some exclusive men's club that Donovan would never be asked to join. There were two secretaries' desks that faced each other, one on the left and one on the right, forming a kind of aisle-way that carried the eye directly to the door on the opposite wall—the office of Senator John Henry Braden.

The aide turned and smiled. "Mr. Donovan, how long do you expect to be with the senator this morning?" The question was worded carefully, and it was asked in an unctuous tone of voice that seemed to suggest, "How long can we hope to enjoy your delightful company?" In reality the question meant something very different: She was asking how much of the senator's precious time Donovan intended to waste, and at what point she could interrupt and tell Donovan to take his things and clear out.

"I'm here at the senator's convenience," Donovan said with a smile of his own. Positioned in front of the senator's door was a somber-looking man striking the unmistakable pose of a security guard: feet shoulder width apart, hands in front, one resting on top of the other, suspended just below the waist. He wore a black jacket with a matching crewneck shirt and slacks, which was a little over the top; a security officer should dress like an employee, not like Johnny Cash. He was thirtyish and lean, with broad shoulders and a muscular neck and jaw. He had thick black hair swept over to the side, forming a well-placed comma over his left eyebrow, and just enough length in back to allow a few curls to fall on his neck.

Man, Donovan thought, *was I ever trying that hard?*

He stepped up to the security guard and held up his FBI credentials.

The man gave it the barest of glances and said, "You'll need to leave your weapon here with me, sir."

Donovan raised one eyebrow. "Sorry?"

"Your handgun—you'll need to leave it with me."

Donovan smiled and held his credentials a little higher. "Maybe you need to take a closer look at this."

"I saw it."

"You're not Secret Service, are you?"

"No, sir. Private security."

"Uh-huh. That explains why you just asked an FBI agent to surrender his weapon. That's a big no-no where I come from."

"It's standard procedure, sir."

"For you maybe; not for me."

"I'm sorry—there are no exceptions."

Donovan stepped a little closer and lowered his voice. "Look—I know you've got a job to do here, and I can see that you're a real eager beaver, but I need to explain something to you: I'm an FBI agent, and an FBI agent will not hand over his weapon to you or anyone else. So what do you want to do now?"

The man never changed his expression. "We seem to have a small difference of opinion."

"Maybe I should just go," Donovan said. "Then you can go to your boss and tell him that the FBI agent he specifically requested was here, but he left—because you wouldn't let him in. Try that—see how it goes over."

The security guard hesitated, then slowly stepped aside.

"Thanks," Donovan said. "I knew we could work out our differences if we just put our heads together."

He knocked softly on the door and without waiting for a response opened it and stepped inside. The office interior was larger than he'd expected, almost like a second foyer, and it sounded like the DC Metro compared to the tranquil waiting area outside. He counted at least eight staff members chattering into Bluetooth headsets, scribbling notations on wall-mounted whiteboards, or clipping columns from the newspapers that seemed to cover every flat surface in the room.

"Senator Braden?"

The senator glanced up from his desk. "Yes?"

"Special Agent Nathan Donovan. You sent for me, sir."

Braden stood up behind his desk. "Oh, yes, Mr. Donovan—come in. Please, take a seat. Brad, I'd like you to stay for this."

Donovan looked the senator over. It was the first time he had actually met the man face-to-face, or had even spoken to him, for that matter—his assignment came through the ADIC at the Bureau's Washington field office. Braden was a tall man, about sixty years of age, with silver-white hair that showed no hint of thinning. His face seemed permanently tanned, and his classic features looked as if they had been lifted from an ancient Roman bust, from his noble brow to his aquiline nose to his deeply cleft chin. His eyes were a hollow blue, capable of communicating the full range of emotions a president requires, from compassionate concern to righteous indignation. He looked trim, even athletic, but that may have been due to the padded shoulders in his black pin-striped Valentino suit. *He is the picture-perfect politician*, Donovan thought, the cardboard cutout you got your photo taken next to on the boardwalk in Atlantic City. There was no doubt about it, John Henry Braden would make a perfect U.S. president—or at least he would look like one.

Donovan took a seat in a leather wingback chair across from Braden's desk. Everyone in the room grabbed handfuls of paper and quickly exited, except for one man who remained behind and took the chair beside Donovan's.

"Agent Donovan, Brad Lassiter—Brad is my chief of staff."

The two men shook hands.

"You come highly recommended, Mr. Donovan. Brad here tells me you're the best and brightest the Bureau has to offer."

"I'd hate to contradict your chief of staff." It was a good answer—one that merited a smile and a nod from the senator. Washington is no place for modesty, Donovan had quickly learned; people with power are busy, and they don't have time to stand around while you twist your skirt into knots.

"I don't need to tell you that this couldn't have come at a worse time. The convention is coming up in a little more than two months, and then we've got the presidential debates; after that it's a horse race all the way to November. We don't need this distraction right now."

"No, sir."

"The voters don't need this distraction either—they need to stay focused on the issues."

"Yes, sir."

"Brad here tells me you're going to take care of this little distraction for us."

"That's my intention, yes."

"Good. This is just the kind of thing the opposition would love to take advantage of—to exaggerate its importance, to draw the eye of the voter away from more significant matters. Don't get me wrong, Mr. Donovan, the war on terror is one of the major themes of my campaign—whether it's terrorists acting from outside our borders or criminals operating from within. I intend to take a strong stand against crime in this country, and I intend to push for significant budget increases for organizations like your own. The people of America need to know that I will pursue terrorists to the ends of the earth, and the citizens of my beloved Virginia must know that I will not allow criminals to operate in my own backyard. Do I make myself clear?"

"I think so, sir, yes."

"Good. I'm glad we had this little chat, Mr. Donovan, and I appreciate you dropping by to see me today. I'll be keeping track of your progress through Brad here, and I look forward to hearing of a speedy resolution to this matter. Good day, sir."

The senator stood up and extended his hand. Brad rose too, smiled at Donovan, and gestured toward the door.

Donovan was stunned; the meeting had just begun and it was apparently over. *What was that?* he wondered. He came prepared to offer a full report, to give a description of the resources that the Bureau had intended to allocate to the case and to discuss his investigative strategy. Instead he got a two-minute sound bite, half policy statement and half pep talk, that he really didn't need to hear. Braden seemed uninformed, almost unaware of Donovan's purpose here. But didn't Braden send for him? Wasn't he the one who requested him to be assigned to this case?

No skin off my back, Donovan thought. If that's all the involvement Braden wanted, so much the better—it just meant one fewer pair of eyes looking over his shoulder. Maybe that's all Braden had time for—to care about the broad strokes and leave the details to somebody else. *So much for micromanagement,* he thought.

Donovan stepped out into the foyer and closed the door behind him.

"Have a nice day," the security guard said behind him. "I hope to see you again."

Donovan headed for the hallway without looking back.

"Mr. Donovan?"

He stopped; it was the young aide who had shown him to the senator's office.

"Mrs. Braden would like a word with you, please."

"*Mrs.* Braden?"

"If you have a moment."

Donovan followed her into another office. There was no one inside.

"Please make yourself comfortable. Mrs. Braden will be with you in just a moment."

The door closed behind him with a soft click.

Donovan looked around the office; it was much smaller than the senator's but just as elegantly appointed. It was clearly a business office, just like the senator's, but the number of potted plants and the personal memorabilia on the desk and walls revealed a definite woman's touch. Donovan had never met Mrs. Braden before either, but he had certainly seen her photograph—and so had just about everyone else in America. Victoria Braden was one of the most photographed women in Washington, and now that she was the definite favorite for the role of First Lady, she was fast becoming the most photographed woman in the world. The camera loved her; she had hair like the mane of a thoroughbred, a deep chestnut brown with striking red highlights. Her flawless skin looked like rose petals, and her almond-shaped eyes and

Cupid's bow lips made her look like a model. So did her sense of fashion; everything she wore seemed to complement her perfectly, and every designer on the East Coast was competing to see whose gown she would favor at the next White House reception or ball. Victoria Braden was about fifteen years younger than her husband, just enough of an age difference to titillate the American public but still fall within the bounds of propriety. Every eye in America seemed to be turning to her, which made her the perfect wife for a presidential candidate like John Henry Braden; it was a match made in a politician's heaven.

Donovan took a seat in an upholstered chair with his back to the door. The leather felt soft and supple, and he squeezed the arms and settled in a little. He glanced at a diploma prominently displayed on the end table to his left and read the top two lines: University of Virginia, Darden Graduate School of Business Administration. *Not bad*, Donovan thought. *She may be a trophy wife, but she's got a few trophies of her own.*

"Coffee?"

Donovan twisted around and looked at the door. Victoria Braden was balancing a delicate bone china cup with a gold rim on top of a book in her left hand. She had today's *Washington Post* tucked under her right arm and an assortment of folders and files in hand; she quietly pushed the door shut with her hip and crossed to her desk. She was dressed in a simple black blazer and skirt, with an open white blouse that showed off the long curve of her graceful neck. It was a simple, even utilitarian outfit, but the tailoring was immaculate and the lines flowed like honey. *This is a woman who's going places*, Donovan thought. *So what does she want with me?*

"Thanks. I'm fine," Donovan replied.

"I don't know how you do it. Personally, I run on caffeine."

"I gave it up when I joined the FBI."

"So you don't have to take a leak in the middle of a surveillance."

Donovan blinked.

"You're not the first FBI agent I've met," she said.

"I guess not."

She gingerly set her coffee cup in the center of the desk. "This is my favorite cup," she said. "It's a fabulous design—I'm thinking of using it for my White House pattern. I lifted it from the governor's mansion after a dinner party."

"You stole government property?"

"It's still government property—I just had it transferred to a different department. The governor's wife had a breakfront full of them; I didn't think she'd miss just one." She gave Donovan a wink. "Always count the silverware when the politicians leave."

"Thanks, I'll remember that."

She opened a manila file folder and scanned it quickly. "Special Agent Nathan Donovan," she read. "I was impressed with your record. Your wife is quite impressive in her own right: an expert in international terrorism and professor of international relations at Georgetown. The two of you make quite a pair."

"Behind every great man there's a great woman," Donovan said.

"Behind or in front—it depends on your perspective. Do you know why I requested you for this assignment, Mr. Donovan?"

Donovan paused. "I understood that the senator requested me."

"As I said, it's a matter of perspective. I was born in the town of Endor—did you know that?"

"No, I didn't."

"I left when I was very young—my parents were bright enough to realize that there were better opportunities for me elsewhere—but still, Endor is my hometown, and I feel a certain responsibility to the people there."

"You sound like your husband."

"Do I? I'll have to do something about that. My point is, the people of Endor deserve to know that their elected officials haven't forgotten them. They need to see that something is being done to protect them."

"And so do the voters of America."

"Why, Mr. Donovan, that sounded almost cynical. Where's your lofty idealism?"

"Sorry," Donovan said. "That's something else I gave up when I joined the FBI."

"Then you are a cynic."

"I prefer to think of myself as a realist."

"So do I. So tell me—realist to realist—what's the situation at the Patriot Center?"

"What would you like to know?"

"I'm asking for your report, Agent Donovan."

"Well, I've been to the crime scene and I—"

"The excavation site."

"Excuse me?"

"Has it been proven that the two additional bodies were, in fact, victims of foul play?"

"There isn't much doubt."

"That isn't what I asked."

Donovan paused. "No, it hasn't been proven—but I think it will be. I believe in calling a spade a spade."

"So do I—but not until somebody proves it is one. In politics perception is everything. If you call my husband's property a 'crime scene' then it is one, and I don't want it to be one until I say so. So far all we've got is an unmarked graveyard—a historical curiosity, just a part of Virginia's rich historical heritage."

"And the two extra bodies?"

"Nobody knows yet—and until they do I want you to say so. Is that understood?"

Donovan nodded.

"What else can you tell me?"

"I have a forensic team in place—an entomologist from North Carolina and an anthropologist out of UVA."

"My alma mater—I approve. Who's the other one you mentioned—the entomologist?"

"His name is Dr. Nick Polchak."

"Is he good?"

"He's the best there is. Between the two of them, I'm hoping to come up with an estimated time of death for each body. Then we'll search the missing persons reports for those time periods and try to come up with a match."

"Is that likely?"

"It depends a lot on how old the bodies are."

"And that hasn't been determined yet."

"No."

"Then it's possible these two bodies are just historical remains—just like the bodies that were buried beneath them."

"I don't think so."

"But it's possible."

"Theoretically, yes."

"I'd like you to emphasize that possibility until we know otherwise."

"Fair enough."

"Your forensic team—this anthropologist and entomologist—they are not to speak directly to the press. Everything is to go through you—is that understood?"

"They've already been informed."

"Good. I don't want some tech head offering second opinions."

"Anything else?"

"Just an answer to my question."

"What question is that?"

"Why do you think I requested you for this assignment?"

Donovan paused. "You want an honest answer?"

"I prefer honesty. It saves time."

"Okay," he said. "I think you requested me because I'm in the spotlight right now—just like you are. From a practical standpoint it doesn't matter who you ask for, because no matter who the Bureau assigns to the case, the full resources of the FBI come with him. You want the spotlight on the Patriot Center—right now, right away, before things get any worse than they are. You're hoping the camera will follow me there so you can say, 'See, America? We told you all about it.' And then when the public gets tired of hearing about it you're hoping the camera will go away again—in fact, you're hoping the whole problem will go away. You don't really care how I handle this from an investigative perspective; you only care about the way it looks to the public. That's why you called me in here today—to make sure I say 'excavation site' instead of 'crime scene.' Your husband is running for president, and you'd just love to get yourself a whole set of those coffee cups, but you've got enemies—enemies who could blow this whole thing out of proportion if it isn't handled correctly. I think that's why you asked for me, Mrs. Braden. You think I might be a little savvier than your average law enforcement grunt. You think I might be able to handle this the way you want it done—and . . ."

"And?"

"And you think you might be able to handle me."

She studied his face and slowly smiled. She walked around to the front of the desk and leaned back against it. She placed both palms on the edge and lifted herself up onto the desk, then wriggled back a little and crossed her legs so that her knees were pointing at Donovan's chest.

Donovan never looked away from her eyes.

"My, my," she said. "You're either a very disciplined man or you're a man who loves his wife. Which is it, Mr. Donovan?"

"Is there some reason you need to know?"

"I like to know people. It comes in handy."

"Me too," he said, rising from his chair. "I'm glad I stopped by." At the door he turned and looked back. "There's something I need to make clear."

"What's that?"

"I stopped by here today purely as a professional courtesy. I don't know what strings you or your husband pulled to get me assigned to this case, but the assignment came through the assistant director in charge. That means he's the boss, and I report directly to him—and only to him. If you have any further questions about the way this case will be handled, please direct your questions to him. Is that clear?"

"Very."

He nodded and opened the door.

"Mr. Donovan."

"Yes?"

"Tell your wife I'd like to meet her sometime."

"Come over for dinner," Donovan said. "We'll use the everyday china."

She smiled. "You have a sense of humor. I like that in a man."

Donovan didn't return the smile.

When he closed the door she picked up the phone. "Hi, Brad. Stop in and see me when you get a moment, will you? I just spoke with Mr. Donovan. We're going to have to keep an eye on him; I'm not sure he's the one we're looking for after all."

8

It was early evening when Nick pulled his car into the parking lot of the Skyline Motel. The lot was narrow, allowing just a single row of cars between the building and the street. The building itself was a single-story structure with white beveled siding and a black shingled roof, built in the days when land was cheap and the motor hotels that lined the highways looked more like long cottages than the corporate high-rises of today. The Skyline had been strategically located on the main intersection of Endor in hopes that the tourists on their way up into the Blue Ridge Mountains would stop off for a quick night's rest. But the tourists turned out to be few and far between; there were better roads up into the mountains, and there were far more entertaining stop-offs than the little town of Endor.

The Skyline's single virtue was that it was the only lodging place in town—which made it the FBI's official residence for anyone associated with the Patriot Center case. Not for Kegan—she was from Charlottesville and had an easy commute; not for the Bureau's forensic tech crew—they all lived near Quantico, and they didn't mind getting up a little earlier in the morning for the privilege of seeing their wives and kids each night. That left just Nick and Marge—and Bosco, of course, who shared his trainer's room. Nick imagined the King stretched out on satin pillows while his trainer camped out on the floor beside him. Then he imagined the motel catching fire and both of them perishing in the flames because the dog didn't smell the smoke—but that was just wishful thinking.

He pressed the Lock button on his key fob, though he wasn't sure why; he could probably leave the car doors open and no one would bother it here. He looked across the parking lot at the only other vehicle —a gleaming white SUV with the name *Fidelis Search and Rescue Dogs* emblazoned on the side. *Impressive-looking car*, Nick thought. *I wonder if it has an engine.*

He started across the street toward the Endor Tavern & Grille, wondering what story Biff had concocted to tell his friends about their adventures the night before. "Biff goes toe-to-toe with the Witch of Endor"—there's a story to tell your grandkids. Nick wondered if Biff would include the part where he wet his pants and ran screaming into the woods. He didn't really blame him for being scared; to tell the truth, he felt a little sorry for him—but he would have paid good money to see how fast the kid cleared that fence on the way back.

At the intersection he glanced across the street to his left; there was the Endor Regional Library and the lights were still on. Nick had a sudden idea, so he turned and crossed the street.

To the left of the library's main door he found an old woman kneeling on the lawn and digging furiously in a flower bed, with a flat of red begonias waiting on the grass beside her.

"I'm too old for all this digging," she muttered, plucking the omnipresent stones from the soil and tossing them over her shoulder.

Nick walked over. "Is the library still open?"

"'Til nine," she said, using her trowel like a lever to pry out a large rock.

"Do people stay that long?"

She looked up at Nick. "You lookin' for books or for company?"

"I'm looking for information."

"That we got. Hold on a minute." She lifted one thick leg and planted the foot squarely in front of her, then put both forearms on her thigh and pushed down, using her leg like a rock ledge to push herself up and draw her other leg up under her. She stood there for a moment, panting and mopping her forehead with the back of her gloved hand.

"Sorry to bother you," Nick said.

"No bother. I'm the librarian—that's what I'm here for."

She was a short woman, maybe five feet tall, and she had that look some old people get—sort of like an old candle, tapering at the top and sagging toward the base. Her torso was pear-shaped, and she covered it with a sleeveless cotton sundress that had no particular color or form. Her upper arms were thick but still solid—the reward you apparently get for years of gardening in rocky soil. Her ankles were almost as wide as her calves, a probable indication that her kidneys could no longer process all of her body's fluids. Her hair looked like it had lost its color a long time ago, and she had apparently quit doing anything about it; she wore it in tight gray curls that clung close to her head. It was difficult to judge her age; Nick would have guessed between seventy and eighty, but he had noticed that the mountains seem to wear people down a little earlier in life—and she looked to Nick like a genuine mountain woman, from her yellowed teeth that had never seen braces to her calloused hands that had seldom seen rest.

She supported herself on Nick's arm as they started toward the library. "Bad knees—got a bit of the rheumatoid."

"Can't you get somebody else to do the digging?"

"Who you got in mind? Besides, it's how I get my exercise. Now what are you lookin' for?"

Nick held the door for her. "Historical records—information on the land around Endor."

"You come to the right place. This is the Endor *Regional* Library—we got records from all around these parts, and I'm just the woman to help you find 'em. If we got it, I can put my finger on it."

"I'm looking for grave registries."

"We got those—I know right where to look."

"Old ones—old enough to list a graveyard that nobody remembers anymore."

"Whereabouts?"

"Where they're building the Patriot Center."

She stopped and thought.

"Do you know the place?"

"Everybody does. Give a soul a minute to think." She seemed to stare off into space for a moment, then abruptly nodded her head. "Know right where to look—be right back."

She disappeared through a doorway that led to a back room.

Nick looked around. It seemed like a typical small-town library, with minimal holdings and even less technology. Nice seating, though; there were a couple of comfortable-looking upholstered chairs where a local kid like Biff could cover his face with his math book and pretend to do his homework while he took a little snooze. *He'd better watch himself here*, Nick thought. *That old bird looks pretty tough—she could toss him out on his ear.* But Biff was probably in no danger; Nick had a feeling he didn't spend a lot of time here.

He spotted a small room that opened off the main library, so he wandered in and looked around. He noticed the walls; every square inch was covered with photographs and newspaper clippings featuring the future First Lady of the United States, Victoria Braden. There was Victoria on a yacht in the Chesapeake Bay; Victoria in a stunning dropped-back evening gown at the Bush 43 inaugural ball; Victoria on the steps of the Capitol beside her husband. Celebrities and famous faces were everywhere: There was Victoria with the Clintons, Victoria with the Bushes, Victoria with anyone and everyone who managed to push or shove their way in front of the camera to get their picture taken with one of the most beautiful women in the world.

Nick scanned a few of the newspaper and magazine clippings. Every one of them was a glowing tribute to one of Victoria's stellar qualities: her beauty, her charm, her intelligence, her generosity, her tireless work for charity or on the public's behalf. Apparently the woman was perfect; there wasn't a single word of negative press anywhere in the room.

Nick shook his head. *This isn't a library, it's a shrine.*

"She's somethin', ain't she?"

Nick turned. It was the librarian, standing and beaming proudly in the doorway.

"Yeah, she's something. Who collected all this?"

"I did. She's from Endor, y'know."

"You're kidding."

"Most people don't know that."

Nick studied one of the photos. "I'll bet she got a few invitations to the prom."

"Oh, she left way before that—when she was just a little girl."

Too bad for Endor, Nick thought. *She would have made a major addition to the gene pool.*

"She going to be First Lady of the United States," the librarian said with a faraway look. "But she'll always be our little Victoria—and she'll never forget Endor."

But I'll bet she's tried. "Did you find the records I asked for—the grave registries?"

Her face dropped. "No, sir, I didn't. I'm sorry to say they just weren't there."

"Are they checked out?"

"You can't check 'em out. They're part of our historical holdings—that's why we keep 'em in the back."

"Maybe if I helped you look."

"You're welcome to try, but it won't do you no good. I been the librarian here for goin' on fifty years—I know every book we got and I know what shelf it sits on. We just don't have no grave registries; I thought we might, but we don't."

"Can you think of any other historical record that might describe a graveyard near the Patriot Center? I'm looking for a burial plot or a list of the people buried there—even a good physical description of the area might help."

She thought for a moment. "Nothing comes to mind—but I'll give it some thought if you like."

"I'd appreciate that. My name is Nick Polchak—I didn't catch yours."

"Agnes Deluca," she said. "Nice to meet you, Nick."

"Well, Agnes, I'm staying across the street at the Skyline. If you come up with anything, you can leave word for me there."

"I'll see what I can find. Mind if I ask you somethin'?"

"Go ahead."

"How come you want to know about a graveyard?"

"I'm afraid I'm not at liberty to say. Sorry."

She held up both hands. "That's all right—I know where my nose belongs and where it don't."

Nick looked at her. "Do you mind if I ask you a question?"

"Not at all."

"You said you've been here for fifty years."

"Been head librarian for fifty years—been in Endor all my life."

"Then you must know everyone in town."

"Can't think of one I don't—'course, those I don't won't come to mind."

"What can you tell me about the young woman who lives up on top of the mountain?"

"You mean the witch?"

"Yeah—the woman people call a witch."

"People call her a witch because she is a witch."

Nick paused. "What makes you think so?"

"You know what she does up there on that mountain?"

"What?"

"On the night of every full moon she wanders the woods, searching for the body of her dead father. She always has a three-legged dog close by her side—at least it *looks* like a dog."

"It's not really a dog?"

"It *looks* like a dog."

"Then what is it?"

She motioned for Nick to lean in closer. "The soul of her father lives in that animal. It's half-dog and half-human—that's why it's only got three legs. The witch and the dog search the woods for her father's body. When she finds it, they'll be reunited forever."

Nick stared. "Okay—I think that's all I need here."

"If you want to know more about the witch, you come back sometime—the stories I could tell you. 'Course, when you talk about the witch, she knows it. Not to worry—I'll make us some tea and we'll put a broom in the doorway. A witch won't never cross a broom."

"It's a date," Nick said. "In the meantime, if you come up with anything on that graveyard—"

"You're at the Skyline. Don't worry, I won't forget."

Nick stepped out of the library. The sun was setting fast now, and the streetlamps that surrounded the intersection were just beginning to blink on. Nick once again started toward the Endor Tavern & Grille and dinner, but he caught a glimpse of a figure standing in front of the Lutheran church and decided to take a look.

There was a winding sidewalk that led from the street corner back to the main entrance, paved in the same Virginia bluestone that the church itself was made of. On the lawn beside the sidewalk a man was stacking more of the flat stones into some kind of shapeless mound.

"People seem to work late around here," Nick said.

"Not much else to do." The man turned and tipped his head down, sliding his small spectacles down his nose and staring over the top at Nick. "I don't believe I know you. I'm Gunner Wendorf—I'm the pastor here."

"Nick Polchak," he said, extending his hand. "*Gunner*—that's an unusual name."

"It's *Günther*, actually, but the folks around here aren't particularly good with glottal stops and guttural *r*'s, so it just became Gunner." He gestured to his stone creation. "What do you think?"

"I'm not sure. What is it?"

"It's supposed to look like the Pool of Bethesda."

"Never been there."

The man shrugged and tossed the stone aside. "Me neither. I could use a cup of coffee and a stale donut—you interested?"

"Sure."

"Follow me."

Nick followed the man into the church and down the main aisle of the sanctuary to his office at the front. The office was small and cramped and the walls were crowded with bookshelves from corner to corner and from ceiling to floor, giving the room the slight musty smell of an old library. There was paper everywhere, and the desk was piled high too. Nick immediately liked the office—it reminded him a lot of his own.

"Take a seat if you can find one," the man said. "I'll see what I can scrounge up in the kitchen."

Nick browsed the bookshelves instead. The books were organized into main subject categories, with little handwritten labels like "Systematic Theology," "Cultural Apologetics," "Grammars and Lexicons," and "Reformation History." There was a section reserved for "Classics," and another devoted to Luther alone. Nick liked the man already; if his mind was anything like his library, he was a man worth getting to know.

"You're like me," the man said, returning with two mugs and a plate with two donuts balanced on top. "You head straight for the books."

"I like to see what people read—it tells me a lot about them."

"I'm the same way. Here, take your pick—they're both as hard as rocks. Sorry, that's all that's left from Sunday school. Never stand between a Christian and a donut."

Nick slid a thick volume from the shelf and opened it. "Now this is interesting—a geology textbook. In fact, you've got a whole section devoted to geology. Hobby?"

"It was my undergraduate major. Thought I might work for the U.S. Geological Survey, but I found something better."

Nick replaced the book. "You know, they should make your office the public library and bulldoze the one across the street."

"You've been to our library? Then you must have met Agnes."

"Yes, I had the pleasure."

"No visit to Endor would be complete without a chance to meet Agnes. She's practically a historic landmark herself around here. She's been around forever—she looked old even when I was a boy."

"You're from Endor, then?"

"Born and raised."

"Then you must know this town inside and out."

"Not as well as Agnes—she's the keeper of the flame of Endor."

"What does that mean?"

"Anything you want to know about the history of this town and its people, she's the one to ask. Every fascinating detail she keeps right in her head."

"How many are there?"

He grinned. "You've got a point there. How about you—where are you from?"

"I'm at NC State down in Raleigh."

"You look too old to be a student."

"I'm a professor."

"Of what?"

"Entomology."

"No kidding. Well, we've got enough strange bugs to keep you occupied around here." There was a lull in the conversation and Gunner took the opportunity to ask, "Is there something I can do for you, Nick? Are you working up your nerve, or is this just a social call?"

"I have a question for you. I think you might be the right man to ask."

"Go ahead."

"What can you tell me about the woman who lives on the top of this mountain?"

"You mean the witch?"

Nick frowned. "I'm a little disappointed."

"Why?"

"You're a scientist after all."

"I don't believe she's really a witch, if that's what you mean. That's just what everybody calls her around here, so I do too."

"What can you tell me about her?"

He paused. "She's a young woman with a very painful past—and if you don't mind, that's all I'd like to say about it."

"Why?"

"You're not from a mountain community, are you?"

"No."

"People in the mountains are a different breed. The land shapes the way they think, the way they feel. People down in the lowlands, they're communal people—you can see your neighbor across the valley and you make a point to get together from time to time. In the mountains you're isolated; every house is tucked away in some little hollow or ravine and people learn to take care of themselves—and they like to be left alone. This is old country; there are stories and legends about every corner of this place, and people have long memories here. Superstitions grow like weeds; somebody calls somebody else a witch, and pretty soon everybody believes it. That's something else about the mountains—stories spread like wildfire here. Endor's newspaper comes out twice a week, and people only read it to see if they got the story right."

"Agnes seems to know a few stories," Nick said.

Gunner smiled. "She knows them all."

"So somebody called this woman a witch, and now everybody thinks she is one. Okay, I can understand that—what I don't understand is why she calls herself one."

He hesitated. "I'm in a bit of an awkward position here, Nick. People don't have a lot of privacy around here, and I like to help protect what little they have."

"Understood," Nick said.

"But if you'd like to talk theology or philosophy or history, I'm your man. Drop by anytime—I'll take you over to the ET&G and buy you a beer."

"You people drink beer?"

"I'm a German Lutheran—we practically invented the stuff."

"Thanks, I may take you up on that. By the way—I met the witch last night."

Gunner's face went blank. "Where?"

"Her place—and I'm going back tonight."

He took off his glasses and wiped them with a tissue. "Mind if I give you a piece of friendly advice?"

"Not at all."

"Be very careful."

"Of what?"

"Just be careful—if not for your sake, then for hers."

9

Nick slowly worked his way through the woods again, holding the flat white box in front of him. He stopped from time to time to listen, but at first detected nothing. Then he heard it: the soft padding of feet drawing steadily closer. He kept walking, knowing that if he stopped the dogs would stop too, and he didn't want them to stop—he wanted to draw them in. Within a few minutes the first of the huge dogs came into view—then the second, then the third. They slowly drew closer, surrounding Nick and bringing him to a standstill just as they had done the night before.

"Hi, boys," Nick said cheerfully. "At least I'm assuming you're boys, since the males of most species tend to be larger than the females. I'd hate to think there are ladies out there that are bigger than you guys are, but hey, who knows? Personally, I'm into bugs."

The dogs showed no reaction to Nick's pleasant greeting.

He turned to the dog on his right. "Nice doggie," he said in his friendliest voice—but the words sounded ridiculous even as he said them; it was like calling an African lion "Mr. Boots." Still, it was a canine, and domesticated canines were known to respond to human affection, so— "Good doggie," he tried again. But there were no wagging tails in this group. They continued to eye Nick warily, studying his every move.

Nick looked up ahead in the woods. "I suppose Her Royal Wickedness will be along any minute now. Have you boys had your dinner yet? I hope not, 'cause I brought you something I think you'll really like." He opened the white box and folded back the lid. He peeled a slice of pizza from the cardboard and dangled it in the air.

"Meat Lover's," he said. "I made a wild guess that you boys aren't vegetarians."

The dogs made no response.

"Here you go—come and get it." He turned to the dog on his left and tossed the slice of pizza so that it landed at the dog's feet; he tossed another slice to the dog behind him. Neither dog moved—not even a sniff.

He set the entire box down in front of the third dog and waved the lid back and forth, fanning the scent toward its face. "C'mon, it's pizza. You guys can't be *that* disciplined. How'd you ever get so big?"

The dog just stared.

Nick stood up and wiped his hands on his khakis. He looked into the woods again; there was still no sign of the witch. "Where's your master this evening? Did she take the broom out for a spin? She must know I'm here by now—what's keeping her?"

Fifteen minutes later Nick was still waiting.

"I can't wait here all night," he grumbled. He looked at the dogs that surrounded him; he only had two choices—he could go forward or he could go back. "Back" didn't seem to be an option—he tried that last night and the dog behind him had barred his way. He looked at the two dogs in front of him; they were standing guard at the ten and two o'clock positions, and that left a small gap between them. He wondered if they would allow him to move forward again. It seemed possible; after all, they had let him come this far.

"Nice doggies," Nick said again. "I'm going to try something here, and I'd appreciate it if you'd just bear with me."

He took a single step forward and nothing happened. "Good doggies," he said with a sigh of relief.

Then he took a second step.

Nick caught a glimpse of black fur streaking in from the left; the dog reached him in a single bound, turning its massive head sideways in midair and seizing Nick by the throat as it sent him crashing to the ground.

He lay on his back, stunned, with the dog standing over him, still gripping his throat in its jaws. Nick's first instinct was to grab at the dog's head and try to push it away, but he knew that could be a fatal mistake; it would only encourage a tug-of-war with Nick's throat as the prize—and that was a contest he couldn't afford to lose. Instead he lay perfectly still, waiting for the dog to make its next move—but the dog did nothing more. It just stood motionless, pinning Nick's neck to the ground like a giant slobbering clothespin.

Nick heard footsteps approaching, but there was nothing he could do. He just stared up into the starry sky, unable to turn his head even to look.

The witch leaned over and glared down at Nick; she cocked her head to one side and pulled her hair back to get a better look at his face.

"You're persistent," she said. "I'll give you that."

"It's one of my better qualities," Nick said.

"Really. I'd hate to see your bad ones."

Nick pointed to the dog's head. "Would you mind?"

"Not just yet."

He frowned. "I don't really care for this view."

"That makes two of us."

Nick twisted a little; when he did, he felt the dog tighten its grip.

"I wouldn't do that if I were you," the witch said. "He won't purposely harm you, but he will not release your throat—under any circumstances—until I tell him to do so. When you twist like that he thinks you're trying to escape, and he won't let that happen. The harder you try, the harder he'll bite—and believe me when I say, he doesn't know his own strength."

Nick tried his best to relax—which wasn't easy given the circumstances.

"Why did you come back here?" she asked.

"Because I need your help."

"I thought we covered this last night."

"No, we didn't—you were rude and told me to go away."

"I was not *rude*," she said. "You were trespassing on my land."

"I had no choice. You don't have a phone."

"I don't want to be interrupted—especially by you."

Nick stopped. He sensed the increasing tension, and apparently the dog did too—he felt it gradually tightening its grip again. He decided to slow down and try again. "You have me at a disadvantage," he said. "Usually when I fight with a woman she doesn't have three huge animals ready to rip out my throat."

"Too bad for them," she replied. "Whenever I fight with a man I find they come in handy."

"I wonder if we could start over. I would really appreciate the chance to talk to you for a few minutes—just a friendly conversation, witch-to-mortal. After that, if you want me to go, I will."

"You're in no position to bargain," she said.

"Please? It's a little uncomfortable down here. Plus your dog is drooling down my neck, which is easily one of the grossest things I've ever experienced—and believe me, I have a very high threshold for 'gross.'"

She hesitated.

"I even brought you a pizza—as a peace offering."

She looked at the open box.

"I got the Witch Supreme," Nick said. "Eye of newt with extra bat wings."

She smiled a little—then she saw the three slices of pizza lying in the dirt. "Were you trying to bribe my dogs?"

"I told them it was for you. They threatened me. It got ugly."

She smiled a little more.

"That smile looks good on you," Nick said.

"Well, don't get used to it." She snapped her fingers, then closed her fist and opened it again; the dog immediately released Nick's throat and returned to its sitting position.

Nick sat up and wiped his neck with both hands, then looked at them.

"Were you expecting blood?" the witch asked.

"Frankly, yes. Extraordinary—an animal with that much power yet is able to exercise that kind of control. Did you train these animals yourself?"

"You said you wanted to talk—so talk."

"Is there someplace we can go and sit down?"

"You're sitting down now."

"You're not making this easy."

"Is there some reason I should?"

"No," Nick said, "I suppose there isn't." He got up from the ground and dusted himself off. "I'm Dr. Nick Polchak. I'd offer you my hand, but I'm afraid it might get bitten off."

He waited, but she didn't respond.

"I didn't get your name."

"I didn't give it."

"Am I supposed to keep calling you 'Witch'? I tried that with a woman once and it ended our relationship."

She paused. "Alena Savard."

"Alena," he said. "That's a perfectly good name."

"Who said it wasn't?"

"The way you kept resisting, I thought maybe it was 'Wanda' or 'Glendora'—you know, something really embarrassing for a witch."

She didn't reply.

"I'm a professor of entomology at NC State down in Raleigh. I'm also a forensic entomologist—that's why I'm here in Virginia. I'm working for the FBI."

"Working on what?"

"Are you familiar with the Patriot Center?"

"You mean that unforgivable scar that destroyed a thousand acres of beautiful Virginia hardwoods?"

"That's the one. During excavation they discovered an unmarked graveyard; by law they have to stop and identify all the remaining graves and relocate them before work can continue."

"Good—I don't care if they ever find them."

"The FBI does."

"Why?"

"Because a couple of the graves contain two bodies—one in a casket and another one buried on top. Apparently somebody had the bright idea of hiding a body by burying it in an existing graveyard—they figured nobody would bother to look for it there. If there are two bodies then there might be more; if there are more we might be talking about a serial killer here—that's why the FBI's involved. We need to find the remaining graves as soon as possible."

"So what do you want from me?"

"I think you have a cadaver dog here—an exceptionally good one."

"What makes you think that?"

Nick smiled. "You know, you're an interesting person. 'The Witch of Endor,' they call you—and it's not just a nasty name that somebody made up—it's something you actually encourage. So much myth and superstition surround you that it's hard to separate fact from fiction. A sheriff's deputy told me that you actually have the power to raise the dead—but when I asked a few questions I realized what he was really describing: You have the power to *find* the dead—or should I say, your dog does." Nick pointed to the three-legged dog seated at her side. "Is that it?"

"*Her*," she corrected. "She has a sex, you know."

"Sorry. When I was down there I should have noticed."

"Why should I help the FBI?"

"Forget the FBI," Nick said. "Help *me*."

"What are you talking about?"

"The FBI hired some woman with a FEMA-certified cadaver dog—King Ding Dong or something. The dog's got all the right credentials, but it just can't smell. They've been working for two days now, and they still can't find any graves."

"Two *days*?"

"That's right—and she won't let me come anywhere near the site because she says my scent is distracting her dog."

"That's silly. She's making excuses."

"That's what I told her. Alena, I can't do my job until we locate those remaining graves, and I can't find those graves without a cadaver dog—a real one, not just one with a colorful wardrobe. If this cadaver dog of yours is trained anywhere near as well as your other dogs, then you could do this job in no time. Please, help me out here."

She narrowed her eyes at Nick. "And why should I help you?"

"Because I came all the way up here to ask you—twice; because I brought you a pizza; because I let your dog use my neck as a chew toy; because I risked life and limb and losing my appendix to a voodoo curse—that's why."

She didn't seem impressed.

"Then do it because you train dogs," he said. "There's a woman down there who has no idea what she's doing, and she's giving people like you a bad name."

The witch considered this. "I'm sorry," she said. "It's just not possible."

"Why not?"

"I don't want people to see me."

"No one has to see you. We can do it at night—right now if you're available."

"We'd have to be back before daylight."

"Absolutely. I can drive you there and bring you back."

"I have a truck," she said. "I can drive myself."

"Even better—then you can go back anytime you want. And while you're there, you can cast a spell on the whole Patriot Center so that no one can ever find a parking space near the front door. What do you say?"

She let out a deep breath. "One hour. I'll meet you there."

10

Nick checked his watch. It was already after midnight, and he was beginning to wonder whether Alena was coming or not. Maybe she changed her mind; maybe she never planned to come at all—maybe she just told Nick what he wanted to hear to make him get off her back and go away. *Strange woman*, he thought, *but those dogs of hers*—if her cadaver dog was half as well trained as those three black behemoths, Nick just might be in luck.

The excavation site looked surreal in the brilliant moonlight. There were no colors except for blues and violets and the deep black shadows that seeped over the ground like pools of oil. The silent blades and cranes and backhoes of the excavation equipment looked like the bones of dead dinosaurs against the nighttime sky, and the four open graves seemed more ominous than they did in the daylight. *What is it about a grave at night?* Nick thought. *It always makes your skin crawl when you can't see the bottom.*

"Let's get started."

Nick jumped. The witch was standing right behind him with her three-legged dog by her side. She was dressed no differently than she was earlier, except that she now wore three bandannas tied around her neck, each with a different color and pattern. Her long black hair still draped like a curtain in front of her face, and she peered out from behind it at Nick. He looked over her shoulder at the parking lot and saw an old red pickup with a white camper shell.

"You sure know how to walk quietly," Nick said.

"I heard you stomping through my woods a mile away," she replied. "I didn't need a dog to find you."

"That's what my girlfriend used to say."

The witch just looked at him.

"It's a joke," Nick said. "Don't witches like jokes?"

"Funny ones."

Nick glanced down at the dog; the animal looked about as impressed as her master. "What's your dog's name?" he asked.

She glared at him. "Why do you want to know that?"

"I just thought—"

"No one knows her name but me, okay?"

Nick shrugged. "Whatever you say."

"Are we going to do this or not?"

"Sure," he said, pointing to the area around them. "We think the graves are probably—"

"Just give me a general search perimeter."

Nick raised one eyebrow. "*Search perimeter*—is that witch talk?"

"Are you going to make wisecracks all night?"

"Probably—but I'll be happy to get out of your way and let you get to work."

"Good. The sooner we get started, the sooner I can go home."

"Where do you want me?"

"Just stay out of our way."

"Should I stay downwind or something?"

She looked at him impatiently.

Nick nodded. "Out of the way—got it. This is the search area here; any unexcavated ground is a possible location for a grave." He moved off to the side and watched.

The witch and the dog moved to the approximate center of the un-excavated area. She walked without any sound at all. *No wonder*, Nick thought, *she's still barefoot*. She pointed at the ground a few yards away from her, and the dog immediately trotted to that spot, turned, and sat down. The witch stood motionless for a moment, then lifted her face to the moon. She slowly raised both arms in front of her with her palms facing up as though she were carrying an invisible load of firewood, then moved her arms up and down a little as if she were testing its weight.

Now she began to walk in circles, making the same lifting motion as she went. It looked silly to Nick—like an outfielder waiting for a pop fly to drop out of the air. After a minute or two she stopped and looked at each arm, turning it back and forth as though she were admiring a new bracelet. She shook them a little and looked at them again.

She slowly lowered herself into a quarter-squat and then rose again, staring straight ahead; she did it over and over until Nick thought she looked like a horse on a merry-go-round.

Now she extended both arms out to the sides and lowered her head as if she were studying her feet; her hair draped down around her head like tinsel from a Christmas tree. She shook her head a little, making her hair dance about—then she stopped and waited. A few seconds later she repeated the ritual again.

Finally she turned to the dog, snapped her fingers, and wiggled one of them. The dog immediately came and stood facing her, attentively awaiting her next command. She knelt down and took one of the bandannas from her neck; she held it open and showed it to the dog, then tied it around the dog's neck and straightened it a little. She waited for a moment—then suddenly clapped her hands together and looked at the dog with a wide-eyed grin. It was the first time Nick had seen the woman really smile, and it caught him a little off guard. Still, it looked good on her. *Maybe if I wear a bandanna*, he thought.

The moment the witch smiled the dog became eager and excited, bobbing its head up and down and shifting its weight back and forth between its three legs like a runner before a race. She reached out with both hands and grabbed the dog by the fur of its neck and pulled it toward her. She rolled onto her back and dragged the dog on top of her, and the two of them lay there playing together in the dirt.

Nick suddenly became aware that his mouth was hanging open and he was squinting hard, though there was barely enough light to see.

What the heck is she doing? It looked like some kind of bizarre ritual—worshipping the moon and then cross-dressing with the dog. Nick began to wonder if he'd made a big mistake. Maybe the woman actually took this "witch" thing seriously—maybe she was trying to call up the spirits from their graves or something. *Terrific*, he thought. *I traded a dog without a nose for a woman without a mind.*

Now the witch got up from the ground and straightened herself. Her demeanor had changed; there was no longer a smile on her face. She snapped her fingers and pointed down and the dog immediately returned to its place by her side. She pivoted and started off briskly as though someone had called to her from across the field, and the dog followed close beside. At the southeast corner of the unexcavated area she stopped and turned, facing the open field. She waited until the dog took a sitting position, then snapped her fingers and dropped her arm to her side. The dog seemed to tense, anticipating something—then the witch made a motion like someone tossing a horseshoe and the dog took off like a shot.

The dog moved quickly at first, darting back and forth just as Bosco had done—but after a few moments she began to slow down, and the area that seemed to interest her became smaller and smaller. The witch walked along beside the dog, circling her, studying her, bending down or squatting from time to time to get a better look at the dog's face. Less than five minutes passed before the dog slowed to a standstill. She lowered her head and sniffed at an area no more than one square foot in size—and then lay down.

The witch immediately called the dog away from the area and pointed again at the ground by her side. When the dog returned to its sitting position she waited a few seconds, then made that tossing motion again. The dog quickly retraced her steps, sniffed at the same area, and lay down again. The witch knelt down in front of the dog and studied her face. She held up both hands and made a shrugging motion, as if she were asking the dog for some sort of confirmation; the dog didn't move. Then Alena broke into an ecstatic grin, as if she had just learned that she won the Virginia lottery—and she pulled the dog on top of her again and they again began to play.

After a few minutes she stood up and looked across the field at Nick. "Are you expecting me to remember where they all are?"

Bingo! "Hang on a minute—I'll be right there."

Nick ran to the tech tent and grabbed a handful of wire flags, then hurried across the field to the witch and her dog. "Where?" he asked.

"Where she was lying."

"Are you sure?"

One dark eye glared at him from behind the curtain of hair.

"Right." Nick pushed a flag into the ground to mark the spot—it felt so good. "Good work—keep going."

"I will, as soon as you get out of the way."

"Sorry, I forgot—the distracting scent."

"You're not distracting her," she said. "You're annoying me."

Nick continued to watch as the witch and her dog combed the field. They worked with remarkable speed and efficiency. Nick checked his watch; on average the dog was locating a new grave every ten minutes, and Nick kept trotting back and forth across the field to mark the spot with another red flag. She was finding so many graves that at first Nick wondered if the dog was making it all up—just picking up a general graveyard smell and sounding the alarm every few yards or so. But as Nick added each additional flag, he observed its position relative to the others, and there was no denying it—the flags were aligning in a definite grid pattern. The pattern was becoming so obvious that Nick could actually anticipate the location of some of the graves—and the dog did not disappoint. She found them all one by one, filling in the grid like a man working a complex crossword puzzle—and she did it all with three legs and a nose.

Nick was beginning to understand now. What looked like meaningless hocus-pocus at first was slowly beginning to make sense to him; there was definite method to the witch's madness. Whenever she snapped her fingers the dog seemed to come to attention. It seemed to be some sort of operant signal, as if to tell the dog, "Pay attention! What comes next is a command." The commands themselves were remarkably subtle: The barest lift of a finger or flip of a wrist sent the dog racing off in a different direction or called it back again. Sometimes she communicated with just a tilt of her head or a slight change in facial expression—the sort of signals a man might easily miss, but the dog never missed a single cue. They communicated without a spoken word, and the effect was eerie. It was almost as if they could read each other's minds—at least that's the way it would appear to any casual observer. "The witch can talk to animals," the deputy had told Nick, and he was right—almost. It reminded him of something he had read once from Arthur C. Clarke: "Any sufficiently advanced technology is indistinguishable from magic."

Nick shook his head. *No wonder they think she's a witch.*

He thought about Marge and Bosco again—the shouted commands, the constant piercing whistle—and he wondered if Bosco was a little slow or if this dog was just a genius. Maybe Bosco was like a confused child with an overbearing mother who kept screaming commands until the child just shut down in frustration. Maybe the difference was talent or maybe the difference was training, but the difference was obviously there—the two dogs didn't belong in the same category. Bosco may have had all the right papers, but this three-legged mongrel seemed to have powers that bordered on the supernatural.

Nick looked at the witch. *Maybe it's not the dog.*

By dawn the dog had found almost thirty graves, arranged in a neat geometric pattern with a straggler or two on each side—*probably latecomers*, Nick thought. The first rays of golden sunlight streamed down the valley from the east, illuminating the little red flags like licks of fire. The witch led the dog around the perimeter of the graveyard twice more, but the dog found nothing else.

"What's going on here?" a voice called out.

Nick turned and looked. Marge was approaching from the parking lot with Bosco on a short leash. She was glaring angrily at the witch and her dog—and at the field of little red flags.

"I requested a second dog team," Nick called back.

"May I ask why?"

Nick rolled his eyes. "I was hoping that between two dogs I might get one nose."

"That isn't funny, Dr. Polchak."

"Nobody thinks I'm funny," Nick said. "Is it me or is it just women in general?"

On the opposite side of the graveyard the witch heard the voices and turned. She immediately commanded her dog to take a sitting position beside her, then lowered her head until her eyes disappeared.

"I was hired to do this job," Marge said. "Who is *that*?"

"*That* is a dog trainer," Nick replied. "You can tell by the dog."

"What in the world is she dressed for? I assumed you wanted a professional."

"I'm not looking for a cadaver dog with fashion sense," Nick said, "I'm looking for a cadaver dog that can actually find cadavers."

"Which I was in the process of doing." Her dog now spotted the witch's dog; he began to emit a high-pitched whine and strain at the leash. "King—*stay!*"

"Your dog failed to find anything," Nick said. "You told me there might not be any more graves here. I can't just take your word for that—it takes a second dog team to confirm a negative finding. C'mon, Marge, this is standard procedure and you know it."

"*She* is not 'standard procedure.' Where in the world did you find her?"

"What difference does it make? She knows what she's doing—and apparently so does her dog." He made a sweeping gesture at the grid of red flags behind him.

Suddenly the dog jerked harder, yanking the leash from Marge's hand and racing across the field toward the witch. "*King!*" she shouted again, but the dog paid no attention to her. She squinted at Nick. "Anybody can stick a bunch of flags in the ground."

"Twenty-nine flags—that's twenty-eight more than yesterday."

"And how many of them will turn out to be false positives?"

"We'll find out when we excavate," Nick replied. "At least we have something to excavate now—that's more than we got from Bosco."

"His name is not *Bosco*," she growled, and brushed past Nick in the direction of the witch.

Nick turned and followed her; the last thing he wanted was a confrontation between Marge and the Witch of Endor. Somebody was likely to get mauled—and based on his track record with these two women, it would probably be him.

On the other side of the field the witch watched warily while Bosco came bounding playfully toward her. She held her right hand palm-down above her dog's head, and the dog sat frozen beneath it. As Bosco approached she turned sideways and stepped between him and her own dog. He tried to go around her and she repeated the maneuver, blocking the dog's way over and over until it finally gave up and stood motionless, staring up at her in confusion. She pulled the hair back from her face and looked down at the dog, establishing eye contact; she snapped her fingers once and then placed an index finger on the dog's haunches and gently pushed down.

The dog sat.

She stroked the dog's head and scratched behind his ears. She roughed up his fur and examined it. She lifted his muzzle and looked into his eyes, then lifted one jowl with her thumb and looked at his teeth and gums.

"You there!" Marge shouted as she charged across the field. "May I ask what you think you're doing?"

The witch stepped back from the dog and lowered her head again.

"Take it easy, Marge," Nick said. "She was only trying to—"

"*Never* touch my dog!" she growled, looking the witch over in disdain. "Do I make myself clear?"

The witch mumbled something under her breath.

"Excuse me? What was that?"

"I said, 'Your dog is dehydrated.'"

"My dog is in perfect health, thank you very much."

"Look for yourself. You can tell by his fur."

She glared at her. "I don't recognize you—where did you get your training? Do you have your FEMA certification? May I see your credentials, please?"

The witch said nothing.

"Now hold on," Nick said. "This is no time to start comparing pedigrees."

"*Pedigree?* Is that some kind of joke? That *thing* has no pedigree—it's nothing but a mongrel. And why would anyone allow this pathetic creature to suffer this way? The humane thing would have been to put it down years ago. I can only hope it won't be allowed to pollute the bloodlines further. Has she at least been spayed?"

The witch raised her head and peered out with one burning eye. "Have you?"

She snapped her fingers and ran toward the parking lot with the dog on her heels.

"Alena, wait a minute!" Nick called after her—but she didn't even slow down.

"I plan to confirm each and every one of her supposed 'findings,'" Marge said, frowning at the field of red flags.

Nick turned on her. "Confirm anything you want," he said, "but whatever you do, *don't touch those flags.* I consider every one of them a positive identification until excavation proves otherwise—and we'll start digging the minute the crew arrives."

She sniffed. "That will make my work difficult."

"Your work isn't difficult, it's impossible—but that's your fault. You'd better get to work, Marge, because the minute my crew confirms Alena's findings, you're out of here—and it won't be soon enough for me."

Nick looked across the field at the parking lot just in time to see the old red pickup with a white camper shell pull onto I-66 and speed off in the direction of Endor.

As the pickup left the parking lot, a Warren County sheriff's car pulled in.

11

Donovan looked out over the group of reporters. "That concludes my prepared statement," he said. "You've all received a copy of our briefing; it contains all the facts I just mentioned. I recognize some of you from the district; I see a few unfamiliar faces too. The FBI would like to thank all of you for making the drive out here today."

The reporters huddled together in a small, roped-off area situated on a rise overlooking the Patriot Center. The site for this press conference had been carefully selected by the FBI's public liaison officer and approved by Donovan himself. This location afforded members of the media a clear view of the entire excavation, allowed their cameramen to shoot with the sun at their backs, and, most important, kept reporters from wandering off where they didn't belong—which Donovan knew from experience reporters had a habit of doing.

The graveyard was now bustling with activity as forensic tech crews began the excavation of the newly located graves. Even in ordinary circumstances the relocation of an old grave was a delicate procedure, requiring the last foot of soil to be removed by hand to keep from collapsing the rotting casket below. Here every bit of soil had to be removed by hand because there was no telling what the next few inches might reveal—and if another double occupant did turn up, the soil above that body instantly became potentially valuable forensic evidence. That's why the tech crews worked slowly and with extreme care, measuring and cataloging everything removed from each of the excavations under Nick's careful direction.

"I'll take your questions now," Donovan said. "As always, the FBI is happy to cooperate with the media and to tell you everything we want you to know."

The younger reporters glanced around the group; the older ones laughed. In the front row, one reporter didn't change expression at all. Paul Decker worked as a stringer for WRTL, a struggling young affiliate trying to hang on to a thin sliver of viewership in the competitive top-ten market of Washington, D.C. WRTL couldn't afford the top talent that stations like WRC-TV could—the really hot-looking anchors working their way up through the smaller markets along the East Coast—and they couldn't afford their own helicopter like FOX 5. WRTL didn't have the deep pockets or the power or the prestige to go toe-to-toe with the larger stations; what they did have was reporters like Decker, hungry and ambitious men working on a pay-per-piece basis who would kill for a regular salary and benefits. WRTL said they wanted local news, but Decker had been around long enough to know that nobody wanted a story about the new Smithsonian exhibit or the latest demonstration on the mall. The stories that sold were sensational—the more sensational the better—and Decker thought that a presidential candidate with his own personal graveyard had definite possibilities.

Decker pressed closer and pointed his microphone in Donovan's face. "Mr. Donovan—Paul Decker, WRTL. How many more of these double graves does the FBI expect to find here?"

"There's no way to tell, Mr. Decker, until we finish the excavations."

"But two of the first four graves contained additional bodies—doesn't that suggest that you'll find more?"

"If you win the lottery, that doesn't suggest you'll win it again. As I said, there's just no way to tell."

"Do you have any theories yet about why these people were murdered?"

"We don't know for certain that they were murdered."

"Can you offer any other explanation for the way they were buried?" Donovan paused. "No, I can't."

"So are we talking about a serial killer here?"

"Whoa, let's slow down a minute. The FBI is involved here because of the discovery of two bodies buried in a similar way—and yes, that raises the possibility of a serial killer, but it's only a possibility. The problem is, these bodies are old—we have no idea how old yet. We've brought in both a forensic entomologist and a forensic anthropologist to help us solve that problem, but we don't have an answer yet."

"Can we interview them?" Decker asked.

"They've been instructed to keep me apprised of any new developments, and I'll be more than happy to pass that information on to you."

"In other words, no."

"In other words, no."

"How do they know where to dig?" a *Washington Times* reporter asked. "Is there a map of this place? A list of the people buried here? Can we get a copy of it?"

"We've been unable to find any record of this graveyard," Donovan said. "That made it a little difficult to locate the remaining graves."

"Then how was that accomplished?"

"The FBI has several ways of searching for clandestine graves. Sometimes we find depressions created when the ground settles—these graves were too old for that. We can use thermal imaging to detect the heat from decomposing bodies—but again, these are too old. Sometimes we can use ground-penetrating radar, but the soil around here is just too rocky. In this case we sought the assistance of a forensic detection dog—sometimes referred to as a *cadaver dog*."

"They can detect graves this old?"

"Fortunately for us, yes. Every little red flag you see behind me marks a grave, and every one of them was found by a cadaver dog just last night."

Decker looked at the yellow crime scene tape that surrounded the entire graveyard. "Any chance of letting us in to get some close-up shots?"

"What's the matter, Mr. Decker? Can't WRTL afford a telephoto lens? Sorry—the entire area is considered a crime scene until we determine otherwise. That means it's off-limits to all unofficial personnel. We can't have people trampling over possible forensic evidence."

"Just one quick shot?"

Donovan looked at the group and smiled. "Perhaps I should remind you all that crossing our crime scene tape would be a violation of federal law. I'm sure none of you need that reminder, but you might want to pass it on to some of your less scrupulous colleagues."

"What does Senator Braden think about all this?" another reporter asked.

"I have no idea. You'll have to ask him that yourself."

"This land belongs to him. The Patriot Center is his project."

"Yes, and I'm sure he's thinking what any other developer would be thinking right now: Where did I put that checkbook?"

Decker waited for the laughter to die down. "This land has been in the senator's family for generations—isn't that true?"

"That's my understanding, yes."

"But you don't believe there's any connection between these bodies and the senator himself."

"None that I know of."

Decker paused. "Did he tell you to say that?"

Donovan looked at him; there was no change in his expression, but there was a definite intensity in his gaze. "No one *tells* me to say anything." He broke eye contact and turned to the rest of the group. "Are there any other questions?"

No one spoke up.

"Look," Donovan said. "You guys are the reporters and I don't want to put words in your mouths—but when you write your stories I'd encourage you to exercise a little restraint. What we have here so far is an old forgotten graveyard, nothing more. As for the two unexplained bodies, well, that's just what they are—unexplained. We'll let you all know the minute we figure this out—but in the meantime, please try not to concoct any wild conspiracy theories, okay? That doesn't help anybody." He threw a glance at Decker with his last comment.

The press conference ended here; photographers began to snap caps onto black, barrel-shaped lenses and fold the legs of tripods with dull metallic clicks. Reporters gathered up their belongings and began to work their way back to their cars, escorted by the public liaison officer.

Decker turned to his cameraman. "Did you get anything worthwhile?"

"Oh, yeah," the cameraman said, "a nice head shot of a talking FBI man telling everybody, 'Go on home, there's nothing to look at here.' I also got a shot of a big field with people digging in the dirt about a mile away—they'll look like ants even in high-def. Terrific stuff—the station oughta pay us top dollar for this."

"You're right," Decker said. "We won't make the 5:00 p.m. with this garbage—we need to find a better angle." He searched the dwindling group and spotted Donovan collecting his notes at the portable lectern. "Mr. Donovan! Hang on a minute."

Donovan looked up and recognized him; he didn't smile.

"I have a follow-up question, if you don't mind."

"Go ahead."

"What's the real story here?"

"What do you mean, Mr. Decker?"

"I can't go back with a story like this. Help me out here."

"Sorry," Donovan said. "I don't write stories; I just relay facts."

"Then give me some more facts. Does the senator know about all this?"

"Does the senator know that he might lose millions in interest on construction loans because his project has been shut down? Think it over, Paul—of course he knows."

"Does he have any explanation for the two bodies?"

Donovan shook his head. "You're just dying to bring Senator Braden into this, aren't you?"

"Why are you protecting him?"

"C'mon, Decker, it's an election year and politicians make easy targets. If you don't like Braden then write about his fiscal policy or his stand on global warming. But don't throw this in his face—it's just not fair."

"I'm just doing my job."

"Which is what, exactly?"

"Telling stories that don't make people fall asleep."

"Ever hear of a bedtime story? Some stories are supposed to make people sleep."

"Not the ones I write."

"Well, that's your business. My business is to conduct a press conference, and I'm finished now—so if you don't have any more questions, I'd like to get back to work."

"Thanks for nothing," Decker said.

"Any time. And Mr. Decker—I meant what I said about the crime scene tape. Right?"

Decker didn't reply—he was already on his way to the parking lot with his cameraman in tow.

"What do you want to do now?" the cameraman asked.

"Beats me," Decker grumbled. "Maybe we could—" He stopped. In the parking lot ahead he saw a gleaming white SUV with the name *Fidelis Search and Rescue Dogs* printed across the side. The rear doors of the vehicle were open wide, where a woman dressed in khaki was grooming a black-and-tan dog.

"C'mon," he said. "I may have found our angle."

The chief of staff rapped his knuckles on the senator's office door. "Sir—have you got a minute?"

"Come in, Brad. What's on your mind?"

"There's something I think you need to see." He leaned over the senator's shoulder and typed in an Internet address on his computer; a moment later the WRTL masthead appeared on the screen with the byline "WRTL: The Stories Behind the News."

"WRTL," the senator read. "Is that the ABC affiliate?"

"No, sir, that's WJLA—but they're both owned by Allbritton, the same people who own News Channel 8. WRTL is a recent acquisition for them; they're targeting a nontraditional demographic—the same people we'd like to reach. That's why I thought you should see this; it just aired at five o'clock." He moved the cursor down to a section titled "Local News" and clicked on the headline "Braden Finds Skeletons in Closet." A small black window opened and a video clip began to play:

"Trish, I'm standing in front of the excavation site for the Patriot Center, the billion-dollar mega-mall and entertainment complex being developed by presidential candidate John Henry Braden. The workers you see behind me, however, are not construction workers. They're a team of forensic experts from the FBI's crime lab in Quantico. Construction on the Patriot Center ceased a few days ago when workers uncovered a forgotten graveyard—unusual in itself, but not enough to involve the FBI. What caught the attention of federal officials was the discovery of two additional bodies—bodies someone buried on top of existing graves. But who did it, and why? Rumors are circulating that a serial killer may be responsible."

"Rumors," the senator said. "Since when are rumors news?"

"When you're the fourth-ranked station in the Washington–Maryland–Northern Virginia market," Brad said. "Watch the next segment."

"I'm here with Marjory Claire Anderson-Forsyth, owner of Fidelis Search and Rescue Dogs, and this is her dog, King. Ms. Forsyth, your dog has an unusual ability—can you tell me about it?"

"King is a forensic detection dog."

"And what is he trained to detect?"

"Human remains."

"He's a cadaver dog?"

"We prefer the term *forensic detection dog*, or sometimes *historical remains dog*."

"The FBI says that this graveyard may date back to colonial times. Is a dog actually capable of finding human remains that are two hundred years old?"

"Definitely."

"That's remarkable. When the FBI arrived here a few days ago only four graves had been discovered, and now there are almost thirty. Were you responsible for this?"

She hesitated. "The credit really belongs to the dog."

"Tell me, Ms. Forsyth, as an expert in finding bodies, do you expect the FBI to find more of these double graves?"

"I really can't say."

"Let me put it another way: Is it easier for a dog to find recent remains than very old ones?"

"Of course."

"I'm told that all these graves were found in a single night—that seems like fast work. Doesn't the speed of these discoveries suggest to you that at least some of the graves might contain more-recent remains?"

She considered this. "That seems reasonable, yes."

The reporter stepped to his left until he was alone in the frame with the busy excavation site visible in the background. As he began his wrap-up, the camera slowly zoomed over his shoulder and gradually came to rest on a man with large glasses sifting dirt through a wire screen and studying the unseen bits and pieces that were left behind.

"Though the FBI refuses to speculate on how and why these bodies were buried here, the unavoidable conclusion seems to be murder. The FBI also refuses to speculate on how many more of these bodies they might find—but experts like Marjory Claire Anderson-Forsyth believe there could be many more.

"The FBI's investigation here is being spearheaded by Special Agent Nathan Donovan—a name familiar to many due to his involvement in the infamous Plague Maker case in New York City a few years ago, in which hundreds of thousands of lives were spared due to his efforts. Buy why is an agent of Donovan's caliber and experience required here? What does the FBI expect to find?

"The missing piece of this mystery might just be John Henry Braden himself. Why were these bodies buried on his ancestral land? Did someone in his family know about it? Does the senator himself know? Until the graves are excavated and the bodies examined, these secrets will lie buried—just as they have for many years. This is Paul Decker, reporting from the Patriot Center near Endor, Virginia."

The screen went black.

"He practically called me a serial killer," Braden said. "That's inexcusable."

"It's a nonstory story," Brad said. "He's got nothing to work with, so he made a story out of what he doesn't know."

"And what happens when he does have something to work with? I thought we agreed to control media access to this. Who was that cadaver dog woman? Why was she allowed to be interviewed? Her comments were irresponsible and inflammatory—the last thing we want to do is create a desire for more of this nonsense."

"I agree. Do you want me to call Nathan Donovan?"

"Call Victoria," the senator said. "Mr. Donovan was her idea—and I'm beginning to think she made a mistake."

12

"Now this is more like it," Kegan said, passing a bucket of dirt up to Nick.

Nick took the bucket and spread the soil evenly on a sifter, a rectangular wooden frame with a fine wire mesh stretched across its bottom. The frame hung down from four hinged arms, one attached at each corner, allowing the frame to swing back and forth like a porch glider and slowly sift the dirt through the mesh. Nick shook the soil through the screen, stopping from time to time to pluck out an almost invisible insect part with a pair of forceps and carefully deposit it into an evidence container.

"You've got to hand it to Marge and Bosco," Kegan said.

Nick didn't reply.

"They may start slow, but once they get going, they really pick up speed."

"You're particularly annoying today," Nick said. "Did I do something to deserve this, or are you just being yourself?"

"I just believe in giving credit where credit is due."

"So do I."

"Well, look around: Two days ago we were sitting on our thumbs staring at an empty field, and today the place looks like Flag Day at the UN. Twenty-nine graves in one night—that's pretty impressive work. Hats off to Marge—I'd like to shake her hand."

"I'd like to shake her too," Nick mumbled.

Nick and Kegan had agreed on a procedure for excavating the remaining graves: They decided to excavate all of the graves halfway first in order to search for additional bodies, since that was the issue that concerned the FBI; after that they could take their time removing the coffins. The forensic technicians carefully removed the soil from each grave layer by layer, collecting and photographing any artifacts found at that site, while the soil itself was stored in plastic containers for later analysis.

So far ten of the graves had been partially excavated, revealing two important facts: None of them contained a second body, but each of them contained a casket. The witch and her three-legged cadaver dog were proving unerringly accurate; every flag she had placed marked the precise location of a grave. There were no "false positives," as Marge had promised. Marge was wrong—Marge had been wrong about everything—but Nick was the only one who knew it, and it was driving him crazy.

"Admit it," Kegan said. "You were wrong about Marge and Bosco."

Nick said nothing.

"I get the feeling you just don't like this woman."

"Really? Your powers of perception are astonishing."

"What have you got against her, anyway?"

"There's an entomological term for people like her," Nick said. "'She has a bug up her—'"

"Dr. Polchak!" one of the techs shouted. "Take a look—we've got another body."

Nick and Kegan hurried over to the grave site; the technician scrambled up out of the hole to allow them a better look. Kegan lowered herself into the knee-deep pit and pulled a bristle brush from her back pocket.

"Coracoïd process of the right scapula," she said, "and here's the head of the humerus. This body has the same orientation as the others: fetal position, left side down." She brushed away the soil six inches above the scapula, exposing a smooth ivory surface. "The cranium appears to be intact," she said. "We're in luck—this is a better specimen than either of the other two."

"We've got another one over here!" another technician shouted from a grave a hundred feet away.

"This must be our lucky day," Nick said. "That's *four* bodies. We just won the graveyard lottery—that doubles our evidence pool."

"I'll get to work on both of them right away," Kegan said.

"Good—and I'll start going through the soil samples."

He started for the tent when his cell phone rang; he opened it and pressed it to his ear. "Nick Polchak."

"Nick, it's Donovan."

"Good timing," Nick said. "I was just about to give you a call. We've got two more bodies, Donovan—that makes four. We just found them a minute ago. You might want to come take a look."

Donovan paused. "I'm off the case."

Nick stopped. "What?"

"I got a call from the ADIC late last night."

"Just like that?"

"Just like that."

"Did they give you a reason?"

"They rarely do."

"But why would they pull you? You haven't had time to screw things up yet."

"My guess is that Braden got cold feet. There was a news report last night that raised questions about his connection to all this, and that's the last thing he wants. I think he's decided to keep his head down, and I won't help."

"So he's shutting down the investigation?"

"He can't do that—only the FBI can make that call. But Braden has a lot of influence and he can pull a few strings. He's probably the one who asked for me to be reassigned, since he requested me in the first place—or his wife did, anyway."

"Victoria?"

"That's right. Do you know her?"

"No, but I visited her shrine."

"Her what?"

"Never mind."

"Anyway, whether it was Braden or his wife, I'm off the case."

"What about me?"

"I picked you, but the Bureau hired you—so you're working for the Bureau until they fire you."

"Will they?"

"No. I told them I had top people in place and they believe me—unless you prove otherwise."

"So who's in charge now?"

"They've already assigned a new special agent in charge—a young guy named Daniel Flanagan. I briefed him early this morning; he's on his way out there now."

"A new boss," Nick groaned. "It took me years to break you in."

"Go easy on this guy," Donovan said. "He's a little green."

"Are we talking who-left-this-cheese-in-the-refrigerator green, or Ireland-in-the-springtime green?"

"You'll know soon enough. Look, do me a favor—keep your balance this time, okay? Try not to turn into the usual neurotic, self-destructive Nick."

"Thanks, I'll write myself a note. How am I supposed to do this without you around? What do I do when I need to bend the rules a little? What happens when I need the boss to look the other way?"

"Here's an idea: You might try following the rules for once."

"No, seriously."

"Look, I'll help you in any way I can. Give me a call if you get stuck and I'll see what I can do."

"Hey."

"Yeah?"

"Has it occurred to you that Braden might have other reasons for wanting you off this case?"

"Like what?"

"You know what. Maybe he wants somebody a little less experienced in charge. Maybe he doesn't want this thing resolved too quickly. Maybe he's got something to hide."

"It's occurred to me," Donovan said, "but we have no way to know—so let's not get paranoid, okay?"

"Sorry—paranoia is a part of my neurosis."

"Keep me posted, Nick. I'd like to know how this thing plays out."

"Right. Gotta go—I think Mr. Green just arrived." Nick dropped the phone into his pocket.

A man had just stepped across the crime scene tape and, after a brief word and a handshake with the sheriff's deputy, headed in their direction. He was definitely young, not more than a year or two out of the academy, with a fresh, scrubbed face and a messy, tousled hairstyle that seemed more appropriate for a club than a crime scene. He was dressed in a standard executive three-button with a white handkerchief in his lapel pocket; he kept fingering the buttons as he walked, as if he was still checking the fit.

"Who's the suit?" Kegan asked.

"Our new boss."

"New boss? You're joking."

Nick looked at her. "We're working for the government, where jokes don't exist—just nightmare after nightmare."

"He's kind of cute."

Nick rolled his eyes. "What is it with you women? Is *everything* cute?"

"Except insects."

"That figures."

"Dr. Polchak," the man called out. "Dr. Nicholas Polchak."

"Present," Nick said, raising one hand.

"I'm Special Agent Daniel Flanagan. Have you spoken with Agent Donovan today?"

"I just got off the phone with him."

"Then I assume you've been apprised of the change in command."

Nick looked him over. "How old are you?"

Flanagan paused. "Why do you ask?"

"Donovan told me you were green, but I had no idea—all you need is a sash full of merit badges."

Flanagan shook his head. "Donovan told me you were borderline psychotic. Is that true?"

"I have no borders."

"He also said you're the best there is."

"He's right about that—but then, you're taking the word of a psychotic."

Flanagan stepped past Nick and extended his hand to Kegan. "You must be Dr. Alexander. I've read your file; it's a pleasure to work with you."

"Thank you," she said with a smile. "Then you must have read Nick's file too."

He glanced at Nick. "Yes, I did."

"I don't know who writes those things," Nick said. "Besides, history is open to interpretation."

"Let's hope so." Now Flanagan raised his voice so that all of the technicians could hear him. "I am Special Agent Daniel Flanagan. As of this morning I am replacing Special Agent Nathan Donovan as agent in charge here—that means you'll all be reporting to me now. I will remain on-site as much as possible; I will be the first one here every morning and the last one to leave at night. If there are any new developments, I want to know about them. I like facts and I like details; if you're not sure whether you should tell me or not, tell me. If there are any questions or problems, bring them to me. If there is anything you need to do your jobs more quickly or more efficiently, let me know and I will get it for you. I look forward to working with each of you. Please resume your duties."

Now he turned to Nick and Kegan. "Agent Donovan briefed me early this morning, but I'd like to be brought up to date on any recent developments. In addition, I expect to be briefed by each of you twice a day—once during the lunch break and once at the end of the day. Questions?"

"Yes," Nick said. "Do I have to raise my hand to use the bathroom?"

"Twice a day might be a bit much," Kegan said. "The excavation of buried remains usually takes anywhere from one to three days, and then there's the lab work after that. I'm not sure I'll have much to report twice a day."

"Nevertheless. Now if you don't mind, I'd like a word with Dr. Polchak alone."

He turned and took a few steps aside and Nick followed. "I'm going to call you Nick," he said. "It'll save time."

"Pals already," Nick said.

"I want you to know, I did read your file."

"And?"

"And I'd like to make a few things clear up front. The FBI operates by a set of procedures—procedures that have been carefully refined over a hundred-year history. I follow those procedures, Nick; I live by them, I serve them, and while you're working for me I expect you to follow them too. Is that clear?"

"I'd like to explain something too," Nick said. "I believe rules are for the obedience of fools and the guidance of wise men. From your little speech back there you sound like a micromanager; if you take that approach here, you'll wear yourself out and you'll drive the rest of us crazy. These are smart people; they know what they're doing. You need to trust them and you need to let them follow their instincts, even if the process bends your precious rules a little. Follow the rules when you have to, Danny, but don't serve them. Serve your people."

Flanagan paused. "It's Daniel."

Nick smiled. "It's Dr. Polchak."

Flanagan slowly smiled back. "Thanks for the advice, Nick. I can't say I'm surprised since, as I said, I read your file. But I'm not sure you understand what I'm telling you here. I wasn't asking for your opinion on management style or investigative procedure—I was telling you mine. And while you're working for me you're going to do it my way—or you won't be working for me long. Are we clear on that?"

"I heard every word you said. I don't agree with one of them."

"You don't have to. Just do what I tell you and we'll get along fine." Flanagan turned and headed for the tech tent. "Five minutes," he said. "Don't keep me waiting."

When Flanagan was out of earshot Nick took out his cell phone again and punched Redial.

"Donovan."

"Why do you torture me?"

There was a pause. "I'm assuming you just met Agent Flanagan."

"Did you pick this guy yourself? What did I do to you?"

"I'm not a king, Nick—I don't get to name my successor. What's the problem?"

"He's an FBI drone, Donovan—he's been here for five minutes and he's already given me the 'rules and regulations' speech. Didn't you tell him about me?"

"I tried to."

"He said you told him I was borderline psychotic—thanks a lot."

"That's a lie. I never said 'borderline.'"

"I can't work under a guy like this—you know that."

"You don't have a choice, Nick."

"I can quit."

"Sure you can. You can go back to NC State and maybe pick up a summer session or two. Teaching. Students. Grading papers. Faculty committees—"

"In case you're unaware of it, extortion is against the law."

"I'm a little busy here, Nick. Is there a reason for this call?"

"I want to talk to Braden—in person."

"What?"

"Senator Braden—I want to talk to him. Can you arrange it?"

"You are psychotic. Braden wouldn't give you an appointment in a thousand years."

"I know. Where does he live?"

"Why do you want to know?"

"Just curious."

"Nick—don't even think about it. Why do you want to talk to Braden anyway?"

"To save us all some time. We just found two more bodies, Donovan,

111

and there might be more. This graveyard is about to turn into an incredibly complicated puzzle, and we're missing a lot of pieces right now. We're going to have to try to identify these people through fragments of bone and teeth and hair. That could take forever—if we can do it at all. You say this land has been in Braden's family for generations; well, then he might have family records—something that might identify the people buried here—maybe even some clue about the victims in the double graves."

"If he does, he'll never admit it."

"Probably not—but I'd like to look him in the eye and ask him. That might tell me something right there."

"Did you run this by Flanagan?"

"This one isn't in the Boy Scout manual, Donovan. Why do you think I'm calling you? You said, 'Give me a call if you get stuck.' Well, I'm stuck—help me out here."

Donovan paused. "What do you need from me?"

"Just tell me where Braden lives and when I can find him there."

"This could backfire on you, Nick."

"But not on you. You're not my boss anymore. I never called you. You know nothing about this."

"If it backfires, it'll come back on Flanagan."

"He can't stay green forever. Think of this as a rite of passage."

There was a long pause on the other end. "Braden lives on a huge horse farm near Middleburg, about half an hour east of you. The place is called Bradenton."

"There's a surprise."

"He'll be there for the next couple of days—he has a second office there and he likes to get out of the district whenever he can. I can't believe I'm telling you this."

"Sure you can. Despite all your bad qualities, Donovan, you're not a Boy Scout. Deep down you and I are a lot alike."

"Thanks—now I feel awful."

"I'll let you know how it goes."

"Hey, Nick."

"Yes?"

"Keep an eye on the wife—Victoria."

"Judging by her photos, that sounds like a good idea."

"I'm serious. I'm not sure which end has the rattle and which end has the fangs."

"Since I'm not a herpetologist, I can only venture a guess: The end with the fangs is the one that bites."

"Yeah—but by then it's too late."

Gunner Wendorf sat at the desk in his office arranging his sermon notes for the following Sunday. He heard a faint scratching sound and looked up; in the doorway he saw a small dog, not much larger than the head of a mop. Its pink wrinkled skin was visible through the sparse clumps of gray hair that sprouted from its body in every direction. Its head was almost bald except for one tuft of pure white hair that stood up straight on top. Its muzzle was small and pointed and had the color of an old man's beard; it had round black eyes that seemed to have no pupils and shone like dots of ink. It had a bulldog's jaw, misaligned so far that its lower canines jutted up on one side and its tongue stuck out on the other—a tiny pink pull tab on a grotesque little package.

When Gunner made eye contact with the dog it barked once, then waited. He snapped his fingers and made a quick gesture, and the dog disappeared into the night.

He turned out the light and followed.

13

Nick knew he had arrived at Bradenton long before he reached the entrance to the property. A stacked-stone wall ran parallel to the road for miles, topped by a split-rail fence in a kind of teepee configuration. Nick found himself staring at the stone wall as he drove, estimating the amount of stone and the number of man-hours necessary to produce such an endless structure. The wall provided no security; it was purely decorative. *That's what a man can do with money and sweat*, Nick thought. *Braden's money and somebody else's sweat.*

Beyond the wall, vast pastures of verdant green rose and fell like ocean swells under the black rail fences. Holding ponds dotted the landscape like glistening gemstones, and Nick thought the neatly painted barns and equipment sheds looked like little milk cartons on a piece of green felt. Suddenly the wall rose into a towering column of stone, marking the entrance to the property. Nick pulled in and stopped his car under an elaborate black wrought-iron arch that spelled out the name "Bradenton" in an old copperplate script, framed by a leaping thoroughbred at either end. Nick looked down the road but saw no sign of a house anywhere. It was apparently concealed behind some hill or even over the horizon; the property must have been enormous.

He drove at least half a mile before the road curved to the right around a grove of towering red oaks. Another quarter mile ahead he could finally see the farmhouse—if the word could be used to describe such a structure. The house was enormous—a sprawling construction of massive wood beams and white stucco walls with slate roofs sliced from the same Virginia bluestone that outlined the property. A hundred yards from the house the road turned from gray crushed gravel to smooth paving stone and the car suddenly fell silent, like a man stepping onto carpet from a hardwood floor.

So this is how the other half lives, was the thought that crossed Nick's mind, but he knew it was nonsense. The other half lived nothing like this—no one did except for a blessed few, and that blessing was almost always handed to them on a silver platter. This was old money; there just wasn't time for one man to earn all this in one lifetime. You could win a dozen lotteries and never afford a property like this, even if it was for sale—and places like Bradenton never were.

The driveway looped like a shepherd's crook in front of the house; in the center was a fountain with a bronze statue of two rearing stallions in apparent combat. Nick parked his car and approached the house. The front door was actually two doors, both very wide, and Nick wasn't sure which one of them would open—so he pushed the doorbell and stepped back a little, waiting for something to happen. After a few seconds the door on the left slowly swung open, and Nick felt a rush of cold air.

"May I help you?"

The man holding the door was not what Nick had expected: He was tall and athletic-looking, dressed in a dark suit with wavy black hair to match. Nick blinked; the man looked more like an Italian swimsuit model than a butler.

"I'm here to see Senator Braden," Nick said.

The man looked Nick over doubtfully.

"You'll have to excuse my appearance," Nick said. "I came directly from work."

"Work?"

"Yes—I'm in charge of the investigation at the Patriot Center."

"Do you have an appointment with the senator?"

"I only need a few minutes."

"Sorry—the senator isn't at home right now."

"I was told the senator would be here for the next couple of days."

"Who told you that?"

"Like I said—I'm in charge of the investigation."

The man considered this.

"Look," Nick said, "tell the senator I have information for him about a recent development at the Patriot Center—tell him it's something he'll want to know."

"You can leave the information with me," he said.

It was Nick's turn to look doubtful. "No offense, but—who are you?"

"I'm head of the senator's security force."

"And he's got you opening doors?"

The man frowned a little. "We have to be careful—you never know who might show up unannounced."

"Well, this information is confidential—for his ears only. I'll leave if you want me to, but I don't think your boss will be happy about that."

The man hesitated but finally opened the door and stepped aside. "Come in," he said. "The senator isn't here, but he's on the property— he's doing a little hunting right now. I can reach him by cell phone; I'll ask him if he wants to see you. Whom shall I say is calling?"

"Dr. Nick Polchak."

"Does the senator know you?"

"Not yet."

"Wait in there—that's the senator's study."

The man disappeared around a corner and Nick wandered through the foyer and into the study. The room was cavernous, with a tall cathedral ceiling and shaved log beams that spanned the room from one end to the other. There was a desk in the center of the room so large that Nick thought anyone sitting behind it would look like a child. The walls were covered with so many framed certificates and diplomas and the display cases were crammed with so many awards that he wondered if the senator could have actually earned them all. *Who knows? Maybe he inherited those too.* To the right of the desk was a seating area, where four small upholstered chairs formed a half-circle around a stately leather wingback—Nick had no doubt whose place that was. In the far right corner, under a brilliant halogen accent light, was a stuffed black bear standing in a ferocious attack position—jaws open, teeth glaring, paws held high. Nick shook his head; he wondered if bears were ever stuffed in a sleeping position, or with their backs turned, running away.

Nick turned to his left, and to his surprise found two men standing at a round table, dressed in dark suits like the man who answered the door—except that they wore white shirts with ties. A set of blueprints was on the table in front of them—and right now they were looking at Nick.

"Sorry," Nick said. "Your boss told me to wait in here."

"Who?"

"Your boss—the guy who answered the door."

Both men grinned. "We're Secret Service," one of them said. "That guy's just some private security flunkie."

"He said he was head of the senator's security."

The man chuckled. "He is, for a couple more weeks—then we take over."

"I thought you people only guarded the president and people like that."

"No, we cover presidential candidates too—starting a few months before the election. Do you mind? We've got a lot of work to do here."

The two men returned to their blueprints and Nick returned to wandering the room—but he kept an ear tuned to their discussion. They were studying blueprints of Bradenton's farmhouse and grounds, identifying the vulnerabilities and deciding where security would need to be enhanced.

Nick pointed to a door in the corner of the room. "Excuse me—is that a bathroom?"

One of the agents looked up. "I think so, yes."

"Do you think the senator would mind?"

"I'd leave the seat down if I were you—Mrs. Braden uses it too."

How convenient, Nick thought. He stepped inside and closed the door behind him.

When he emerged again the security guard was waiting for him in the doorway. "Dr. Polchak—the senator will see you."

Nick looked at the office. "Here?"

"No—I'm to take you to him. Do you ride?"

Nick blinked. "If you're driving, I'm riding."

"Horses, Dr. Polchak. This is a horse farm."

"I'm not very good with large animals," Nick said. "Have you got anything with wheels?"

"We'll take the Land Rover. Follow me."

They exited by a back door into a parking lot between the house and a long outbuilding with multiple doors—stables, Nick guessed. They climbed into the car and started down a gravel road that led away from the farmhouse; a half mile later the gravel road ended and they continued to drive across open fields. Nick kept wondering where the property would end, but there seemed to be no end in sight.

"I didn't get your name," Nick said.

"Riddick—Chris Riddick."

"The two guys in the senator's study—they said they were Secret Service."

Riddick didn't respond.

"And I understand you're private security. When did you sign on?"

"About three years ago."

"When Braden started to draw more attention?"

"That's right."

"When does the Secret Service take over?"

Riddick paused. "A hundred and twenty days before the election."

"That's only a few weeks from now."

"Thanks, I figured that out."

"When the Secret Service takes over, what happens to you?"

Riddick jerked the steering wheel to the left, throwing Nick up against the passenger door. The Land Rover lurched up and over a small rise, then bounded down the slope on the opposite side. Just before a stand of tall hardwoods he slammed the brakes, bringing the car to a skidding stop.

Nick released his grip on the dashboard and looked at Riddick.

"This concludes your jungle adventure—please watch your step on the way out."

Riddick opened his door and got out. "This way."

Nick followed him toward the trees; as he approached, he heard a flurry of wings and saw a gray-and-white bird rise from the grass just a few yards away. There was an echoing blast followed by a puff of feathers—then the bird fell silently back to earth.

"Thanks for flushing that one," Braden said, stepping out from the shadow of the trees. He thumbed the lever on his over-and-under, and the shotgun folded in half; he pulled two smoking hulls from the barrels and dropped them into his left jacket pocket. "Rock doves," he said. "You can't eat 'em, but they're good for target practice. They're in season year-round—they're a nuisance species."

"Who are they bothering?" Nick asked.

"Senator, this is Dr. Nick Polchak," Riddick said. "He says he has news for you."

Braden approached and eyed Nick warily. "This had better be good, Polchak—you're interrupting my personal time, and I don't get much of it. Let's have it."

"We found two more bodies at the Patriot Center."

"More of those double graves?"

"That's right. The bodies were deposited exactly like the others: in shallow pits on top of existing graves. That makes four, Senator—if the remains all indicate foul play, the Patriot Center case will be officially classified as a serial killing."

"The papers will be all over that."

"No doubt."

"What else have you got?"

"Not much. We've excavated twelve graves so far—at least deep enough to know that there are no extra bodies in eight of them; that still leaves us seventeen more to go. The remains have all been shipped back to Quantico for analysis. We should get preliminary results in a couple of days. We've got four bodies so far—you should expect more."

"You drove all the way out here just to tell me that?"

"No. I came out here to ask you something."

"And what's that?"

"What can you tell me about this graveyard?"

Braden paused, then looked at Riddick. "Chris, I wonder if you could give Dr. Polchak and me a little privacy."

Riddick straightened. "Senator, are you sure that's a good idea?"

"Well, son, since I'm standing here holding a twelve-gauge shotgun, I think we can afford to take a chance, don't you? Why don't you wait in the car."

"That's a good idea," Nick said. "You can review the driver's manual while you're waiting."

Riddick reluctantly left and Braden turned to Nick again. "Who exactly are you, anyway?"

"I'm the lead forensic specialist on this investigation."

"You're with the FBI?"

"No—I was hired by the FBI. I'm a forensic entomologist."

"And you think I might have information about this graveyard—information I haven't yet revealed. I don't believe I like the sound of that."

"I think you might have information you don't know about."

"And how's that?"

"I understand you've got deep roots here—dating back to Jamestown, I believe."

"The Bradens are one of Virginia's founding families. I'm very proud of that."

"I'm sure you are. A family like yours keeps records: birth certificates, baptismal records, marriage covenants, title deeds—burial records too. It must be quite a collection after four hundred years—a small library, I would imagine. Somewhere in all that information there could be a mention of this graveyard. I've checked with the regional library in Endor—they have no grave registries for the area around the Patriot Center. Maybe you do."

Braden looked at him without expression. "It's Nick, isn't it? Mind if I call you Nick?"

"Everybody seems to," Nick said. "Sometimes I wonder why I got a PhD."

"Well, Nick, I'm gonna tell you something—not because I need to, because the fact is you're working for me and I don't owe you a thing."

"I thought I was working for the FBI."

"You go right on thinking that. The truth is, this slowdown at the Patriot Center could cost me millions—and I don't have millions to lose right now, because in case you haven't heard, I'm running for president. That takes money, Nick—a whole lot of it. I don't need deep roots right now, son; I need deep pockets. Nobody wants this fiasco taken care of more than I do, so yes—I have family records—and I've already been through them. If I had anything more to tell you, I would have told you already."

Nick watched his eyes as he spoke.

"Any more questions?"

"Just one—but I don't think you'll like it."

"I've got thick skin, son—I've been dragged across the Senate floor a time or two."

"In your records, is there any mention of bad blood with some other family? Some kind of family feud, perhaps?"

"You're asking about those four extra bodies—you're wondering if someone in my own family might be responsible for that."

"Whoever buried them had to know the graveyard was there. That limits the field considerably."

"Yes, it does. But as I said, my family has no record of that grave-yard—so that eliminates my family, doesn't it?"

Nick paused. "If you say so."

"Are we done here, Nick? Is there anything else?"

"Just one more thing: I understand your wife has pretty deep roots here as well."

"Victoria? That she does."

"She's from the town of Endor, isn't she? Would you mind if I spoke with her? She might know something that you don't."

Braden smiled. "I can promise you that. I doubt Victoria knows anything more about this graveyard matter, but you're welcome to ask. She'll be in her office; she usually is—Chris can take you to her. C'mon, I'll walk you to the car."

"Mind if I ask one last question? It's a little off the subject."

"Go ahead."

"Why do humans hunt—for pleasure, I mean?"

"This is Virginia, son—this is hunt country. Turkey, fox, deer, black bear—we hunt it all here."

"Insects kill only for food or defense. It's something I've never understood about our species. You're shooting birds just for target practice—wouldn't a clay pigeon work just as well?"

"Wouldn't be the same."

"Why not?"

"A target's too predictable—you just load and fire. But you never know what a living thing will do next."

"No," Nick said. "You don't."

Braden looked at him. "A forensic entomologist—what is that, exactly?"

"We study necrophilous insects—insects that consume bodies after they die."

"Sounds disgusting."

"It's a necessary part of nature—it keeps the fields from piling up with dead birds."

Braden extended his hand and Nick took it. "You just dropped in on a U.S. senator unannounced—not many men can say that. Don't make it a habit, son—I made an exception for you."

"Why did you?"

"Because I want your people to know that I'm behind them. I want this thing resolved too—as soon as possible. Now get back to work."

14

"Mrs. Braden? Am I interrupting?"

Victoria Braden looked up from her desk. "You must be Dr. Polchak—Johnny called and told me you were coming." She rose and met Nick halfway across the room. Nick glanced around her office. It was smaller than her husband's and clearly more functional; there were far more books and papers and fewer stuffed bears.

"Please," she said, gesturing to a seat and then returning to her own. Nick watched her as she walked. She was easily the most beautiful woman Nick had ever seen: tall, poised, and every bit as stunning as her photographs—a quality few people possess. He shook his head—it was like visiting the *Homo sapiens* exhibit at some museum. The Bradens seemed to be perfect specimens of the human species; in fact, everything about this place was perfect—the perfect woman and her perfect husband in the perfect home. *Definitely the deep end of the gene pool*, he thought, and he suddenly felt strangely self-conscious.

They both sat down and looked at each other. Victoria smiled and waited. "You're the most beautiful woman I've ever seen," Nick said.

"Well—thank you. You're very kind."

"Why do you suppose people get flustered in the presence of beauty?"

Victoria blinked. "Is that what you came here to ask me?"

"No, but you seem like a good person to ask."

She paused. "I've never really thought about it before. I suppose it's because beauty is desirable—to be close to beauty is to be close to something you want. When you want something badly but can't have it, you get flustered."

"But why is beauty desirable? In the insect world, beauty usually indicates danger. Bright colors or patterns warn predators or attract prey. Among insects, desiring beauty is a good way to get eaten."

She smiled. "Are you feeling flustered, Dr. Polchak?"

"Yes—and it really annoys me."

"Then let's talk about something else. My husband tells me you're looking for information."

"I understand you're from Endor."

"That's right—though I moved away when I was very young."

"Do you have any family records? Any kind of family history?"

"My background is a little different from my husband's. My biological parents died when I was just a baby; I was adopted by a childless couple. My biological parents came from very old Virginia families, but due to my early adoption I have only a few of their family records—just genealogies and things like that. I don't think that's what you're looking for, is it?"

"I'm looking for information about the graveyard we're excavating at the Patriot Center."

"What sort of information?"

"Who's buried there? When did they die? Who else might know the location of that graveyard?"

"Did you ask in Endor? They have the regional library there."

"It was my first stop."

"What about UVA? They have some extensive historical collections there—especially dealing with Virginia history."

"It's worth a try, but Virginia is a big state with a long history—since you're actually from Endor I thought I'd try you first."

"I'm afraid I won't be much help."

Nick paused. "Would you help me if you could?"

She didn't answer.

"Sorry," Nick said. "I know that's an awkward question."

"That's one word for it."

"What I meant was—"

"I know what you meant, Dr. Polchak. You're wondering if my husband and I might be withholding information—if there might be some skeleton in our closet that we'd rather not reveal just prior to a presidential election. Is that the basic idea?"

"Something like that, yes."

"Do you have a specific reason for wondering about this, or are you just generally suspicious?"

Nick looked around the office. "I can see that you take a great interest in your husband's affairs."

"They're my affairs too."

"May I ask what your official capacity is—other than 'wife'?"

"I serve as office manager and political strategist. I also handle media relations."

"Who does the hiring and firing?"

"I do, in general."

"Did you fire Nathan Donovan?"

She hesitated. "That was my husband's decision. I agreed with him, though I found the decision . . . disappointing. Why do you ask?"

"I've known Donovan for years; he was your best shot at solving this thing. Firing him was a bad decision—so bad that it made me wonder if you really want this thing solved at all."

She tilted her head to one side and studied Nick's face as though she were trying to remember his name. "Believe me, we want it solved—and we want construction to resume on the Patriot Center just as quickly as possible. But there are aspects to this that you may not have considered."

"Such as?"

"How much do you know about Virginia?"

"I've been here once or twice."

"Did you know Virginia has produced more U.S. presidents than any other state?"

"No, I didn't."

"Do you know why? We breed them here."

"You breed them?"

"The very same way we breed show dogs and feeder cattle and thoroughbreds. In Virginia good breeding is everything, and breeding is all about appearance—it's about stature and bearing and length of bone."

"Are we talking about horses or presidents?"

"Both. My husband is about to become the next president of the United States. Do you know why?"

"As I recall, it has something to do with voting."

"Voting is simply registering a decision that's already been made. Do you know why people want my husband to be president? Because he looks like a president; he sounds like a president; he carries himself like a president. Johnny was born to be president, Dr. Polchak—it's in his breeding."

"And you were bred to be a First Lady?"

"According to the last Gallup poll, 71 percent of Americans think so."

"I hate to sound naive, Mrs. Braden, but I like to think the American public is a little more sophisticated than that. They care about substance too."

"Substance is important, but let's be honest: I have substance—I have degrees in business and political science—but substance didn't get me on the cover of this month's *Vogue* and *Vanity Fair*. And like it or not, that's what people will remember on Election Day: my face—my evening gown—not my résumé."

"Point taken."

"Good breeding will put my husband in the White House, Dr. Polchak, and as I said, breeding is about appearance—that's the aspect you may not have considered. I requested Nathan Donovan because it created the right appearance. It told the American public that we were willing to deal with this issue in a forthright manner—that we were willing to send in our best and our brightest. Unfortunately, Mr. Donovan's current celebrity status seems to have attracted the wrong kind of publicity. Johnny is extremely cautious about negative appearances, so he requested Mr. Donovan's immediate transfer. I considered the decision regrettable, but necessary."

"I appreciate the position you're in," Nick said. "I still think it was a bad decision."

"Perhaps, but it's done—so let's move on. The question now is: How do we deal with the situation at the Patriot Center?"

"Are we talking about appearance or substance?"

"You take care of substance—let me worry about appearance."

"I'm glad to hear you say that, Mrs. Braden, because there's something you need to understand about me. I didn't grow up on a horse farm in Virginia—I grew up in a dying little factory town north of Pittsburgh. I don't have stature or bearing or 'length of bone'—whatever that is. I'm a little too tall and my arms are too long; I've got big feet and bad eyes; I pick my clothes at random and I have to wear glasses the size of portholes. I don't have any breeding at all, Mrs. Braden. I'm all substance—that's all there is to me. So if you need somebody to create the right appearance for you, you'd better fire me too—but if you want this thing figured out, I'm your man."

Victoria smiled. "Why, Dr. Polchak—you don't sound flustered anymore."

"I guess I've grown comfortable in the presence of beauty."

"Congratulations. Most men never do."

She glanced down at the papers covering her desk and Nick took the hint. He walked to the door and then stopped and looked back. "You know, there's another strange thing about beauty."

"What's that?"

"Human beings associate it with goodness. Have you noticed that? The wicked stepmother is ugly, but Cinderella is a knockout. Why do you suppose they do that?"

"I'll bet you have a theory."

"I do. I think they're hoping to find substance behind the appearance. But that's just my theory. Who knows? Our species does some very strange things."

Riddick looked down at the bouquet of velvety pink roses that he clutched in his left hand. He spread the stems apart a little and picked off a wilted petal. He smoothed back his hair with his right hand, lifting the coal black comma from his forehead momentarily before it dangled back down again. He straightened his shirt collar, stepped into the doorway, and rapped his knuckles on the wooden frame.

Victoria Braden looked up from her desk.

"I got these from the garden," Riddick said. "I thought you might like them."

Victoria gave the roses the barest glance and returned to her work. "I hope those weren't the floribundas—we've got a garden reception for the DAR coming up, you know."

"Want me to put them in a vase for you?"

"Just leave them in the kitchen—I need the desk space in here."

Riddick took a step into the room. "Have you got a minute?"

She looked at him impatiently. "Is it important, Chris? I've got a lot on my plate today, and people seem to keep dropping by."

"It's important to me." Without waiting to be invited he took the seat directly across from her desk and settled in.

Victoria rose from her own chair and walked around to the front of the desk, as if to say, "Don't get comfortable."

Riddick glanced down at her legs.

She folded her arms tightly across her chest and said, "What's on your mind, Chris?"

"The future—my future."

"What about it?"

"A man can't live in the past, Vic—even if there are some very pleasant memories there. A man has to think ahead."

"And you've been doing some thinking."

"That's right."

"Good for you. Everyone should have new experiences."

"Now don't be like that. I like you better the way you used to be—friendly."

She glared at him. "What do you want?"

"The same thing any man wants: job security; a decent wage; a place where he belongs."

"I think you know where you belong. We've been over that."

"I thought I knew—I'm not so sure anymore."

"What does that mean?"

"I've been working for you for almost three years now—that's a long time. I think that kind of loyalty deserves a reward, don't you?"

"You've been paid for your services."

He smiled. "Not all of them. But that's okay, I'm not complaining—some work is its own reward."

She walked around behind him and closed the office door; when she returned she said, "How dare you—I told you never to bring that up in my presence again."

"And I never thought I would. But like I said, I've been doing some thinking."

"And?"

"Everybody around here seems to have a ticket on the Braden train—except me. Brad looks like a shoo-in for White House chief of staff; I figure Sandy for a senior adviser or deputy chief of staff, and probably Luis for press secretary. I'm sure you'll hang on to both of your assistants, and you'll probably hire at least one more."

"You've got it all figured out, don't you?"

"Well, that's the thing—I can't figure out where I fit in. A few weeks from now the Secret Service will take over my job, and they sure won't ask for any help from me—in fact, they probably won't let me near you anymore."

She raised one eyebrow. "Wouldn't that be too bad?"

"It would, Vic, it really would. I've worked for you for three years now and I feel like part of the family. There are things that family members know—things that should stay within the family."

Victoria narrowed her eyes and lowered her voice to a rumbling growl. "I would really, really hate to think that you're threatening me."

"Why would I threaten you? I'm responsible for your security. That's all I want, Vic—security. Yours *and* mine."

"What is it you want, Chris? Just say it."

"I want a job. Not stuffing envelopes in some White House mailroom—I want something up front, something with a little class and a decent paycheck."

"I'm not sure we have a position for an ex–security guard."

"Find one. I'm a multitalented guy, Vic—but I don't need to tell you that. The fact is, I wasn't really hired because of my security guard skills, now was I? At least that wasn't the only reason."

Victoria stared at him for a long time before she spoke again. "All right—I'll see what I can do. You'll have to go through the same personnel process as everyone else; we'll need a financial disclosure form from you, and the FBI will have to run a background check."

"Sure. Whatever you say."

"One more thing, Chris. You're right, I didn't hire you because of your 'security guard skills'—I hired you because you're pretty, and I like pretty things. But times have changed; I've changed. I've got a future now, and you're just a part of my past—a part I'd like to forget. I'll find you a job, but it won't be like your old one—that job is gone forever. Am I making myself clear?"

"Too bad," Riddick said. "I really enjoyed that job."

"Never mention it again—I mean it, Chris. Now get out."

Riddick slapped the arms of his chair and stood; Victoria returned to her desk without looking back. He shut the office door quietly behind him and stepped out into the foyer.

It worked—he had a job now—but Riddick was not a fool, and he knew exactly what would happen next. Few men knew Victoria Braden better than he did—maybe no one did, including her husband. No doubt about it, she was one of the world's most beautiful women—but inside that pretty head was a set of microprocessors ticking off zeros and ones, estimating angles and calculating odds. Of course she had offered him a job—it was a simple matter of "keep your friends close and your enemies closer." She would keep him securely within the Braden family until the election—but the day after the election he would find his suitcase out on the sidewalk and there would be no retirement party. And sure, he could tell his story to the press about his steamy affair with the new First Lady in her younger days—and he would just sound like a thousand other disgruntled ex-employees trying to settle a score or make a buck. Yes, he had a job—but not for long. He had bought himself four extra months, nothing more. Worst of all, he had made an enemy out of Victoria Braden— and that was a dangerous thing to do.

But Riddick had learned a lot from Victoria in the last three years, and he was calculating a few odds of his own. In four months his threat would lose all power. He needed something else, something more—and he needed it soon.

15

Nick opened the door of the Skyline Motel and stepped inside. The lobby was like a time capsule—it reminded Nick of a blue-collar recreation room from the early sixties. The walls were covered with fake pecan paneling that was printed with a wood-grain pattern, but its surface was as smooth as glass. The carpet was a pale avocado green, about the same quality found on the fairways of a miniature golf course. Lanterns with black iron scrollwork and yellow scalloped glass hung from chains in the corners of the room. The furniture was green and gold vinyl with thin wooden arms—a sort of doctor's-waiting-room style that was so out-of-date it was almost retro. In the center of the lobby sat a folding card table and two chairs, where night after night Nick found the Skyline's proprietors sipping coffee and making no discernible headway on a thousand-piece jigsaw puzzle.

The man looked up as Nick entered. "Evenin', Dr. Polchak."

"Evening."

"Would you like a cup of coffee?" his wife offered. "I'll fetch it for you."

"No thanks. I was just about to have dinner." He held up a grease-stained paper sack and a thirty-two-ounce cup with Captain Jack Sparrow on the side.

The woman frowned at Nick's dietary selection. "You need a woman bad."

"Tell me about it. I just met the world's most beautiful woman today."

"Who's that?"

"Victoria Braden."

Her eyes widened. "Victoria Braden? She's from right here in Endor."

"So I hear."

"I wish she'd stayed here," her husband commented. "That one's a real looker."

"What he needs is a woman who can cook," his wife replied.

Nick started down the hallway toward his room. "That's what I kept thinking today: 'But can she cook?'"

"I sure hope the dog's all right," the man called after him.

Nick stopped and looked back. "What?"

"The dog—it's been whinin' all day."

Nick came back a few steps. "What dog are we talking about?"

"The only dog we got here—the FEMA lady's dog. You know, Marjory Claire what's-her-name. I'm sorry, but that's more names than I can remember. You two are the only tenants we got right now."

"Bosco? He's been whining all day?"

"Dogs get lonely too," the woman said. "Marjory's been gone all day—she's probably out doing more news interviews. Did you catch the one last night?"

"I've been trying to forget it all day."

"Marjory's practically a celebrity now. Everybody's been talkin' about her—that was a Washington TV station, y'know, not just little ol' WAZF over in Front Royal. Marjory said that dog of hers found every one of those graves—imagine that."

"That is hard to imagine," Nick said. "You say Marge has been gone all day?"

"Haven't seen hide nor hair of her."

"And she left her dog here? Locked up in her room?"

"Judgin' by the sound of it. Why?"

"No reason." He glanced over at the front desk. "You know, I just remembered—I locked my key in my room this morning. Have you got a spare?"

"Sure, let me get it for you."

"Don't bother, I can see it from here. I don't want you two to miss out on any of the action there."

Nick stepped behind the front desk and scanned the rack of room keys; there were two keys on every hook except for two of the rooms. He took the spare key to his own room to keep from arousing suspicion, then took the key to Marge's room as well. He lifted one of the keys from an adjacent hook and placed it on Marge's to cover the empty space.

Nick stopped at the card table as he passed and lifted a puzzle piece from the corner. "See that one over there? The one with a little bit of orange?"

"This one here?"

"This piece fits on the right side."

The man took the piece from Nick and tried it; it snapped perfectly into place. He squinted up at Nick. "How'd you do that?"

"I don't know. Thanks for the key—I'll bring it right back."

He went down the hallway to his room and opened the door—then quietly closed it again and continued down the hallway to Marge's room. He listened at the door for a moment; he could hear the tinny, echoing sound of Bosco clawing at the metal grating of his crate—but nothing else. He quietly knocked and waited, but there was no response. He used the spare key to open the door and let himself in.

There was Bosco, locked in his dog crate in the corner of the room—but there was no sign of Marge anywhere. The dog became agitated and began to whimper at the sight of Nick. Nick walked over to the cage and bent down to quiet the dog; he was met by the stench of feces and urine. He looked into the cage and saw a pair of aluminum food and water bowls; both were empty. Nick had a bad feeling; even if the dog lacked a nose, it was still a very expensive and well-groomed animal. It was conceivable that Marge might overlook the dog for a couple of hours, but not like this—she would never neglect the animal's basic needs.

He took a quick look around the room. There was no sign of a disturbance. He found a set of car keys on the dresser; Nick remembered seeing the white SUV in the parking lot when he pulled up. He found no purse or pocketbook; Marge had apparently taken it with her, suggesting that she had left on foot and of her own free will.

But she didn't return—and Nick had a feeling he knew why.

He knelt down in front of the dog crate again. He opened the door just enough to slide out the aluminum water dish, then took it to the bathroom and filled it. He returned it to the cage, then peeled the wrapper from his burger and crumbled it into the other dish.

"This may have to hold you for a while," Nick said. "There's something I need to take care of."

He left the room and hurried back down to the lobby.

"Find your key?" Ralph asked as Nick headed out toward the parking lot.

"Yeah, thanks," Nick said. "By the way—where's the nearest hardware store?"

Nick pulled his car up close to the gate until his headlights illuminated the lock and chain. It was raining lightly; tinsel strands of water streaked through the brilliant light. He got out of the car and took a pair of red-and-gray bolt cutters from the backseat; he positioned the jaws on the hasp of the padlock and cut through it like butter. He dragged the chain off the poles with a ratcheting sound and tossed it aside; he swung the double gate open wide and got back into his car, then drove on into the witch's lair.

The gravel road was just a single lane, and it wound back and forth like a snake with dense trees and thick brush surrounding it on both sides. The rain made visibility poor and Nick drove slowly. He had no idea where the road went, but he knew it was his best bet; roads are built to go somewhere, and he would get a lot farther driving through these woods than walking—he had learned that the hard way.

He had driven almost a mile when he sensed motion on his left; he looked and saw one of the huge black guard dogs lumbering along beside his car with its great jowls flapping like the canvas of a ship. Nick looked out the passenger window; there was the second dog, and he had no doubt that the third was close behind. He glanced down at his gas gauge and was relieved to see the needle on three-quarters of a tank.

About a quarter mile ahead, the road abruptly widened and Nick found himself driving into the center of a large circular clearing. On his right he found a series of kennels—narrow concrete slabs surrounded by chain-link fences, lined up side by side like the keys on a piano. Each of the kennels contained half a dozen dogs of various shapes and sizes, and every single dog began to bark furiously the moment Nick's car came into view.

On the left Nick saw a double-wide trailer, more politely referred to now as a "manufactured home"—but the change in moniker didn't improve the quality or appearance. It looked to Nick like a saltine box lying on its side. It had a barely sloping roof covered with some kind of black composite—just a few rolls of overlapping tar paper to shed water. The trailer's walls looked flat and smooth and monotonous. There were no shutters or fasciae, and the windows had no moldings or sills—they were nothing but glowing rectangular holes cut in the sides of the box. The entire unit was surrounded by a rusting corrugated apron that peeled back at one corner to expose a narrow I-beam resting on a column of cinder blocks. In the center of the unit the roof projected out about three feet, forming a small overhang that sheltered the only door.

Not exactly a witch's castle, Nick thought. He pulled up in front of the trailer and parked; his headlights illuminated two vehicles: Alena's red pickup with the camper shell and a white Chevy TrailBlazer.

When he stopped the engine, the barking of the dogs became deafening. He looked at the kennels and tried to count them, but there were too many and they wouldn't stand still—the frantic animals were roiling like maggots on a corpse. The black dog outside the driver's door planted its two huge paws on the window and began to make a deep, bellowing bay. Nick leaned away from the window—he wasn't sure the glass would support the dog's weight. The dog outside the passenger door reared up on its hind legs as well, and then Nick felt the car rock back a little; he looked in the mirror and saw the third dog straddling the trunk and howling through the rear window.

A few seconds later a porch lamp switched on and the door to the trailer swung open. Alena stepped out and looked at the car. She charged up to the driver's-side window and stared in at Nick, and Nick offered a feeble wave back. She stood in the rain for a few moments as if she were considering what to do next—then she snapped her fingers and made a wide, sweeping gesture, and every dog in the compound fell instantly silent.

When the guard dogs backed away from the car and assumed sitting positions, Nick cautiously rolled down his window a few inches.

"What do you want?" Alena demanded.

"I need to talk to you."

"You just don't get it, do you?"

"Things have changed, Alena. We need to talk—now."

She glared at him in silence.

"Please, let me come in. I promise, I won't hurt you."

She rested one hand on the massive head of the dog beside her. "I know." She finally nodded, then turned on her heels and headed back into the trailer without a word.

Nick looked at the dog—it was still sitting outside his door, staring at him without expression. He wondered what the dog was thinking; he wondered how disciplined he really was. Alena had given him the "sit" command, but Alena was no longer there—was the command still in effect? Would the dog remain in its sitting position until instructed to do otherwise or was it a free agent now—free to make its own decisions? He looked into the dog's eyes. *Insects have no expressions*, he thought—no moods or dispositions to tell you what they plan to do next. But this was a much larger animal with a more highly developed brain; surely he should be able to look into the dog's eyes and tell *something*.

He looked again, and he thought he saw the dog smile.

The trailer door opened again with a bang. "Are you coming in or not?"

Before Nick could open his mouth the door swung shut again. He looked at the dog, took a deep breath, and slowly opened his door.

The dog made no movement toward him. Nick briefly considered allowing the dog to sniff the back of his hand but decided not to press his luck; he climbed out of the car and moved quickly into the trailer.

When he stepped through the door he found himself facing a wall that ran the length of the trailer; the double-wide was apparently made of two separate units joined in the middle, giving the interior a long, tunnel-like appearance. He looked to his right and saw a kitchen and a narrow breakfast nook tucked against the far wall; he turned to the left and found a simple living room occupied by an old sofa sectional, a coffee table, and crowded bookshelves lining the interior wall. At the end of the room was a doorway—*probably to the bedroom and bath*, Nick thought.

Alena was nowhere in sight, but there was a figure seated on the sofa looking back at Nick: Gunner Wendorf.

"I didn't expect to see you here," Nick said.

"I suppose not," Gunner replied.

Nick paused. "Come here often?"

"From time to time."

Nick was hoping for a little more in the way of explanation, but Gunner offered nothing else. Just then Alena entered through the doorway with a white hand towel and threw it at Nick; it landed across his left shoulder like a sash. Alena moved to the sofa and stood beside Gunner with her fists on her hips, glaring at Nick with one wary eye.

"Thank you," Nick said. He used the towel to blot his face and neck and dry his hair. Alena waited until he was finished, then held out a plastic bag with both hands.

Nick looked down at the bag. "I'm not radioactive—that radiant glow is just good health."

She held the bag and stared at him until he dropped the towel inside, then she sealed the bag and set it aside.

She turned to him again. "Well?"

"I wasn't expecting you to have company," Nick said. "If you don't mind, I'd like to have a word with you in private." He looked at Gunner. "Is that okay with you?"

"That's up to Alena," Gunner said. He reached out and took her right hand. "Are you okay with this? Do you feel safe?"

"I'm not afraid of him," Alena said.

"I don't think you need to be," Gunner said. "I've met Dr. Polchak before, and I believe him to be an honorable man." He looked at Nick. "Am I right?"

"I braved wild animals to get here," Nick said. "That should tell you something."

Gunner turned to the coffee table where there was a small mahogany box lined with maroon-colored satin; it held a glass bottle with a round lid, four small glass cups, and a pillbox-sized container made of brass. Gunner quietly closed the lid, stood, and tucked the box under his left arm. "I still owe you that beer," he said to Nick.

"I'm looking forward to it."

Gunner stopped in the doorway and looked back at Alena. "If you need anything else, you know how to reach me."

"Send in Acheron when you go," she said, then took a seat on the sofa.

A few seconds later, the huge black dog came trotting into the trailer and sat down next to Alena.

She looked up at Nick. "Just so you know: Before you could ever lay a hand on me, Acheron would tear out your throat."

"I got a sample of what Acheron could do the other night," Nick said. "Believe me, I'm happy right where I am."

"Sit," she said, pointing to the sofa.

"Is that an invitation or a command?"

She didn't reply.

Nick looked down at the dog. "*Acheron.* If I remember my mythology, Acheron is one of the rivers that surround Hades—the 'river of woe,' isn't it? It's an unusual name—how did you happen to pick it?"

"He picked it," she said.

Nick raised one eyebrow. "He picked it?"

"That's right."

"You were taking a big chance, weren't you? Most dogs would have picked 'Woof.'"

Again, no response.

Tough room, Nick thought. He turned to the bookshelves and began to examine the books. "How do you happen to know Gunner?"

"I live here, remember?"

"I thought you hated the folks down in Endor."

"Most of them. How do you know Gunner?"

"I stopped by his church the other day. I was looking for information about a mysterious woman who lives alone up in the mountains. People say she's a witch."

She paused. "What did he tell you?"

Nick looked at her. "Apparently a lot less than he could have." He slid a book from the shelf and opened it. "Gunner thinks you can tell a lot about people by their books; I agree with him. Take this book, for example: *Scent and the Scenting Dog,* by William Syrotuck. It has chapters on 'The Human as a Scent Source' and 'Atmospheric Factors and Airborne Scent.'"

"So?"

"Not exactly a book of spells and incantations, is it? This doesn't look like a witch's library at all; in fact, it's the sort of library that might belong to a behavioral scientist."

Alena frowned and got up from the sofa. She took the book from Nick's hand and replaced it on the shelf, then turned to him and shook the hair back from her face. "What is it you want, anyway?"

Nick blinked. Alena was standing only a foot away from him, looking directly up into his eyes. This was as close as he had ever been to her; it was the first time he had seen her face in the light and both of her eyes at the same time. She was beautiful, and Nick was more than a little surprised. In the dark shadows of the woods, she created such an eerie image that Nick had imagined the worst. He had assumed that the hair hanging down over her face was intended to cover some hideous blemish—but he

saw no blemish here. He had assumed that her skin would be pale and sal-
low, but now he realized that it only appeared that way by contrast with
her jet-black hair; up close he could see that she had a light tan and a spray
of fine freckles across the bridge of her nose. Her most striking feature
was her eyes—they were large and almond-shaped, and they were an
astonishing shade of emerald green. One eye alone had looked haunting
in the moonlight; both of them together were almost overwhelming.

"You should pull your hair back more," Nick said. "You have a very
nice face."

She immediately dropped her head and shook her hair down a little.
"I asked you what you want."

"For starters, I want you to trust me."

"Trust you? How did you get up here tonight?"

"I drove."

"I'm not stupid—I saw your car, remember? How did you get through
my gate?"

"I cut the lock off."

"What? Who gave you the right to—"

"I did it for your own good. If you'd shut up and listen for a minute,
I could explain."

She raised her eyes again—they were still overpowering, but this time
they were filled with anger. "You climbed my fence and I told you to go
away. You came back again and I had to have my dog take you down.
You talked me into helping you, and you said no one would ever know,
and I had to stand there and be insulted by that—that *woman*."

"I'm sorry about that," Nick said. "I never meant for—"

"And now you cut the lock off my fence! What does it take to get
through to you, anyway?"

"I had to walk all the way back to Endor the first time," Nick said.
"The second time I had to lay there and let your dog slobber all over
me—and now I have to stand here and let the 'river of woe' stare at me
like a lunch meat buffet. Do you think this is some kind of fraternity ini-
tiation, Alena? Do you think this is fun for me?"

She hesitated. "Then why are you here?"

"Because I think your life might be in danger."

Her eyes softened. "What?"

"The woman you met at the Patriot Center—the obnoxious one with the dehydrated dog—I think she might be dead."

"You think she *might* be?"

"Let me ask you something: Would you ever leave one of your dogs locked in a cage all day without food or water—without letting it out to relieve itself?"

"Never."

"Do you think she would?"

Alena considered. "No—even she's not that evil."

"Well, I found her dog locked up that way this evening."

"That doesn't mean she's dead."

"Her car is still in the parking lot."

"Maybe she's in a hospital somewhere—maybe she just went off her rocker. I could believe that, after meeting her."

"You're right, she might turn up somewhere—if she does, she'll eventually come back for her car and the dog. I'll put the word out—I'll ask around and see if anybody knows where she is. But if she doesn't show up by tomorrow, I'm going to the police."

Alena studied Nick's face. "You don't think she's coming back, do you?"

"No, I don't."

"You think somebody killed her."

"Yes."

"Why?"

"It smells that way."

"What?"

"Instinct—I just have a feeling."

"But why would somebody want to kill her?"

Nick looked at her. "Because somebody thought she was you."

16

Alena opened her eyes and looked at the clock. She blinked once, testing her eyelids to see if they were heavy enough to sink shut again, but they remained open. She listened and heard the wind howling through the woods; she could hear the oaks and hickories rocking back and forth, sweeping the night sky with their great leafy brooms. A powerful gust caught the trailer broadside and flexed the metal wall with a soft boom; she squeezed her eyes shut and pulled the sheets tighter around her neck.

The wind began to tease the trailer, buffeting it with sticks and twigs and the brittle shells of old acorns, making ticks and clicks and soft dull thumps everywhere. She heard something land on the roof and slowly roll across—or was it walking? The harder she listened, the more each sound seemed to take on life: The ticks on the walls became tapping fingers; the pummeling wind contained muffled voices; the shadows that flashed across her window became figures stealing by.

She felt a drop of cold sweat run down her back, but still she kept the sheets pulled tight. She stared wide-eyed into the darkness and tried not to listen while she strained to hear even more.

She heard a sound under the trailer, where she had never heard a sound before. It was a thumping, dragging, scraping sound, and it seemed very much alive. A dozen hopeful explanations hurried through her mind: a possum or raccoon escaping the wind; a rabbit or ground squirrel that couldn't reach its burrow in time; even a tiny field mouse, its size amplified by the thin, hollow floor. Now the darker explanations began to creep into her mind: the hideous, the deformed, the slithering, the nameless ancient fears that only come out at night. She could feel something under her, staring up at her, feeling along the floor with its cold dead fingers for a crevice or a crack.

The thumping stopped as suddenly as it had begun, and the room fell silent, except for the sound of air exiting her lungs in short, trembling gasps.

She heard a high-pitched whine from the direction of the kennels. It was the whimper of one of the younger dogs, probably cowering from the wind—or was it something in the wind? She could imagine the dog pacing back and forth in its kennel, its head slung low and its hackles standing on end from fear. She heard another whine—a lower one this time, from one of the older and more experienced dogs that should have known better. Now the rest of the dogs began to slowly join in a rising lament of whimpering moans and howls.

She sat up on the edge of her bed and listened.

From somewhere deep in the woods she heard a bellowing yelp and then an abrupt silence. In the kennels, every dog fell silent.

She threw off the covers and ran from the bedroom. She flung open the door of the trailer so hard that the spring snapped and the door crashed back against the trailer wall. She flew barefoot past the kennels and toward the trees in the direction of the dog's yelp. The wind beat her like surf, throwing her off balance and tossing her hair in every direction. She came to the edge of the woods and crashed into the brush without hesitating; the leafy branches slapped at her face and arms, and brambles tore at her nightgown, trying to hold her back—but she ran wildly, frantically, trying to reach the echo before the last reverberation faded away.

She broke through the brush into a small clearing; there, on the ground, she saw the body of a beautiful golden dog lying on its side. She staggered up to it and looked down; its eyes were dull and lifeless and there was a dark pool under its head. She squeezed her eyes tight and clenched her fists; she threw back her head and let out a mournful wail, but the sound was instantly swallowed up by the wind. She sank to her knees beside the dog; she lifted its massive head and cradled it in her lap, stroking its soft fur and sobbing. *Who would do this? Why would they take him away from me? Don't they know that I'm alone now—that I have no one else in all the world?*

She heard a branch snap and looked up.

She listened and heard nothing more, but she sensed a definite presence. Someone—something—was watching her from the woods. She heard the quiet crunch of leaves and then it abruptly stopped—like someone taking a cautious step closer. She gently laid the dog's head back on the ground and struggled to her feet. She wiped her eyes and face, staring into the trees and listening. She felt her grief slipping away, and fear crawling over her like a creeping vine.

She looked back toward the trailer but saw no sign of it through the dense brush. She tried to remember how long she had been running—how far she was from safety—but in her panic she had lost all sense of time and distance. She took one tentative step toward the trailer and listened—

She heard another crunch from the woods.

Terror flooded over her like a breaching dam and she took off back through the woods, plunging madly through the brush, searching for the light from the kennels and listening for footsteps behind her—but it was all one cacophony of crashing branches and frantic panting and crunching feet. She imagined someone running behind her, matching her stride for stride, slowly gaining, reaching out his fingers, touching the fringes of the soft cotton gown fluttering out behind her—

She broke through the brush and into the clearing. She caught her ankle on a grapevine and almost lost her footing but managed to stay upright. More than anything in the world she wanted to turn and look back, to know and understand the terror that was pursuing her—but she didn't dare. She ran screaming for the trailer, her heart pounding in her throat, unable to feel her legs or the ground under her feet. She ran with everything in her, but the trailer seemed an infinite distance away. She was utterly exhausted; she imagined her strength failing completely, collapsing to the ground, unable to move—the horrible image was enough to keep her going a few more steps.

She reached the open trailer door and scrambled inside, doubled over and panting like a spent mare. She staggered across the living room and through the doorway into the bedroom beyond. She stumbled to the far corner of the room and turned, sliding down and wedging herself tightly against the walls, wrapping her arms around her shoulders and staring back at the doorway, waiting for the pursuer who would never come.

She looked across the room at the floor-length mirror and saw a terrified ten-year-old girl with long black hair and green eyes. The little girl buried her face in her arms and began to cry.

Alena woke up in her bed, sobbing.

17

Nick looked down at Kegan, who was kneeling inside a newly opened grave and probing in the soil with a pointed trowel. "Have you seen Marge lately?" he asked.

"Not this morning."

"What about yesterday?"

"No, now that you mention it. Why?"

"She said she wanted to confirm these sites, but I haven't seen her around. Ask around, will you? See if anybody's seen her."

Kegan smiled up at him. "You miss her, don't you?"

"It's hard to describe the feelings I have for her."

"Don't laugh," she said. "I've read about things like that: You despise someone so much that you suddenly begin to like them."

"I just realized something," Nick said. "I'm in love with you."

"Dr. Polchak! Dr. Alexander!"

Nick and Kegan turned. At the tech tent a courier from the FBI crime lab at Quantico was waving at them with a manila envelope.

"That should be our test results," Kegan said.

"It's about time. Let's take a look."

Kegan took the envelope from the courier and spread the papers out on a folding table in the shade of the tent. The courier looked at her and asked, "Have you got anything for me to take back?"

"Those," she said, nodding to three corrugated evidence boxes lined up on a nearby table. Each measured one-by-one-by-three, and each contained an entire set of bones recovered from a grave, as well as soil samples and any artifacts found nearby.

"Anything else?"

"I've got something," Nick said. He reached into a knapsack and took out two zippered plastic bags, each containing a few strands of hair. "I want a DNA sequence run on both of these—both mitochondrial and Y-line—and tell them I want to know the haplogroup too. Have you got all that?"

"Got it." The courier took the bags and the first of the evidence boxes and headed for the parking lot.

"Where'd you get those samples?" Kegan asked.

"It's a surprise."

"Nick, tell me—I should know."

They were interrupted by another voice: "Nick! I want to talk to you—*right now!*"

They looked up and saw Danny Flanagan charging across the field toward the tent.

"Uh-oh," Nick said under his breath.

"Nick—what did you do now?"

"I demonstrated problem-solving abilities and exercised personal initiative."

"What?"

"I dropped by to see Senator Braden yesterday."

"You *what?*"

"Do me a favor," he whispered. "Act like it's something you would have done too."

"Nick," Danny said, "I was just informed that you paid an unscheduled visit to Senator John Braden yesterday. Is that true?"

"Let me think," Nick said. "Yesterday was such a long day."

"Are you out of your mind?"

"I can't tell you how many times I've been asked that."

"Who gave you permission to do that?"

"I didn't think I needed permission."

"I thought I made myself clear yesterday."

"Is there some FBI regulation that says I shouldn't pursue a possible source of information in the course of an investigation? Kegan, help me out here—is there any reason I shouldn't have interviewed Senator and Mrs. Braden?"

Kegan's mouth dropped open. "You saw *Victoria* Braden? What was she wearing?"

Nick rolled his eyes.

"Exactly what information were you looking for?" Danny demanded.

"We need to identify these bodies," Nick said. "We could use some help."

"And you think Braden knows who they are?"

"This is his property—he could have family records. C'mon, Danny, it was a logical assumption."

"It's *Daniel*—and if you wanted to inquire about the senator's family history then you should have gone through proper channels."

"What channels?"

"First of all, *me*. I would have cleared it with the Bureau, and they would have made the request through the senator's chief of staff—"

"And by that time we'd all be buried here. You would have told me no or the Bureau would have put it on the back burner or Braden's chief of staff would have shelved it until next month's staff meeting. That's how 'channels' work, Danny—you should have learned that by now."

"You were just looking for a shortcut."

"As I recall, the shortest distance between two points is still a straight line. Besides, I didn't want the information secondhand—I wanted to ask Braden myself."

"Why?"

"To find out if he was lying."

Danny looked at Nick in astonishment. "Now you're *suspecting* the senator of something?"

"Of course I am—and you should too. Are we supposed to consider Braden above suspicion just because he's a politician? There's an irony for you."

Danny glared at Nick. "Have you got any more bright ideas like that?"

"Not yet, but I'll let you know."

"Well, you'd better. From now on I want these things cleared through me first, understand?"

"I didn't want to bother you with details."

"I told you yesterday: *I like details.*"

"And I told you that's micromanaging, and you'll drive us all crazy that way—me, anyway."

"That's a risk I'm willing to take. Is there anything else you two haven't told me? Are there any other developments I should know about?"

Kegan held up the manila envelope. "We got the first anthropological evaluation from Quantico."

"When did that happen?"

"Just a few minutes ago," Nick said. "Let's not get paranoid here."

"What do the reports say?"

"We were just about to go over them."

"Good—fill me in."

There were four separate reports, each one labeled with a designator indicating the victim's location in the graveyard and the date of discovery.

"Victim 2-6-18-08," Kegan read. "This was the first body discovered. Not many surprises here; the victim was male, roughly six feet in height, right-handed."

"How can you tell that?" Danny asked.

"You tend to favor your strong hand, so the muscles become stronger; that thickens the muscle attachments on the wrist and arm."

"What about the cause of death?"

"Still undetermined. There were no cut marks on the bones and no sign of ballistic injury. There's a note here that suggests blunt-force trauma to the skull might be indicated, but I'm not sure how they could tell—the skull was smashed flat, remember?" She scanned the rest of the page. "Apparently the assumption is based on the analysis of the second set of bones." She picked up the second report and began to study it.

"4-6-18-08—also a male, a little shorter in stature and heavier in build. Approximate age at time of death forty to forty-five. Here we go: The cause of death is listed as 'blunt-force trauma to the head.' The skull was intact on this one; the victim was struck from behind, and the diameter and shape of the fracture suggest a large, smooth weapon was used—maybe an ax handle or a club."

"Could it have been accidental?"

"It's possible—a tree limb maybe—but it takes a lot of force to crush a skull." She looked at the next report. "No—it was no accident."

"Why not?"

"Because the third victim died the same way—a blow to the back of the head. The same cause of death, the same method of disposal. That's no accident—they were definitely murdered."

"How old are these skeletons?" Nick asked. "Did they find anything that could give us a postmortem interval?"

She looked. "They tested the bones for nitrogen levels; their best estimate is between twenty and fifty years."

"Can't they narrow it down any more than that?" Danny asked.

"The older the body, the harder it is to tell," Kegan said. "Once the soft tissues are gone and the body is fully skeletonized, age becomes very difficult to estimate."

"Twenty to fifty years—that doesn't give us much to go on."

"It tells us something important," Nick said. "All four bodies are in the same age range; that means one killer could be responsible for all four, and he could still be alive."

"All three," Kegan corrected.

"Excuse me?"

"The fourth skeleton—one of the two we found just the other day—it's two hundred years old."

"What?" Nick took the report from her hand and looked at it.

"The cause of death was the same—a blow to the back of the head—but the condition of the skeleton was different. On the first three bodies there were still shreds of fabric surrounding the bone. They were synthetic fibers—synthetics break down a lot more slowly than natural fibers like cotton or silk, and none of them existed before the early twentieth century. On the fourth body there were no fibers at all, and that suggests greater age. There were artifacts that helped date the fourth body as well: four buttons made of ivory—they were commonly used in the eighteenth century but rarely since. There were also fragments of brass near the feet."

"Shoe buckles?" Nick suggested.

"That's what they think at Quantico. Low nitrogen levels, absence of synthetic fibers, and datable artifacts—it all adds up to two hundred years, more or less."

"Then we've got two different killers here," Danny said, "a historical one and one that might still be alive."

"And we're not finished excavating yet," Kegan said. "Who knows what else we might find."

"What's taking so long?"

"It's a slow process, Danny. The soil above every grave could contain forensic evidence—we have to go through it one shovelful at a time. We're excavating, not gardening. It could take a few more days still."

"Somebody knows about this graveyard," Nick said almost to himself.

"Well, obviously."

"I mean they not only know its location—they know what it was used for two hundred years ago. Who would know that?"

No one had an answer.

"Could the victims be connected in some way—the old one and the new ones?"

"We're still waiting on mitochondrial DNA results," Kegan said. "That might tell us if any of them were related—at least if they shared a common female ancestor."

"Let me know as soon as you get them," Danny said. "Is there anything else?"

Kegan flipped through the reports. "Nothing out of the ordinary."

"Okay," Danny said. "What do we know so far?"

"First of all, we know we're talking about murder now," Nick said.

"And second, we know that one killer is probably responsible for all three of the recent murders—the similar ages of the skeletons make it possible, and the common modus makes it almost certain. Third, we know the killer is a copycat—he learned his technique from somebody who lived a long time ago. That means he has historical knowledge of the area and he's probably a native."

"I'll get the behavioral science services unit to start working up a profile," Danny said.

"That's a good idea, Danny—this guy doesn't fit the traditional serial killer profile."

"You two keep me posted—I'll see you both at the noon briefing."

They watched as Danny took out his cell phone and headed off across the field.

"That concerns me," Nick said.

"He's only trying to do his job."

"No, not that—he never asked me what Braden said. I wonder why?"

"What *did* Braden say?"

"He said he has no information about this graveyard. Mrs. Braden said the same thing."

"Do you believe them?"

Nick paused. "Actually, I do."

Kegan leaned closer and grinned. "You never told me—what was she wearing?"

"I have no idea."

"You didn't even *notice*? What are those glasses for, anyway?"

"Not fashion assessment."

Kegan shook her head. "It defies explanation."

"I'm a man," Nick said. "That's all the explanation I need—now let's get back to work."

18

"Are there any other developments I should be aware of?" the senator asked.

"No, sir. I think that about covers it for now."

Braden sat in his wingback chair with his forearms resting on the padded leather and his legs crossed casually at the knee. Victoria and Brad sat across from him in low-backed Savannah chairs covered in cotton twill. All of them stared at a triangular black conference phone sitting on a pedestal table between them.

"Good work, Danny," Braden said. "You don't mind if I call you 'Danny,' do you?"

"No, sir, that would be just fine."

"Well, I appreciate the update. You're doing good work out there, son—I'll make sure the director knows about it."

"Thank you, sir, I really appreciate that."

"You keep me posted on any further developments, hear?"

"Yes, sir—you'll be the first to know."

Brad leaned forward and pushed a button on the center of the phone. "What do you think, John?"

"I think we've got one certified mess out there, that's what I think."

"It might not be as bad as it sounds," Victoria said.

"Now how do you figure that, darling? I count four dead bodies, and there might be more."

"Bodies that could be fifty years old," Victoria said. She turned to Brad. "We need to make sure we emphasize that."

"The media will say twenty," Brad replied.

"That's pure speculation on their part, and we should say so. Whoever did this probably died years ago—that's what we want to stress. We need to set this whole thing in the past—make it sound like nothing more than a historical curiosity."

The senator winked at his wife. "What do you think of our new boy Danny?"

"He'll do," Victoria said. "He's young and he's eager to please. He'll be a lot easier to handle than Nathan Donovan."

"Let's hope so. We need to stay a step ahead of this situation—I don't want to be learning about it from the morning papers."

"We need to be informing the papers ourselves," Victoria said. "We should send out regular press releases—get the information to the reporters before they dig it up themselves."

"What do you want to tell them?"

"Everything we know—with a certain editorial slant, of course. 'Four bodies have been found so far; the FBI has no reason to think there will be more. The bodies are estimated to be as many as fifty years old; so far the FBI is at a loss to explain them.' Brad, I want you to get me some information on how they date these skeletons. Put one of the research assistants on it—have them call the FBI or one of the local universities. Find out how much guesswork is involved—how much margin for error there is. Twenty, fifty, two hundred years—it sounds like they're guessing to me, and if they are, I want to be able to say so."

Brad didn't reply.

Victoria looked at him. "Is there a problem, Brad?"

"I think there's a question of strategy here—something we need to address. The question is, how much attention do we want to draw to this? I understand your approach, Mrs. Braden—total transparency—but I think it could backfire on us. We could start a feeding frenzy if we're not careful."

"Just the opposite," Victoria said. "A feeding frenzy occurs when there's not enough for everyone to eat. The instant a reporter senses that you're withholding information, that's when he'll take a bite out of you."

"I'm not suggesting that we withhold information—I'm suggesting that we look the other way."

"Draw attention to more important matters," the senator said.

"Exactly. We're in the middle of a presidential campaign and we've got a platform to push. Who can blame us for that? Immigration reform, renewable energy mandates, the international nuclear threat, homeland security—every one of those subjects is more important than what's going on at the Patriot Center. Let's talk about what's significant—direct the public's attention where it belongs."

"I just did a sit-down with *Harper's Bazaar*," Victoria said. "I went into that interview with two talking points: immigration reform and preschool education for the poor. You know what they wanted to talk about? Whether I was wearing a Zac Posen or a Nina Ricci at the Kennedy Center last week. So I told them all about the gown—the way it's made, the way it fits, the way the stupid thing rides up on anybody bigger than a size six. I didn't 'direct their attention where it belongs,' Brad, I told them more than they wanted to know—and you know what happened? *They changed the subject.* The question here isn't, what do *we* think is important? The question is, what do *they* think is important? And if they think what's important is a little graveyard at the Patriot Center, then believe me—it is."

Brad looked at the senator for a ruling. So did Victoria—but her look was a little more determined, and her eyes communicated a subtext that her husband couldn't miss.

The senator paused. "I think we should follow Victoria on this one. She's got a lot of experience with the media, and I trust her instincts."

Mrs. Braden flashed her husband a quick wink.

"It's your call," Brad said with a shrug of resignation. "I'll get on the first press release right away."

"Make sure I see it first," Victoria said. "Remember—I want a certain editorial slant."

"You've got it—anything else?"

"Yes. I want to pay a visit to Endor."

Both men looked at her in astonishment.

"Sweetheart, I trust your instincts, but don't you think that might be going a bit too far? I requested that Mr. Donovan be removed because he was attracting too much publicity—what will happen when your pretty face shows up out there? Talk about a feeding frenzy."

"The problem with Nathan Donovan wasn't too much publicity—it was the wrong kind. Think about it, Johnny: Who covers the FBI? Crime scene reporters do. But crime scene reporters don't cover me— I get the reporters from Lifestyle and Fashion, and isn't that just the kind of publicity we're looking for? We don't want someone asking, 'How many more bodies might be out there?' We want them to ask, 'How big is that mall going to be?' Besides, I won't visit the Patriot Center—I'll visit Endor. It's my hometown, and it's right next door— just close enough but not too close."

Brad turned to her. "What would this visit accomplish, Mrs. Braden?"

"Ask Johnny," she said. "He understands."

The senator smiled at his wife. "I believe my wife is referring to a technique commonly employed by our nation's chief executive: When a situation is deserving of the president's attention but it's too contro-versial to allow a personal appearance, he sends the First Lady instead. She has a softer presence. She conveys compassion and concern. No one wants to embarrass her with awkward questions. They respect her—they treat her with kid gloves."

Victoria looked at Brad with a pouty face. "You wouldn't want to make me cry, would you, Brad?"

Brad grinned. "No, ma'am, I wouldn't want that. Okay, I'll set it up. When would you like to make this visit?"

"The sooner the better. Get the PR team moving on it, and have Cassandra meet me in my office—we'll start working up a schedule of events." She rose from her chair, blew a quick kiss to her husband, and started for the door.

"I do have one more question," Brad said.

"Yes?"

"What happens if they find more bodies?"

"It won't matter," she said.

"It won't matter?"

"They found an old graveyard, that's all—it happens all the time. As for the bodies, nobody knows who they are or how they got there. It's a mystery—and that's exactly the way we want to leave it until after the election. We want them to get those caskets out of there so they can get back to work on the Patriot Center, but as for the bodies—we want the FBI to take them back to some laboratory and puzzle over them for a few months. Four bodies, five bodies, ten bodies—it doesn't matter. Time is all that matters here, Brad—it's all about time."

Victoria turned and left the room; her heels made a receding *clack* on the slate floor as she crossed the foyer to her office.

"When are you going to learn to trust Victoria?" the senator said with a sly smile. "We might as well face it, son—the woman is smarter than both of us combined."

Nick trotted up the shallow stone steps of Alderman Library, the largest and oldest collection of books and rare manuscripts at the University of Virginia. He squeezed past a group of students exiting the building with their ever-present cell phones pressed against their ears and entered the lobby, a cavernous room with a twenty-five-foot ceiling and towering arched windows that made it look even taller. On his left there was a coffee shop, offering both companionship and chemical enhancement for each student's study needs; across the aisle there was a rectangular study area lined with padded vinyl chairs. On the right there was a grid of low cubicles equipped with charcoal gray computers, and across the aisle he found what he was looking for—the reference desk. Nick crossed to the desk and approached the first worker he saw, a young man in a blue scrubs top with the letter *V* embroidered on the breast pocket and a pair of crossed sabers below.

The student glanced up. "Need some help?"

"Yes," Nick said, "I'm looking for a master's thesis titled 'The Utility of Arthropods in Medicolegal Investigations.' It was completed at Penn State University."

The young man looked at him blankly. "I—don't think we have that one."

"I didn't expect you to keep it on a shelf next to *Seventeen*. I want to know if you can find it for me."

The student began to slowly peck at a computer keyboard. "Um— I'm not sure what to look under. Let me see if I can find someone who could—"

"Never mind," Nick said. "You can go back to *Facebook* now."

Nick walked down to the opposite end of the reference desk where he found a woman seated at a computer. Her hair was a dyed reddish-orange and pulled back in a simple ponytail with short strands that dangled down over her forehead. She wore black-framed glasses with the logo "D&G" encrusted in rhinestones on the temples, and a silver post protruded from the right side of her nose. She wore a navy UVA hoodie even though it was almost summer, which was no surprise to Nick since she was a woman and the library was kept at the temperature of a meat locker.

She looked up as he approached. "May I help you?"

"Yes—I'm looking for a doctoral dissertation titled 'Systematics, Morphology, and Ecology of *Chrysomya rufifacies*, the Hairy Maggot Blowfly.' Can you find it for me?"

"Where was it done?"

"Penn State."

"Which one? Penn State has twenty-four campuses."

"The main campus—University Park."

Her fingers began to skitter across the keyboard. "Let's try Dissertation Abstracts Online—they cover every American dissertation accepted at an accredited institution since 1861 and selected master's theses since 1962. Do you need an abstract or is this just an author search?"

"I'd like an abstract."

"The abstracts only date back to July of 1980."

"It's more recent than that."

"Can you give me a subject heading? It sounds like entomology."

"Good guess."

"Hmm—it looks like 'Biological and Environmental Sciences' is the closest subject heading they've got. I'll do a Boolean search on 'hairy-maggot-blowfly'—isn't that what you said?"

"Good memory too."

"It comes with the territory."

"The guy at the other end of the desk must come from a different territory."

"Here we are: 'Systematics, Morphology, and Ecology of *Chrysomya rufifacies*, the Hairy Maggot Blowfly.' I just sent the abstract to the printer. Would you like me to order the complete dissertation for you?"

"That won't be necessary. I wrote it."

She looked up. "You don't have a copy of your own dissertation?"

"Of course I do—I keep it on my nightstand. I just wanted to see if you could find it."

She paused. "What is this, some kind of test?"

"You could say that. I'm looking for a grad student to do some research for me—someone who knows their way around a library."

"How did you know I'm a grad student?"

"You have that hungry look."

She looked down at the computer screen. "Author: Dr. Nicholas Polchak."

"Call me Nick."

"I'm Carlyn Shaw. What kind of research are you looking for, Nick?"

"Historical research. For starters, I'm looking for colonial-era grave registries for the area around Endor."

"Endor? Where they're building the big mall?"

"That's the place."

"I've read about that. Does this have something to do with that graveyard they've uncovered there?"

"As a matter of fact it does. It seems we've got a meadow full of caskets and no idea who they belong to."

"'We'?"

"The FBI."

"You're with the FBI?"

"No, I'm a professor of entomology at NC State. I'm assisting the FBI."

"Did you try the local library in Endor? That's where I'd look first. Small towns take a lot of pride in their history—you'd be surprised what you can find there."

"I tried. No luck."

"Well, then you've come to the right place. UVA has fourteen libraries with five million volumes between them—some really good special collections too."

"That's why I'm here—and that's why I need you. I don't have time to do all the digging; I need someone like you to do it for me."

Carlyn considered his offer. "How much?"

"A couple of days, maybe a week or—"

"Money, Nick—I'm a grad student, remember?"

"What's the going rate for research around here?"

"Whatever the market will bear."

"I'll pay you thirty bucks an hour, and I'll trust you to keep your own time card." He extended his hand to her. "Deal?"

She looked at it for a moment before she took it. "Deal. Now—tell me exactly what you're looking for."

Two hours later, Nick stepped into the Endor Regional Library and looked around. *Not exactly UVA*, he thought—but then, to be fair, it wasn't designed by Thomas Jefferson. The library was empty except for a handful of hyperactive after-school kids furiously flipping through picture books in the Juvenile section. He spotted Agnes behind the circulation desk; the old woman seemed to keep turning this way and that, as though she couldn't decide which direction to head first.

Nick approached. "You seem to be in a hurry today."

"She's coming," Agnes said solemnly.

"Who's coming? Where?"

She looked at him in wonder. "You don't *know?*"

"I'm working for the government—we're always the last to know. What's up?"

"Victoria Braden—she's coming here—to Endor!"

"No kidding. When?"

"In just a couple of days. Imagine—our own little Victoria is coming home!"

"You're in for a surprise," Nick said. "She's not so little anymore."

Agnes looked around the library in desperation. "There's so little time and so much to do."

"You'd better polish the altar and fire up the incense burners."

"I'm sorry, Nick, I just don't have time to chat with you today—can you come back another time?"

"I just have one quick question: Remember the grave registries I was looking for? You said you'd ask around for me. Has anything turned up yet?"

"I'm sorry—there's just no trace of them."

"Because I asked at UVA, and they told me that the regional library would be the best place to look."

"It is—but I'm afraid we just don't have them. If anyone would know, I would. Now if you don't mind—"

"Sorry, I'll let you get back to your preparations. Don't forget the sacrificial ox."

But Agnes was already scurrying off.

20

Nick left the library and looked across the street, where Ralph and Edna Denardo were busy draping the lampposts in front of the Skyline with patriotic red-white-and-blue bunting. He looked to his left; in the parking lot behind the Resurrection Lutheran Church he saw Gunner Wendorf's white Chevy. He crossed the street and entered the church. The Gothic arched door stood wide open, though no one was anywhere in sight. *It figures*, Nick thought. Theft probably wasn't much of a problem in a town the size of Endor—after all, there wasn't much to steal.

He stepped through the narthex and into the sanctuary, where he heard the sound of an electric drill and spotted Gunner kneeling by a pew near the chancel. Nick stuffed his hands into his pockets and walked down the aisle; Gunner had just driven a Phillips head screw into the side of a pew and was tapping in a hardwood plug to conceal the hole.

"You look like you know what you're doing," Nick said.

Gunner looked up. "The pews keep falling apart—too many sleeping people." He dropped the hammer and screwdriver into a metal toolbox and hoisted himself to his feet.

"I didn't mean to interrupt," Nick said.

"I'm glad you did—I could use a break."

"Do you take outside jobs? I've got a deck that's falling apart back in Raleigh."

"Sorry—I've got my hands full here. I cover a lot of ground."

Nick smiled. "That's what I was thinking last night when I saw you at Alena's."

Gunner smiled back but didn't reply.

"I suppose you were a little surprised to see me too," Nick said.

"As a matter of fact, I was."

"You're probably wondering what I was doing there."

"The thought crossed my mind."

"I'll tell you if you'll tell me."

Gunner shook his head. "It's not that simple, Nick. There's a clergy confidentiality issue here; you see, Alena is a member of my congregation."

"A witch in the church? You people are really reaching out."

"She's not a witch—you know that."

"She seems to think so."

"No, she doesn't—I think you know that too."

Nick nodded. "Can we sit down for a minute? I need to talk to you."

They both took a seat on the newly repaired pew. Gunner wiggled in a little to test the quality of his work.

"These things are just as uncomfortable as I remember," Nick said. "Nobody could sleep on this."

"That's sort of the idea." He waited for Nick to continue.

"I want to tell you why I was at Alena's last night," Nick said, "even if you can't tell me."

"Oh? How come?"

"I think somebody else needs to know."

"Why me?"

"Because I have a feeling you care about Alena's welfare—and because I think I can trust you."

"You're definitely right about the first," he said, "and I like to think you're right about the second too. Go ahead—what's on your mind?"

"There was a woman hired by the FBI to locate all the graves at the Patriot Center. I called her 'Marge'—she had a cadaver dog."

"Sure, the woman on TV."

"You saw that?"

"Everybody did. I told you, news travels fast in a small town. She's staying over at the Skyline where you are, isn't she?"

"She was. I have a feeling she's dead."

Gunner did a double take. "Dead? How?"

"I think she might have been murdered."

"By whom?"

"By someone who saw that interview; by someone who didn't want those graves to be found; by someone with something to hide."

"Have you told the police?"

"Not yet. I plan to in the morning. I wanted to wait a day and see if she'd turn up first."

"Why are you telling me this?"

"Because Marge didn't find those bodies, Gunner—Alena did."

"What?"

"I went up there the other night. I told Alena that Marge just couldn't do the job. I talked her into coming down and helping me with that three-legged dog of hers. She didn't want to come at first; she finally agreed, but only if I promised not to tell anyone she was there. Alena found every one of those graves, but Marge took credit for it—I think that's why Marge is dead and not Alena."

"That means Alena is in danger. We have to go to the police."

"Alena is safe as long as no one knows about her involvement. You said it yourself: News travels fast in a small town. If we tell the police, how long will it be before everybody else knows? No—right now our best chance of keeping Alena safe is to keep her out of it."

Gunner thought about that. "If you're right, then you took a big chance even telling me. What if I turned out to be the town gossip?"

"Are you?"

"No."

"I didn't think so. I have to trust you, Gunner—I need your help."

"Tell me what I can do."

"Look—I understand 'clergy confidentiality' and all, but is there anything you can tell me about Alena? This isn't just idle curiosity. If I'm going to figure all this out, then I need to understand what's going on here."

Gunner took a minute to consider his words. "I've known Alena since she was a little girl," he said. "I knew her father—his name was Ken Savard. The land on the top of this mountain has been in Alena's family longer than anyone can remember. Ken and Alena moved up there when she was just a little girl—just the two of them."

"And the mother?"

"Divorced, I think, maybe deceased—I never got the details. I'm not sure Alena even knows."

"What did her father do for a living?"

"He worked over in Front Royal at the Canine Enforcement Training Center—that's where the Customs and Border Protection people train all the drug-sniffing dogs that they use along the borders; ATF trains bomb-sniffing dogs there too. How much do you know about detection dogs?"

"I've worked around them; I've seen what they can do. I know they can be trained to find narcotics, people hiding in cars, large amounts of currency—things like that."

"Most of that started in the '70s—before that, dogs didn't really specialize. If you had a convict on the loose, you sent for a bloodhound; if you had a body to find, you sent for a bloodhound. It was sort of a 'one dog fits all' approach—but Alena's dad helped change all that. He thought dogs should specialize—he thought they could be more effective if they concentrated on detecting only one thing. That's what he did at the CETC: He developed methods for training dogs to perform specialized tasks. They say he taught them to do some amazing things."

"Is that where Alena learned to train dogs? From her father?"

"That's where she got her start—but to tell you the truth, I think she's done things her father never dreamed of."

"I've seen a sample of what she can do," Nick said. "Those guard dogs of hers—and that three-legged cadaver dog—I've never seen anything like them. She never says a word to those dogs, but they seem to know exactly what she wants them to do."

"People around here say she can talk to animals. She can't, of course—she just knows how they think. It's a gift, in a way. I suppose it's what happens when you withdraw from people and pour your life into dogs; you learn to think like a dog instead."

"What happened to her father?"

"He was quite a celebrity around here for a while. The newspapers picked up on what he was doing, and pretty soon people started coming to see him. Then one day he disappeared."

"Disappeared?"

"Vanished without a trace—Alena was about ten at the time. There was a big storm one night. Her dad heard a noise in the woods and went to check on it. He never came back."

"What happened to Alena? What did she do?"

"She stayed up there."

"Alone? She was only ten years old."

"I know—talk about impressive stuff. Alena practically raised herself, with a lot of help from people like me and my wife—Rose is her name. We heard what happened to her father and we went up to see her. We tried to get her to come down to Endor, but she just wouldn't do it."

"Don't you have Child and Family Services out here?"

"Sure. They placed Alena in a foster home—she ran away. They put her in another home—she ran away again. She'd head back up to the top of the mountain and hide out in her woods for weeks at a time. That's awfully hard on a little girl; after a while the authorities got tired of chasing her down, and we started to realize that we were doing her more harm than good. Social Services sort of forgot about her, so Rose and I took over; we decided it was best to let her stay in her home and just try to take care of her there. It's all we could do; you can put a kid in a foster home, but you can't make her stay. Alena just refused to live in Endor."

"Why?"

"Because she hates the people here. When her father vanished, no one called; no one raised a finger to help. They left her up there to take care of herself; she might have starved if Rose and I hadn't gotten to her first."

"Why didn't anyone help?"

"The stories."

"What stories?"

"These are the mountains, Nick. People are deeply superstitious here—it's sort of in their blood. There were too many stories about Alena's father: the man who could talk to animals, the man who could raise the dead—"

"I've heard the same stories about Alena."

"Exactly—but when her father disappeared the stories got worse. Some people said that he turned into an animal himself and ran away; some said that he was like Enoch in the Bible, only it was the devil who took him away and not God."

"That would be pretty tough on a ten-year-old girl."

"The stories almost killed her. It's hard to blame her for hating Endor—I guess maybe I would too. She's been living up there ever since, just her and her dogs. That's the same trailer she lived in with her father, and those are the kennels he built."

"Did her father leave her any money? How does she live?"

"Her father didn't have a dime—just a thousand acres of Virginia mountaintop. Alena makes a living finding dogs for the CETC. About four times a year dog breeders from all over the country bring their puppies in. The trainers there test the dogs and buy the ones that have the qualities they're looking for."

"Can you make a living that way?"

"A good pup is worth about forty-five hundred bucks, and Alena knows what they're looking for. She manages to sell quite a few—enough to get her by."

"She seems to have a few of her own."

"Thirty or so, last time I counted."

"Where does she get them all?"

"Animal shelters—she takes the ones they're about to put down. She brings them back to her place and trains them. The ones that are good enough she sells to the CETC; the others she keeps or finds homes for. They're a mangy lot—there's not a purebred in the bunch—but brother, the things they can do. Alena can look in a dog's eyes and tell you its gift—the natural ability it has that can be developed with the right training. It's spooky sometimes."

"She told me her dogs pick their own names."

"That's right. They tell her who they are—get the idea?"

Nick shook his head. "She's an amazing woman."

"Yes, she is."

"Beautiful too."

Gunner stared into Nick's eyes.

"I just meant—I couldn't help but notice, that's all."

"My wife and I love Alena as if she were our own daughter," Gunner said. "I go to her whenever she sends for me. I sit with her; I talk to her; I let her take Communion. You put her in danger, Nick."

"I didn't mean to."

"That doesn't matter. The point is, you did—and that makes you responsible for her safety."

"I understand."

"I'm not sure you do. Alena is vulnerable—she's lonely, and she's isolated, and someone with the wrong motives could take advantage of her. She's been deeply hurt all her life; I don't want to see her get hurt again. I have to trust you too, Nick—I have to know you'll look out for her."

"That's why I'm here, Gunner—that's why I was at Alena's last night. I'm not sure what happened to Marge yet—maybe she took a trip somewhere, maybe she got depressed and just took off. Who knows? Bosco the Wonder Dog just got his butt whipped by a three-legged mongrel—maybe she went shopping for a new dog. It's only a hunch I have about Marge, but I wanted Alena to know—just in case."

"She needs more than a warning."

"I know that too. I'm going back up there tomorrow morning—after I talk to the police about Marge."

"You won't mention Alena to the police."

"Not a chance. Marge kept Alena out of the picture—I want to leave it that way."

"So how can I help?"

"You can help me think," Nick said. "If I am right about Marge, then we've got a killer loose—and the same guy who killed Marge knows the story behind the bodies at the Patriot Center. It looks like the murders there were spread out over a period of thirty years, and that graveyard isn't far from here. That means the perpetrator was almost certainly a local—someone from Endor or one of the other towns nearby."

"That makes sense."

"You've been around here a long time, right? You must know just about everybody in town."

"Everybody in Endor—half the people in Front Royal too."

"Then help me out here. Who do you know who might be capable of murder?"

Gunner began to chuckle.

"Did I say something funny?"

"To someone in my profession, yes."

"So what's the joke?"

"You know what I like about being a pastor, Nick? I don't have to go around spouting some nonsense like 'Human beings are basically good.'"

"I thought pastors were supposed to believe that."

"Not the ones who read their Bibles. I'd like to believe it—unfortunately, there's just too much evidence to the contrary. The Bible treats people as *fallen*—made in the image of God but corrupted in a fundamental way. Fatally flawed, you might say—that's the human dilemma, and nobody is exempt. You asked, 'Who do you know who might be capable of murder?' The answer to your question is, 'Everybody—every man, every woman, and even the children by a certain age.'"

"Must be a tough town."

"No tougher than anywhere else. People are people, Nick. That's the problem; that's the human dilemma."

"Everybody," Nick said. "That doesn't help me a lot—I'm trying to narrow the field."

"Maybe you shouldn't."

"What do you mean?"

"Keep an open mind—especially when it comes to the human capacity for evil. That's what I try to do; there are fewer surprises that way. Everybody has the capacity to do evil—all they need is the right frame of mind."

"Okay," Nick said. "Then who do you know who might have the frame of mind?"

"Let me think about that one," Gunner said. "I have to be careful. Pastors tend to hear a lot of confessions. If I start pointing the finger at everyone who's ever admitted a bad attitude to me, I'll be pointing out half the people in town."

"I'm not interested in bad attitudes," Nick said. "I'm looking for someone who has a reason to kill."

"Who doesn't?"

"Excuse me?"

"I know people who've been robbed of their life's savings; parents who've lost kids to drunk drivers; wives who've been abandoned by husbands after thirty faithful years of marriage. Everybody has a reason to kill somebody; most people don't do it. It isn't just about reason—it's about what's going on in your heart, and that's what God wants to change."

"Now you're starting to preach."

"You're in a church—what did you expect? To believe what I believe and not want to tell you about it would be the worst kind of hypocrisy. If you had cancer, wouldn't you want the doctor to tell you? And if there was a cure, wouldn't you want to know? That's what I tell people: You're a part of the human dilemma too, and I think there's a cure. Let's grab that beer sometime; we can talk more about it then."

"Thanks." Nick got up from the pew and stretched. "You said you go to Alena whenever she sends for you. How does she send for you if she doesn't have a phone?"

"She sends a dog—a little one, about so high. Ugly little cuss. His name is Ruckus."

"The dog knows where you live?"

"He knows what I smell like. He stops here first; if I'm not home, he'll search all over town until he finds me."

"Sort of like 'call forwarding,'" Nick said.

"Yeah, something like that."

"What about that three-legged dog that always seems to be with her?"

"That's Trygg—she's the most special of all."

"Why?"

"Has anyone told you the story about the witch who wanders the woods at night in search of her father's soul?"

"I think Agnes told me that one."

"Well—that one happens to be true."

21

Nick rapped his knuckles on the trailer door; it sounded tinny and hollow, like the door of a cheap car.

Alena opened the door and looked at him. "What did you do this time, knock down my fence?"

"I brought you a gift," Nick said, holding out a small package.

"It's a little early for pizza."

"You're obviously not a college student. May I come in?"

She hesitated but eventually opened the door and took the box.

Nick stepped into the trailer. In the living room he saw half a dozen puppies of various shapes and sizes—as Gunner said, "not a purebred among them." They were curled up on the sofa and wandering the floor; one was sniffing at a spot on the carpet while another was gnawing on a rawhide toy. Alena walked to the sofa and scooped up one of the puppies along the way. She sat down and set the puppy on her lap, then rolled it over onto its back and began to massage its pink tummy and the undersides of its legs.

Nick watched. "What is this, a day spa for dogs?"

Alena gave him a look—half boredom, half disgust.

"Sorry," Nick said. "I tend to be a wise guy. I've spent my whole life developing the habit, and I'm probably not going to change for you. May I ask what you're doing?"

"Touching."

"I can see that. Why?"

"Some of these dogs will become service dogs, that's why. They'll be around people and they'll be in public places—you don't want a dog to bite someone just because someone accidentally touched a sensitive spot. This is part of his socialization, okay?"

"Did you learn that from your dad?"

She looked annoyed and didn't reply.

Nick started toward the sofa but stopped when his eye caught a framed certificate hanging on the wall. "Well, what do you know."

"What?"

"A diploma—and it isn't from Hogwarts. 'Alena Savard, BS in Behavioral Science, Virginia Polytechnic Institute and State University.' You've got a college degree."

"So?"

"You don't exactly advertise it."

"What am I supposed to do, wear my diploma around my neck?"

"They call me *Dr.* Polchak. You're a Virginia Tech graduate—did you put yourself through college?"

"It's no big deal. I'm still paying off the loans."

"It's a very big deal," Nick said. "I hope you're proud of yourself— you should be." He took a seat on the sectional across from her. One of the puppies rose from its slumber, trotted over to Nick, and curled up next to his thigh. "Friendly dogs," he said.

"They're young—they don't know any better."

"Maybe they know who they can trust. I hear animals have pretty good instincts."

"Instincts can be mistaken. That's what brains are for."

Nick pointed to the package beside her. "You haven't opened your gift yet."

"What is it?"

"Well, you could have your gift-sniffing dog check it out. Personally, I'd open it."

She opened the box and removed a small silver object—a combination padlock.

"It's the least I could do," Nick said.

"Do you know the combination?"

"You know, you're a very suspicious person. Here, let me have it—
I'll put it on the gate when I leave."

"And when will that be?"

Nick smiled pleasantly. "Later—I hope. Do you mind if I ask a
favor?"

"What kind of favor?"

"I'd like you to say my name."

"What?"

"My name—it's 'Nick.'"

"I know what it is. Why do you want me to say it?"

"Because I'm not a dog, I'm a man. You can't just snap your fingers
and give me a command—I'm a little more complex than that. Go
ahead, try it—just say, 'Nick.'"

"This is stupid."

"Just once."

"Okay, *Nick*. There—are you satisfied?"

"It would sound a little better if you didn't vomit it up, but it's a start."

"Is that what you came all the way up here for?"

"No—just a friendly visit."

Alena glared at him. "I can't just sit here with you all day—I've got
work to do."

"Tummies to rub?"

"No—dogs to train."

"Great! Mind if I tag along?"

"Why?"

"Know what I do for a living? I study the insects that are attracted to
decomposing human flesh. They find bodies the same way that dog of
yours does—only they do it by instinct, and you have to teach the dog.
I'd love to see how you do that."

She hesitated. "Is that the only way I can get rid of you?"

"It's all that comes to mind."

"Will you stay out of my way?"

"Don't I always?"

She shook her head in resignation. "Grab a puppy and come on."

They set the last of the puppies in the grassy clearing. Alena opened a sealed bag and took out a six-inch length of PVC pipe with holes drilled in the sides and a cap on either end.

"What's that?" Nick asked.

"Death."

"Excuse me?"

"This is a scent vial; it contains the scent of decomposing human flesh."

Nick held out his hand. "May I?"

She handed him the vial. "Don't touch the sides—you'll contaminate the scent."

Nick held the vial by one end and carefully sniffed. "Yep, that's the real thing all right."

"No, it's not."

"It's not?"

"Where would I get the real thing? This is called Pseudo Corpse Scent—there's a company in St. Louis called Sigma-Aldrich that manufactures the stuff. They make three kinds of death scent: putrefying remains, post-putrefying remains, and submerged remains. Every kind of victim gives off a different scent, and you have to train the dog to find the specific kind of victim you're looking for. There's actually a fourth scent too—they make one called 'distressed body.'"

"What's 'distressed body'?"

"It's a living person who's under intense stress. The stress changes their blood chemistry and their skin gives off an odor that a dog can detect. 'Distressed body' simulates that odor; Sigma-Aldrich just came up with it a few years ago."

"So your dog can find the living too?"

"Sometimes—but only if the victim is just less than dead."

"Actually, insects are the same way. The line between life and death is so fine that sometimes they have trouble telling the difference. Blowflies won't land on a living, moving, breathing human being, but they will if you're wounded and unconscious. It's like they figure, why not? You're just less than dead—might as well get started."

"How do insects find the dead?"

"Different species are attracted to a body at different stages of decomposition. As the body dries out it emits different chemical indicators, and each one attracts a different kind of insect. They pick up the scent through the air, just like your dog does—only they have smell and taste receptors all over their bodies."

He bent down and began to look through Alena's equipment box.

"Hey—keep your nose out of my stuff."

"I'm supposed to be learning here." He took out a second plastic bag containing a short length of PVC pipe. "What's this one?"

"Submerged remains."

"That's interesting. When a body decomposes in a wet environment it forms a waxy substance called *adipocere*—that must be what the dog is detecting." He held the bag up to Alena. "Do you mind?"

"Knock yourself out—if you're not careful, you will."

Nick opened the bag and sniffed. "It smells just like the other one. I can't tell the difference."

"That's because you only have about five million olfactory cells in your nose; a dog can have two hundred million—one-eighth of its brain is dedicated to smell. Dogs have an incredible ability to distinguish scents. You walk into a kitchen and smell beef stew; a dog walks into a kitchen and smells beef, carrots, peas, potatoes—it's called 'odor layering.' He can even smell the salt—even in a dilution of one in ten million."

"Question," Nick said. "If a dog's sense of smell is so much more sensitive than a man's, how come a dog will stick its nose in your crotch?"

She squinted at him. "Are you always like this?"

"What? That was a good question."

She set the scent vial down on the ground and placed one of the puppies in front of it. The dog sniffed at the vial once, then cowered and backed away.

"See what he's doing? A lot of dogs are instinctively repulsed by the smell of death. He's out—he'll never make a cadaver dog."

"Just like that? No second chances?"

"It isn't something he can learn. He was either born with it or he wasn't—and he wasn't. It's not his gift." She picked up the dog and looked into its eyes. "No—he doesn't have it in him. I should have seen it before."

"Wait a minute," Nick said. He picked up a second dog and handed it to her. "Try this one—but look at it first and tell me what you think it'll do."

She took the dog and looked into its eyes. "This one's all play and no work—he'll have the opposite problem." She set the dog in front of the vial and watched; the dog took the vial in its mouth and began to run off. She reached down and lifted it by the scruff of its neck. "Some dogs love the scent of death—they're no good either. You're looking for a dog that doesn't care—a dog that will treat it just like any other smell."

She tested three more puppies; the third one sniffed at the vial and made no response at all. Alena looked at its face. "He might make it, he might not."

"You're tough," Nick said. "I should have you take a look at some of my grad students."

"There's no sense wasting your time. They either have it or they don't."

She handed the dog to Nick, who held it awkwardly against his chest while she set up three cinder blocks about ten feet apart. She hid the scent vial inside the center cinder block, then took the puppy back again.

Nick looked down at his chest; there was a large wet spot on his shirt. "This is why I don't like mammals."

Alena smiled. "You're right: Animals do have pretty good instincts."

Nick shook his head. "Now she gets a sense of humor."

Alena set the dog down a few feet from the cinder blocks, then reached into her pocket and took out a small, round, mahogany-colored object; she pointed it at the dog like a key fob.

"What's that?" Nick asked.

"You'll see."

They watched while the dog wandered aimlessly around the cinder blocks. After a few minutes it approached an empty block and sniffed at it; Alena did nothing and the dog wandered off again. A few minutes later it approached the center cinder block; the instant its nose neared the concrete, Alena worked her thumb, and the object in her hand made a crickety clicking sound—*CLICK clack*. She immediately ran to the dog and lavished it with affection.

Nick pointed to the clicker. "May I see that?"

She hesitated, but handed it to him.

Nick adjusted his glasses and looked at it. It was a glossy round buckeye with a thumb-sized slot carved into one side; projecting out of the slot was a thin tab of gunmetal steel. He pushed it with his thumb—*CLICK clack*. "It's beautiful," he said, handing it back.

"My father used to make them."

"This is classic operant conditioning. You're using that clicker to reinforce the behavior you're looking for."

"That's right." She moved the dog away and set it down again. This time it returned to the cinder block in half the time, and Alena once again hit the clicker and showered it with praise.

"He learns fast," Nick said. "I've had freshmen who need a semester to get that far."

"He's just imprinting on the cinder block—now we have to tell him what he's really looking for." She moved the vial to the first cinder block and released the dog again; it immediately trotted to the same cinder block as before and waited for its reward—but this time there was none. The dog seemed confused. It pawed at the block and stared, but eventually lost interest and wandered away. When it finally approached the block concealing the scent vial—*CLICK clack*—Alena once again operated the clicker and praised the dog.

"That's how it works," she said. "You keep moving the vial until the dog learns to find the scent source and not the cinder block. Then you start hiding the vial in other places: in the woods, hanging from a tree, buried underground. You keep making it more and more difficult and you use the scent in lower and lower concentrations until the dog can find it anywhere—if he has the gift."

"How long does the training take?"

"It depends on the dog. These pups are really too young to train. I usually wait until they're about a year—before that they're adolescents and they have a hard time paying attention. They just want to play."

"Say no more."

"That's basically all there is to it."

"I have a feeling there's a lot more to it than that."

"There's time—days and weeks and months and years. The training never stops."

"Even for your three-legged dog—the one you call 'Trygg'?"

"Who told you her name?"

"Gunner."

"You talked to him again?"

"This morning, before I came up here."

She frowned. "What did he tell you this time?"

"He told me about your father and the Canine Enforcement Training Center in Front Royal. He told me that your father disappeared one day and that you've lived up here by yourself ever since—that you basically raised yourself. He also told me why you hate the people down in Endor, and I can't say I blame you."

"Gunner's got a big mouth," she grumbled.

"He told me that he and Rose love you like a daughter, and it's pretty clear that they do. He also said that I put you in danger, and that makes me responsible for your safety."

"You don't owe me anything."

"I owe you a lot—so does the FBI. We couldn't have found those graves without you."

Alena shook her head. "You didn't come up here just to learn about cadaver dogs, did you?"

"No. I thought if I spent a little time with you, you might trust me more."

"Why does that matter?"

"Because I might need your help again."

She didn't respond.

"Look, Marge still hasn't come back. I told the police about her this morning; they picked up her dog and they're beginning a search. I think Marge is dead, and I think the guy who killed her is connected to the Patriot Center murders—but we have to find him using twenty- to fifty-year-old bones, and that's very hard to do. If it's the same killer, then Marge might be our best way of finding him—but we have to find Marge first. That's why we need you."

"I don't want to get more involved," Alena said.

"You're already involved. The guy who killed Marge wanted to stop the person responsible for finding those graves—that's you. As long as he doesn't know about you, you're safe—but how long will that last? The only way to keep you safe forever is to find that guy before he finds out about you, and I need your help to do that. This isn't for Marge, Alena—it's for you."

"But if I help you again, somebody is bound to find out."

"We can work at night, just like before. I'm sorry to have to ask you this, Alena, but I told Gunner I'd try to keep you safe—and this is the only way I know to do it."

She paused. "Let me think about it."

"Fair enough—I need to get back to the Patriot Center anyway." He turned and started off toward his car. A few yards away he turned and looked back. "Hey—can I tell you something without offending you?"

"I doubt it."

"I like insects better than people."

She glared at him. "Is that supposed to make me feel better about myself?"

"No—it's supposed to make you feel better about me."

22

"You're late," Danny said. "The briefing is supposed to be at noon—on the dot."

Nick pulled out a chair and sat down. "I never do anything 'on the dot.'"

"I do."

"Well, there are medications for that." He nodded a greeting to Kegan.

"It's not like you to be late for work," Kegan said. "You're usually the first one here."

"I couldn't tear myself away from Endor," Nick said. "There's so much to do."

"I hear Victoria Braden is visiting there tomorrow."

"You should see the place—crepe paper everywhere. It looks like a Polish wedding."

"I'm sure I don't need to mention this," Danny said, "but you will *not* be visiting with Mrs. Braden tomorrow. Correct?"

"I've decided to break things off," Nick said. "She was getting too clingy."

Kegan grinned. "You wish."

Nick turned to Danny. "Are we going to do this briefing, or are we going to keep discussing my attendance record? I've got things to do."

Kegan held up a manila envelope. "We got the first DNA reports back from the lab this morning."

Nick reached for the envelope, but Kegan held it back.

"Have you reviewed the results yet?" Danny asked.

"Yes, I have." She glanced at Nick. "All of them."

"And?"

"There are two sources of DNA in the body, Danny. You can get it from the nucleus of a cell—that's nuclear DNA—or you can get it from the mitochondria. Nuclear DNA degrades rapidly—it would be almost impossible to get a good sample from bones this old, so we used mitochondrial DNA from the teeth. Teeth are almost indestructible—they're the toughest biological evidence around. The only problem is that you can't tell as much from mitochondrial DNA."

"Why not?" Danny asked.

"Because it's passed directly from mother to child—it lacks the father's DNA sequence. That means you can't use it to, say, test for paternity—but since a mother and her children share identical mitochondrial DNA, you can at least use it to tell if two people have a common female ancestor."

"And what did the tests show?"

"Are you ready for this? All four bodies are consanguine—they have a common lineage."

"Are we talking brothers or cousins or what?"

"There's no way to know," Nick joined in. "All it means is that they share a common female ancestor somewhere in the past—a mother, or a grandmother, or even somebody who lived hundreds of years ago. Mitochondrial DNA doesn't change—it mutates very slowly." He looked at Kegan. "Did you say all *four* bodies?"

"That's right."

"Then all four victims have a familial link. That could be huge."

Danny looked at Nick. "I hate to have to ask this, but—why?"

"Motive, Danny—somebody knocked off four members of one extended family. It suggests some kind of family feud or something—that could narrow the field of suspects quite a bit."

Danny turned to Kegan again. "What else did the tests show?"

"They're running the DNA profiles through CODIS—the Combined DNA Index System—to see if they get a match with any unsolved cases. No results yet."

"Well, let me know if you hear anything. Is there anything else?"

She glanced at Nick, who shook his head almost imperceptibly. "That's all for now," she said.

"Okay. You two get back to work—*both* of you. But keep me posted."

When Danny was a safe distance away, Kegan leaned across the table to Nick. "I'm not going to cover for you, Nick."

"You just did."

"I mean I'm not going to keep doing it. Danny's the boss—he has a right to know what's going on—and by the way, so do I. We got the results on those two hair samples of yours. Are you going to tell me about them?"

"You first."

She looked around for Danny again, then slid the report from the envelope. "Sample number one: from the head area of an adult female, probably Caucasian. Brunette in color, shoulder length, chemical analysis indicates the presence of a colorant. A few of the hairs still had intact roots, so serology was able to get a DNA sample."

"Good. What did the profile show?"

"Nothing. There's no connection between this hair and the bodies we've recovered so far—at least through the maternal line. C'mon, Nick, tell me—whose hair is this, anyway?"

"Victoria Braden's. I took it from a hairbrush in her husband's bathroom."

Kegan's mouth dropped open. "Victoria Braden colors her hair?"

"Would you try to focus here?"

"Then the other sample—that's from *Senator* Braden?"

Nick nodded.

"Why don't you want Danny to know about this?"

"Are you kidding? Danny had a cow when I stopped by to see the Bradens—what would he do if he knew I was having their DNA tested?"

"But you asked the Bradens about this place, and they said they knew nothing about it. You told me you believed them."

"I do. But there could be some connection in their pasts that they don't even know about—or they could be very good liars. Hey, they're politicians—they've had a lot of practice. What did the senator's test show?"

"The same thing—no connection, at least along maternal lines."

"What about the other test I asked for—the one to determine their haplogroup?"

"Why did you order that test? How does it help us to know the Bradens' ethnic backgrounds?"

"I'm not sure yet. What did the tests show?"

She checked the report. "They tested for the four major historical population groups: Indo-European, Sub-Saharan African, East Asian, and Native American. According to his DNA, Senator Braden's ancestors were pure Indo-European. Isn't that what you'd expect? Wasn't his family at Jamestown?"

"What about Mrs. Braden?"

Kegan looked. "This is interesting: Markers on Mrs. Braden's DNA show a mix of Indo-European, African, and Native American ancestry."

Nick arched one eyebrow. "That is interesting."

Kegan slipped the reports back into the envelope and looked at him. "Nick, you know that haplogrouping is controversial—it borders on ethnic profiling. Why do you care about this?"

"I don't. Personally, I come from a long line of horse thieves and swindlers; the Polchaks don't have a genealogy, we have a rap sheet. I don't give a rip about ethnic background, Kegan—but the Bradens do. Victoria Braden said something that I found very interesting: She said that good breeding is all about appearance. That's all I'm trying to do here—separate appearance from reality."

"You need to be very careful with this," Kegan said. "Ancestry may not matter to you, but it does to some people."

"It'll be our little secret."

"What about Danny?"

"I'll tell Danny—when the time is right."

"And when will that be?"

"Hopefully never."

"I mean it, Nick—I won't keep covering for you. I know you like to work outside the box, but it's not fair to me. No more secrets, okay?"

"Thanks for covering for me this time." He got up from his chair.

"Nick."

"What?"

"You're not thinking of confronting Victoria Braden with this, are you?"

"What good would that do?"

"Then you're really not planning to talk to her tomorrow?"

"In Endor? Fat chance—she'll have a whole town full of people trying to talk to her already."

23

"I can't tell you all how good it feels to be home. I left the town of Endor when I was very young, and now that I'm back and I've seen how beautiful this town is, I feel cheated—cheated out of the opportunity to grow up here, to graduate from Endor High, and to have each and every one of you as a neighbor."

The good people of Endor responded with grateful applause.

Home, Riddick thought. *Victoria belongs in this dump the same way Bradenton belongs in a trailer park.*

Riddick stood behind Victoria Braden and off to her right, allowing him an unimpeded view of the crowd. He studied their faces, looking for the disgruntled and the potentially unstable—but all he saw was adoring smiles and affirming nods. *Sheep*, he thought. *She could tell them to hand over their wallets and the fools would probably do it. Who knows? Maybe she will.* He watched their hands too; he searched for hands that moved too quickly or hands that slipped into purses or pockets—but the hands just applauded warmly or dabbed at tearful eyes. *There's one born every minute*, he thought. *Looks like most of them were born here.*

Victoria Braden stood behind a portable lectern on the steps of a band gazebo at Endor Recreational Park. The gazebo had been constructed half a century ago with the intention of hosting summer concerts in the park, but Endor had no band and the gazebo fell into disrepair—until word was received of Mrs. Braden's intended visit. The gazebo was quickly reshingled and freshly painted and now stood crisp and white, draped in patriotic banners and American flags.

Chris Riddick, by contrast, was dressed in his usual dark suit and crewneck shirt, which allowed him to disappear—and that's exactly what he felt like doing right now. The small park was packed with bodies, exactly as Braden's organizers had planned it, so that no camera angle could suggest so much as an empty corner. It took every citizen of Endor to pull it off, and more than a few from the neighboring towns of Linden and Riverton and Front Royal—but they would have all come anyway. Little Victoria had come home, and this was their chance to see the next First Lady of the United States.

"I want to thank the Endor High School marching band for that rousing rendition of 'Hail to the Chief.' I should remind you that 'Hail to the Chief' is the official presidential anthem, reserved only to announce the president of the United States. I'm afraid playing it for me was a breach of protocol—or at least a little premature."

The audience erupted in laughter.

Riddick looked at Victoria and almost smiled. *You're good, sweetheart—really good.* She rarely glanced down at her notes; it gave the audience the impression that she was speaking straight from her heart, though in fact her text was always prepared in advance and she rarely departed from it. But even when she did, her instincts were unerring; she knew what she wanted from an audience and she got it. *You always get what you want*, Riddick thought. *You just get tired of the things you get.*

The day had begun with a humiliating "Welcome Home" parade up Main Street—a pathetic stretch of potholes lined with appliance stores and thrift shops and gift boutiques promising tourists "authentic mountain crafts." Next came a visit to "Endless High," followed by a mind-numbing "high tea" with the wife of the mayor. At each event Riddick did what he always did—stand in the corner and look formidable and protect Mrs. Braden from dangers that didn't exist. Somehow Victoria managed to throw herself into every event, smiling and waving and listening enraptured to boring drivel with eye contact like a laser-guided weapon—and everywhere she went the cameras clicked softly, capturing every caring moment.

"Some of you may not know this, but 'Hail to the Chief' was first used to announce the president at the inauguration of James K. Polk. It seems that Mr. Polk was a short man, and his wife was afraid that he might arrive unnoticed. Fortunately, my husband doesn't have that problem; when John Henry Braden walks into a room, people know he's there. John is a man of stature—you're going to notice that between now and November whenever he stands alongside another candidate. You'll notice his stature—not just in height but in principles, in values, in ideas that will make this country an even greater place to live."

Riddick could sense the climax coming. He knew the formula by heart: Once she mentioned "principles and values," she was about to bring it home.

"I want to thank you all for coming out today; I want to thank you for making me feel so much at home. I will never forget Endor. This town is a part of me, and I'll take it with me wherever I go—with your help, God willing, to the White House. Thank you—thank you all so much."

A tremble in her voice—a tearful farewell—one final wave, and—cut! It's a wrap, boys. Break it down and set up the next shot.

Riddick stepped up beside Victoria as a signal to well-wishers not to get too close.

"How was it?" she whispered, smiling for each of the photographers as they squeezed to the front of the crowd.

Riddick placed one hand in the small of her back. "Flawless, as always."

She immediately moved away and turned to her assistant. "What's next?"

"Some of the photographers are asking for more time."

"Which ones? I'm not interested in the locals."

The assistant checked her notes. "There's one from the *Post* Arts & Living section; there's *DC Style* and the *Washingtonian* too."

"Good. Find them and let them know—tell them it's 'by invitation only.'"

"Where do you want to set up?"

She looked around the area. "Let's take a walk—do a little window-shopping. If we don't get away from this crowd, we'll never stop being interrupted."

She left the gazebo and headed for the sidewalk with Riddick close by her side. She nodded a friendly greeting to each person as she passed, but in between smiles she cocked her head toward Riddick and said, "Don't ever—*ever*—touch me in public again. Do you understand?"

Riddick paused. "What if I'm taking a bullet for you?"

"Then do it in midair—but don't touch me. It sends the wrong message."

"Maybe that's the message I wanted to send."

She accelerated her pace and widened the distance between them.

For the next hour they moved from gift shop to gift shop, allowing the photographers to capture her image in every conceivable setting. There was Victoria studying the engraving of Monticello; Victoria resting in a rocking chair beside the kindly old proprietor; Victoria looking thoughtfully out the window with the shadows of the mullions cast dramatically across her face. Riddick watched, imagining how he might pose her if he were a photographer himself. He slowly shook his head; the camera never got tired of her, and it was easy to see why.

When the last of the photographers was finally satisfied, Riddick and Victoria stepped out onto the sidewalk. Victoria waved to the rest of their entourage to catch up with them while Riddick lit a cigarette.

"I wish you wouldn't smoke," she said.

"Concerned about my health?"

"I could care less about your health. It reflects badly on me."

He dropped the cigarette and crushed it out. "I don't know how you do it, Vic."

"Do what?"

"Handle all the attention. Smile for all the photographers. Act like you're listening when you're not. I'd feel like screaming at the end of a day like this."

"It doesn't matter how you feel," she said. "It only matters how you look. I thought you would have figured that out by now."

"Victoria! There you are!"

Victoria turned; standing behind her was an old woman no more than five feet tall, with curly gray hair and a broad grin that exposed the tips of twisted yellow teeth.

"Well, hello there," Victoria responded, smiling warmly and extending her hand.

The old woman eagerly took Victoria's hand with both of hers, holding it with one and stroking it with the other. "I've been trying to see you all day, but it's just been impossible! I waved to you in the parade but I don't suppose you saw me. I called your name over and over again—but I guess everyone else did too. I came to the high school but you were already gone. I was at the park, of course, but there were so many people and a little soul like me—well, I just couldn't squeeze through! I started to get all panicked—I thought, *What if Victoria goes away and she never meets me?* The thought was almost too much to bear!"

"Aren't you sweet," Victoria purred. "What's your name, dear?"

"Agnes," she said, "but I don't suppose you'll call me that."

"I'd be proud to, Agnes."

The old woman suddenly released Victoria's hand and threw her arms around her waist, pulling her in close and squeezing her tight. Riddick immediately stepped forward, but Victoria looked at him and shook her head. She wrapped her arms lightly around the old woman's shoulders and patted her on the back. A few seconds later Victoria let her arms fall to her sides, but Agnes continued to hold on.

Riddick stepped up behind her. "Ma'am."

The old woman released Victoria and turned to him.

Riddick handed her a business card. "If you'll write to me at this address, I'll see that you get an autographed photo of Mrs. Braden—would you like that?"

"Oh, I have all sorts of photographs of Victoria—ones she hasn't even seen yet." She turned back to Victoria. "I'm sorry for being such an old fool. It's just that—well—I never thought I'd get a chance like this. I thought I might never see you again."

Victoria put her hand on the old woman's shoulder. "You're no such thing. In fact, I think meeting you has been the highlight of my visit to Endor."

Tears began to well up in the old woman's eyes. "I have something to show you, Victoria—something I made just for you—something I know you'll want to see."

"What's that, dear?"

"It's at the library—right across the street there. I wonder, could you come with me and see it?"

Victoria glanced at her watch.

"I promise, it will only take a moment. Please? It would mean so much to me—and to you too."

Victoria smiled. "I think we can spare just a moment for Endor's finest citizen, can't we, Chris? All right, Agnes—lead the way."

They crossed the street to the library. Agnes unlocked the main door and Riddick went in first while Victoria and Agnes waited outside. He stepped out a few seconds later and said, "It checks out—you can go in." Agnes allowed Victoria to enter first—but when Riddick tried to follow she held up a hand and stopped him. "If you don't mind, what I have to say to Victoria is personal."

"I'm sorry, ma'am—that isn't allowed."

"It's all right, Chris," Victoria said. "Wait outside."

"I don't think that's a good idea, Mrs. Braden. It isn't procedure."

"We're making an exception for Agnes. I'll be right back."

They disappeared into the building and left Riddick standing there, staring angrily at the closed door.

Agnes led Victoria into a small room just off the lobby. Victoria looked at the walls; they were covered with photographs and magazine covers and newspaper clippings of her.

"Well—I must say I'm flattered." She moved quickly around the room, pausing to look at a few of the photographs. "This is quite a collection, Agnes. You put a lot of time and effort into this. You're right—this is very special to me." She glanced at her watch.

"Oh, this isn't what I wanted to show you." Agnes took a key from around her neck and unlocked a lower drawer, then took out a large scrapbook with a brown leather cover; she set it on the table in the middle of the room and opened it to the first page. "This is what I want you to see."

Victoria looked. The page was filled with faded black-and-white Polaroids of a beautiful baby girl. "What a lovely child. Is this your granddaughter?"

"That's my baby girl."

"She's beautiful. Where is she now?"

Agnes smiled up at her. "She's right here, Victoria."

Victoria blinked. "I'm sorry?"

"I don't expect you to remember—you were only six months old at the time."

She stared at the photographs. "Are you saying that's me?"

"I don't expect you to remember me at all—a child can't remember its mother after only six months."

"I think there's been a mistake," Victoria said. "I left Endor when I was just a baby."

"That's right, dear—that's when I gave you away."

"What?"

"I loved you, of course—more than you'll ever know. But I wanted something better for you, and I knew I couldn't give it to you. I was dirt poor, you see, and I was raising a baby all by myself. I know it's hard to believe now, but I was a pretty little thing back then—I had all kinds of boys sniffing around my door. There were two of them in particular—well, I just couldn't choose between them. And when I told them I was in a family way, they both ran for the hills. I can't really blame them; they were just boys. But that left me to raise you by myself, and—"

"Wait a minute. I know all about my birth parents—they were killed in a car crash."

"That's the story I made up—that's the story I told your new parents."

Victoria began to turn the pages of the scrapbook. On the next page she found a birth certificate; the date of birth was the same as hers, but the name was different.

"Beulah Deluca?"

"I named you after your grandmother—isn't it lovely? But your new parents liked 'Victoria' better, and I suppose it's done you just fine."

On the next page was a baptismal certificate and a lock of delicate hair tied with a pink ribbon. The following page contained a single sheet of paper—it seemed to be some kind of genealogical chart.

"I've seen this before," Victoria said. "This is my family tree."

"I'm very proud of that," Agnes said. "It took months to make it all up."

"You—made it up?"

"See, I wanted to find you a good family—but to find you a good family you needed to come from a good family, and mine just wouldn't do. I'm a librarian, sweetheart—I just looked up some old Virginia families and dropped you into one. That way you got a good start *and* a good finish. What more can a mother give her little girl?"

Victoria turned the page—there were her adoption papers. She looked at the bottom and recognized her parents' signatures. "You're listed here as my foster parent."

"What else could I tell them? I don't exactly fit in that fine family tree. I told them your real parents died in a car crash, and I guess that's what they told you. Didn't that work out nice?"

Victoria's head was spinning. It had to be a mistake—but there were records. It could all be a lie, but the birth certificate contained a footprint and there was a lock of hair—it could all be verified. She turned and looked at Agnes as if for the first time. She studied her face: the shallow forehead, the thinning hair, the mottled flesh, the sagging neck and chin—

"I—I have to go," she stammered, turning for the door.

"But honey, wait—there's so much more to see. I have another whole scrapbook to show you!"

Victoria shook her head and kept moving forward.

"Victoria! Victoria!"

She stopped in the doorway and looked back. She saw the old woman smile.

"Welcome home, sweetheart."

She stumbled across the lobby and out the front door. She took only a few seconds to collect herself before hurrying down the sidewalk toward her waiting entourage.

Behind her, the library door opened again and Riddick stepped out.

"Oh, yeah," he said with a grin. "Welcome home."

24

"Mind if I join you?"

Nick looked up from his dinner. He didn't recognize the man smiling down at him.

"You're Dr. Polchak, aren't you? You're the bug man Nathan Donovan called in at the Patriot Center."

"And you are?"

"Paul Decker, WRTL."

"You're a reporter."

"Hey, you're quick. Can I sit down, or do I have to stand here and watch you eat?"

Nick glanced around the Endor Tavern & Grille. "I see a lot of empty tables."

"A reporter never eats alone." He pulled out the chair across from Nick.

"That's because reporters don't eat—they just suck blood."

"Now, that's no way to talk. Mind if I ask you a question?"

"Are you looking for an interview?"

"Always."

"Then talk to the FBI liaison officer at the Patriot Center—he'll be glad to oblige."

"I was hoping to interview you."

"If he gives his permission—in writing—I'll answer any question you've got."

"I just want to know if there have been any recent developments at the Patriot Center. I haven't been there all day—I was stuck here in Endor covering Mrs. Braden's visit."

"Lucky you."

"Do you have any idea how boring this town is?"

"Poor baby, you had to follow Victoria Braden around all day. I can think of more boring places to point a camera."

Decker looked down at Nick's plate. "What is that? Is it any good?"

"Are you a reporter or a restaurant critic?"

"I'm a guy who hasn't had dinner yet."

"I believe the menu refers to this as 'Number Five.'"

"How is it?"

"They're off by three."

Decker leaned in closer and lowered his voice. "What's this I hear about your cadaver dog trainer disappearing?"

Nick looked at him. "I don't know. What did you hear?"

"C'mon, Nick—can I call you Nick?"

"No. A man has to draw the line somewhere."

"Well, for starters, I heard the police are looking for her."

"Where did you hear that?"

"From a sheriff's deputy at the Patriot Center."

"Elgin," Nick said. "He's a nice guy, but he needs to learn to keep his mouth shut."

"It would have been public knowledge in another day or two."

"But you're planning to make it public before that."

"That's my job. News is all about timing. Get the story a day early and it's news; get it a day late and it's history. It's a lot like your job if you think about it."

"How do you figure that?"

"There might be a serial killer around here somewhere. Maybe he'll have a change of heart and confess; maybe he'll get tired of all the publicity and turn himself in. But you're not willing to wait for that to happen, are you? You want to figure it out now, whether he's ready to talk or not."

"There's a slight difference," Nick said. "I'm trying to dig up dirt on the bad guy—you're doing it to the people in charge. People can get hurt that way."

"Is that what you think happened to the cadaver dog trainer?"

"Why would you think that?"

"Doesn't it seem like an odd coincidence that she disappeared the day after she did that interview with me?"

"You did that interview?"

"That's right."

"Tell me something, Decker. Did the FBI give you permission to interview her?"

"Are you kidding? They gave me permission to stand in their nice little playpen and ask polite questions. You don't get a story that way."

"But you might get the facts, if you're interested in that sort of thing."

"I love facts—when they make a good story. I understand she was staying at the Skyline Motel, where you are."

"I believe that's public knowledge."

"And she disappeared the day after the interview—right after she found all those graves. Think she went on a bender somewhere?"

"It's possible."

"But she left her dog behind."

"Maybe he's not a party animal."

He smiled. "You know, I like you. You and I are a lot alike."

Nick pushed his plate away. "There goes the rest of my appetite."

"You didn't like her, did you?"

"Who?"

"Marge—that's what they tell me you called her. I'll bet she loved that."

"You should hear what I'll call you when you leave."

"Can you think of anybody else who didn't like her?"

"I'd talk to the dog if I were you—he had means, motive, *and* opportunity."

Decker paused. "Then you think she's dead too?"

Nick leaned toward him and rested his elbows on the table. "You know, our jobs do have something in common: A criminal investigation is about timing too—it's about who did what and when. That's what I'm trying to figure out here, and I just might be able to do it if people

like you don't screw it up for me. So if you've got a job to do, go do it—
but don't expect any help from me. Elgin never should have talked to
you; Marge shouldn't have either, but they were both too inexperienced
to know any better. I don't have that problem."

Decker grinned. "Good speech—can I quote you?"

"How? We never met."

Decker got up from the table. "Well, if we had met, it would have
been a pleasure. Tell me, do you eat here every night?"

"There aren't many options in Endor."

"Then maybe I'll see you here tomorrow."

"I thought you were eager to get back to the Patriot Center."

"I'm eager to find a story," he said. "I have a feeling there might be
one around here."

Nick watched him as he left. The last thing he needed was a reporter
snooping around Endor. How long would it be before he heard about
the "Witch of Endor" and began to get suspicious? Maybe he'd never
make the connection—but Nick kept thinking about something Decker
had said: "You and I are a lot alike." What bothered Nick most was that
it was true; Decker was the kind of guy who wouldn't stop digging
until he found what he was looking for. The problem was, when he
found it, he would broadcast it all over northern Virginia.

Nick's cell phone rang. He opened it and pressed it to his ear. "Nick
Polchak."

"Nick, it's Carlyn down at UVA."

"How's the research going?"

"Good and bad."

"I was hoping for a little more detail."

"I checked for the grave registries like you asked me to—no luck. I did
find two sources listed in the online card catalog that might possibly have
included those registries—but the books themselves are both missing."

"Any record of when they were last checked out?"

"They're part of a special collection, Nick—they can't be checked out."

"They were stolen?"

"Or lost, or misshelved—all I know is that I can't find them. I can't even say for sure that the grave registries were inside—but they might have been."

"Who else might have a copy of those books?"

"I did a query with the Library of Congress; I'm also checking with the Library of Virginia down in Richmond and the Virginia Historical Society, but I wouldn't get your hopes up. Special collections contain a lot of one-of-a-kind books."

"So you have nothing to tell me. How much has this cost me so far?"

"Wait, there's more. When I couldn't find the grave registries I began to ask myself, 'Where else might the location of a graveyard be mentioned?'"

"And did your self come up with anything?"

"Yes—oral histories."

"Oral histories?"

"They started collecting them back in the thirties—personal recollections and reminiscences. You know, 'My mother told me that my grandfather once said . . .' UVA has some terrific collections, along with a lot of diaries and memoirs and random information like that."

"How does that help us?"

"Formal histories tend to be written around grand themes, like politics and economics and so on. These collections are more slice-of-life stuff—simple descriptions of what people did on a day-to-day basis. They're fascinating—by far the best way to get a feel for what life was really like back then."

"I believe we were talking about graveyards."

"Well, think about it: People are born, they live, and they die—and when they die they're buried, and then there are funerals and graveside vigils. I figured somebody might mention a death in the family—and where they were buried."

"That's good. So what did you find?"

"There was a ton of stuff. I had to wade through volumes and volumes of—"

"Thirty bucks—that was my final offer."

There was a pause on the other end. "Now where did I put that excellent information?"

"Blackmail doesn't become you," Nick said. "C'mon, Carlyn, a deal's a deal."

"Well, it was worth a try. I found two mentions of graveyards in the area around Endor. Here's the first one: 'In the year of our Lord seventeen hundred and ninety, the soul of our beloved son Jacob Mallory was laid to rest in the old cemetery, by the great oak overlooking the dog's leg.'"

"The *dog's leg*," Nick said. "It sounds like some kind of landmark."

"Listen to the second one: 'Dear Sara, God rest her soul, now watches the sunrise over the waters of the dog's leg.' I think it's a lake, Nick—a lake shaped like a dog's leg. You know, a dogleg—like on a golf course."

"Was there anything else?"

"That's it. Sorry there's nothing more specific—there must be all kinds of lakes in the mountains around Endor."

"Yes, but names tend to stick around here. If they used to call it 'the dog's leg,' they probably still do. I'll ask around. Thanks—that was good work."

"And speaking of money."

"Oh, yeah—now where did I put that excellent check?"

"Nick—you wouldn't do that to me."

"Stiff a blackmailer? What kind of person would do that?"

"Nick, I was kidding."

"A professor benefiting from a grad student's work without reward? Unheard-of."

"Nick."

"Don't worry, Carlyn, you'll get paid—but I'm not done with you yet. There's something else I need you to find."

25

Alena pulled her truck over to the side of the road and shifted into neutral. "There it is," she said, pointing out the passenger window. "Dogleg Lake."

Nick looked out his window; beyond the railing and down a steep slope he saw the glimmer of moonlight on water through the pines.

"You're sure that's the one?"

"How many lakes shaped like a dog's leg do you think we have? It's been called that as long as I can remember."

"Let's take a look. Can you get us down there?"

"I'm still not sure I get this. Why are we looking for a graveyard here? What does this have to do with the Patriot Center?"

"It has to do with Marge," Nick said. "She did that interview—she said she found all those graves—and *then* she disappeared."

"So?"

"Let's assume that someone killed her. Why would they do that?"

"Like you said, to keep her from finding any more graves."

"Yes, but she already found all the graves—she said so in the interview. Why would someone kill her after she was already finished? They wouldn't—unless there was something else she still might find."

"Unless there was something *I* might find."

"Unfortunately, yes."

"But—in a different graveyard?"

"It's the only thing that makes sense to me. The killer used the same double-grave technique three times; it worked for him, so why would he change? He apparently learned the technique from someone who used it a long time ago—maybe an ancestor who left a little 'oral history' of his own. He decided to use a historical graveyard because no one would ever look there—it was already forgotten. But would he bury all of his victims in the same graveyard, or would he diversify a little—spread out his risk of discovery? I think that's what he did; I think that's why he went after Marge. He saw what she could do, and he was afraid she might do it again—somewhere else."

"But you don't even know if there are any more victims."

"No—and if it wasn't for Marge, I wouldn't even be looking. That was the killer's big mistake: He didn't have to do anything—he played a card when he didn't have to. C'mon, let's see what we can find. We need to get you home before daybreak."

The truck shifted back into gear with a *thunk*. There was a gap in the railing where a narrow gravel path left the road at a precarious angle. Alena jerked the wheel hard and steered the truck onto it. The right front wheel dropped suddenly, throwing Nick against the passenger door.

"Do you know where this road goes?" Nick asked.

"Down."

"Thanks." He twisted around and looked through the grating into the camper shell; he saw Trygg standing calmly in the center of the truck bed, with her three limbs smoothly absorbing the shocks like the legs of a photographer's tripod.

"Incredible," Nick said. "How does she do that with only three legs?"

"That's one more than you've got."

Alena showed no signs of slowing down, though the road whipped back and forth like a kite's tail. The well-worn gravel rolled under the tires, causing the tail of the truck to spin out on every curve with a shuddering crunch.

"I was just wondering," Nick said. "If you've been on your own since you were ten, who taught you how to drive?"

"I taught myself."

The truck skidded to the right; Nick stuck his head out the window and found himself staring over the edge of a fifty-foot overhang.

"I want to *find* a graveyard," he said. "I don't want to be buried in it."

"Do you want to drive?"

"Yes."

"Well, it's my truck, so shut up."

To Nick's relief the road gradually leveled out and began a wide arc around the edge of the water.

"Now where?" she asked. "This is a big lake."

"The western side."

"How do you know that?"

"The history said, 'Sara watches the sunrise over the waters of the dog's leg'—you can only see the sunrise *over the water* from the western side. It said there was a 'great oak' there; we could look for one, but I doubt we'll find it. That was two hundred years ago—a lot of great oaks could have come and gone since then."

"Should we look for a clearing?"

"Hard to say. The graveyard would have been in a clearing originally, but that was a long time ago. It depends on how long it's been forgotten. I'll tell you where to stop; just drive along the shoreline—*slowly*."

Nick watched the trees as they passed; he wasn't sure there would be any trace of the graveyard at all after all these years. He searched for a spot where the trees were less dense or the pattern of growth seemed different. He made his best guess and told Alena to pull over.

She opened the back of the camper shell; Trygg stepped onto the tailgate and smoothly jumped down.

"How did she lose that leg?" Nick asked.

"It was chewed off, just above the paw. Some moron down in Chester Gap left her staked out in the yard when she was in season. I found her in a shelter there; she asked me to help her, so I did."

"What happened to the rest of her leg?"

"I took it off."

"*You* took it off?"

"You have to, or the dog will keep trying to walk on the stump."

Nick made a low whistle. "Never mess with a witch."

"That's what I've been trying to tell you."

He was about to lift the tailgate when a second dog stepped out of the darkness. It was a tiny dog with pink mottled skin and just a few twisted wisps of fine gray hair. It was more skin than Nick had ever seen on a dog, and he couldn't help sneering—it looked like a ninety-year-old man in a bathtub. Its jaw stuck out to one side and its tongue stuck out on the other; the effect was comical. "What is that thing?" he asked. "It looks like Yoda on a bad hair day."

Alena glared at him. "Is that supposed to be funny?"

"Sorry—he just caught me a little off guard. What did you bring him along for?"

"Protection."

Nick almost laughed, but he caught himself just in time. "Does he have a name?"

"Of course."

Nick waited. "I could ask him myself, but I don't speak Dog."

"His name is Ruckus."

Nick held out the back of his hand but the dog showed no interest. "Is he friendly?"

"Unless I tell him not to be."

"What happens then? Don't tell me—he raises a ruckus."

"He can tear your sock off without removing your shoe."

"You're joking."

"Would you like a demonstration?"

"No, I believe you—besides, if something went wrong I wouldn't want you giving me first aid."

Ruckus bounced down from the tailgate and the four of them walked to the edge of the trees.

"Might as well start here," Nick said. "How do you want to do this?"

"Just give us some room," she said, summoning Trygg to her side.

Alena began just as she had done at the Patriot Center—by lifting both arms in the air and walking in slow circles.

"What are you doing?" Nick asked.

"Lessons are extra," she said.

"Fine—put it on my bill."

She glanced over at him. "I'm testing the air—the temperature, the humidity."

"Why?"

"A dog can work longer in cooler temperatures; humidity will keep the scent down low."

She held out her arms and gently shook them; she squatted down a little and straightened again.

"Why are you doing that?"

"I'm feeling my joints. No rain tomorrow."

Nick had read about people who could predict the weather with uncanny accuracy due to their ability to sense changes in barometric pressure. It was more than folklore; there was a scientific basis for it. It was like putting a balloon in a vacuum chamber: When the pressure goes down, the balloon expands—and so do the tissues that surround human joints. *Remarkable woman*, Nick thought again.

Alena lowered her head and dangled her long hair in front of her face. She shook it.

"You're checking the direction of the wind," Nick said.

"The wind will move the scent away from the actual source—you have to allow for that."

When she completed her assessment she called Trygg to face her, then took one of the three bandannas from around her neck and showed it to the dog.

"What's the bandanna for?"

"It's her uniform," she said, slipping the bandanna over the dog's head. "It tells her that she's in work mode now; it reminds her to stay focused."

"Like the orange vest that Bosco wore. I guess he needed a cap and trousers too."

"It also serves to remind her what she's looking for. She was trained to detect three different kinds of remains, remember? Putrefying, post-putrefying, and submerged."

"What about 'distressed body'?"

"We're not looking for a living person—I left that one at home. Each bandanna has a distinct pattern; this one tells her we're searching for older remains. Now are we going to talk all night or can we get to work?"

"Wait a minute," Nick said. "We're not just looking for an old graveyard here, we're looking for double graves. Is there any way to tell your dog to search for the most recent remains she can find?"

"No—but she'll respond more confidently to a stronger scent, and that might indicate a more recent grave. I'll ask her about it—maybe she'll help."

"Ask politely," Nick said. "Tell her it would be a real time-saver for us—I'd hate to have to excavate another whole graveyard."

Alena squinted at him. "Do you have permission to excavate these graves if we find them?"

Nick shrugged. "Are we going to talk all night or can we get to work?"

Alena moved to a position downwind and began to work back toward the trees; it wasn't long before Trygg zeroed in on a section of ground and lay down.

Nick looked at Alena. "Bingo?"

"Bingo."

He pulled a flag from his back pocket and marked the spot.

Alena and Trygg worked quickly, systematically covering and re-covering the area, narrowing their focus and eliminating sections of ground that yielded no results. Nick sat on the ground beside Ruckus and watched. *Gunner was right*, he thought. There was an almost psychic connection between Alena and this dog. She seemed to be able to look at the dog and know what it was thinking. As Nick watched the dog, he began to pick up things too—at least he thought he did. He noticed that the dog had a kind of body language that changed from time to time: the way she carried herself, the way she moved her tail, the way she pricked her ears or laid them back. He could see each change, but he had no idea what meaning to assign to it; it was like watching a man use sign language without knowing what each signal conveyed. Somehow, Alena had figured it out—and so had the dog.

Nick looked down at Ruckus. "Come here often?"

Ruckus stared straight ahead.

"It would take a lot of beer before you started to look good."

"I heard that," Alena called over. "You're about to lose your socks."

"We were just talking," Nick called back. "He says his real name is 'Eduardo,' but he was too ashamed to tell you."

Alena finally let out a laugh.

Bingo, Nick thought.

When Alena and Trygg had exhausted the area in front of the trees, they began to work their way deeper into the woods; by five o'clock they had finished. There were a total of seventeen graves in the old forgotten graveyard beside Dogleg Lake—but only one of them interested Nick.

"You're sure this is the most recent one?"

"That's what Trygg told me."

"No offense, but—exactly how did she tell you that?"

"By how fast she found it—by the look she gave me—by how pleased she was with herself. If this one isn't recent then they're all old, because she treated the rest of them the same."

Nick looked around the area: Little red flags dotted the open ground and gradually disappeared into the woods as if they were tiny creatures crawling off to hide. "I still can't believe that dog of yours. She's absolutely amazing." He looked at Alena. "You know, you're amazing too."

She brushed the hair back from her face. "Thank you—Nick."

"It sounded better that time. Now that didn't hurt, did it?"

"A little."

Nick looked toward the lake and spotted Trygg stretched out peacefully beside the water. She no longer wore the red bandanna with the polka-dot pattern. *It figures*, Nick thought. The bandanna was probably like a necktie, something the dog wore to work but couldn't wait to get out of at the end of a hard day. "You can't blame her for being tired," he said. "She sure put in a long night."

Alena looked up. She immediately clapped her hands and summoned the dog to her side.

"Why don't you let her rest for a while?" Nick said. "You know—'let sleeping dogs lie.'"

"She wasn't resting." Alena waited until Trygg sat motionless beside her, then made a quick tossing motion; the dog returned immediately to the lake and began to sniff along the edge of the water.

"What's going on?"

"Wait." Alena dropped her head and let her hair hang down over her face. She watched the tips of the long strands drift in the direction of the lake. She waited; after a few seconds the strands hung motionless, pointing directly at the ground—and then they began to drift back toward her body.

"Now," she said, and looked up—just as the dog lay down again beside the water.

"There's one more grave," she said.

"Where?"

"Out there somewhere—in the lake."

26

"Hello again."

Agnes didn't bother to look up. "Library closes in five minutes—checkout's closed already."

"That's all right, I'm not looking for a book. I was wondering if I could have a word with you alone."

Agnes looked at the man. He was tall and handsome, dressed in a black blazer and a crewneck shirt.

"Remember me?" he said with a smile.

"You were with my Victoria today."

"That's right. I didn't get a chance to introduce myself this afternoon. I'm Chris—I've been your daughter's chief of security for almost three years now."

"Security?"

"Yes, ma'am, that's my job. Your daughter has become quite an important person, you know. She has to be careful; she needs someone to look out for her."

"Then—she told you about me?"

"She was barely out the door before I knew all about it. You should have seen her—she was so excited."

"Really? I wasn't sure—she seemed in such a hurry when she left."

"I think she was just overwhelmed at first. Imagine how she must have felt—meeting her own mother for the very first time. She thought you were dead—she didn't even know you existed—that's a lot for a person to take in all at once."

"I didn't mean to upset her—I wouldn't hurt her for the world."

"The important thing is that you told her. She's so glad you did."

"She is? She said that?"

"She sure did. Your daughter and I have become very close in the last three years—she tells me everything. That's why I'm here tonight. She asked me to come; she sent me."

"Why didn't she come herself?"

"Like I said, your daughter has become a very important person. She can't just jump in a car and drive off by herself. There's always a driver and at least one assistant and, of course, there's always me—and then there are the reporters and the photographers who follow her wherever she goes. What you told her today was very personal, and she wants to keep it that way. That's why she sent me instead."

"What does she want?"

"She wants me to say thank you and to tell you how much she loves you—and she wants me to tell you she's sorry."

"Sorry for what?"

"For the way things have to be right now. She'd just love to tell everyone about you, but news like this would be very distracting just before an election. She hopes you understand."

"I do—of course I do. I know Victoria can't have an old sow like me around—that's why I did what I did. I only wanted her to know, that's all."

"She also wants you to know how sad she is."

"Sad? Why is she sad?"

"She feels cheated. It's like she said in her speech today: She didn't get to grow up here. Now she meets you and she feels like she missed out on even more. She has no photographs, no mementos—she feels like her entire childhood is one big blank."

"I have plenty of photographs. She can see them anytime she wants."

"She told me all about the wonderful scrapbook you put together for her. I sure wish I'd had a chance to see it. I wonder—is there any chance I could take a look?"

"I'd be more than happy," Agnes said. "You come with me."

Riddick followed Agnes into the small room off the lobby and watched as she unlocked the lower drawer and pulled out the leather-bound scrapbook. He noted the drawer's location and looked at the lock; it was a simple single-tumbler device that any moron with a bobby pin could pick. He looked at his watch. *Closing time, Grandma—time to go home so I can get to work.*

He watched over her shoulder while Agnes turned the pages, showing him the photographs, the birth records, the adoption papers. He shook his head in amazement and grinned from ear to ear. *Poor Victoria,* he thought. *Looks like you're not the purebred you thought you were—no wonder you just about had a coronary today. Poor little Victoria—or should I say, poor little Beulah? Given away by her own mother to a family on the other side of the tracks. Hey, who says you can't make a silk purse out of a sow's ear? Your folks sure did. Man—what would happen if the wrong people got their hands on this? Can you imagine, Victoria? 'Cause I sure can.*

"This is just wonderful," Riddick said. "Are these documents originals?"

"Every last one."

"I don't suppose you have any copies? I'd love to surprise Victoria with them—I know she'd die to have them."

"Oh, no, I couldn't. These things can never leave this room."

"I understand completely."

"Would you like to see the other scrapbook too?"

Riddick looked at her. "What scrapbook is that?"

"Victoria left in such a hurry, I never got to show it to her." She bent down to the drawer again and pulled out a second scrapbook almost equal in size to the first. She set it in front of Riddick and began to turn the pages.

Riddick threw back his head and laughed.

"How's it goin' at the Patriot Center, Elgin?"

Sheriff's deputy Elgin Tate swiveled around on his barstool and looked at the table behind him. "Evenin', Mr. Decker—didn't see you sittin' there."

"Thought I'd stop off for a quick one on the way home."

"Haven't seen you here before."

"First time. Good crowd—looks like a popular place. I asked where all the sheriff's deputies go after work—cops always know the best watering holes. Can I buy you one?"

"I was just about to head home to the wife."

Decker pushed out the chair across from him with his foot. "Sit for a minute. Don't make me drink alone."

"Just one then." Elgin moved from the crowded bar to the table.

"So how was your day?"

"No complaints."

"What's new at the Patriot Center? Find any more bodies?"

"Nah. Looks like four is all there is—now they're just haulin' up all those coffins."

"I bumped into that bug man up in Endor. What a character."

"Nick? Real smart fella—a little strange, though."

"Did you get a look at those glasses of his? Spooky."

"He puts in a long day's work, I'll give him that. I'm usually there before sunup, and sometimes Nick's already there."

"I did a little interview with him this evening. He says he thinks that cadaver dog woman might be dead."

"He said that?"

"Not directly, but he sure hinted at it. Do you think it's possible?"

"It's a little early to think that. Did Nick say why?"

"Let me run a theory by you. See what you think of this: Suppose somebody saw Marge on the evening news admitting that she found all those graves. Suppose somebody saw that interview—somebody who didn't want any more graves to be found—so they killed her. What do you think?"

"I think it would be a real shame. Marge didn't find those graves."

"What?"

"Nah—that dog of hers couldn't smell fish in a bucket."

"But she said she did."

"Nah. She was just wishin' real hard."

"Then who found the graves?"

"The witch."

"Who?"

"Yep—saw her drivin' out one mornin' just as I was pullin' in. Musta worked all night. Nick was there—he could tell you."

"Did you say *witch*?"

"The Witch of Endor. The woman's got powers; she can talk to animals; she can raise the dead."

Decker looked at him for a long time before he finally waved to the bartender. "Let's get you that drink," he said.

27

Victoria sat down on the plush rolled-arm settee, slid off her black-and-silver Giuseppe Zanottis, and slowly massaged her heels. She looked at her closet, which spanned one entire wall of the dressing room. She tossed the shoes onto the closet floor and watched them tumble to a stop. She looked at all the other pairs of shoes—dozens of them—perfectly aligned heel-to-heel and toe-to-toe on their own little slanted shelves. She wondered who put them away every morning; she wondered who picked up all the dresses and blouses and slips she left hanging from chairs and doorknobs every night.

Beulah.

The name kept haunting her—she couldn't get it out of her mind. Twice that afternoon she had turned and looked, imagining that someone had whispered the name behind her—but there was no one there.

Beulah.

She began to undress, then stopped and looked at herself in the closet mirror. She stood up a little straighter; she turned her head from side to side and looked at her cheekbones and jawline. She lifted her chin and patted the skin of her throat with the back of her hand.

She felt numb—the kind of aching emptiness you feel after fear and panic have left you dry. She kept thinking about Agnes—about her *mother*—and she couldn't bear to put the two thoughts together. She thought about the scrapbook again—the photographs, the birth certificate, the adoption papers signed by the only parents she ever knew. She kept wondering if it could somehow be a mistake—a joke—a ploy—but the look on the old woman's face told her it was all true. She tried to

imagine her first six months of life in some trashy trailer park in Endor—
she couldn't do it. She remembered lying in bed as a little girl, feeling a
proud sense of destiny as she imagined her noble ancestors—and it was
all just a fiction compiled by a librarian with no husband and no future.
She felt robbed—she felt *raped*—as though a part of her own soul had
been stolen.

Her thoughts were interrupted by a soft knock on the bedroom door;
she pulled on a robe and wrapped the belt around her waist. Halfway
across the bedroom, the door opened slightly and her husband slipped
his head inside.

"Darling? A word?"

"Come on in, John."

The senator stepped into the bedroom and shut the door quietly
behind him. He was dressed in a crisp cotton bathrobe with wide
lapels and square-cut shoulders that looked good enough to hold a
press conference in. He was clean shaven as always—the senator
always shaved twice a day to avoid that incriminating Nixon shadow.
His hair was neatly combed and fixed, and it occurred to her that she
had almost never seen his hair mussed—as though the wind was
somehow cooperating with his press agent. She glanced down at his
legs and noticed a sharp crease in his pin-striped pajamas. *Starched
pajamas*—something really bothered her about that, and she wasn't
quite sure what it was. She tried to remember if it had always bothered her, but she couldn't.

"What's this I hear about Endor?" the senator asked.

She felt a cold jolt in her gut. "What do you mean?"

"I hear you're planning to move there."

"What?"

He grinned. "From what they tell me, every living soul in town fell
in love with you today—one man can't hope to compete with that."

She let out a breath. "That's not funny, John."

"Is anything wrong?"

"It was a long day, that's all."

He walked to the end of the bed and sat down. "I caught your speech. I thought it was perfect. Was that Evan's work?"

"He wrote the rough draft—I added a few touches of my own."

"I thought so. I can always tell. So what did you think of your hometown?"

"A grimy little backwater with no economy and substandard housing and education—I wish we could bulldoze the place so we could save the tax dollars on infrastructure. The mountains are full of these little hovels."

"Not exactly a glowing assessment."

"But fair."

"Still, I think you were right to go there. You got a lot of good press coverage today—and those are cameras that weren't at the Patriot Center. You met a lot of people too, and every one of them is in our back pocket now."

You met a lot of people, she thought—but she could only remember one.

The senator smiled. "So you won't be moving home just yet?"

"I told you, that's not funny. Look, I was just about to take a bath—is there something you need?"

"Just wanted to check in. I don't see a lot of you these days."

"Well, the schedule's pretty tight." She walked to the door and opened it, then turned to him and waited.

He nodded and got up from the bed; in the doorway he stopped and looked at her. "I just don't want us to end up like some of the others," he said. "You know—holding hands but leaving fingernail marks."

"Thanks, I'll add it to the agenda."

He turned to leave but she stopped him; she leaned forward and kissed him on the forehead. "Some other time," she whispered.

She shut the door firmly behind him.

She walked into the bathroom and twisted both handles on the Jacuzzi, sending a torrent of water cascading into the deep white basin. She almost felt sorry for Johnny—almost. She wasn't naive enough to believe that the junior senator from Virginia had simply fallen in love with her eight years ago; he was an ambitious man and it wasn't that easy. John Henry Braden saw in her the same things the cameras saw: beauty, grace, and poise. He needed those things—not to fill his soul but his ticket. She wasn't angry or resentful, because she knew in her heart that she had struck the same bargain. Johnny was a handsome man, a successful man, but he was empty: a beautiful package that had nothing inside—at least, nothing that called to her. They were just two images that complemented each other well; two faces that voters could remember; two travelers on a journey to the same place.

But now everything had changed. She wasn't the woman Johnny thought she was; she no longer filled out the image—and she wondered what would happen if he ever found out. She felt sick to her stomach; she didn't understand what was going on inside of her. This morning she'd felt no need to be loved by John Henry Braden—but this evening she did.

She slipped off her bathrobe and let it drop to the floor—then she heard the bedroom door open and close again.

"Johnny?"

There was no answer.

She shut off the water and listened.

"Johnny, it's been a long day."

Still no answer.

She put the robe back on and cinched it tight. She walked to the bathroom door and poked her head around the corner; there was Chris Riddick, sprawled out on her chaise lounge with a grin on his face and his hands folded behind his head.

She charged into the bedroom. "How dare you come into my private quarters without my permission!"

"Nice outfit," he said. "A little casual, but then I suppose this is an unscheduled meeting."

"Get out of here!"

"Or what—you'll call your chief of security? I'm already here."

"You're fired. I want you out of this house in ten minutes."

He just looked at her and smiled.

She ran her fingers up the front of her bathrobe and closed the neckline a little. "I'll call my husband—he was here just a minute ago."

"I wouldn't do that if I were you—Beulah."

She sank down on the edge of the bed.

"You never have understood my job," he said. "I sure hope you pay more attention to the Secret Service than you do to me. See, my job is security: I walk into a room before you do; I keep people from getting too close; and I never, *ever* allow you to meet with a stranger alone—even if you want to. It's just too dangerous; you never can tell what a stranger might do—or say. So what I do is stand right outside the door—that way I can listen in and make sure nothing goes wrong. See?"

She nodded.

"It's a thankless job, believe me. There are lots of things I do that you probably aren't even aware of. When you spilled coffee on your dress the other day, who drove home and got you another one? I did. When you broke a heel on your way up the Capitol steps, who ran over to the Old Post Office Pavilion and bought you another pair? I did. And when that sweet old woman at the Endor Library showed you all those nice pictures and you ran off like your hair was on fire, who went back to say thank you?" He grinned. "I did."

"What do you want?"

"The same thing as always: security." He reached over and picked up a large manila envelope from the floor. "Family records are precious," he said. "You of all people should know that. What if there was a fire? You could lose everything: baby pictures, birth certificates—everything. The smart thing to do is to make copies." He tossed the envelope; it landed beside her on the bed.

She opened the envelope and took out the copies.

"Convenient place, a library—it has a copier and everything. You can do whatever you want with those. I've got plenty more."

She tossed the envelope aside. "Okay, you know. Now what?"

"*Beulah,*" he said with a grin. "It didn't grab me at first, but it kind of grows on you. I can see it embroidered on a bowling shirt, or maybe tattooed on some auto mechanic's forearm."

"What do you want, Chris?"

"Nothing."

"Nothing?"

"Just what I asked for before: a job with a salary, that's all. And—"

"And what?"

"I think I deserve benefits too, don't you? That's what I want: a salary plus benefits."

"What kind of benefits?"

"The personal kind. The kind I had before."

"Chris—"

"That's not asking so much, is it? I mean, it's not like I'm asking for something new—they were voluntary benefits a couple of years ago. That's all I want, Vic: my old job back. You give me a salary plus benefits, and I give you security. You'll never have to worry about the rest of those copies and where they might turn up."

She stared at him for a long time before she finally said, "No."

"No?"

"Do whatever you want with them. Sell them to the *Post* or the *Times*—I don't care."

"Are you sure that's wise?"

"I can survive this. Think it over, Chris—this isn't about me, it's about something that happened to me when I was just a kid. It makes me look better, not worse: Look how I started out—look at the adversity I've had to overcome—that's the way we'll spin it. Show everybody the copies if you want to; you'll be doing me a favor. Hey, I might even show them myself."

"And what will John Boy think?"

She hesitated for just an instant. "He'll get over it. He'll have to. He needs me to reach the White House; he'll never do it without me."

"But think of the humiliation," Riddick said. "Beautiful Victoria Braden is really Beulah what's-her-name. I didn't catch the last name, did you? Oh, that's right—you don't really have one. Momma isn't sure who Daddy was."

"It's *Braden*," she said. "That's the only name I need."

"What about all that 'good breeding' you always talk about? What about your membership in the Mayflower Society and the Colonial Dames of America? I don't think they take trailer trash, do you?"

"They need me more than I need them."

He just looked at her.

"Is that all you've got, Chris? Was that your best shot? Then we're done here—pack your bags and get out."

He nodded. "That's pretty much what I thought you'd say. You're a smart girl, Vic—it's one of the things I like about you. You know what you want and you know how to get it—and you don't let anything get in your way. Don't take this the wrong way, but I wasn't surprised to find out where you really came from."

"No?"

"It explains a lot about you. You've got the survival instincts of a pit bull, and somehow I never thought that came over on the *Mayflower*. You're right, you can survive this—you'd rather not face all the embarrassment, but it wouldn't stop you. I never thought it would." He reached down to the floor again; he picked up a second manila envelope and set it in his lap, then looked at Victoria.

She glanced down at the envelope.

"A salary," Riddick said, "plus benefits."

"Never."

He smiled. "You know, you left that library awfully fast this afternoon. You must have had a lot on your mind—you didn't even see me standing by the door. You probably didn't hear Momma calling after you either—she kept saying, 'Wait! I have more to show you!' I thought she just meant there were more pages in the scrapbook, but I was wrong—there was a second scrapbook. Shame on you, Victoria—your momma made a whole scrapbook for you, and you didn't even bother to open it." He tossed the envelope onto the bed. "You should have. You really don't understand your family history until you do."

She opened the envelope. She pulled out a stack of copies and began to read. Her mouth dropped open.

"Talk about a page-turner," Riddick said. "I couldn't put it down."

She turned the pages with trembling hands. Her breathing became shallow and erratic. She kept looking up and staring at the wall as if she were searching for something written there.

"It explains a lot, doesn't it? A lot about a lot of things."

The papers slid off her lap and scattered on the floor. "I—I need some time to think about this."

"Sure you do—it's a lot to take in, in one day. I'll get out of your hair and give you a chance to think." He got up and went over to her; he brushed the hair back from her forehead and kissed it. She made no effort to stop him, and she showed no recognition of his touch.

"I'm really not asking much—just my old job back, that's all. Your secret is safe with me—but from what I hear, that mother of yours is the town gossip. I'd think about that if I were you."

He walked to the door. "Sleep tight, Vic. Don't stay up too late reading. And don't worry—I made extra copies of those too."

28

Nick removed the first two feet of earth with a spade; he didn't dare go deeper for fear of damaging any remains he might discover. He was on his hands and knees now, poking through the soil with a pointed trowel like a soldier probing for land mines. Maybe there were no remains—in which case he would spend the rest of the day troweling his way down inch by inch until he struck the wooden planks of a coffin lid six feet below. Maybe Trygg got it wrong this time—maybe it was asking too much of a cadaver dog to pick the most recent remains from a grave-yard full of ancient corpses. How could the dog even know what was expected of her? He knew the answer: *The witch can talk to animals.* From what Nick had seen so far, he almost believed it.

He stood up in the shallow pit and stretched. It was almost noon and the sun was already high overhead. The day was hot and still; wisps of morning mist still clung to the trees, making the humidity oppressive. He unbuttoned his dripping shirt and peeled it off, then draped it over the handle of the spade to dry. He walked to the lake and knelt down; he scooped up some water and drank. He looked at his hands; the water was cold and clear, but he knew this mountain lake wasn't as pristine as it looked on the surface. Somewhere under all that water there was a decomposing body.

Nick and Alena had talked about it all the way back to her trailer just a few hours ago. Trygg had alerted on a scent blowing in from the lake, but the odor of ancient remains submerged beneath several feet of water would have been too faint for the dog to detect—the wind would have dispersed the weak scent too widely. But the dog did pick up the scent—that meant the odor was strong and the remains must be fresh, probably still in a putrefying state—and Nick had a feeling he knew who the remains belonged to. He needed to find that submerged body—but he had another body to check out first.

He went back to the grave and began to dig again. Even if he did find human remains here, he knew he couldn't excavate the grave by himself—he needed Kegan's help for that. But he couldn't exactly ask for her help just on the hunch that they might be there—he needed to know first. He actually found himself wishing that he could tell Danny about all of this—that way he would have the full resources of the FBI at his disposal. He could excavate the entire graveyard and dredge the lake for the submerged body too. But how was he supposed to tell Danny? How could he explain how he just "happened" to find another lost graveyard without mentioning Alena? Gunner was right: Nick got Alena involved in all this, and now it was Nick's responsibility to keep her out of it—even if it did make his work painfully slow.

Half an hour later the trowel hit something solid—but not with a *plink* as it did when it struck one of the endless fragments of stone. Nick scraped away the soil with his fingers until he saw the smooth ivory surface of bone. He needed to be certain this was not just some random fragment or the bone of a predator that had tried to dig down to the casketed remains. He carefully scraped away more dirt and found what appeared to be the iliac crest of a human pelvis staring back at him.

He continued to remove dirt from around the bone. He found shreds of fabric—a sure sign that the remains were fairly recent. He carefully pushed the pieces of fabric aside and dug deeper until his fingers felt something hard and smooth—the dislocated head of a humerus, perhaps. But when he tugged on it, the object gave way in his hands. He picked it up and looked at it; he blew on it and brushed the dirt away. It was spherical, just smaller than a golf ball, with a notch cut in one side. In the center of the notch was a kind of metal tongue. He pushed down on it with his thumb.

CLICK clack.

Nick parked his car in the Patriot Center parking lot and headed directly for Kegan. He found her in the tech tent sealing up yet another corrugated evidence box.

She looked up as he approached. "Where have you been? I haven't seen you all day."

"I had something I needed to look into."

"Sounds mysterious." She looked at him—at his stained and dripping shirt, at the brown blotches of dirt ground into his knees, at the little lines on his face where rivulets of sweat had washed away the dust. "You've been digging. Where?"

"What are you doing after work?"

"Why?"

"You should be knocking off here soon—have you got any plans?"

"Yes—I plan to drive back to Charlottesville and take a nice hot bath. Why?"

"I was wondering if I could interest you in a little extracurricular activity."

"What kind of activity?"

"If you're going to ask a lot of questions it will only slow us down. C'mon, what do you say? Just you and me—and all your digging tools."

"Nick—what's going on?"

"I stumbled across something I want you to take a look at."

"You never 'stumble across' anything. You were looking for something."

"All right, if you insist on being picky, I stumbled across something while I was looking."

"What did you find?"

"Another double grave."

"Here?"

"No—in another graveyard."

"What graveyard? Where?"

"I'll explain on the way. Are you going to help me or not?"

"Polchak!"

They both turned and looked; Danny was hurrying toward them across the field.

"That doesn't sound good," Kegan said.

"I don't have time for this now," Nick groaned. "Do me a favor—"

"Forget it. You're on your own this time."

"Fine—just get your tools together."

Danny charged directly up to Nick and squared off with him toe-to-toe. "Would you mind telling me exactly what you know about this 'Witch of Endor'?"

Nick did a double take. "What did you say?"

"You heard me."

"Where did you hear about the Witch of Endor?"

"From a waitress at Denny's this morning—apparently I'm about the last one to know, and based on my past experience with you, I can't say I'm surprised."

"Oh, no—Look, I have to go."

"You stay right where you are."

"Danny, I need to know exactly what you heard."

"No, you need to tell me exactly what *you've* heard—and I mean everything. The story I'm hearing is that our original cadaver dog team didn't find these graves."

"That's true."

"And that the graves were actually found by some woman who lives way up in the mountains—a woman with supernatural powers who can talk to animals."

"That's not true—at least not all of it. Her name is Alena Savard. She's a dog trainer—she's got a cadaver dog that's almost psychic. I heard about her; I went up to see her when Marge couldn't do the job; she came down and helped me out one night, that's all."

"You went to see a *witch*?" Kegan said. "Boy, I knew you were desperate, but—"

Danny turned to her. "Did you know about this too?"

227

"She didn't know anything," Nick said. "I couldn't tell her—I couldn't tell you—I promised Alena I wouldn't tell anybody."

"Why?"

"It's complicated."

"We had an agreement—no more secrets."

"I had an agreement with Alena too, and hers came first—this happened before you were even assigned here. Look, Danny, I can't talk now—I have to go."

"You're not going anywhere, mister. If you're withholding information about a criminal investigation, I can have you arrested."

"I'm not withholding information—I just don't have time to talk right now. If Alena's involvement has become public knowledge then her life could be in danger."

"Then take me to her. I'll post an agent—I'll provide protection."

"She's got a thousand acres up there—how many agents are you planning to post, and for how long? She doesn't need an armed guard, she needs to help us solve this case—that's the only way she's going to be safe long-term. She's a recluse, Danny—I need to go up there and convince her to come down, and it'll be a lot easier if you're not with me. C'mon, let me go—it'll be dark soon. I need you to trust me."

"*Trust* you? Are you out of your mind?"

"I need until tomorrow morning—give me until then to convince her to come down. There's a lake in the mountains up above Endor called Dogleg Lake. Ask anybody in Endor—they can tell you how to find it. Meet me on the west bank at sunup and I'll explain everything—and bring the crew with you."

"Give me one reason why I should trust you."

Nick turned to Kegan. "Tell him, Kegan. Tell him I might be stubborn or obsessive or just plain crazy sometimes—but he can trust me."

Kegan shrugged. "He's right, Danny, you can trust him. He's right about the 'just plain crazy' part too, but you probably already know that."

Danny glared at Nick and slowly shook his head. "Sunrise—the west bank of Dogleg Lake. And you'd better be there, Nick—because if you're not, I'll get a warrant for your arrest."

Nick rapped on the door frame of the pastor's study. Gunner looked up from a copy of *The Bondage of the Will* and slid his glasses down to the tip of his nose.

"Got a minute?" Nick asked.

"For you, always. What's up?"

Nick sat down on the edge of an old leather chair. "We've got a problem."

"Alena?"

Nick reached into his pocket and pulled out the faded and weathered buckeye. He held it up. "Do you know what this is?"

Gunner held out his hand and Nick tossed it to him. "Sure—it's a clicker. Did you get this from Alena?"

"No—I got it from her dad."

It took a moment before the meaning sank in. "When? Where?"

"A couple of hours ago—at an old graveyard down by Dogleg Lake. I found his body in a double grave, Gunner—just like the ones at the Patriot Center."

"*You* found him? Then Alena—"

"She doesn't know yet. That's why I'm here. I'm going up there, and I'd like you to be there when I tell her. I don't know how she'll take it."

"I do," he said, "and you're right—I should be there. Just give me a minute to call Rose."

"Make it quick," Nick said. "Her father's murderer is still out there—and he knows where Alena lives."

29

He dropped from the chain-link fence into the low grass, then turned and pointed his flashlight into the woods ahead. A fragile mist was already beginning to collect on the ground, lying like a veil around the trees and brush, as cicadas and wood crickets chanted their midnight lament.

So this is where she lives, he thought.

He started forward into the woods, pointing the beam ahead of him, but it was swallowed up by the darkness around him.

How long did they think they could keep it a secret? The woman who really found all those graves—the one they call the witch—the one they say has the power to raise the dead. How long did they think they could keep it a secret from me?

He stuck to the clearings as much as possible, picking his way through the brush when necessary. He felt a thin filament of spiderweb stretch across his face and the skitter of tiny legs on his cheek; he brushed it off and kept moving.

I have to find this woman. I have to get to her before the others do. We'll see what powers she really has.

He heard a sound to his left. He turned and pointed his flashlight; he saw a great black shadow and the eerie green glow of eyes staring back at him. He waited but the eyes came no closer; he started forward again and the eyes moved with him. He heard another sound on his right—then another behind him. He turned and saw two more pairs of glowing eyes watching his every move. He felt a knot of dread in his stomach but he forced it down.

There's always something, he reminded himself. *Some barrier, some obstacle, something to keep me from getting the job done—but I've faced worse than this. She's crazy if she thinks this will stop me.*

230

He started again with renewed confidence, trying his best to ignore the three sets of eyes that slowly tightened the circle around him—but in less than a minute the three dogs had encircled him completely and blocked him from taking a step in any direction.

He waved the flashlight like a club at one of them. "Get back, dog!"

The dog let out a subterranean growl.

Then he heard another sound—a small, whisking sound, like raking in shallow leaves, coming from somewhere in the darkness ahead. A moment later a tiny dog appeared and planted itself directly in front of him, challenging him, shattering the night with its incessant piercing yap. He pointed the flashlight at it and looked: It was ugly and hairless, with bulging black eyes and a jaw that jutted out to one side. He swung his right foot back and kicked the little dog, sending it tumbling into the darkness with a howling yelp.

The instant he did he felt a searing pain in the back of his left leg; the dog behind him had lunged forward and sunk its teeth into his hamstring, causing the muscle to spasm and the leg to instantly collapse. He threw back his head to scream—but before he could make a sound, the lead dog leaped forward and took him by the throat, sending him crashing to the ground and smothering the sound of his cry. The two dogs pinned him to the earth, one holding his throat and the other his leg, while the third dog took a middle position and fixed its eyes on the man's soft and unprotected belly.

He grabbed the muzzle of the dog at his throat and tried to pry it off—but when he did, the dog only tightened its grip. He felt himself getting light-headed; he wondered if the animal was crushing his carotids, cutting off the blood supply to his brain. He let his hands drop limply to the ground and lay paralyzed, staring up helplessly at the stars.

Nick and Alena heard the yelp from Ruckus and hurried through the woods. Alena knew every inch of the forest and ran through the brush like a gazelle; Nick stumbled along behind her, tripping over roots and rocks and catching the tree limbs that whipped back in his face as Alena let them go. Nick could hear Gunner running heavily somewhere behind him, but it was slower going for the older and heavier man, and the distance was increasing between them.

Alena got there first, checking to make sure that Acheron, Phlegethon, and Styx held the intruder safely in check—then she looked around in the darkness for Ruckus. There was no sign of the little dog. She raised her hands over her head and clapped once; nothing happened.

Now Nick stumbled into the clearing behind her, panting and pushing his glasses back up onto the bridge of his nose. He saw the man lying motionless on the ground, surrounded by the three black behemoths.

"Been there, done that," he said under his breath.

He spotted a flashlight glowing like a firefly in the grass; he picked it up and shined it down on the man's face. He shook his head. "And you wonder why people don't like reporters. Alena, this is Paul Decker—he's a reporter with WRTL."

Decker looked up at him. "Is that you, Polchak?"

Nick pointed the flashlight at his own face. "I've always heard that a dog's mouth is very clean—not anymore."

"Get these dogs off me, will you? One of them's biting my leg."

"I've got a few questions first. Who told you about Alena?"

"That sheriff's deputy named Elgin told me—I met him at a bar the other night."

"How did he know?"

"He said he saw her the night you found all the graves—he said he was pulling in just as she was leaving. I guess he just put two and two together."

"Was there anybody else around when you two were talking?"

"It was a bar. What do you think?"

"Great," Nick said. "And how did you know to come up here?"

"How did you?"

Nick looked at Alena. "What's the command for 'The buffet line is now open'?"

"Okay, okay—I just asked around town. I'm a reporter, for crying out loud. I just asked, 'Where can I find the witch?'" He pointed with his eyes. "Is that her?"

In the darkness behind Nick, Alena continued to search for Ruckus. She clapped her hands for the third time before the little dog finally came limping out of the brush. She dropped to her knees and felt the dog's shoulders and legs.

"Uh-oh," Nick said. "You did a big no-no."

Alena jumped to her feet and charged forward in a fury. She twisted the flashlight out of Nick's hand and shoved him aside, then pointed the beam in Decker's face.

"Did you kick my dog?" she demanded.

"Are you the witch?"

"I said, 'Did-you-kick-my-dog?'"

"What's your problem, lady? I only wanted to talk to you."

She raised her right hand and made a fist; both dogs began to slowly tighten their grips.

"I'd consider your answers very carefully if I were you," Nick said. "Trust me, I've had some experience in this area."

Alena glared down at him. "Do you know what a 'crush bite' is? It's the way dogs bite—not by puncturing the skin like cats do, but by crushing and tearing. A dog this size can bite with a force of four hundred pounds per square inch—what do you think he'll do to your windpipe if I give him the command?"

"Get these dogs off me right now," Decker demanded. "These are dangerous animals—I could call the authorities and have them destroyed."

"Wow," Nick said. "I was just wondering if it was possible for you to get any stupider. Apparently it is."

Alena knelt down beside him and glared directly into his eyes. "You're right," she said, "these are dangerous animals. I've taught them to hunt the way their ancestors did—in a pack. That one grabbed your leg to keep you from escaping; I had to train him not to follow his instincts and tear your hamstring out. I trained this one to go for your throat but not to crush it. That was a very difficult skill for him to learn—it's like learning to carry an egg on your tongue. And this one down here—the one who's drooling over your potbelly right now—he's the one who would kill you. The other two are just supposed to paralyze you—to hold you down and stretch you out nice and tight while their partner disembowels you."

"You're out of your mind," Decker said.

"I'm a witch," she whispered. "What did you expect?"

"I'll see you in court, lady. This is a violation of the First Amendment—you're infringing on the freedom of the press."

She slowly rose to her feet. "There's only one way to deal with a man like you."

At that moment Gunner came crashing through the brush into the clearing and collapsed to his knees, panting. "Alena—don't!"

But Alena ignored him. She snapped her fingers and pointed to Ruckus, then to Decker. The little dog trotted over and positioned itself beside the man, then looked up at its master for the final command. Alena held out her left hand and raised her little finger.

Ruckus lifted his left leg and sent a jet of water onto Decker's head.

Gunner heaved a sigh of relief.

"Hey!" Decker shouted as loudly as his constricted throat would allow. "What the—What's he doing?"

"What a coincidence," Nick said. "I was just thinking of doing the same thing."

"Tell him to stop that!"

"Tell him yourself. Give him that line about 'freedom of the press'—that one really impressed me."

Decker reached up for the little dog—but when he did he felt his throat tighten. He dropped his arm to his side again; he had no choice but to lay there until the dog had finished his business at his leisure.

"That's quite a bladder for a little dog," Gunner said. "I'm jealous."

"I know what you mean," Nick said. "That's a performance any man would admire."

"Are you going to let me up or not?" Decker growled.

Nick squatted down beside him. "Let's get a couple of things straight first: Number one, as of tonight Alena is assisting the FBI in an investigation—that means she'll be subject to the same interview restrictions the rest of us are. If you want to talk to Alena, talk to the public liaison officer at the Patriot Center first. Got it?"

"Whatever."

"And number two, when you climbed that fence you became guilty of trespassing, and the First Amendment won't protect you there. If I ever see you up here again, I'll make sure charges are filed and your credentials are pulled—and if Alena catches you up here again, you'll get worse than that. And you know what, Decker? These are trained security dogs and this is posted private property—I don't think a jury in the world would convict her."

"I'm still going to do this story."

"Go ahead, scuzzball—the damage has already been done. Just don't come back here unless you're invited. Do we understand each other?"

Decker blinked his assent.

Nick looked up at Alena and nodded; she snapped her fingers, then closed her fist and opened it again. The dogs immediately released their grip and took sitting positions beside her.

Decker stood up and wiped himself off. "All I wanted to ask you is—"

"My dogs will escort you back to the fence," Alena said. "And if you feel like kicking one of these dogs, please—go right ahead."

The three of them watched in silence until Decker was well into the woods. Alena scooped up Ruckus and cradled him in her arms.

"Is he all right?" Gunner asked.

"Nothing seems to be broken."

"He's a tough little guy," Nick said.

"I told you—it's his gift."

"It could have been worse, Alena. It could have been you."

"He was just a reporter."

"This time."

"I told you before, I can take care of myself."

"Is this the way you want to spend your life—listening for sounds in the woods every night? Wondering if somebody else has climbed your fence? Wondering if they're coming for you?"

She shrugged. "That's what I do anyway."

"You shouldn't have to," Gunner said. "Listen to Nick, Alena. Somebody's going to come looking for you—the same guy who came looking for that FEMA woman. Please—help the FBI find him before he finds you. Everybody knows about you now; there's no reason for you to hide anymore—no reason you and Nick have to sneak around at night."

"Every time I help him, things get worse."

"Sometimes things get worse before they get better," Nick said, "but they will get better—and they'll improve a lot faster if you help."

"What do you want me to do?"

"Come with me to Dogleg Lake in the morning. Help us find the body in the water. You and Trygg can pinpoint it for us—without your help we'll have to search the whole lake."

"Why is that body so important?"

"Because it's Marge's body—I'm sure of it. The lake water's cold—that slows down decomposition—and the body's only been there for a couple of days. So far we've had to track this guy with nothing but a pile of thirty-year-old bones. This time we have a fresh body—a chance of finding forensic evidence that could lead us right to him."

"You can find the body without me," she said. "It'll just take a little longer."

"It could take a lot longer, and in the meantime somebody could be looking for you. Marge disappeared the day after her interview, remember? Well, news about you has been circulating for about a day now. We don't have time to mess around, Alena—we need to move fast."

"Listen to him," Gunner added. "Nick's making sense."

Alena considered their words. "I can't go down there—not in the daylight—not when people will see me."

"The FBI will declare the area a crime scene. We'll cordon off the whole place—no one will be allowed in except you and me and a handful of FBI personnel. Believe me, it's the safest place for you to be right now."

"The safest place for me is with my dogs."

"We're talking about a murderer," Nick said, "and that little dog can't protect you. I'm afraid the others can't either—they're big, and they're smart, but they're not bulletproof."

"Don't ever say that. Ever."

"I'm sorry. You need to hear it."

"I want you both to go away. I can't go back down there. I won't— and you have no right to ask me to help you again. I've helped enough." She turned and started back through the woods.

"Alena, wait," Gunner said.

"Then help yourself," Nick called after her. "You want this guy more than I do."

Alena turned and looked at him. "What's that supposed to mean?"

"Whoever killed Marge needed a place to dump her body fast. He took it to the old graveyard by the lake, but he knew he couldn't bury it like he did the others—not while people are looking for graves—so he dropped it in the lake instead. He knew about the graveyard, Alena—the one you helped me find last night."

"So?"

"I went back there this morning. I started excavating that grave— the one you said had the most recent remains. You were right, just like always. There was a second body—one that wasn't supposed to be there."

Alena waited.

Gunner took a step closer. "We didn't want to tell you like this."

"Tell me what?"

Nick reached into his pocket and pulled out the buckeye; he pushed on it with his thumb.

CLICK clack.

Ruckus barked once.

Alena sank to the ground, and Gunner hurried to her side.

30

Riddick led the mare from her stall and tied the lead to a wooden post in an open section of the stable. It was a magnificent animal, a classic reddish-brown bay with a black mane and tail. He took out a soft-bristled brush and began to stroke the mare's forelock and face, being careful to avoid her eyes. Then he switched to a medium brush and moved to the neck, working his way down to the powerful shoulders with a brush in one hand and a grooming mitt in the other.

I'm definitely getting one of these, he thought. He imagined himself sitting in the saddle, holding the reins loosely in his lap while the mare cantered smoothly around the exercise arena. He was a good rider—for someone who grew up in the suburbs of Virginia Beach and never saw a horse outside of a petting zoo. But he used to ride with Victoria, and she had taught him well. She taught him how to keep his shoulders back and how to keep constant pressure on the irons with the balls of his feet; she taught him how to push his heels down to stay square in the saddle and how to hold the reins to keep a constant light pressure on the bit. Victoria grew up on a horse; she knew how to ride, and now Riddick did too—and he was looking forward to riding again.

"Is she ready?"

Riddick turned. Victoria was dressed in khaki breeches with knee-length riding boots and a black blazer over a white cotton blouse; she was working her slender fingers into a pair of pigskin gloves. Her hair was pulled back in a simple ponytail today—something Riddick rarely saw and few cameras were ever allowed to record.

"Almost. Thought I'd give her a once-over first."

"Good." She took a quilted saddle pad and threw it across the mare's back.

"Want some company? I could saddle the Appaloosa."

"I prefer to ride alone. You'd slow me down." She glanced around the stable for any sign of listening ears. "I thought this might be a good place to have a little talk, Chris. I can't have you popping in and out of my bedroom ever again. Are we clear on that?"

"What's on your mind?"

"I've been thinking about what you said the other night—about those two scrapbooks and what they contain—about what would happen if people found out."

"And?"

"You said that the old woman is the town gossip, and that I should think about that. What did you mean?"

"Just food for thought."

"Don't get coy on me, Chris. What did you mean?"

He looked at her. "I think you know what I meant."

"What I want to know is, what are you willing to do about it?"

He paused. "What do you want me to do?"

"Not a thing. That old woman is my biological mother, Chris—believe it or not, that means something to me. Besides, I don't think she's a problem. After all, she's kept this secret for over forty years; if she wanted to tell someone she would have done it a long time ago. She wants to see her little girl make it to the White House; I think she wants it even more than I do. She's no problem; the secret's safe with her."

"Then why did you bring it up?"

"Because—I want to know how far you're willing to go." She turned to the wall and lifted an English saddle from a rack.

Riddick reached out to take it from her.

"Don't." She hoisted it onto the mare's back and folded down the saddle flaps. "You said something else I've been thinking about—you said you weren't asking much. You're wrong about that, Chris—you're asking for everything."

"No more than I'm entitled to."

"You're not 'entitled' to anything—you get what you earn around here. That's the way it works in the big leagues, and that's what you're really asking for: You want to play with the big boys now—isn't that right?"

"I guess you could put it that way."

"Good. There's a woman who lives in the mountains above Endor. She lives all by herself in the woods. The people there think she's a witch. That's what they call her: the Witch of Endor."

"Nice little hometown you've got there."

"People get some crazy ideas in their heads, don't they? Take you, for example: You think you've got a free ticket to Washington just because you know something that I don't want revealed. Sorry, Chris, it's not that easy. You can have Washington—we can work something out—but you'll have to earn it."

"How?"

"This woman—the one they call the witch—she's a dog trainer. She has a cadaver dog that can find almost anything—even bodies buried hundreds of years ago. You know the graveyard at the Patriot Center? She's the one who found every one of those graves—and the four bodies that weren't supposed to be there. They thought a different woman found the graves at first—everybody did. That woman has disappeared; the FBI thinks someone killed her."

"Where did you hear all this?"

"From the nice young FBI agent in charge of the investigation."

"So now you own an FBI agent."

"Don't be silly—no one 'owns' an FBI agent. He simply keeps me informed as a professional courtesy, that's all."

"What does this have to do with me?"

"You disappoint me, Chris—I thought you were smarter than that. Think about the scrapbooks: Do you know who killed the four people they found at the Patriot Center?"

"I've got a pretty good idea."

"So do I—but the FBI doesn't know, and we don't want them to. All they've had to work with so far is four very old skeletons, and that's not enough for them to figure out who did it. But they just found another body—in a different graveyard—and there could be more. Every time they find another body, they find more evidence, and that puts them one step closer to figuring it all out. Guess who found that fifth body, Chris? The witch did—the Witch of Endor. She's the real problem here."

"What are you asking me to do?"

"I'm not asking you to do anything. I'm just telling you my problem, that's all—I'm just telling you what's weighing on my heart. That's what women do, Chris. They find a man they feel close to and then they share their burden with him. If the man really cares, he'll do something about her problem—without waiting to be asked. That's how she knows if he really cares—if he does something."

She turned her back to him and stepped in close until they were almost touching. She looked back at him over her right shoulder. "Help me up, will you?"

She fit her left foot into the stirrup. He put his hands on her waist and lifted; she slowly rose up in front of him and swung her right leg over the saddle.

Chris looked up at her. "When?"

"I have no idea what you're talking about. But my problem is getting worse every day—if anyone cares."

He nodded.

She tugged on the reins and backed the horse away. "Oh, and Chris—muck the stall while I'm gone, will you? I gave the stable boy the day off."

31

The bass boat cruised silently across the lake. Trygg balanced on her three legs in the shallow bow with her head draped over the edge and her nose hovering just above the water. The dog's head swung slowly from side to side like a pendulum, and the walls of her nostrils flexed in and out as she tested the air for scent. She wore a different bandanna this time—a green one with a checkered pattern—the one that reminded her to search for submerged remains. Alena knelt in the bow beside the dog, studying her eyes and the movements of her body, watching for any sign of an alert.

Nick sat on the casting deck behind them, steering the boat with two foot pedals; they used an electric trolling motor to keep gasoline fumes from obscuring the scent. He glanced back over his shoulder; on the distant shore he could see Kegan and Danny and the FBI's forensic tech crew excavating the remains of Alena's father. He looked at Alena. Her eyes were red and swollen; she had cried most of the night while Gunner sat beside her and held her and Nick watched helplessly from across the room. Nick knew she was exhausted and he knew she deserved to be left alone to grieve, but he had no choice; they had to find this body soon—for Alena's sake. Nick knew that a decomposing body was like a ticking clock; with every passing hour valuable forensic evidence would be lost. So far they had been trying to find a killer with nothing but a handful of ancient bones. The bones of Ken Savard were more recent, but even they were already more than two decades old. But Marge—she had been dead only a day or two, and the killer's hand-prints might still be all over her body—if they found it in time.

But mountain lakes can be deep, and the pressures at greater depths can keep a body from bloating and rising to the surface—it could stay down there for weeks, even months. Deep lakes can have thermal layers where icy water at the bottom slows the process of decomposition, keeping the body submerged. And this killer wasn't stupid—he might very well have taken the time to weigh the body down, in which case it would remain submerged even if it did bloat. That could be a big problem, because mountain lakes have craggy bottoms littered with rotting tree stumps, where a body can stay hidden for years. But they didn't have years to wait; they needed to find this body now, and Nick knew they might never find it without Alena's help.

Nick also knew something about grief: He knew that the worst way to have to face it was to just sit there and feel it until it finally cooled down like a dying fire and you succumbed to exhaustion and sleep. Alena needed something to do—she needed a distraction—and this was probably as good as any.

He caught a glimpse of motion to his right and looked; he saw the quick flash of a tail as a bass snatched an insect from just above the water and dove for safety. *Good spot for fishing*, Nick thought. *Let's hope it's as good for us.* There was a steady breeze blowing across the lake from northeast to southwest. They had divided the lake into quadrants and were covering one section at a time, keeping the boat pointed into the wind to allow the dog to pick up the scent as the breeze carried it forward. Nick knew the body could be almost anywhere, depending on how big a hurry the killer was in when he dumped it. He was hoping for a find in the shallow water near the shore. He knew the scent would be stronger there; the body would be easier for the dog to find and easier for the divers to recover. But they had already covered most of the shoreline without success; now they were in deeper water, and Nick didn't know what Trygg's detection threshold was. How deep was too deep? He had no idea; he just hoped that the dog's psychic powers were operating at full strength that day.

"She needs a break," Alena said suddenly, then rolled onto her back on the cut-pile carpet of the foredeck. Trygg immediately turned and jumped on top of her and the two of them began to play.

"You don't have to do this," she said to Nick without looking up.

"Do what?"

"Keep me out here while they're digging up my father's bones. That's what you're doing, isn't it?"

Nick paused. "I suppose I could tell you, 'It's a long way back to shore—we might as well stay out here until we're finished,' but there's no sense trying to lie to a witch. Yes, that's exactly what I'm doing. You shouldn't have to see that."

"It doesn't matter. I've been preparing for this since I was ten years old."

"You know, down in Endor they say there's a woman in the mountains who wanders the woods at night with a three-legged dog, searching for the soul of her father."

Alena stopped and looked at him. "Did you ever wonder why I have a cadaver dog? Not many people do."

"People keep some strange pets," Nick said. "Me, I have giant hissing cockroaches from Madagascar."

"My father disappeared when I was ten. There was a storm one night; he heard a noise in the woods and went to check on it. He never came back, and I never knew what happened to him—until last night. I found Trygg in an animal shelter in Nineveh—they were about to put her down. I walked up to her and said, 'I need someone who can help me find my father.' She looked at me and said, 'I can learn to do that—that's my gift.' And she was right—she's the best cadaver dog in the world."

"It's a good thing she wasn't overly modest," Nick said.

"Why should she be? If you've got a gift you should say so—you should put it to use. We've been over every square inch of our land together, and there's a thousand acres of it. We did it at night when no one would see us. I always thought that one night—that I would be the one to—"

She stopped.

"She eats dogs too," Nick said.

"What?"

"That's another story I heard down in Endor. The woman in the mountains—she goes to animal shelters and feels all the puppies. She takes the fattest ones back to her lair and eats them—with their blood."

"Who told you that?"

"Sorry—I have to protect my sources."

"That's disgusting. I check the puppies for congenital joint defects, that's all. They told you I *eat* them?"

"That's right."

"With their *blood*?"

"I threw that part in. I thought the story needed something."

"Thanks," she said. "Those idiots don't need your help."

Nick watched while Alena and Trygg played together. Alena rolled back and forth and roughed up the fur on the back of the dog's neck; she took off one of her bandannas and gave the dog the knotted end so they could play tug-of-war.

"Why do you do that?" Nick asked.

"What?"

"Wrestle around like that—you do it every time the dog finds a body. Why?"

"It's her reward. It's what she lives for."

"Wrestling?"

"Play. Touch. Love—that's what motivates her. She doesn't care about finding bodies—she wants to please me and she wants to play. At the CETC they use a little white towel rolled up and taped at both ends. They have a room there with a whole wall full of holes. A trainer stands behind the wall with the towel; inside one of the holes is a sample of cocaine or heroin. When the dog detects the scent, he walks up to the hole and the man sticks the towel out—that's the reward. The dog could care less about finding drugs; all he wants is the towel. That's all the dog ever does—he spends his whole life searching for that little white towel. Funny, isn't it?" She looked up at Nick. "What's your little white towel?"

"I'll have to give that one some thought," he said. "What's yours?"

245

"Finding my father's body," she said. "Now what?"

"Dogs are too easily pleased," Nick said. "If I were a dog, I'd renegotiate my contract. I'd tell my trainer, 'Hey, you sniff out the drugs and I'll hand you a towel—see how you like that.'"

She laughed a little.

"You'll be okay, Alena. You just need a new towel, that's all."

"Like what?"

"Like finding the man who killed your father."

"I'd like that," she said. "I'd like that a lot." She released the dog and snapped her fingers, and the dog immediately resumed her position in the bow.

Nick looked out across the lake; they had been working most of the day and they had a lot of water still to cover. He tried to think like the killer: Where would he dump the body? There didn't seem to be a logical place. He tried to imagine the body underwater: the bacteria running amok in the gut, producing methane and carbon dioxide that bubbled toward the surface in tiny specks of gas along with *putrescine* and *cadaverine* and the other malodorous by-products of death.

It seemed incredible to Nick that a dog could detect the chemicals in such tiny concentrations—*but so can insects*, he thought. Blowflies and flesh flies constantly hover in the sky, testing the air for tiny clusters of scent molecules, then follow the scent to the source. On a warm, clear day a blowfly can find a body within minutes of death—sometimes within seconds. If a fly can find a body, why not a dog?

A fly can find a body.

Nick looked to his right again and waited; a few seconds later he saw another splash of water in the same place as before. "Over there," he said, working the pedals and bringing the boat around.

"Where?"

"There—see the ripples? Blowflies are picking up the same scent molecules that your dog is trying to find. The flies are coming in low, searching for the source, and the fish are picking them off."

"Blowflies? How could a fly find the body before Trygg does?"

"Because there are thousands of them all over the lake and there's only one of her. I'm lining up downwind from that spot—get Trygg to confirm the location for us."

Nick approached the spot slowly; when he did, Trygg sniffed at the water and lay down.

"Bingo," Alena said.

"I couldn't have said it better."

Nick dropped a weighted hand line into the water to take a sounding; when he felt the weight touch bottom he tied a red buoy to the other end and let it go. "C'mon," he said. "Let's get back to the others and tell them to send in those divers." He tipped the trolling motor out of the water and started the outboard—fumes didn't matter anymore.

32

"We found it," Nick called out as he cut the engine and let the bow ride up onto the shore.

Danny pointed to the red speck bobbing in the distance. "Is that the spot?"

"That's where the scent exits the water," Nick replied. "The body should be nearby, but tell your divers they might have to do a little looking."

"Why?"

"They have to do a little math: They have to consider the wind speed and the depth of the water, and then they can do a rough estimate of the location of the body—it's in about thirty feet of water, by the way. But the current can move the scent around, and the deeper the water, the greater the margin for error. There's no way around it, the divers will still have to search—but we've narrowed it down to a very specific area. It shouldn't take them long."

While the two men were talking, Alena stepped off the boat and headed directly for the excavation site. Kegan was seated at a small folding table covered with evidence bags and fragments of bone. She looked up at Alena as she approached and recognized her; she immediately stood up and covered the table with a plastic tarp.

"Ms. Savard, my name is Kegan Alexander. Thanks for your assistance today."

"Are you the anthropologist? Are you the one who dug up my father's bones?"

"I am," Kegan said. "I'm so sorry."

"What can you tell me? I want to know."

"We'll have to do a thorough examination of the remains before—"

"Don't put me off. What can you tell me now?"

"I really don't like to speculate."

"Look—this is my father, and I've been searching for him since I was ten years old. I want to know what happened to him, and I don't want to wait another second—okay? Now can you tell me how he died or not?"

Kegan paused. "Yes, I can."

"Well?"

"He died from a blunt trauma wound—specifically, a blow to the back of the head."

Alena pointed to the table. "Show me."

"Ms. Savard, please—I really don't think that's a good idea."

"I think I should decide that, don't you?"

"I'm not sure you're in the right frame of mind to—"

"Show her," Nick said, approaching from behind.

Kegan looked at him. "Are you sure?"

Nick put his arm around Alena's shoulders and looked at her. "Are you?"

She nodded.

"Then show her," he said. "She has a right to know."

Kegan lifted the tarp from the table and revealed the collection of bones and plastic evidence bags containing remnants of clothing and samples of soil and a couple of unrecognizable objects encrusted with dirt and rust. Alena's eyes went directly to the skull. She shuddered.

Nick pulled her in closer. "You okay?"

She mouthed the word *okay*, but nothing came out.

"Did your father have a dentist?" Kegan asked.

Alena nodded. "In Front Royal."

"Good—then we might be able to get dental records. Do you have anything personal of your father's? An old toothbrush? A hairbrush?"

"I have everything he owned—everything he used. I keep it all in sealed plastic bags to preserve the scent. I used it to train my dog to find him. Why?"

"We might be able to do a DNA match—to make a definite ID."

"Please don't do that."

"Do what?"

"Hold out hope—I'm past that. This is my father—I think we both know that." She put her index finger on her top right incisor; the same tooth on the skull had a gold cap. "He called it his 'gold mine.' He said I would inherit it if he ever . . ."

Her voice trailed off.

Nick silently held up one finger and made a small circular motion; Kegan turned the skull around to reveal a caved-in section on the back.

"It's the same wound we found on the skulls at the Patriot Center," she said. "A single, powerful blow to the back of the head caused by a blunt instrument—a club, a bat, something like that. Considering the similar ages of the skeletons, I think we're talking about the same killer— he may have even used the same weapon. But there is one difference."

"What's that?"

Kegan looked at Alena. "I've estimated your father's height at around six-foot-two. Is that about right?"

"Yes."

She pointed to the wound. "Look at the position of the fracture on the skull—see how low it is?"

"So?"

"The blow was made by an overhead stroke—that's the only way to generate enough force to fracture the skull. Now, you and I are about the same height—so if I brought a club down on your head, the fracture would be up high—near the crown. But Nick is taller, so if I took the same swing at his head, the wound would be low—just like it is here. The other four victims were all shorter than your father, so their wounds were all higher than this."

"Then the killer must be a short man," Nick said.

"Very short, I would say—but very powerful. It takes a lot of strength to deliver a blow like this."

Alena began to unconsciously extend her hand toward the skull.

Nick took her arm and turned her to face him. "This could be a breakthrough," he said. "Short and powerfully built—that's a big addition to the killer's profile."

Alena looked back at the table; Kegan had already covered it with the tarp again. "What happens to my—what happens now?"

"Your father's remains will be sent to the FBI crime lab for further analysis. Can you tell us precisely when your father disappeared?"

"The day, the month, and the year—the hour if you need it."

"That could prove useful in helping us date the other skeletons. They've all been in the same soil, subject to the same temperatures and weather conditions. Can you describe what your father was wearing when he disappeared?"

"I can tell you exactly."

"That will help when they're doing the fiber analysis. Thank you, Ms. Savard—I can't imagine how hard this must be for you, and you've been very helpful. When we're finished with the analysis, the remains will be released to you for final disposition. Is that all right with you?"

She nodded blankly and looked up at Nick. "Take me home."

"Sure."

Alena looked around for Trygg; she glanced down at her feet and found her lying under the table. She squatted down and stroked the dog's back. "She found him at last—but I think she knows. I think she's as disappointed as I am."

"C'mon—let's get you home."

On the way to the truck Nick's cell phone rang; he pulled it out and answered it. "Nick Polchak."

"Nick—it's Carlyn down at UVA."

"How's it going down there?"

"Good. How did the 'lake shaped like a dog's leg' turn out? Did you find it?"

"I sure did—I found the graveyard too. That was nice work, Carlyn—I owe you for that one."

"Nothing says 'thank you' like a check."

"I'll keep that in mind. Have you got anything else for me?"

"Well, that depends."

"What does that mean?"

"It means I've hit a dead end on historical research. I've looked every-where—I mean *everywhere*—and I just can't find any further reference to historical graveyards in your area."

"You didn't call just to tell me that."

"No, I didn't. Remember when we first met? I told you the best place to look for that kind of information would be at the local library—and you said you'd already looked."

"Endor Regional Library—it was my first stop."

"Did you look carefully?"

"I asked the head librarian. She's been there for fifty years—she knows every book in the place."

"Maybe not. I ran across a study done by the Virginia Historical Society about five years ago—it was an inventory of historical records in Virginia public libraries. Those grave registries are there, Nick—at least they were five years ago. I'd go back and ask that librarian again—or bet-ter yet, I'd look myself."

Nick paused. "I think that's a very good idea."

"About that check."

"It's in the mail."

"I've heard that before."

"Thanks, Carlyn—if you get any more brainstorms like that, let me know."

He closed the phone and looked at Alena. "We need to make a stop in Endor."

She shook her head. "Not me."

"It won't take long. It should be dark by the time we get there—no one will see you."

"You've told me that before. Take me home first—then you can go to Endor."

"I don't like the idea of you being alone—not right now."

"I told you—"

"I know—you can take care of yourself."

"I'm not going to Endor, Nick. You won't change my mind—I will not set foot in that town."

Nick shook his head. "Okay, you win. But I want you to promise me that you'll stay in the trailer until I get back—and keep those dogs of yours close."

"I always do."

They started for the truck again when Nick heard a voice calling behind him.

"Nick! Wait up!"

He turned and saw Danny jogging toward them. He looked at Alena. "Why don't you wait for me in the truck? I'll only be a minute."

Alena and Trygg went on ahead while Nick waited for Danny to catch up.

"Where are you two going?" Danny asked.

"I'm taking Alena home—she's had a long day. Don't worry, I'll keep an eye on her."

"Nick, who are you kidding? Have you got a sidearm? Could you hit anything with it if you did? I want to post a couple of agents up there—I can have them out here in the morning. C'mon, it's for her own good—no arguments this time."

"Okay," Nick said. "She won't like it, but I'll let her know."

"That's an amazing dog she's got there. Tell her thanks on behalf of the Bureau, will you?"

"I will."

"You know, I never got to ask you: How did you find this graveyard in the first place?"

Nick hesitated. "I did a little digging in the library. I ran across some historical references to a graveyard by a lake shaped like a dog's leg."

"Clever. Did you come up with that all by yourself?"

Nick blinked. "You pulled my cell phone records, didn't you?"

Danny looked at his PDA. "Carlyn Shaw—master's candidate in

Economic History at the University of Virginia. Did you know she graduated from high school second in a class of 698? That's one smart cookie."

"Now aren't you the clever one. Actually, I'm glad you mentioned her—I've been meaning to give you this." Nick took a folded piece of paper from his pocket and handed it to Danny.

"What's this?"

"A payment requisition—I promised her thirty bucks an hour. Believe me, it was a bargain."

Danny looked at the sheet and nodded. "Okay, I'll put this through—she earned it. So tell me: Were you planning on sharing this information with me or just keeping it to yourself and sticking me with the check?"

"I wasn't 'keeping it to myself'—it just wasn't relevant anymore. You've got the graveyard; does it really matter how I found out about it?"

"Is there anything else I should know about, Nick? While it's still relevant, I mean."

"Nothing comes to mind."

"Who was that on the phone just now?"

"Why ask me? You've got my phone records."

"That's right, I do." He checked his PDA again. "What a coincidence—Carlyn Shaw at the University of Virginia. What did she want?"

"She wants a check from you. I told her it was in the mail, so put a rush on it, will you?"

"Anything else?"

"Tell the Bureau if they've got any sense they'll get down to Charlottesville and hire that woman—they could use people like her. Throw some money at her; she's probably up to her neck in student loans, and she won't pay them off with a history degree."

"Thanks for the advice—I'll pass it on. What are your plans this evening?"

"Why? Do you want to hang out with me?"

"Just curious."

"I'm planning to stick close to Alena. We haven't found this guy yet—and I have a feeling he'll be looking for her."

Two hours later Carlyn heard a knock at her apartment door. She shut off the water in the kitchen sink and shouted, "Who is it?"

There was no answer.

She wiped her hands on a dish towel and walked to the door. "Who's there?"

There was a second knock.

She looked through the peephole and didn't recognize the sandy-haired man in the dark suit standing on her porch. She checked to see that the chain was securely fastened before she reached for the doorknob; as an additional precaution, she braced the door with her right foot.

She opened the door until the chain went taut. "Yes?"

"Carlyn Shaw?"

She hesitated. "I'm her roommate."

"Have you been roommates long?"

"Why?"

The man smiled. "I've always heard that people start to look alike when they live together. It must be true—you could be her twin." He held up a copy of her driver's license and showed her the photo.

"Okay, so you know who I am. Who are you?"

"My name is Daniel Flanagan." He held up his FBI credentials. "I don't like to shout it through a door—it makes the neighbors nervous."

She checked his credentials and looked at him. "You look pretty young to be an FBI agent."

He shrugged. "I'm a junior G-man. Want to see my whistle?"

"Thanks, I'll pass. What do you want?"

"I'd like to talk to you for a moment. May I come in?"

She didn't answer.

"Look, I really am an FBI agent."

"I know what you are, Mr. Flanagan—I just don't know *who* you are."

"Good answer. Do you know a Dr. Nicholas Polchak?"

Again, no answer.

"Maybe I should ask your roommate."

"I know Nick. You already know that—otherwise you wouldn't be here."

"Well, I'm Nick's boss. Nick works for me."

She looked doubtful.

"We're excavating a graveyard at the Patriot Center. I'm the special agent in charge. Nick is a forensic entomologist we hired to help with the investigation. He's a tall man with big funny glasses—a real wise guy. Does any of this sound familiar?"

"So what do you want from me?"

"I want to know what you've told Nick."

"You're his boss—why don't you ask him?"

Danny let out a sigh. "Look, Nick is a real smart guy, but he doesn't play well with others. We hired him to help us with this investigation, but he likes to run his own show—he likes to play games. So he hired you, but he doesn't always fill me in on what you've told him. That's all I want, Ms. Shaw—I just want to know what you've told Nick. If I'm going to resolve this case, I need to know what Nick knows."

She considered his words.

"I know you spoke with him on his cell phone just this afternoon. May I ask what you discussed?"

"Ask Nick."

"I did—he told me you called to ask about payment. Was that the entire purpose for your call?"

She didn't answer.

Danny was losing patience. "Look, I don't blame you for being cautious—given the circumstances, I would be too. But I'm Nick's boss, so you don't really work for Nick—you work for me." He took a piece of paper from his breast pocket and showed it to her. "See this? It's a requisition for payment—*your* payment. Nick gave it to me this afternoon and asked me to put it through."

She looked at it. "He said it was in the mail."

"Well it's not—not until I sign off on it. I'm the boss, so I pay the bills. And if I'm paying you for services rendered, then I think I'm entitled to benefit from those services, don't you? I'm not trying to twist your arm here, but fair is fair. Nick isn't paying you—I am. So would you mind telling me what I'm paying you for?"

She paused for a few seconds, then unlatched the chain and slowly opened the door. "What do you want to know?"

"Take it from the beginning," he said. "Just tell me what you told him—and don't leave anything out."

33

Nick knocked quietly on the door frame. "Gunner?"

There was no answer from the darkened room.

He knocked again—a steady, insistent rap like the dripping of a faucet. "I know you're in there, I can hear you breathing. It's me—Nick. I need to talk to you."

Nick heard the rustling of fabric, and then a lamp switched on.

Gunner sat up in bed and squinted against the light. "Nick—what are you doing here?"

"You said if I ever needed to talk I could stop by."

"I didn't mean in my bedroom in the middle of the night."

"You should have been more specific." Nick pointed to a lump in the bed beside Gunner. "Is that your wife?"

"I hope so."

"Charming woman. Can we talk?"

Gunner looked at the clock beside the bed. "It's eleven o'clock."

"At NC State the kids are just waking up now."

"Well, we're not kids and this isn't NC State. How did you find out where I live?"

"It's a small town—I just asked the first guy I saw. They told me you were just up the hill from the church."

"How did you get in?"

"The front door was unlocked."

"That doesn't mean you can walk right in."

"I knocked, but no one answered."

"That's because we were asleep."

Nick shrugged. "Not anymore."

At that point the lump in the bed began to stir. "Gunner, roll over—you're talking in your sleep again."

Gunner placed one hand on the lump and gently shook. "We have a visitor, Rose."

The woman jerked the sheet up to her neck and scooted against the headboard like a squirrel backing off hot pavement. Nick immediately took off his glasses—a precaution he had learned to take long ago when approaching the very young or the very nervous, and this woman was definitely in the second category. It was probably unnerving enough for her to find a strange man standing in her bedroom at eleven o'clock at night—it might be better if the stranger wasn't ogling her with eyes the size of softballs.

"Rose, I'd like you to meet Dr. Nick Polchak. Nick, this is Rose."

Nick began to extend his hand and cross the room, but quickly thought better of it. He was blind without his glasses, and he imagined himself stumbling into a dresser or nightstand—or even worse, onto the bed.

Rose looked at her husband. "Are you sick? Did you send for a doctor?"

"I'm not that kind of doctor," Nick said. "I'm a forensic entomologist. I study the insects that inhabit—"

"Nick. *Don't.*"

He stopped. "I'm a college professor."

"Nick is a friend of Alena's," Gunner said. "I told you about him—he's the one who went up there with me last night."

Rose tossed the covers aside and reached for her robe. "Well, why didn't you say so? Do you boys want coffee?"

"Thanks," Nick said. "That would be great." When Rose slipped by him in the doorway he said, "Sorry for the intrusion, Rose."

She patted him on the arm. "One man in my bed and another one waiting at the door—it's just another night at the Wendorf house. Relax, Nick—any friend of Alena's is a friend of ours. You boys talk—I'll get the coffee."

Nick slipped his glasses back on and looked at Gunner. "I like her."

"Me too. What's on your mind?"

"I want you to help me break into the library."

"What?"

"Will you do it?"

"Why would you want to break into the library? Agnes can let us in tomorrow morning."

"This can't wait until tomorrow—and I don't want Agnes to know."

"Why not?"

"She lied to me, Gunner. I asked her for grave registries for the area around Endor, and she told me they weren't there. I happen to know they are—I just found out this afternoon."

"Maybe she was just mistaken."

"I asked her to double-check. She said she knows every book in the library, and after fifty years as head librarian I'm sure she does. It was no mistake, Gunner—she was lying."

"But why would Agnes lie?"

"There's something she doesn't want me to know."

"What?"

"That's what I need to find out. Your church is right across the street from the library—that makes you next-door neighbors. Endor is a small town; I figured there's a pretty good chance you have a key."

"You're asking me to unlock the door and let you in?"

"That isn't necessary. You could just loan me the key—and a flashlight if you have one handy."

Gunner looked at his watch. "The library closed two hours ago."

"The place is dark. No one would see me come or go."

"Do you have a warrant? Is this against the law?"

"No, I don't have a warrant, and yes, this is against the law. Look, I'm one of the good guys—I may be bending the law a little, but it's for a good cause. I need your help, Gunner. You don't have to be directly involved if you don't want to—just give me the key and look the other way."

Nick held out his hand.

He approached the front door of the library, sticking close to the hedge to blend into the shadows. He peered through the glass; the library was dark except for a faint glow of light from one small room. He put one hand on the glass and felt it give a little; he tested the door and found it unlocked. *That was easy,* he thought. *Life in a small town—must be nice.*

He slipped through the door and carefully closed it behind him, though he wasn't sure why; he probably could have left it wide open and no one in Endor would have raised an eyebrow. Still, there was no sense advertising his presence—this was breaking and entering after all, and people who represent the law aren't supposed to do that sort of thing.

He listened but heard no sound; he switched on the flashlight but kept the beam low to prevent it from being seen by anyone passing by on the street. He shined the beam along the base of the walls, search-ing for the card catalog—if the grave registries were still in the library, that would be the first place to look. It was an older public library, and he knew the library's collection wasn't likely to be online yet. That was a good thing—that meant he wouldn't have to boot up a computer and fill the room with a monitor's glow. Halfway along the far wall he found it—an old wooden card catalog lined with row after row of little square drawers, each with its own alphabetical identifier in a tiny brass frame.

Why would the old woman lie? he kept thinking. *What's she trying to protect—or who? Carlyn said she couldn't find the same records at the University of Virginia, even in their historical collections; she said the books had been taken from the shelves. Was Agnes responsible for that? Would she really go that far? If so, would she leave the grave registries on the shelves here in Endor and risk someone stumbling across them? That made no sense—she would have destroyed them, and she would have pulled the cards from the catalog too.*

Suddenly his whole idea seemed doubtful; what he probably needed to do was to find Agnes and press her until she admitted the reason for her lie. But he had no way to apply leverage to the old woman—if she was determined to keep her little secret she could do it. Besides, there was no sense second-guessing himself now—he had come this far, and he might as well have a look while he was here.

Halfway to the card catalog he crossed the open doorway of a dimly lit room. He stopped and looked inside; the glow emanated from a half-dimmed light focused on a table in the center of the room. He stepped into the room and shined his flashlight along the walls, illuminating the hundreds of photos and magazine covers of Victoria Braden that covered the room like confetti. He looked at the table in the center of the room and saw a large old book with a leather cover. He stepped to the table and took a closer look; it wasn't a book at all—it was an album or scrapbook of some kind, and the table was covered with loose photographs, newspaper clippings, scissors, and glue. He picked up one of the clippings and read the headline: "Victoria Braden Comes Home." He turned the scrapbook back to the very first page, then bent over the table and began to read.

Minutes passed.

"Unbelievable," he whispered. "So that's what this is all about."

He flipped the pages back and forth, studying every photograph and notation. He was so absorbed in the text that he never heard the footsteps slowly approaching from behind; he never heard the thick feet plant themselves solidly in a wide stance; he never heard the muscular hands tighten their grip on the baseball bat and slowly raise it overhead; and he never heard the flat, crunching *thud* of the wood as it crushed the back of his skull.

His lifeless body slumped forward on top of the scrapbook. A powerful pair of hands gripped his collar and pulled him off the table and onto the floor, then began to slowly drag his body across the smooth linoleum toward the loading dock.

"I'm getting too old for all this digging," Agnes groaned.

Nick and Gunner crossed the street and approached the library from behind. They kept the flashlight off to avoid being spotted.

"I can't believe I'm doing this," Gunner whispered.

"You didn't have to come—all you had to do was give me the key."

"And when you got caught, how would you explain the key? I agreed to this, so I'm part of it—I might as well come along."

"Kind of fun, isn't it?"

"Pastors aren't supposed to do this kind of thing."

"What, support the law?"

"I thought we were breaking the law."

"Ironic, isn't it?"

As they neared the loading dock they suddenly saw the outline of a figure moving in the shadows. Nick held out a hand and both men stopped. He put one finger to his lips; they moved closer to the building and crept forward. As they got closer they could make out two figures—one dragging the other across the loading dock toward a waiting pickup truck. Nick switched on the flashlight and pointed it at the face of the standing figure; a pair of startled eyes stared back.

Nick slowly lowered the beam of the flashlight, following the line of her stumplike arms to her blunt gnarled fingers clenching the jacket collar of a man's body. He saw the head slumped forward and the tangle of hair damp with blood; he saw the shoulders shrugged high and the arms hanging limp at the sides; he saw the legs dragging loose and lifeless; and he saw a smear of blood marking a trail back to the library door.

Gunner's mouth dropped open. "Agnes—what in heaven's name have you done?"

34

The dogs heard Nick's car approaching before Alena did. Those in the kennels lined up along the chain-link fences and began to bark viciously; inside the trailer, Ruckus bounded off the sofa and began to scratch at the door.

Alena opened the door and stepped out. She looked toward the opening in the woods and waited; a few seconds later she saw the flicker of headlights filtering through the trees, and then Nick's car emerged with its three-dog escort trotting alongside.

Nick's car pulled up in front of the trailer and stopped. Alena commanded the dogs to be silent and take sitting positions, and they immediately obeyed. When Nick's window began to roll down she leaned forward and said, "Where have you been? This is why I wouldn't go to Endor with you. You said it would only take a minute, but—" She drew a sharp breath and stumbled back from the car.

It wasn't Nick. It was his car, but someone else was driving it—a tall man with wavy black hair.

The three guard dogs instantly sensed her fear and threw themselves at the car. Acheron was closest to the driver's window; he turned his massive head sideways and lunged for the man's throat—but a split second later a gunshot exploded and the dog dropped silently to the ground.

Alena looked down at her dog in horror, then at the man still pointing the gun out the window.

"Call them off or I'll kill every one of them," he said.

Alena blinked in disbelief.

The man turned and aimed the gun at the rib cage of Phlegethon, who was snarling and sprawling across the passenger-side window.

"No!" Alena hurriedly gave the command to "withdraw," but she had to repeat it twice before the last of the dogs reluctantly obeyed.

Alena dropped to her knees and buried her face in Acheron's thick fur. She tried to wrap her arms around the dog's huge neck, but the lifeless form was so heavy that she could barely squeeze her arm underneath. She began to sob uncontrollably—a poisonous brew of sorrow, terror, and rage.

The man opened the car door; he had to shove the dog's body aside to step out. He looked down at her. "So you're the Witch of Endor. Funny, you don't look like a witch to me."

Alena glared up at him. "This is Nick's car."

"Yeah—I found it in front of his motel, so I borrowed it. I heard about these dogs of yours, and I figured I might get a warmer reception if I showed up in a familiar car. Sorry about the dog—I warned you." He walked around the trunk of the car toward the kennels, giving a wide berth to Styx, who was staring at him and emitting a low growl. "Man, these mutts are big. What do you feed them, anyway?"

"Put the gun down and I'll show you."

He looked back at her. "Put them in the kennel."

"What?"

"Both of them—lock them up right now or I'll shoot them both."

Alena hurried to an empty kennel and opened the gate; she snapped her fingers and pointed inside, and Phlegethon and Styx obediently trotted in.

Alena shut the gate and looked at him. "Are you the man who killed my father?"

"Me? I haven't been around that long—but I know who did."

"Who?"

"Let's try not to get sidetracked here, okay?" He approached the kennels and looked at the line of dogs seated obediently in a row behind the fences. "Which one is the cadaver dog?"

"What?"

"You heard me."

Alena didn't answer.

The man raised the gun and took aim at the first dog in line. "Is it that one?"

She still didn't answer.

He pulled the trigger and fired—the dog slumped over onto its side. The other dogs in the kennel scattered at the sound of the gunshot but quickly returned to their sitting positions.

"Stop it!" Alena screamed.

"Which one is the cadaver dog?" he demanded again. "Better tell me now—you might have a few dogs left."

Alena bolted into the trailer with Ruckus at her heels.

Riddick lowered the gun when he heard the flimsy door bang shut. He turned and looked at the trailer. "C'mon, that's not going to get you anywhere."

Inside the trailer, Alena ran to her bedroom and threw open a closet door. The shelves were filled with stacks of sealed plastic bags containing shirts, socks, trousers—everything her father had ever touched, carefully sealed to preserve his scent.

Outside, Riddick crossed to the trailer and shouted, "Don't make me come in there after you!"

Alena rummaged frantically through the bags, searching for one in particular. She found it on the top shelf—a bag containing a small white hand towel. She pulled it from the shelf and looked at the bag; in handwritten letters on the front was a single word: NICK.

"I don't have time to play games!" Riddick shouted. He raised his gun and aimed at the trailer. He fired three shots into the trailer wall, aiming high so that the bullets would strike above Alena's head. The bullets punched through the thin wall like an ice pick through tinfoil.

In her bedroom, Alena heard the shots and felt splinters of wood and chunks of drywall rain down on her; one shot caught the corner of a mirror and sent shards of glass flying across the room. She covered her head and dropped to the floor; Ruckus stood beside her and barked indignantly at the trailer wall.

"Stop wasting my time!" Riddick shouted. "You've got ten seconds to come out of there!"

Alena ripped open the bag and pulled out the towel. She held it out to Ruckus and let him take in the scent; the dog ran its nose back and forth over the rough fabric, then looked up at Alena. She snapped her fingers and pointed toward the door.

Riddick swung the gun around toward the kennels and pointed it at Phlegethon's head. "I'm about to shoot another one of your dogs, and it's a big one this time. I'd get out here if I were you."

"Stop it!"

Riddick turned and looked. Alena was standing in the trailer doorway; a small dog squeezed past her ankles and raced off toward the woods. Alena let the door swing shut behind her and charged toward the man. "Who dares to set foot on my land?" she said, slashing an X across her chest with one finger and making a menacing mystic sign.

Riddick frowned. "What's that supposed to mean?"

"It's the curse of Charon. I have summoned him to ferry you across the river to Hades—soon."

He let out a snort. "You expect me to buy this 'witch' stuff?"

"Wait and see."

"Sorry, I don't have time to 'wait and see.' Now—which one is the cadaver dog?"

"Why do you want to know?"

"Because I'm going to kill it, that's why. I can't have it finding any more bodies." He turned to the kennels again and aimed the gun at the next dog in line. "Is it that one?" He began to squeeze the trigger.

"No!" Alena shouted. "Not that one." Her eyes passed down the row of dogs and rested momentarily on Trygg. The dog stared intently back at her, and Alena thought she could read the meaning in her eyes. "Open the kennel door," Trygg seemed to say. "Don't let us die this way. He can't shoot all of us. One of us will get to him first. Open the door, Alena—give us a chance."

Alena looked at the kennel doors—there were six of them. Phlegethon and Styx were both in the last kennel. They were by far the strongest dogs, but they were large and slow moving and there were only two of them—the man would shoot them both before they ever cleared the kennel door. She was a fool to allow them to be locked up in the first place, but she didn't know any better. If she had known then what she knew now, she would have given the "attack" command and one of them might have reached him; at least they would have had a fighting chance.

The fiercest dogs were all in the third kennel; if she could only open that door—if she could give them the first shot at the man, maybe they would occupy him long enough for her to open the remaining doors. All the dogs together might overwhelm him—but how many of them would he kill first? How many could she bear to lose? She glanced at the first kennel and saw the lifeless form lying on the concrete; her eyes began to fill with tears. Then she glanced at Trygg again, and this time the dog seemed to say, "Do it, Alena. Have courage—we do."

"Well?" Riddick said. "Which one?"

"They're all cadaver dogs," Alena said. "All of them—every last one."

Riddick looked at her. "You're lying."

"Am I?"

Alena suddenly charged toward the third kennel. She prayed she might somehow make it to the door and fling it open before the man realized what she was doing—but before she was even halfway there the man shouted, "Stop right now or I'll kill you where you stand!"

Ten feet from the kennel she stumbled to a stop and turned to face him; she extended both arms as if to make a shield. "You've got a problem," she said.

"Oh? What's that?"

"You didn't come here just to kill my dogs—you have to kill me too."

Riddick didn't reply.

"But to kill me you'll have to shoot me, and then my blood will be on the ground. There are thirty cadaver dogs here that all know my scent, and any one of them will be able to find my body wherever you try to hide it in these woods. You'll have to kill all the dogs—every one of them. How many bullets will that take? How many have you fired already? Five? Six? How much ammunition did you bring?"

Riddick nodded. "I hadn't thought of that. You're right, I do have a problem—but it's only a small one. I can still kill you—I'll just have to do it someplace else."

Alena said nothing; she knew he was right. "Why are you doing this?"

"You've upset a very important person, lady—someone who doesn't want your dog sniffing out any more graves."

"Who?"

"That's none of your business. I want you to walk over to the car and get in the trunk—right now."

Alena's mind raced. She knew she was out of options. If she got in the trunk she was dead; the man could shoot her and dump her body anywhere, and the authorities would have no idea where to look. But if she refused to get in the trunk she was dead too—the man preferred not to kill her here, but he would if he had no other choice. She was dead either way, and there was nothing she could do about it—but she had no intention of dying before she learned the truth.

"Who killed my father?" she demanded. "I won't get in the trunk until you tell me—you'll have to kill me here."

Riddick shook his head. "You really want to know?"

Alena nodded.

"Okay," he said with a shrug. "There's a sweet little old librarian down in Endor. Her name is Agnes. She must be eighty years old—a real grandmotherly type, the kind you'd expect to find putting up preserves or knitting in front of a fire. That's who killed your old man—she took a baseball bat and bashed his brains in, along with half a dozen other poor suckers over the years. Satisfied?"

"Why would she do that?"

"That's a deep, dark secret," Riddick said.

"But—why my father?"

"Because he had a cadaver dog, and people who can bring back the dead are dangerous to have around. Now—get in the trunk."

Alena was devastated. She finally knew the truth—but only half of it. She knew *who* but not *why*, and that was almost worse than knowing nothing at all. Why would a woman kill half a dozen men? What kind of secret was worth that? She would have given everything to know—but she had nothing left to give. She had nothing left to bargain with, and she couldn't bring herself to beg.

She was going to die—she knew it—but if she had to die, she was going to make it as hard on the man as possible. She had no intention of buying a few additional hours of life by climbing into that trunk and making his work easier for him. No—she would make him kill her right here, and she would make sure her blood hit the ground and mingled with the dust—and he could scrape it and wipe it all he wanted, but he would never remove the scent.

She imagined the kennel door ten feet behind her. She would turn and lunge for it and throw the gate wide open. She knew that the moment she turned, the man would fire, but with luck he would shoot her in the back and not the head, and she still might have the strength to make it to the kennel and give the dogs their chance. If not—well, she was dead anyway.

"Let's go," he said.

"Yes. Let's go."

She spun around and dove for the kennel gate. She tensed every muscle in her body, anticipating the blast of the gunshot and the impact of the bullet slamming into her flesh—but to her astonishment she reached the kennel and slid her fingers into the chain-link fence. The latch on the gate was a foot to her left—she had never expected to get this far. She fumbled madly for the latch, and in the back of her mind she felt a desperate flicker of hope. There was no gunshot—no slam of a bullet into her spine or skull. It might work—she might make it.

As she reached for the latch she heard heavy footsteps behind her and a muttered curse. She felt a crushing blow to the back of her head and saw a searing flash of light.

Then everything went black.

35

Agnes slumped forlornly on the edge of the loading dock while Nick and Gunner stood over the body. Nick shined his flashlight down at the lifeless face.

"He's not from Endor," Gunner said. "I don't recognize his face."

"I do. His name is Daniel Flanagan—he was the FBI agent in charge of the investigation at the Patriot Center."

"What was he doing here?"

"The same thing I was, I imagine—trying to figure this thing out. I hate to see this. Danny was a good kid—a little overeager, maybe, but very bright. He must have talked to my research assistant down at UVA. If he did, he had access to the same information I have. He must have put two and two together and come up with the same answer I did—he just got here first."

Gunner looked at him. "Nick—what if you had gotten here first?"

"The thought occurred to me," Nick said. "Thanks for not trusting me with the key." He ran the flashlight up and down the body, searching for wounds, then got down on all fours and put his left cheek to the ground, studying the back of the skull where it rested in a small puddle of black liquid. "He appears to have been killed by a blow to the head; the back of the skull is crushed in—just like the victims at the Patriot Center."

Gunner turned to the old woman. "Agnes, did you kill this man?"

The old woman sat quietly with her hands folded in her lap, staring down at her plump feet dangling over the ledge in front of her. "Couldn't help it," she mumbled. "He was pokin' his nose where it don't belong."

"That's no excuse for taking a man's life. This man was a human being made in the image of God. Was he married? Did he have children? Do you have any idea of the pain you'll cause—"

Nick put a hand on Gunner's shoulder; he walked over and took a seat beside Agnes. "Where was he poking his nose, Agnes? What was Danny looking at that you didn't want him to see?"

Agnes didn't answer.

Nick glanced down at her thick, meaty forearms and gnarled hands. "What did you hit him with? You might as well tell me—they'll find the weapon anyway."

"Louisville Slugger," she said. "Stan the Man autograph."

"Stan Musial—you've had that for a long time, haven't you?"

Again, no answer.

"What did you plan to do with the body? You dragged it out here to the loading dock; you must have been planning to take it somewhere."

Agnes just shrugged.

"Did you plan to bury it on top of another grave or just dump it in the lake like you did with Marge?"

No reply.

"Agnes, there were three men buried at the Patriot Center who were all killed the same way Danny was—by a blow to the back of the head. They were all killed within your lifetime. Did you do that, Agnes? Did you kill them all? Stan the Man's been around long enough."

Nothing.

"And what about the man who was buried at Dogleg Lake? Did you kill him too?"

Agnes had nothing to say.

"I think you killed them all," Nick said. "You're old enough, and you're strong enough, and you're just about the right height—and Danny over there proves you've got the wherewithal to kill a man. You knew where those forgotten graveyards were located—you're the town librarian—you had access to all the historical records. What I want to know is, why? What are you trying to hide? We're talking about murder here, Agnes. I have to call the police—you know that, don't you? I have to notify the FBI too. Danny was a federal agent, and they take a very dim view of losing one of their own. They're going to ask you all these questions and a whole lot more, and they won't be nearly as nice as I am. Why don't you talk to me first? Maybe I can act as a go-between and make things a little easier for you."

When the old woman still refused to answer, Nick got up from the loading dock and looked at Gunner. "Well, there's one way to find out where Danny was 'pokin' his nose.'"

"How?"

Nick pointed to the smear of blood leading from the body back to the library door. "I'll be back in a minute," he said to Gunner. "Keep an eye on her—and I wouldn't turn my back if I were you."

Nick entered the library and followed the bloody trail to a small room just off the lobby. He immediately recognized it—it was the "shrine" to Victoria Braden. But what would Agnes be trying to hide here? It was a shrine after all—a public place, a place that welcomed visitors and admirers. But maybe there was more to this shrine than met the eye; maybe Danny somehow violated this sacred place; maybe he took a peek behind the altar and found something he wasn't supposed to see.

Bingo.

The crimson streak ended at a table in the center of the room. There was an open scrapbook lying on it; both facing pages were spattered with dots of blood. Nick took a pen from his pocket and used it to carefully turn the pages, examining the contents of the scrapbook from beginning to end. "Unbelievable," he muttered. He felt the hair stand up on the back of his neck, and more than once he turned to look behind him.

A few minutes later he pushed open the library door and stepped onto the loading dock again.

Gunner looked up. "Well?"

Nick walked down the short stairway and stood in front of Agnes. "I found the scrapbook," he said to her. "I read it from cover to cover. Was it really that important, Agnes? Was it really worth the lives of five people?"

"What scrapbook?" Gunner asked. "What did you find in there?"

"You were right about human nature, Gunner—apparently anyone is capable of murder. But you were wrong about something else: There are still secrets in a small town. Agnes here has a little secret she's been keeping for years: It seems Victoria Braden is her daughter."

"What? Agnes—is that true?"

"It's true," Nick said. "She's got the birth certificate and the adoption papers to prove it. Apparently she wanted to give her daughter a better life than she had, so she forged a whole new ancestry for her. She turned little 'Beulah' into a bona fide Virginia blue blood—the kind of woman who might catch the eye of a U.S. senator."

"It's unbelievable."

"Not entirely. I visited Victoria Braden; I managed to get a sample of her hair and I ran a DNA test to determine her haplogroup."

"What's that?"

"Mitochondrial DNA is passed from mother to child. It never changes, but random mutations occur over time—mutations that are specific to certain people groups. There might be a mutation that only Native Americans possess—so if I test your DNA and I find that mutation, I know that somewhere in your ancestry there was a female of Native American descent. Victoria Braden's haplogroup showed a mixed ancestry—not the simple Indo-European descent you'd expect. I knew Victoria wasn't what she claimed to be; this just explains it."

"But how could Victoria keep this a secret for all these years?"

"I'm not sure she even knows." Nick looked at Agnes. "Have you ever told her, Agnes? Does Victoria know that you're her real mom?"

"Told her just the other day," Agnes whispered. "When she came to visit Endor—when she came home."

Gunner sat down beside the old woman. "Agnes—how could you carry this burden all by yourself all these years? How could *you* keep it a secret?"

"I'll bet it wasn't easy," Nick said. "I have a feeling three different men were about to uncover that little secret over the years. That's why you killed them, isn't it, Agnes—to keep your daughter's real identity a secret?"

No response.

"What about Alena's father? That was a little different, wasn't it?"

"It was that dog of his," she mumbled. "He could find the graves."

"That's why you had to kill Marge too—you thought she found all the graves at the Patriot Center, and you were afraid she might find even more. Are there more, Agnes? How many more?"

She didn't reply.

"There's still something I don't understand," Nick said. "We found *four* bodies at the Patriot Center—but the fourth victim was two hundred years old. It was the same cause of death and the same manner of burial. You couldn't have been responsible for that one, Agnes—Stan the Man doesn't go back that far. But you knew about that body—you must have. You weren't just copying the killer's technique—all four of those men were from the same family. What's the connection there?"

Nick was interrupted by the sound of a sharp *yip*. He turned and found a tiny dog staring up at him with black bulging eyes and its little wry jaw jutting out to one side.

"It's Ruckus," Gunner said. "Alena must need me." He snapped his fingers and gave the "away" command, but the dog didn't move. He repeated the command, but Ruckus just continued to stare up at Nick.

"Wait a minute." Nick walked a few steps away and the dog turned to watch him. "He's looking for me, not you. Alena must have sent him to find me."

"Go," Gunner said. "Alena wouldn't do that unless she's in trouble. I'll wait here with Agnes."

Nick pulled out a pen and a scrap of paper. "Call the local police and tell them what happened—this is their jurisdiction. Then call this number too—it's in Washington. Ask for Nathan Donovan. Tell him about Danny and explain everything to him—he'll know what to do."

"You'd better get going," Gunner said.

"I'm going now. I'm parked right across the street—I can be up there in a couple of minutes." He turned to leave, then glanced down at the homely little messenger still staring up at him. "How do I tell him to go home?"

"Like this," Gunner said, snapping his fingers and demonstrating the command.

Nick repeated the sequence and the little dog took off up the mountain.

Nick hurried across the street to the parking lot of the Skyline Motel, but when he got there he found the parking lot empty—there was no sign of his rental car anywhere. His mind raced—could he have parked it somewhere else? That was impossible. The Skyline was situated at the exact center of town and everything was within easy walking distance from there; it was the only place he had ever parked in the entire town of Endor.

A flurry of explanations flashed through his mind: Maybe he had inadvertently blocked a fire access and the car was towed away; maybe the rental car company had retrieved the car without notifying him; maybe Biff and his buddies from Endor High had hot-wired it and taken it out for a vengeful joyride. But he quickly rejected each potential explanation, because his mind told him that they weren't explanations at all—they were just wishful thinking. There was only one reason his car would be missing: Someone had stolen it, but he had no idea who.

Then he thought about the little dog again, and he knew why his car was missing.

He felt a cold chill flutter down his spine.

Alena wouldn't do that unless she's in trouble, Gunner said.

He needed a car. He reached into his pocket, then let out a groan. His cell phone—he must have left it in the rental. He looked at the Skyline and at the ET&G across the street—all the lights were off. He looked back at the library. Gunner was still there—he had a car—it was the quickest way.

Nick turned toward the library and ran.

36

The winding road through the woods seemed endless—infinitely longer than when Nick drove it before. It had seemed to take forever to borrow Gunner's car—to explain the situation, to hurry up the hillside and get the keys from Rose. It all took far too long and he didn't have time to waste—and he had a bad feeling that Alena didn't either.

He knew something was wrong the instant he reached the chain-link fence. The gate was open wide. Alena would never leave it that way, and Nick was the only other person who knew the combination. But whoever took Nick's car didn't need it, because he had left the bolt cutters lying on the front seat in plain view. *Terrific*, he thought. *I give you transportation* and *a way in. Is there anything else I can do for you?* Now, as he approached the trailer, he noticed something else. The dogs should have gone wild at the sound of his approach just as they always did, but the sound they made this time wasn't furious or defiant—it was a strange cacophony of lamenting howls and whimpering wails.

Nick skidded to a stop and ran for the trailer. He saw Alena's truck still parked beside it, and for a moment he hoped she might be inside and all would be well—but then he saw the furry black lump lying lifeless and still in front of the trailer door, and he knew for certain that something was terribly wrong.

He threw open the trailer door and stumbled inside.

"Alena!"

He scrambled through the tunnel-like living room and into the bedrooms in the back.

"Alena!"

There was no one there.

When he stepped into the second bedroom he felt a crunch under his feet; he looked down and saw clumps of broken gypsum and shards of shattered glass covering the floor. He searched the walls and found the source—high up, near the ceiling. He ran back into the living room and looked at the wall on the opposite side; he found three jagged holes and three more that aligned with them on the exterior wall. They were bullet holes—someone had fired into the trailer three times.

Nick hurried outside and knelt down beside the lifeless dog. He combed his fingers through its thick black fur until he found a tangled wet clump on the animal's thick breast. He felt the spot and found another bullet hole—the huge dog had apparently been felled by a single large-caliber bullet through the heart.

Nick could see the whole picture in his mind: Someone had used his car to approach the trailer without raising Alena's suspicion. The three huge guard dogs would have detected the car in the woods and accompanied it into the clearing as always, but Alena had probably called them off—after all, it was only Nick. When the man finally had revealed himself, the dogs had attacked—and the man had fired point-blank.

He slowly rubbed the dog's fur again. *Acheron*—the leader—the one that always guarded the driver's-side door. Nick closed his eyes and shook his head. Did Alena have to witness this? Did she have to stand there and watch in horror as some stranger she thought was a friend destroyed one of her beloved dogs? It would have been like losing a child for her; it would have broken her heart.

But what happened next? And where was Alena now?

Nick got up from the ground and ran to the edge of the woods. "Alena!"

He listened, but there was no reply.

"Alena! It's Nick! It's all right, you can come out now!"

He waited but heard no sound from the woods. No one approached.

Where is Alena?

Nick knew that there were only two logical possibilities: Alena was alive or Alena was dead. Someone had wanted to find her badly—someone with a gun—and he was obviously willing to use it. He fired at least once into the dog and three more times into the trailer wall—he wasn't fooling around. But the shots into the trailer were high, almost at ceiling level. He was either the world's worst shot or they were only warning shots, meant to flush her out but not to kill.

Or meant to flush her out and *then* to kill. There were a thousand acres of forest up here; plenty of places to hide a woman's body where it might never be found.

Where is she?

If she was alive and nearby she wasn't answering—maybe because she was wounded or unconscious. But Nick knew that was unlikely; whoever the perpetrator was, he didn't come all the way up here just to wound her and leave her to identify him later. Though the thought made him sick to his stomach, his mind told him that Alena was most likely dead—but how would he ever know for sure?

He looked across the clearing at the kennels.

He raced back into the trailer, through the living room and into the first bedroom, and pulled the cotton pillowcase from the bed pillow. He held it by one corner and hurried it back out to the kennels.

As he approached the first kennel, he spotted another form lying dead and still on the concrete pad, and his heart skipped a beat—for a split second he thought it might be Alena. But the form was too small—it was another of Alena's precious dogs. The other dogs in the kennel were seated in a circle around it, as if they were keeping vigil.

He draped the pillowcase over a post and moved from kennel to kennel, searching through the dogs for one in particular; he found her in kennel number three. She was a mottled gray mongrel with only three legs; she was a drab and forsaken-looking beast; she was a deformed and damaged animal—but she also happened to be the finest cadaver dog Nick had ever seen. Trygg knew every inch of these woods; she had spent years wandering over them every night in search of Alena's father.

But tonight was different—tonight she had to find Alena.

Nick opened the kennel gate a few inches and pointed at Trygg. "Come!" he commanded, but the dog didn't respond.

"Come on, girl! Let's go! Come on! Come to me!"

The dog just stared.

Nick tried to imagine what Alena would do. He remembered her operant command, the one that always preceded the actual instruction. He snapped his fingers once—but he had no idea what to do next. What gesture or motion commanded the dog to "come"? He snapped his fingers and wiggled one finger—nothing. He snapped his fingers and pointed to the ground at his feet—nothing. He snapped his fingers and backed up, waving both arms like a man parking a 747—the dog sat down.

He was starting to get angry. This was one of the most talented dogs on the planet, but it couldn't understand a simple spoken command— a command that even a moron like Bosco could probably comprehend. Nick felt like a stupid tourist in a foreign country who didn't know a single word of the language; all he could do was shout in English and hope that his listener would somehow figure it out.

He opened the gate wider; if the dog wouldn't come out on her own, Nick would just have to go in. The idea seemed simple enough in his mind: He would just walk over to Trygg, hook one finger under her collar, and pull—the dog would get the idea and follow. And the other seven dogs would just sit politely and watch their companion being manhandled by a stranger, after which they would all lick Nick's face and present him with a framed certificate for a job well done.

Idiot.

They were dogs—*big* dogs—*trained* dogs, and he had no idea what they were trained to do if someone dared to invade their private domain. Whatever it was, it probably wouldn't be pretty. He remembered Acheron taking him by the throat and pinning him to the ground—what part of the body were these dogs trained to attack? Nick closed the gate a little; he had body parts he would rather not see in a dog's mouth.

Nick just stood there, helpless and frustrated, wondering what to do next.

In desperation he swung the gate open wide and looked directly into Trygg's eyes. "Okay," he said, "I don't speak your language and you don't speak mine—but I'm a smart guy and you're a smart dog, so we should be able to work this thing out. I know you don't speak English—at least I don't think you do—but your master trained you to understand some very subtle gestures and expressions and body language. So I'm just going to talk to you the way I would anybody else, and I'm going to use the same inflection and the same mannerisms I normally use—and I'm just going to hope that you'll somehow figure out what I mean. You ready? Okay, here goes: I'm afraid something has happened to your master—to Alena. I'm afraid she might be dead, and if she is, you're the only one who can find her. I need you to come out of that kennel and help me, and I need you to do it right now. I want you to come out of there and sit right here beside me—see where I'm pointing? I want the rest of you dogs to stay where you are—that means you and you and especially you, big guy—this is just between Trygg and me. Okay, Trygg, that's my whole spiel—now it's up to you. Are you going to help me or not?"

He put his hands on his hips and waited. A few seconds later Trygg trotted out of the kennel, circled around behind him, and sat down by his side.

Nick started to say, "Good dog," but somehow it sounded insulting. Instead he said, "I knew you'd listen to reason. Let's get to work."

He took the pillowcase from the kennel post, wadded it into a ball, and held it under the dog's nose.

"I hope this helps," he said. "I know that you're trained to find dead people—but I'm hoping she's less than dead."

Trygg sniffed at it for a few seconds, then looked up at Nick as if to say, "Got it."

Nick walked to the edge of the woods, then turned and looked back. He pointed into the trees and said, "Go find her. If her body's around here, that's where it'll be. Go ahead, girl—take me to her."

But Trygg rose and trotted down the road a little and stood perfectly still, staring into the distant darkness.

Nick walked to the spot and looked around. Trygg was a cadaver dog, not a search-and-rescue dog—she was trained to detect the telltale odor of blood and bone and decomposing human tissue, but the ground seemed undisturbed and Nick saw no sign of fluid or tissue anywhere around.

"What is it, girl? Is there something here—something I can't see?"

Nick hooked a finger through the dog's collar and pulled—Trygg resisted. He tugged harder until the dog reluctantly followed him to the edge of the woods. He led the dog into the trees a little and released her again—she immediately turned and trotted back to the same spot in the clearing, where she again stood staring down the road.

Nick didn't understand. The dog showed no interest in the woods at all, though that was surely the place anyone in his right mind would have chosen to hide a body. He looked down the road—was there something there? If so, he would have surely passed it on the way up. He walked down the road a little but still saw nothing. He turned to the dog and made a big shrugging gesture with both hands.

"I don't get it," he said. "There's nothing here—at least nothing I can see. What are you trying to tell me?"

Then he remembered something: The "alert" that the dog was trained to perform whenever she detected the presence of remains was to lie down—that was her way of communicating a find. But Trygg was standing, and suddenly Nick understood what the dog was telling him: *There's nothing here. I detect no presence of death.*

Nick heaved a sigh of relief. *She could still be alive.*

But his relief was short-lived. Where was she now? Alena had obviously been taken away by force, but not enough force to draw blood—Trygg would have detected it. That meant she was alive and relatively unharmed when she was taken—but Nick knew that was no guarantee of continued health and well-being. Alena wasn't a kidnapping victim; no one intended to exchange her for ransom. She had been taken for the same reason that her father had been killed—because of her ability to find the dead. Whoever took her wanted her dead, and they were probably just looking for a better place to dump the body.

Nick sat down and looked at the dog. "You saw the guy who took her, didn't you? I wish you could tell me who it was. You keep staring down this road—does that mean they left together? A fat lot of good that does me; I need to know where they are now."

Cui bono? he thought—a Latin phrase that means "Who stands to gain?" Who else would want Alena dead? Who had something to gain from her death—or something to lose if she kept on living?

He thought about Agnes again, and he thought about the scrapbook.

He jumped up from the ground and ran into the trailer. He searched the countertops and end tables until he found the keys to Alena's truck. As he was about to leave, he noticed a small peg rack on the wall beside the door. Four wooden pegs projected from it, each one holding a brightly colored bandanna printed in a distinct pattern. Nick stopped and looked at them—then swept up all four and ran for the truck.

37

Victoria Braden sat at her office desk with the door securely locked. It was very late, and she had an exhausting agenda the next day, but she couldn't tear herself away from the stack of photocopies that lay on her desk.

She'd been over them at least a dozen times and there was nothing new to find in their contents, but still she kept reading them again—like a man staring at an X-ray that revealed a malignant tumor. She shuddered at the realization of what these pieces of paper implied; she trembled at the thought of what would happen if it ever became public knowledge. The photocopies from the first scrapbook—the one that revealed her true background and identified the old librarian as her biological mother—she could survive that revelation. But this—this would mean the end of everything she had worked for: the election; the presidency; the White House—everything.

Through the office door she heard the main doorbell ring once, followed by an insistent knock. She looked at her watch. Who in the world would be visiting Bradenton at this hour? A few seconds later she heard the knock again, even louder this time. She listened for the sound of the dead bolt unlatching and the hinges squeaking open, followed by the sound of Chris's deep voice dealing with this arrogant intrusion. It never came.

But the knock came again—and this time it was almost pounding.

She immediately gathered the photocopies and dropped them into a desk drawer, then shut the drawer and locked it with a brass key; she tugged on the drawer pull twice to make certain it was secure. She went to her office door and unlocked it; she opened it a few inches and peered out. A second later she saw the foyer light switch on, and she saw Johnny in his bathrobe and pajamas headed for the door. The sight of the soon-to-be president of the United States answering his own door in the middle of the night made her feel indignant; in another month the Secret Service would be crawling all over this place, and no one would get near that door without credentials and a full security clearance—but until then all they had was Chris.

Chris—he wasn't even a decent security guard, and he expected to be a player in the big game? What a joke. Victoria had made a few mistakes along the way, and Chris was definitely one of them; but she had always learned from her mistakes and moved on—that's what it took to survive in Washington. And Victoria was a survivor; she had learned her lesson; she had moved on, and she wouldn't make that mistake again.

But where was Chris tonight? She wondered—but part of her didn't want to know.

Across the foyer she saw the door open and a man stepped into the doorway—a man she recognized. He was wearing large glasses that flashed white in the bright foyer light. Beside him was a dog—a dog with only three legs.

She wrapped her robe tighter and stepped out into the foyer.

"We need to talk," she heard the man say to her husband.

"This is completely unacceptable," the senator replied. "I told you never to come here again. Now you get out of here before I—"

Both men stopped and looked at her as she approached.

"Victoria, you needn't concern yourself with this. I was just telling Dr. Polchak to—"

"It's all right, Johnny," she said. "I don't think Dr. Polchak would have come here at this hour unless it was very important." She glanced at Nick and froze; tucked under his left arm was a large leather scrapbook. She stared at it for a few seconds, then looked up at him.

Nick met her eyes and nodded. "*Very* important. In fact, it's a matter of life and death."

"Very well then," the senator said, stepping aside to allow Nick to enter. "We'll talk in my study—but if you don't mind, leave that ugly cur outside. What a pathetic-looking creature."

"I'd like to keep her with me," Nick replied. "She's a service dog."

The senator grimaced. "A service dog? What service could that mongrel possibly provide?"

"She's sort of a seeing-eye dog. She picks up things that I have trouble spotting."

They moved to the senator's office and took seats—the senator in his usual captain's chair, and Nick and Victoria across from him. The dog sat quietly on Nick's left.

"Now what's this all about?" the senator demanded.

Nick held up the scrapbook and looked at Victoria. "Do you know what this is, Mrs. Braden?"

"I'm not sure I do. May I see it?"

Nick handed it across.

Victoria set the scrapbook in her lap and slowly turned the pages without changing expression. She recognized the documents immediately. It was the same scrapbook her mother had shown her at the Endor library—but how did Polchak get it?

When she finished she looked up at Nick and said pleasantly, "Yes, I'm familiar with its contents. Why do you ask?"

"Is your husband familiar with its contents too?"

She felt a quick twist in her gut but managed to conceal it perfectly. "It's just a bit of family trivia. I'm not sure John would be interested."

"It's a little more than 'trivia,' Mrs. Braden."

The senator turned to his wife. "What have you got there, darling?"

Victoria closed the scrapbook and smiled at her husband. "Just a few old family mementos that were presented to me during my visit to Endor. Nothing of interest, John—I'll tell you about it later if you like."

"A man was murdered tonight," Nick said. "Danny Flanagan—the FBI agent in charge of the investigation at the Patriot Center."

Braden sat up straighter. "Murdered? How? Where?"

"At the Endor Regional Library, just a couple of hours ago."

Victoria felt a wave of nausea.

"How do you know this?" Braden asked.

"I was there. I found the killer preparing to dispose of Danny's body."

"Is the killer in custody?"

"Yes. We'll have a full confession soon."

"Has a motive been established for this terrible deed?"

"A very clear one."

Victoria's face felt hot and she wondered if it showed. Polchak's answers weren't answers at all—they were assaults, specifically designed to prod her for a response. She kept her eyes fixed on her husband, but she could feel Polchak staring at her from the side.

The senator hesitated for an instant before asking his next question: "Is this murder connected in any way to the investigation at the Patriot Center?"

"Your compassion for Danny is touching," Nick said. "His mother lives in Lexington and he's survived by two married sisters—in case you're interested. His skull was smashed in with a baseball bat, by the way."

"Victoria and I will convey our sincere condolences," Braden said. "We're not without compassion, Dr. Polchak. We both liked Danny very much, but you have to understand the larger circumstances here. The situation at the Patriot Center is potentially explosive; I need to know about any event that could have bearing on it."

Nick nodded. "You're right, Senator—you deserve to know." He looked directly at Victoria. "Don't you think he deserves to know?"

Victoria turned and looked at Nick's face; his umber eyes, magnified by the thick lenses that covered them, darted about like a pair of synchronized swimmers. Victoria was used to being stared at by men—but not like this. These eyes were different; they moved over her, through her, watching the way she sat and moved and even the way the muscles shifted under her skin. Polchak made her feel like a specimen on a microscope slide. His questions were more than simple queries; they were like jabs from a metal probe that he systematically administered while he watched to see which way the specimen would crawl. Polchak knew the contents of the scrapbook, and he knew that she did too; he was offering her the chance to admit it rather than have it exposed through awkward confrontation. But it was more than politeness or nobility; he was testing to see how much her husband already knew—and what she might be trying to protect.

Before she could reply, they were interrupted by a knock on the office door. It was Chris; he poked his head in and said, "I spotted a truck outside. Is everything okay in here?"

"Where have you been?" the senator demanded. "You're supposed to be a security guard. What exactly are we paying you for, anyway?"

"Sorry. I was out—I had an errand to run. I thought you two would be in bed by now."

"We were, until Dr. Polchak here decided to pay us a visit."

Chris stepped into the room and looked at Nick.

Victoria watched Chris's face. It showed surprise—alarm—appre-hension. *Fool*—he was giving away way too much information, and Polchak wouldn't miss a thing. Even she felt exposed by those eyes of his, and her composure was almost perfect—Chris must have looked like a fish flopping on the floor.

The senator glared at Chris. "You're interrupting a very sensitive conversation. Now if you don't mind—"

"Let him stay," Victoria said. "Chris is our chief of security after all—at least for another few weeks. I think this issue involves our security, don't you?"

Braden looked at his wife doubtfully, but she gave him a reassuring nod. Chris's interruption was a godsend; she couldn't be expected to reveal family secrets with a low-level employee in the room. Besides, she didn't know how far Polchak was intending to go with this, and Chris's imposing physical presence might serve to remind Polchak of what could happen if things got too far out of hand.

"Pull up a chair," the senator grumbled reluctantly. "But do us all a favor and keep your mouth shut."

Chris dragged up a chair equidistant between Braden and his wife and sat down.

All of them stared at Nick.

"Who murdered Danny Flanagan?" the senator asked.

"An eighty-year-old woman named Agnes. She's the head librarian in Endor."

Chris jerked forward in his chair. *"What?"*

Victoria turned on him before he could say another word. "I believe my husband told you to shut up. If you wish to remain in the room, *do so.*"

Chris slumped back with a look of astonishment on his face.

"An eighty-year-old woman," Braden said. "I find that unbelievable."

"So did four other men—and one woman. That's probably how she was able to sneak up on them: Nobody expected a grandma to pack such a wallop."

"Are you saying this woman is responsible for other murders as well?"

"That's right. We found three of her victims buried on top of other graves at the Patriot Center. The fourth we found near a lake outside Endor. The woman—well, we found her *in* the lake."

The senator blanched. "The Patriot Center? Then this old woman—"

"Is your serial killer. I'm afraid so, Senator—she murdered each of them over a period of about forty years. She apparently dug the holes and buried them herself; great little gardener, that one."

"But—why? What in the world did she have to gain?"

Nick slowly turned and looked at Victoria. "Do you want to take that one, or should I?"

Victoria was trapped; the best she could do was to postpone—to get Johnny alone where the issue would be simpler to defuse and the man would be easier to handle. "I'll deal with it," she said. "But if you don't mind, I'd like to ask you to leave first. This topic is very personal—I'm sure you understand."

"I need to ask you something first," Nick said.

Braden cut in. "We'll be more than happy to answer any—"

"Your wife," Nick said bluntly. "I need to ask her."

"Dr. Polchak, I assure you that anything you can learn from my wife you can also—"

"John," Victoria said firmly. "Go ahead, Dr. Polchak. Ask your question."

"A woman disappeared tonight—I'm trying to find her, and I think you might be able to help."

"Who is this woman?"

"Her name is Alena Savard. She lives alone in the mountains above Endor. She's the one people call 'the witch.'"

Braden leaned forward in his chair. "The Witch of Endor? Danny told us about this woman—the one who found all the graves at the Patriot Center. Is she in some way connected to—"

"John. *Please.*" Victoria kept her eyes on Nick, but she could feel Chris tensing like a coiled spring beside her. "I've heard about this woman, but mostly through rumors—I doubt that much of what I've heard is true. I've never met her personally."

"She was kidnapped a couple of hours ago—taken from her trailer by force."

"How terrible. How can I help?"

Nick paused. "I thought you might have some idea where she is."

"Me? How would I possibly know that?"

Nick glanced down at the scrapbook in her lap.

She nodded with her eyes. "Do you think this woman's disappearance is related to the deaths of those other people?"

"I think Alena Savard was kidnapped for the same reason the others were killed—to keep something secret."

"But you said the old librarian was responsible for all those deaths."

"That's right—and that's what I can't figure out. There was a fourth body discovered at the Patriot Center, remember? Only Agnes wasn't responsible for that one—that body was two hundred years old. Something else is going on here, Mrs. Braden, and I was hoping you could help me understand what it is. Someone else besides Agnes has a secret to keep—a very old one. I need to know what—"

Nick suddenly stopped; he turned and looked down at the floor beside him, then quickly looked around the room.

"Is something wrong, Dr. Polchak?"

"My dog—where's my dog?"

"Right here," Chris said. The dog was stretched out on the carpet beside him; Chris slumped down low in his chair, allowing one arm to dangle down over the side, casually stroking the dog's back.

Nick stared at the dog, then at Chris.

"Riddick!" the senator shouted. "Don't you know any better than to touch a seeing-eye dog? You're distracting the animal from its duties!"

Chris shoved at Trygg with his toe, but the dog refused to move. "I can't help it—the old mutt just came over and flopped down beside me."

"It's okay," Nick said. "She's just friendly, that's all." He pulled off his glasses and began to rub at the bridge of his nose.

Victoria watched him. Something was wrong, but she had no idea what. Polchak suddenly seemed flustered, as if something unexpected had just taken place. He was covering his eyes, taking time to think; something was going on in that mind of his that he didn't want to reveal.

A few seconds later he slid his glasses back onto his nose and looked up. "Mrs. Braden, do you have any information at all about the whereabouts of Alena Savard?"

"I'm sorry," Victoria said. "I sincerely hope you find her."

Polchak stood up and started for the door—then stopped and looked back at the dog. "Trygg—come!"

The dog looked up at him but didn't obey. Nick walked over to the dog, hooked a finger under her collar, and pulled; only then did the dog rise to its feet and follow.

"Not a very obedient animal," Victoria said.

"She's a female—they can be unpredictable. Sorry to bother you all. I'll be going now."

"Wait," the senator called after him. "The Patriot Center—the investigation—what happens now?"

"Ask your wife," Nick said. "The two of you will have to work that out together."

Nick let himself out.

They watched until the door shut behind him.

"What a nutcase," Chris said. "If you ask me, he's—"

"Get out," Braden commanded.

Chris got up and left without any further word, leaving the senator and his wife staring at one another across the empty room.

38

The minute the truck was out of sight of the house, Nick pulled off the road and turned off his headlights. He slumped forward and rested his head on the steering wheel. His mind scrambled, trying to formulate his next logical move—but a terrible realization kept creeping in, crowding out his other thoughts: *The dog was lying down.*

Alena was already dead.

Adrenaline flooded his system; his entire body trembled and he felt like vomiting.

Trygg was lying at Riddick's feet—that was her alert. She detected the odor of death on Riddick's hands or shoes or clothing. Riddick admitted that he was out earlier this evening; he said he had an errand to run, an errand that the Bradens seemed to know nothing about. But wait a minute: Only the senator asked about Riddick's absence, not Victoria—did she know where he went? Apparently the senator knows nothing about the scrapbook and his wife's true identity; maybe she thought she could keep it that way. Maybe it's not just Mommy's little secret anymore—maybe it's her daughter's too now, and maybe Riddick is helping her keep it. But would Victoria be willing to go as far as her mother did?

Nick twisted around and looked back through the rear window into the camper shell; he saw Trygg balancing on three legs in the center of the truck bed, staring back at him. He looked at the dog, and for the first time Nick thought he could read the meaning in the animal's doleful eyes. It was as if she was saying, "Where are we going? That was the guy back there."

"I know," Nick said aloud, "and we'll go back for him—I promise."

He shook his head; he was talking to a dog. It made no sense—or maybe it did. Trygg reminded Nick of the child prodigies he had read about in studies—the one-year-olds who had memorized the faces of all the U.S. presidents before they had even learned to talk. That was Trygg's problem: The dog knew far more than she was able to communicate. She had detected the scent of death, but was it Alena's scent or someone else's? The dog was trained to detect the telltale odor of tissue and fluid and blood—but which one was it? Alena once told him that a dog's chief ability was to distinguish between scents; where a man smells only beef stew, a dog detects the individual odors of carrots, potatoes, and meat. But which is which? Only the dog knows, and she has no way to tell. Did Trygg detect the odor of Alena's dead body already beginning to putrefy? Or was it only her blood—in which case Alena might be wounded but still alive? The dog had no language to communicate the things that she undoubtedly knew.

But the dog could find Alena. She could at least track the scent she had detected on Riddick's shoes or hands or clothing. She could find the source of that scent, and Nick would just have to hope for the best when they found it—and hope they got there before it was too late.

Trygg had picked up the scent of Alena's blood or decomposing body, but there was no scent at Alena's trailer—that meant Alena was alive and probably unharmed when she was taken. Riddick could have killed her and dumped her body anywhere along the way—or he could have brought her here to Bradenton. It was a definite possibility. A human body is a difficult thing to dispose of, and hastily dumping a body in an unfamiliar area is a sure way to have it discovered quickly; bringing it here would give him time to think. There were hundreds of acres of land at Bradenton—plenty of places to bury a body, and all on private land where no one would ever look.

It's worth a try, he assured himself—but he knew that anything is worth a try when you have no other options.

He pulled the truck into a grove of river birches until it was out of sight of the road and then killed the engine. He took a handful of knotted bandannas from the seat beside him and switched on the cab light to examine them. He remembered what Alena had told him: The dog was trained to distinguish four different kinds of remains. The first bandanna was red with a polka-dot pattern—the one Trygg wore at the Patriot Center when she searched for skeletonized remains. Nick set it aside—it wasn't the one they would need here. The second bandanna was green with a checkerboard print—the one Trygg wore when she searched the lake for submerged remains. Nick set that one aside too.

That left only two: an elaborate blue plaid and a bright orange print with a series of wavy black lines. He looked at each of them: *putrefying remains* and *distressed body*. One of them told the dog to search for Alena alive and the other to search for her dead—but he had no idea which was which. And how "distressed" did Alena need to be before the dog could find her? The dog would never find her alive and unharmed; she had to be just less than dead.

He made a random guess—the blue plaid—and stuffed the other bandanna in his pocket.

He climbed from the cab and opened up the back of the truck; Trygg stepped onto the tailgate and silently leaped to the ground. Nick squatted down in front of the dog and held the blue bandanna in front of her face.

"I hope I've got this right," Nick said. "See this? This means we're going to work now. I want you to search for the same scent you just found inside—got it?" He looped the bandanna around the dog's neck and stood up. "We'll circle around behind the house and check the stables and outbuildings first—that's our best bet. He wouldn't have dumped her out in the open and he wouldn't have taken her in the house; he would have hidden her until he figured out what to do next. Come on, let's go."

Nick walked a few yards away but the dog didn't follow. He turned back and said to her, "Look—I know how smart you are, so there's no use playing dumb. If you can detect the scent of table salt in a dilution of one part in ten million, then you can figure out a simple spoken command. Now we don't have time to mess around, so—"

He snapped his fingers once and said, "Come!"

Trygg immediately rose and followed.

Nick nodded with satisfaction. "Your first word. Momma will be so proud."

They stayed in the shadow of the trees as they made a wide arc around the house; Nick could see the lights still burning in Braden's office. He wasn't surprised; by introducing that scrapbook he had undoubtedly kicked off a discussion that would last well into the night. He wondered how Braden was taking the news that his made-in-heaven wife was a little more down-to-earth than he thought; he wondered how the senator's spinmeisters would reveal to the public that the future First Lady's mom was a serial killer responsible for multiple murders, including the murder of a federal agent. And these weren't genteel and ladylike murders either—not just a sprinkle of arsenic on the pot roast or a few sleeping pills dissolved in the tea. No—these were bat-bashing, skull-cracking, corpse-dragging murders—the kind that stick in people's minds for a long, long time.

The Braden campaign seemed doomed—it seemed impossible to Nick that anyone could recover from that kind of negative publicity— but if anyone could manage it, the beautiful Bradens could. There was a lot of money on the line in a presidential race and a lot of powerful people were involved. The Bradens had probably already made a few calls, and somewhere in Washington right now an army of strategists was already calculating the best way to distance the Bradens from these unfortunate events. *Politicians are survivors*, Nick thought. In his experience they were harder to kill than a cockroach, probably because they share a common characteristic: When the lights go on, they disappear.

It took fifteen minutes to circle around behind the house and come up behind the first of the outbuildings—a rustic old grain silo that had apparently been preserved to keep Bradenton looking like the working farm it hadn't been in years. If the silo was empty it would be an excellent place to hide a body—but Trygg circled it once and simply looked up at Nick.

Next they came to a large tack shed. Nick pulled up a handful of grass and tossed it into the air to test the direction of the wind; they approached from downwind to allow Trygg to pick up any scent that might be drifting in the breeze, but the dog made no alert. Nick found the door unlocked and they entered; they searched the interior carefully but found nothing there.

They worked their way from building to building, allowing the dog to sniff every crack and crevice for any indication of scent. Nick began to wonder if he was doing something wrong; maybe the dog needed some further instruction—maybe she thought they were just out for a walk. But then he remembered the scene in Braden's office, where Trygg simply picked up the scent, walked over to Riddick, and lay down with no instruction from Nick at all. *She knows what she's doing*, Nick told himself. *This is what she was trained to do. All I need to do is stay out of her way and watch.*

Or so he hoped.

Next they came to the long stables and Nick hesitated at the open door. He could hear the sounds of the horses breathing and stamping in their stalls. He knew the horses would quickly pick up Trygg's scent, and he knew they would find the scent unfamiliar—but he didn't know how they would respond. The last thing he wanted was an entire stable of horses panicking and bolting from their stalls; that would bring everyone in the house running, and he would have a difficult time explaining his presence there—especially to Riddick. He took Trygg around the outside of the building instead and let her sniff at the walls and foundation; he hoped that the generous cracks in the board-and-batten siding would allow any scent to pass through. Trygg took her time, searching the entire building carefully, but once again found nothing.

Not far from the house was an old hay barn, clad in siding weathered gray from age and the bleaching effects of the sun. The barn had twin doors that were framed in flat wooden trim and crisscrossed with a decorative X; each door was supported by a pair of metal wheels at the top that allowed it to be rolled aside. Nick shoved hard against one of the doors and it slowly began to give way—but the rusted wheels made a loud groaning squeak and he stopped. He looked back at the house and held his breath—Riddick could easily have heard the sound from this distance—but he saw no porch light switch on or door swing open, so he tried the barn door again, pushing it a little at a time, easing it open until there was a space just wide enough for the two of them to slip through.

He heard a skittering sound at his feet; he looked down and saw half a dozen startled barn rats scatter in every direction. He quickly reached out to silence the dog, but Trygg just stared at the rats disinterestedly, as if they were nothing but dust balls blowing across the floor. To Nick's surprise he was able to see reasonably well; the old plank roof was so thoroughly split and cracked that it allowed long shafts of moonlight to illuminate the floor, and the dust that lingered in the air made the beams of light appear almost solid—like the columns of a great stone building.

He looked around the barn; it appeared to have been abandoned long ago—just another decorative element on the Bradens' faux farm. The stalls that lined the walls were empty except for a crumbling hay rake and a few other relics rusting from decades of disuse. The floor was compacted dirt covered by a thin layer of scattered straw. The walls were bare except for the occasional coil of rope or dust-encrusted oil lantern; there seemed to be no bins or closets of any kind—no place where a body might be concealed—but Nick still allowed the dog time to wander the barn and sniff each corner thoroughly.

Nothing.

They squeezed out the door and Nick carefully eased it shut again. He looked around the grounds; there were only a couple of outbuildings left and he was beginning to lose hope. Maybe he was wrong; maybe Riddick wouldn't have taken a chance on bringing Alena here. Maybe he did dump her body somewhere along the way, knowing that it would eventually be discovered but counting on the fact that no one would connect the murder to him. Riddick was probably right—there was no physical evidence that would implicate him. Nick's rental car, wherever it turned up, would probably be found wiped clean of prints—and there would be no evidence at Alena's trailer except for the tire tracks from Nick's own vehicle. There were bullets that could be recovered from the two dead dogs, but Riddick wasn't stupid enough to hang on to the gun—they'd never get a ballistics match. What was Nick supposed to tell the authorities—"I know he did it because a dog told me"? He could level the accusation, he could try to raise suspicion, but he knew none of it would stick.

He walked slowly toward the next of the outbuildings with Trygg by his side. There was nothing else to do but finish what he had started—but he had the sinking feeling that he was finished already.

Suddenly his shadow appeared on the ground before him in a field of brilliant blue—someone had switched on a security light back at the house. Nick snapped his fingers and took off running, hoping that the dog would follow and that he could reach the outbuilding before they were spotted. Just as he ducked into the shadow of a small shedrow barn, he heard a door swing open behind him. He pressed back against the side of the barn and peeked around the corner; in the distance he saw Riddick exit the Braden house and walk across the grass toward the old abandoned hay barn. Nick adjusted his glasses and looked carefully—he had nothing in his hands.

As Riddick approached the front of the barn, Nick lost sight of him; the barn itself was blocking his view, but he could hear the squeaking of the metal wheels atop the doors—Riddick was opening them. He was apparently entering the barn—but why? Of all the outbuildings Riddick might be expected to visit, the hay barn would be last on Nick's list—there was nothing inside. Nick did a quick mental review of the interior of the barn and the objects he had seen there—he could think of nothing that might interest the man. Then why was he there?

He surely went to the barn for some reason: either to drop something off, or to bring something back, or to pay a visit to something inside—or possibly some*one*. The thought gave Nick a glimmer of hope. He'd know soon enough; he sat down and waited, making sure Trygg stayed deep in the shadows behind him.

Minutes passed.

Nick waited—but as he waited he found his hope slipping away. He had already been inside the barn, and there was no place to hide a body there. Even worse, Trygg had already searched it too—and one of the finest cadaver dogs on the face of the earth had found no trace of Alena Savard.

39

Alena opened her eyes but saw nothing—everything around her was black. She couldn't be certain that her eyes were even open; she blinked hard twice to make sure. Maybe she was dreaming; maybe she was still asleep and only imagining herself waking up—but when she felt the throbbing pain in her skull she knew this was no dream.

She was lying on her right side with her arms pulled tight behind her back. Her right shoulder ached terribly and she tried to twist her arm out from under her body—but when she did she found that her wrists were bound together with some kind of sticky tape. She lifted her head and felt bits of grass and debris clinging to her cheek; she seemed to be lying on a hard dirt floor. When she moved her head, the pain in her skull became excruciating, radiating from the crown downward in agonizing waves. She felt her stomach begin to heave, but when she tried to open her mouth to gag she realized that another strip of tape prevented her lips from parting. The thought of choking to death on her own vomit horrified her, and she put her head down again and lay perfectly still, breathing slowly through her nose.

She tested her legs—they were taped together at the ankles. Her right side was almost numb and she wanted to try to sit up, but not until she was sure that her nausea was under control. She lay still for a few more seconds, steeling her nerve and steadying her stomach—then all at once swung her legs around and brought herself up to a sitting position. She almost fell back again; it felt as if someone had driven a railroad spike through the center of her brain. She sat quietly sobbing with her head hunched over her knees, praying for the pain to stop and for someone to help.

Where am I?

She tried to think back, but her mind was still thick and muddled by the pain. She could remember sitting in her trailer; she remembered hearing the sound of a car outside—Nick's car. But it wasn't Nick inside the car, it was a stranger—a man she had never seen before. Acheron attacked—the man pulled out a gun—he fired! She remembered now: Acheron was dead—no, *two* of her dogs were dead. The memories came flooding back all at once and she shut her eyes hard to fight back the grief.

She remembered running toward the kennels, the sound of heavy footsteps behind her, then a flash of light and a searing pain in her head—a pain that was even worse now. The man must have hit her with something—maybe his gun—then tied her up and brought her here. But where was *here*? Where was the man now? And what was he planning to do to her next?

Nick—where are you?

She stared into the blackness around her; she could see now that the room was not completely dark—faint, pencil-thin shafts of light radiated down from above. She looked up; the flat ceiling looked to be about eight feet over her head, and it didn't appear to be one solid surface. Dots and dashes of light penetrated the ceiling everywhere, suggesting that the ceiling was constructed of strips of wood with thin gaps in between.

She tucked her taped ankles under her thighs and rocked forward onto her knees, then with great difficulty struggled to her feet, tottering precariously as she fought to keep her balance. Now she knew how Trygg must feel. Standing was difficult one limb short, and it was even more difficult to move—she had to travel in short broken hops, and each time her feet hit the floor a blast of pain echoed through her skull.

With just a few short hops she bumped into a wall. She turned her face to the side and felt the surface with her cheek; it was made of smooth wooden planks. She turned her shoulder to the wall and shoved against it, but the wall was solid—it didn't budge an inch. She began to hop forward, rubbing her shoulder and arm along the wall as she went, hoping to find a window or a door—some way she might get out. In just a few steps she came to a corner; she turned and followed the next wall, then the next, until she was back where she started again. She leaned her back against the wall to rest, drenched in sweat and breathing hard through her nose. She had hoped to find a nail or a splinter projecting from the wall somewhere, something sharp enough to allow her to cut through the tape that bound her wrists and ankles, but she found none. It was a small, square room, no more than ten feet on a side, and there were no doors or windows anywhere. No way in, and no way out.

How did I get in here?

She looked up again, and this time she noticed bits of dust and dirt drifting down in the blue-white shafts of light like tiny angels descending from heaven. Suddenly she understood: She was looking up at the floor. This wasn't a room at all—it was some kind of pit.

She slowly slid down the wall until she rested on the dirt floor again. There was nothing she could do other than wait—but she was terrified at the thought of what she might be waiting for. There was no sense letting fear get the better of her, though; she tried to calm herself, deliberately slowing her breathing and trying to project her thoughts to a better place.

Then she heard a loud rolling squeak from somewhere above her—like the sound of a closet door that had slipped off its track. She pulled her feet under her and struggled upright again; she looked up and waited. A moment later she heard heavy footsteps on the wooden planks over her head; the steady shafts of light were suddenly shattered into a thousand bits of confetti, and pieces of dirt and straw drifted down on her head. Someone was standing directly over her now. She rammed her shoulder against the wall but it made no sound at all; she jumped up and down and stamped her bound feet, but the dirt and straw absorbed the impact. On the third jump she came down askew and lost her balance, falling silently onto the floor. She looked up and saw the figure's shadow moving away—he was leaving! In panic she filled her lungs with air and emitted the loudest muffled scream her sealed lips would allow—a kind of piercing groan that savaged her vocal cords but made dismally little sound. She did it again and again until her voice began to fail—and then she saw the ceiling begin to move.

It lifted from one end, opening like the lid of a lunchbox; dirt and straw rained down everywhere, and she shut her eyes and turned her face away.

"You're awake," a man's voice said. "I was beginning to wonder if I hit you harder than I thought—not that it matters much."

She instantly recognized the voice—it was the man in Nick's car. She squinted and looked up at him; she could see nothing but a towering silhouette standing and staring down at her.

He squatted and dropped down into the room beside her.

Alena scooted away until she collided with the wall; she felt as though a python had just been dropped into the pit.

"It's an old threshing floor, in case you're wondering. Sorry about the rats. Have you bumped into any yet? Sorry—maybe I shouldn't have mentioned them."

She used the wall to struggle back to her feet again.

The man stepped closer and looked her up and down, then held up one finger and wiggled it. "Let's see the head."

She turned away.

He grabbed her by the jaw and jerked her closer. He twisted her head to one side and ran his fingers roughly over the crown of her skull—it hurt terribly.

He rubbed his fingers together. "You're okay—not even a drop of blood." He turned her head forward again and brushed the hair back from her face. "The Witch of Endor," he said. "So how come people think you're a witch? You look pretty much like any other woman to me—better than most."

Alena wished she could drive a knee up into his groin, but her ankles were bound tight. All she could do was twist her face away from him and shove one shoulder into his chest, hoping he got the idea.

He released her and let her fall back against the wall.

"Your boyfriend was here looking for you, in case you're interested. You know—the weird guy with the funny glasses. He stopped by a few minutes ago—that's why I thought I'd better check on you—but you look okay to me."

She turned her back to him and nodded to her bound wrists.

"Sorry," he said. He walked to the wall and looked up; he squatted down a little and leaped, grabbing the ledge and pulling himself smoothly up out of the pit and onto the barn floor. "By the way, your boyfriend had one of your dogs with him. A three-legged dog and a blind man—what's the deal with you and cripples anyway? If you ask me, a woman like you could do better—but hey, it's none of my business."

He dusted himself off and looked down at her. "Look, if it means anything to you, this is nothing personal. You just stuck your nose where it didn't belong, that's all. You'll stay here for another couple of hours. Things happened kind of fast tonight, and I need time to figure out what to do with you next. Might as well get some sleep—there sure isn't much else to do."

He stepped to the side and lifted one end of the threshing floor, swinging it over and down until only a small opening remained—then he stopped and stuck his head inside. "One more thing," he said. "That piece of tape over your mouth is supposed to keep you quiet. If I ever hear you trying to make noise like that again, I'll have to kill you—understand?"

She nodded.

He dropped the floor into place with a resounding thud.

Alena covered her face against the dust again. She heard the sound of dirt being scattered over the planks above her, and the pit grew darker as the penetrating shafts of light became thinner and fewer. She heard the sound of receding footsteps, then the groaning squeak of the door, and then silence.

Her legs gave way and she sank to the floor.

A three-legged dog! Nick is here and he brought Trygg with him! He's searching for me—but how will he ever find me? What if he was already here? What if he came when I was still unconscious? What if he already gave up and left? And what if he hasn't searched this barn yet—what if he still comes by? How will I know it's him and not the other man—the one who said he'd kill me if I make another sound? I can't even scream—I can't take the chance.

Alena felt a knot tightening in the back of her throat. She was beginning to understand the full extent of her dilemma: Nick was searching for her, but he brought the wrong dog. Trygg was a cadaver dog, not a search-and-rescue dog—she was trained only to detect the scent of death. "Not even a drop of blood," the man said—that meant there was no scent for the dog to find. Nick and Trygg could have already searched this barn; Nick could have easily missed an old dirt-covered threshing floor, and Trygg could have walked right over it without ever finding the scent—at least not the scent of death, and she would alert on nothing else.

Alena stopped. *Trygg is here to find me, but she has nothing to find. There's only one answer: I have to give her something to find.*

I have to bleed.

She struggled to her feet again. If there was only some way she could scrape the skin from her knees or elbows, but it was impossible. She couldn't swing her legs and she couldn't bend her arms at all—she'd never be able to generate enough force to break the skin. She rubbed her shoulder against the wall again. She felt no cracks or splinters at all—the boards had been polished smooth through years of use. She could rub up against them all day and never take off the skin.

She turned and faced the wall. There was only one other option—her nose. She had to drive her face into the wall hard enough to cause her nose to bleed.

She slowly leaned forward until her forehead touched the wall, measuring the distance. She straightened again, cocking her head back a little to make sure her nose would take the full brunt of the force—then she stopped. The throbbing in her skull felt like a knife stabbing into her brain—how could she purposely ram her face into a wall? The pain would be unbearable.

But she had no choice.

She stood there for a full minute, summoning up all of her anger and determination—then she squeezed her eyes tight and slammed her head like a hammer against the wooden surface.

She felt an agonizing blast of pain and saw a brilliant flash of light—then she felt herself falling backward in space. She hit the ground head-long but never felt the impact—she seemed to be moving in slow motion, as if she were lowering herself onto a feather bed. She found herself lying on her back in the dirt a few seconds later—or was it a few minutes, or even an hour? What if Nick had come looking for her while she was unconscious? The thought made her frantic. She tried to focus her thoughts, but every heartbeat sent a mind-numbing pulse of agony through her head—and now her face hurt too.

She turned her head to the left and rubbed her face against her shoulder. She felt nothing—no steady trickle of fluid leaking from her nose. There was no blood—either the force had been insufficient or she had misjudged the angle. She thought about struggling to her feet and trying again—but when she did, she burst into tears and lay weeping on the floor.

She wasn't sure she could even get to her feet again without passing out—and even if she did, how could she ever bring herself to drive her face into the wall with even more force than before? The misery in her head would force her to pull back a little more each time she tried, and then she would only be slowly beating herself to death.

Maybe that's the answer, she thought. *Kill myself and let Trygg find my body.* That's what the dog was trained to do, after all—that's what she was good at. If Alena could just will herself to die, then Trygg could find her putrefying remains—or maybe she could drown herself and let Trygg find her submerged remains. That's it—she could just drown in her own tears, and then—

My tears.

Alena turned her head and rubbed her face against her shoulder again. This time she felt thin fluid draining freely from her nose, but it still wasn't blood. It was tears—the by-product of a distressed victim.

Alena couldn't make herself bleed—she couldn't even get to her feet—but she could amplify her distress. She could let her mind run wild; she could call up every personal demon and revisit every dark corner of her tortured life until she radiated terror and pain. If Nick and Trygg had visited the barn while Alena was lying peacefully unconscious there would have been no scent of distress—but she was awake now, and she could change that.

It was worth a chance. No—it was her *only* chance.

The storm is all around me and I'm running through the woods. Somewhere ahead of me I hear a bellowing yelp and then silence. I come to a clearing and find the body of a beautiful dog lying on its side. I sink to my knees beside the dog; I lift up its beautiful head and hold it in my lap, stroking its soft fur and sobbing. Who would do this? Why would they take him away from me? Don't they know that I'm all alone now—that I have no one else in all the world?

She clenched her fists and her body began to stretch as tight as a wire; sweat began to run down her forehead and form shallow salt pools in her eyes.

I hear a branch snap and look up. Someone is there, watching me. I take off running again, running for the trailer—but something is running behind me, matching me stride for stride, slowly gaining on me, reaching out its fingers—

I stop. I turn. I face the thing and I look into its eyes—

The people of Endor—the ignorance, the prejudice, the stories that make my blood run cold. The loneliness—the fear—the awful sounds that come from the woods at night. The dreams—the hopes that never come true. Daddy, why? Where did you go, and why don't you ever come back? My beautiful Acheron dead on the ground. The skull of my father staring up at me from a flimsy folding table—

Alena writhed in the dirt as heat from her anguished body caused molecules of scent to lift from her skin and slowly drift away.

40

Nick watched from the shadows of the shedrow barn and waited for Riddick to reappear. After several agonizing minutes he finally heard the squeak of the hay barn doors again and saw Riddick emerge from behind the barn and head back toward the house. Nick adjusted his glasses and looked carefully: Riddick had nothing in his hands. He had taken nothing with him when he went to the barn, and apparently there was nothing he went there to retrieve. So why would he visit an empty barn, especially at this hour of the night?

There was only one way to find out.

He waited until Riddick disappeared into the house and the security light switched off again, returning the entire area to darkness. He took Trygg by the collar and pulled her to her feet, then started for the barn. He had to take another look—Riddick's visit to the barn was like a neon arrow pointing to the site. But what was the point? Nick had searched there already and the barn was empty—and to make matters worse, Trygg had already searched there too. Why would she pick up a scent this time that she hadn't detected before?

Nick stopped and looked at the dog.

He reached into his pocket and fished out the other bandanna—the orange one with the wavy black lines. He looked at the blue plaid bandanna that hung around the dog's neck—what was it telling the dog to do? What kind of body was it telling her to concentrate on, living or dead—and what if it was the wrong kind?

He thought about the encounter in the senator's office again; Trygg had alerted on Riddick's feet without wearing any bandanna at all.

Maybe that was the answer—maybe he should just take the blue bandanna off and let the dog do what she did before.

But would she do what she did before? Could he be sure of that? This was different; this was a formal search situation and the bandannas were part of her training—would leaving them off just tell the dog that she didn't really need to try? The dog was probably confused already—was it worth taking a chance on confusing her any more?

Then he remembered—beside the lake, when the dog lay down by the water—she wasn't wearing any bandanna at all. There was nothing to tell her to search for submerged remains, and yet she did—all on her own. Now he understood: The bandannas told the dog to specialize—to look for one specific scent and ignore all others. Without the bandannas the dog was a generalist, detecting human remains of every type. Nick shook his head. He had been telling Trygg what *not* to look for, and in the process she might have walked right past her own master's body.

He squatted down in front of the dog and took the blue bandanna from around her neck, then tossed both bandannas aside. "You're a free agent now," he whispered. "I want you to search for everything this time—everything, no matter how small. Have you got that?" He looked into the dog's eyes. "C'mon—let's go take a look at an empty barn."

Nick took one final look at the house before quietly rolling the barn door open. He slipped inside again, and this time he closed the door behind him. He looked around the cavernous barn. It looked exactly as it had before; nothing seemed to have changed; nothing seemed to have been moved. For an instant he considered calling out, "Is anybody in here?" but he remembered the proximity of the house and quickly decided against it. He looked down at the dog but had no idea what to tell her to do, so he just snapped his fingers and made a vague "take a look around" gesture with his left hand.

Nick went from stall to stall, carefully searching every dark corner and concealing shadow this time—but there was nothing to find. There were no spaces big enough or dark enough to conceal a human body; if there were he would have spotted them before.

At the end of the barn he found something: an old wooden ladder lying on its side against a wall. *Why would the barn need a ladder unless*—he looked up and saw a small hayloft on the barn's left side. Nick felt an anxious surge of hope; he hurriedly hauled up the ladder and positioned it against the edge of the loft, then climbed up the ladder and looked—but the loft appeared to be completely empty. To make absolutely certain, he climbed up onto the loft and poked his foot into every corner. Nothing—the hayloft was nothing but a vacant platform.

He walked back to the ladder and looked around; from this vantage point he could see every beam and rafter in the barn. He could see the contents of every single stall too, and there was no doubt this time— the barn was empty. He had no idea why Riddick would have chosen to come here in the middle of the night, but apparently it had nothing to do with Alena. He looked down and saw Trygg standing motionless in a shaft of faint moonlight near the center of the barn; apparently she wasn't having any luck either.

Then he noticed something: Trygg was standing in moonlight but she cast no shadow. Nick squinted hard and saw the reason: Trygg wasn't standing at all—she was lying down.

Nick hurried down the ladder. He grabbed the dog by her collar and yanked her to her feet, then dragged her to the opposite side of the barn and released her; she immediately trotted back to the same area, sniffed at the ground, and lay down. Nick went over to the spot and looked at it; the ground under his feet had a different feel here, and the weight of his body made some of the dirt seem to settle in long thin lines. He dropped to his knees, and when he did the lines became even more pronounced.

The floor is hollow!

He bent down and swept the dirt and straw away with his forearm, revealing a series of long wooden planks laid side by side. It was a platform of some kind—a false floor. He continued to clear the dirt away until the entire wooden platform was exposed, then lifted one end and dragged it aside, revealing a deep black pit below. He shoved his head into the opening and blinked, allowing his eyes to adjust to the deeper darkness—and when they did he saw a body lying on its back in the center of the pit.

"Alena!" he whispered.

There was no response.

"Alena, it's me—Nick!"

The body didn't move.

He took the wooden ladder from the hayloft and lowered it into the pit, then scrambled down and knelt beside Alena. He felt her face; it was hot and she was drenched in sweat, but her body was rigid from head to toe as if she were locked in a grand mal seizure—or as if she had died and rigor had set in. Nick placed two fingers under her jaw and checked her carotid just to make sure—he found a pulse. He took her by the shoulders and gently shook her, but she still didn't respond. He gently peeled the tape from her mouth, then rolled her onto her side and freed her wrists and ankles. He laid her on her back again and took her hands, rubbing them and shaking them vigorously.

"Come on, Alena. Come back to me."

She slowly opened her eyes and looked up at him without recognition.

"Hi," he said. "Remember me?"

She reached up and touched his face. "Nick."

"You know, you're a hard woman to locate. I think you take this privacy thing a bit too far."

"How did you ever find me?"

"Trygg found you. Sorry it took so long. It was the bandannas—I couldn't remember which one told her to do what."

"The blue one. It's for 'putrefied remains.' The orange one—that's 'distressed victim.'"

"That explains why we missed you on the first pass—I was telling her to look for the wrong thing. She went right to you this time; lucky thing you were 'in distress.'"

"Yeah. Lucky me." She looked over Nick's shoulder and saw Trygg staring down at her from the edge of the pit. "Nick—that man—he killed Acheron. He hit me—he brought me here—"

"We'll talk about it later," Nick said. "Right now we need to get you out of here. Can you walk?" He helped her to a sitting position.

"My head," she groaned.

Nick gently felt the top of her head. "You've got a real goose egg there, but I don't feel any blood. Look, I'm sorry—I know you don't feel up to this, but we've got to get you out of this barn before Riddick decides to come back again." He helped her to stand and walked her to the ladder, then stayed close behind while she slowly climbed one rung at a time. When they reached the barn floor Alena crawled onto the dirt and sat with her arm around Trygg while Nick replaced the threshing floor and swept dirt over its surface again.

"That should do it," he said, dusting off his hands. "It'll look like no one was here—at least until he opens it up again, and we'd better be long gone by then. Come on, let's get out of here."

Nick eased the barn door open and looked at the house; the interior lights were still burning but he saw no sign of activity. Alena was woozy and wobbly on her feet; Nick kept his arm around her to steady her as they walked. He closed the barn door behind them and looked to the left and right, estimating the shortest distance back to the truck. The way he had come was definitely longer—the shortest route would be to continue in the same direction around the house, past the final outbuilding and along the edge of a field of tall grass. He looked at Alena and pointed; when she nodded they took off, making their way as fast as Alena's aching head would allow.

Fifty yards ahead they passed the final outbuilding—the one that Nick and Trygg didn't have time to search. It was a long, narrow building surrounded by a tall chain-link fence. It looked somehow familiar to Nick, as though he had seen it before or one just like it. He tried to remember, and then it occurred to him.

It was a kennel.

He straightened a little and felt the wind blowing across his face.

It was blowing from left to right; it was blowing toward the kennel.

"Hurry," he said to Alena, no longer bothering to whisper.

"I can't," she groaned. "My head feels like it's going to explode."

"Try," Nick said. "See that building?"

Alena glanced over at it and recognized it immediately; she looked down and watched the movement of the wind through her hair, then looked up at Nick: "Too late."

All at once the kennel erupted with the sound of barking dogs, as if someone had just removed the MUTE on a television turned up to full volume. There were at least a dozen dogs, all howling and yowling and baying in furious protest at the scent of an intruder.

"Do we smell that bad?" Nick asked.

"It's Trygg—she's coming into season."

"Terrific," Nick said. "Right when we pass a fraternity house."

The security light behind the house switched on again and the entire area lit up like a Friday night football field.

"Run!" Nick said. "We've got to make it to that tall grass before he spots us."

"I can't," she said.

"We don't have a choice." They ran side by side with Nick's arm still around her waist; he caught her when she stumbled and dragged her when her legs went limp. They reached the edge of the field just as they heard the door open behind them. They collapsed in the grass and lay panting; Alena hooked one arm around Trygg's neck and pulled the dog down beside her. Nick twisted around and looked out through the tall grass; he could see Riddick standing in the center of the lawn and turning back and forth, searching for the source of the intrusion.

"Stay down," Nick said. "When he goes into the barn to look for you, we'll have to run for it. It'll take a minute or so before he finds out you're gone—maybe we can get to the truck by then."

"Do you think we can make it?"

"We'd better—because he'll be coming after us."

A few seconds later Nick saw Riddick turn and charge across the lawn toward the hay barn. "Get ready," he told Alena.

He watched Riddick throw the barn door open and duck inside; he could hear the piercing shriek of the wheels even above the barking dogs.

"Now!" Nick said, grabbing Alena by the arm and hauling her to her feet.

They stumbled forward through the tall grass. The thick strands wrapping around Alena's ankles made progress exhausting and agonizingly slow. She stumbled more than once, then finally collapsed on all fours and vomited in the grass.

Nick squatted down beside her. "Take a minute—catch your breath."

"Go on without me," she whispered.

"Not a chance."

"I mean it—take Trygg and go."

Nick paused. "You know, I never realized what a whiner you are."

She turned her head and looked at him. "What?"

"Look at Trygg—she's only got three legs, and you don't see her complaining."

"I got hit on the head. It feels like my brains are coming out my ears."

"What a drama queen. Should I send the dog out for an ice pack?"

"You know, you're really starting to make me mad."

"That's the general idea. Can we go now?" Nick poked his head up from the grass and looked back at the barn—still no sign of Riddick. "Let's go—we won't have long."

They started forward again, keeping to the tall grass, working their way past the house and up the road toward the grove of trees where Nick had ditched the truck. Nick glanced back as he ran, watching the barn door for any sign of Riddick; when Riddick finally did appear, Nick dropped into the grass and pulled Alena down with him. "He's back—he knows you're gone and he knows I'm the one who took you. He has to find you again—his life depends on it."

Nick poked his head up just enough to see; he saw Riddick turn to his right and start across the lawn toward the kennels.

Nick turned to Alena. "What kind of dogs are those, anyway? Can you tell by the way they bark?"

She listened. "The big ones are July hounds or English Fell hounds—maybe a Bouvier or two. I hear a PennMaryDel in there—you can always tell their voice. The higher pitches are beagles—why?"

"Are they good trackers?"

"They're foxhounds, Nick—what do you think?"

Nick took her by the arm. "I think we'd better run."

Nick looked at Alena. "Are you sure you should be driving?"

"Do you know these roads as well as I do?"

"No—but if you drive the way you run, we could have a big problem."

"I'll be okay."

The pickup truck sped down the narrow road away from Bradenton; the stacked stone walls that lined both sides of the street looked like nothing but gray streaks of paint in the truck's brilliant headlights. The engine emitted a constant high-pitched whine, and the dashboard rattled and clicked until Nick wondered if the old Toyota would shake itself apart.

He glanced at the speedometer. "How fast will this thing go?"

"I don't know, but it sure beats running."

They had made it safely to the truck before the hounds could reach them; they hurriedly loaded Trygg into the back and sped out of the grove of river birches and left the indignant hounds baying in the moonlight behind them. They had seen no further sign of Riddick, but Nick knew exactly where he was—he was not far behind them, driving just as fast as he could to try to stop them before they could tell anyone what they now knew.

Alena looked in her side mirror. "Is he following us? Can you see him?"

Nick leaned out the passenger window and saw a pair of glowing pinpoints in the distance. "I see headlights," he shouted. "What kind of car was he driving?"

"Beats me—I woke up in a dungeon."

"Well, we should know soon enough."

"Who is he, anyway? What did he want with me?"

"His name is Chris Riddick—he works as a security guard for John and Victoria Braden. He wants to kill you."

"Why?"

"It's a little complicated. There's an old woman who lives in Endor. She's the librarian there—her name is Agnes. Do you know her?"

"I know who she is—she's the one who killed my father."

"Who told you?"

"That man—the one you called Riddick. What I want to know is, why did she do it?"

"To keep your father from uncovering a secret."

"What secret?"

"That Victoria Braden is actually her daughter."

"But—how could my father have uncovered that?"

"He couldn't—but apparently a couple of other men could have over the years, so Agnes killed them. She only killed your father to keep him from finding their graves. I'm guessing that Riddick was after you for the same reason. I think the Bradens were involved; maybe they didn't want the information coming out just before the election."

"The Bradens? I don't understand."

"Neither do I. I'm still piecing it together."

Alena abruptly jerked the wheel and steered the pickup onto a smaller road.

"Where are you going?"

"Back to my place. I know a shortcut."

"That's no good. We need to find a police station."

"Great idea—just tell me where to turn."

Nick stopped. His entire focus had been on reaching the truck and getting Alena out of there before Riddick knew she was missing; he hadn't thought at all about where they would go next. "We could look for a town," he suggested. "Pull off someplace where there are lots of people around—maybe a mall or a restaurant."

"There are no malls around here—why do you think they're building the Patriot Center? There's practically nothing between here and

Endor, and nothing's open this time of night anyway. There's a thousand acres of forest at my place and I know every inch of it. If we can just get there a few seconds before he does we can duck into the woods and hide—I know places that he could never find."

Nick considered her idea. "Okay—we'll go to your place. We'll hide out there until he gives up and quits looking for us—then we can contact the authorities."

"I think that car is getting closer. Are you sure it's him? Can you tell?"

Nick looked out the window again and saw the headlights turn off onto the same smaller road that they had—and they were definitely closer now.

"It has to be him—he'll be on us in another couple of minutes. Step on it—maybe we'll get lucky and pass a cop along the way."

They raced past a green sign pointing to I-66 West.

"You just missed the freeway entrance!"

"I saw it," she said. "We don't want the freeway."

"Why not? It's the fastest way."

"Maybe for him. We'd never outrun him on the freeway—not in this old wreck. What's he driving?"

"Looks like a silver BMW 550i sedan. Probably belongs to the Bradens—it's too pricey for his pay grade."

Just then a car shot past them from the opposite direction. The headlights illuminated the truck cabin for an instant and Nick saw Alena's face clearly for the first time; there were purplish-black bruises under both of her eyes and across the bridge of her nose. "Did he do that to you?"

She looked at her reflection in the rearview mirror. "I bumped into something."

"Were you driving at the time?"

"I don't want to talk about it. Did you get a look at that car? Was it a cop?"

Nick turned and saw red taillights fading in the distance. "I don't think so. He's not stopping, and a cop would pull us over for sure at this speed.

Why is it you can never find a cop when you need one?" He looked and saw that the car behind them was steadily gaining even though Alena had the gas pedal pushed to the floor.

"An *old woman* killed my father?" she said under her breath. "But why in the world would she—"

"Watch the curve!"

Alena jerked the wheel and the truck swerved wide, crunching and grinding onto the shoulder and fishtailing twice before the tires finally grabbed the asphalt and straightened again. "Stop yelling! I saw the stupid curve, okay?"

"Were you planning to turn, or did you know a shortcut across that field?"

"Can you do any better?"

"I can't do much worse."

She glared at him and pointed to her nose. "See this? I did this to *myself*—I slammed my own face into a wall to make my nose bleed. Now do you really want to make me angry?"

Nick settled back in his seat.

"We need to find a gravel road," she said.

"Why?"

"Because the graders come through every spring and level the road surface here—it leaves a layer of loose gravel on top. We could lose him—it's like driving on marbles if you don't know what you're doing."

"Do we know what we're doing?"

She turned sharply and the car veered onto an even smaller road—a narrow gravel two-lane that wound back and forth and began to climb steadily into the mountains.

"Do you know where this road goes?" Nick asked.

"Up."

"Thanks."

He looked out his window and saw that the hills were quickly becoming steeper and there were no protective guardrails anywhere in sight. "Do we have air bags?"

She didn't answer.

"I'll bet he has air bags."

"Nick, *shut up*."

He turned and looked back; the BMW was so close now that he could see Riddick's silhouette hunched behind the wheel. "We've got to widen our lead," he said.

"Thanks for the helpful tip. Got any bright ideas?"

"I'm working on it."

Suddenly they heard the engine rev and felt the truck lurch forward, as though a giant had lifted the truck by the bumper and let it drop. It was Riddick—he had closed the gap between them and bumped them from behind.

"He's trying to push us over the edge!" Alena shouted.

"Slam on the brakes and make him run into us," Nick said. "It might wreck his engine—then we can pull away."

"Trygg is in the back—the collision could kill her. And what if we wreck our truck but not his engine? Then we *can't* pull away."

"Good point. I'll keep working on it."

"How close is he right now?"

Nick looked. "Our bumpers are almost kissing. Why?"

"Hang on!"

Alena steered the truck directly toward a sheer drop-off, then at the last possible moment cut the wheel hard and let the tail swing into the turn. The cab slumped precariously to the right as the rear wheel slipped off the shoulder and spun in midair before the truck pulled itself back onto the road.

"Did it work?" Alena shouted.

"That depends. Were you trying to make me wet my pants?"

"Did he go over the edge?"

Nick looked again. "No, but it looks like he's stopped. I think he dropped a wheel off the shoulder—he's trying to get back up onto the road."

"That should buy us a few minutes."

"Let's hope so—I think we're going to need it."

They followed the winding road up into the mountains for another fifteen minutes, constantly cutting across the inside lane to pick up speed while praying that no cars were approaching from the opposite direction. Nick kept watch out the passenger window, searching for any sign of headlights rounding the bend behind them. Then he noticed something; they seemed to be slowing down. Even though Alena had the accelerator pushed to the floor, the truck was gradually losing power.

"Can't we go any faster?" he asked.

"It's the altitude. Old truck, old carburetor—there's not enough air."

"This is no good—he'll catch up to us for sure at this pace."

"The back road into my place is just a few miles ahead."

"Is there a gate?"

"Just like the one on the other side."

"Is it locked?"

"Yes."

"Ram it—we sure don't have time to stop."

A few seconds later, Nick saw the trees light up in the distance behind them. It was Riddick—and he was coming fast.

"He's back."

"There's the gate—hang on!"

"I hate it when you say that." Nick braced himself against the dashboard.

She cut the wheel hard and accelerated directly into the gate. The metal poles bent back like pipe cleaners and the chain-link fence stretched like a fishnet under the weight of a record haul—until it suddenly gave way and snapped, raking over the hood of the truck and curling away from the road. Alena sped up the road toward the trailer—but before the truck had even rounded the last bend they could see Riddick's headlights lighting up the woods behind them.

"This is going to be close," Nick said. "When we reach the clearing just stop the truck anywhere—we'll grab Trygg from the back and make a run for the trees."

"Got it."

Seconds later the truck burst from the woods and sped into the clearing. Alena slammed on the brakes and skidded to a stop midway between the trailer and the kennels—and when she did she saw the lifeless form of Acheron still lying near the trailer door.

Nick threw open his door and jumped out. "Let's go! I'll get the dog!"

Alena opened her own door and looked at the kennels, where thirty anxious dogs stared back at her, eagerly wagging their tails.

"I'll get the others," she said.

"What? Alena, don't—there isn't time!"

"I'm not leaving them," she shouted, starting toward the kennels.

Nick dropped the tailgate and let Trygg jump out, then turned and ran toward Alena. He reached her just as she was lifting the latch on the first of the kennels; he grabbed her by the wrist and spun her around.

"Leave them! Come on!"

"No! He'll threaten them just like he did before—he'll kill them all if we don't come out of the woods!"

"That's a chance we have to take!"

"I won't leave them locked up again! I won't let them die like this! Let go of me!"

Nick looked back at the road—he could see Riddick's headlights flickering through the trees and he could already hear the sound of the BMW's approaching engine. What was he supposed to do now—throw Alena over his shoulder and carry her kicking and screaming into the woods? She was right—Riddick would use the dogs as hostages and he would kill every one of them to try to force Nick and Alena out of hiding. Alena knew it, and Nick did too—the difference between them was that Nick was willing to let it happen. The lives of a few stray mongrels in exchange for the lives of two human beings: That was an acceptable price to him—but not to Alena. These dogs *were* her life, and there was no sense arguing about it.

He let go of her arm.

Alena turned back to the first kennel and Nick hurried over to the second—but before either of them could lift the latch on the gates, Riddick's BMW shot out of the woods and skidded to a stop behind them.

Riddick jumped from the car and charged toward them with a gun in his hand. Trygg began to bark viciously, crouching low and preparing to attack.

Riddick aimed the gun at the dog. "Call him off or I'll kill him—do it now."

Alena snapped her fingers and commanded the dog to be silent.

Now Riddick pointed the gun at Nick. "I knew you were going to be trouble. How did you find her, anyway?"

Nick didn't answer.

Riddick glanced down at the dog. "So that's why you brought the dog along. He's the one, isn't he—he's the cadaver dog."

"She," Alena corrected.

Riddick shook his head. "You'd never think a mutt like that could do anything."

"Appearances can be deceiving," Nick said. "I thought you would have learned that from the Bradens."

Riddick shrugged. "I guess good breeding isn't everything."

"It isn't anything," Alena said. "What matters is what's inside you."

"Well, here's what's inside me."

He widened his stance and slowly raised the gun.

42

"I wouldn't do that."

The voice came from the direction of the trailer. All three of them turned and looked. Nathan Donovan was standing in the doorway with his own gun raised and leveled at Riddick's head.

Nick heaved a sigh of relief. "How long have you been standing there?"

"Got a call from your pastor friend," Donovan said without taking his eyes off Riddick. "Where've you been, Nick? I've been waiting here for hours."

"I've been a little busy," Nick said.

"Me too. Ever heard of a cell phone?"

"I left it in my car."

"That's the bad thing about a cell phone—you have to have enough intelligence to keep it with you."

"Someone's a little grumpy."

Donovan addressed Riddick now. "I know you—you're that private security guard I met in John Braden's office. I hate to break it to you, ace, but you just blew your chances for a job as security guard at the Patriot Center. Too bad—I think you were qualified."

Riddick didn't reply—he just stared at Donovan and blinked.

"I've seen that look before," Donovan said. "Right now you're running through your options, and you just don't have many. You can shoot Nick if you want to—"

"Donovan. Hold it."

"Relax, Nick—he won't do it. He knows that if he does I'll put a bullet through his head."

"That's a big comfort," Nick said.

"Now he's wondering if he can get off two shots—one at you and one at the lady there. It's possible, if he speed-fires—but he knows I'll still kill him where he stands, so what's the point? What he's really dying to know is if he can turn and get off a shot at me before I fire at him. Let me answer that one for you: No—it's just not possible. The way I see it you're pretty much screwed—and you know it too. So here's what I want you to do: Slowly lower your arm to your side and let the gun drop to the ground. Don't bend your arm; don't turn toward me; don't make any sudden moves. And if I even think I see the look in your eye that I've seen a dozen times before, I'll empty my clip into you—and believe me, at this range I won't miss. Do it right now—lower the gun slowly—let it drop. C'mon, kid, you've used up your stupid quota for the month—do something smart for a change."

Riddick hesitated for a moment—then slowly lowered his arm and let the gun fall from his hand.

The moment he did so, Alena lifted the latch on the gate and swung it open wide. The hysterical dogs immediately scrambled from the kennel and began to bark furiously at Riddick—all but one. The enormous black Phlegethon spotted the only armed man left among them and broke away from the pack to charge across the clearing at Donovan.

"Whoa!" Donovan shouted, taking a step back. "Call off your horse! Tell him I'm one of the good guys!"

Alena clapped her hands loudly, but Phlegethon was in a frenzy and failed to respond to her command. He continued to lumber forward, quickly gathering speed, and Donovan had no choice but to turn his gun on the advancing dog. He fired a warning shot into the ground, but the dog didn't even flinch—so he raised the gun and pointed it directly at the dog's head.

"Don't shoot him!" Alena screamed. *"Please!"*

Donovan looked incredulously at Alena, then down at the charging animal that was almost on top of him—and at the last moment he raised the gun and pointed it into the sky.

Alena kept clapping until the "Return" command finally penetrated the huge beast's frantic mind. Phlegethon instantly pulled up—but not before his momentum carried him into Donovan's legs and knocked him off his feet.

Riddick looked down at his own gun lying in the dust—but before he could reach for it, Nick made a headlong dive and landed almost on top of it, covering it with his crossed arms.

Riddick turned and bolted into the woods.

Donovan sat up in the dirt and stared at the woods while Phlegethon apologetically licked his face. "Now I have to run after him, and I *hate* running after people."

"Don't bother," Alena said. She walked from kennel to kennel, lifting each latch and opening the gates until the clearing was filled with barking dogs. She snapped her fingers once and made a quick spreading motion.

Every dog fell silent.

She walked over to the spot where Riddick had just disappeared into the woods, with all of the dogs following eagerly behind her. She snapped her fingers again and this time made a great swirling motion, then lunged forward and slung both arms as if she were flinging batter from her fingers—or casting a powerful spell.

Every dog took off racing into the woods, with little Ruckus in the lead and the lumbering Phlegethon bringing up the rear.

Alena looked at Donovan. "There's no hurry," she said. "He'll be there whenever you want him."

Riddick ran wildly, crashing blindly through the thick underbrush with his arms out in front of him to try to separate the branches and clear a path ahead. He had to run—he had to make it deep enough into the woods so that Donovan couldn't find him without help, and by the time help arrived it would be daylight. By then he would be far away and he could hole up somewhere and figure out what to do next.

There was a bright moon out, but the woods were thick and only broken shafts of moonlight could penetrate the dense canopies of the trees, leaving large areas of forest floor hidden in thick shadow. Riddick smashed his way through unseen branches and ripped through briars that tore little chunks of flesh from his arms and legs; once he stumbled headlong into a shallow ravine that unexpectedly dropped away beneath his feet. But each time he fell he struggled to his feet again and kept moving forward; he couldn't afford to slow down now—his life depended on it.

He kept thinking about Victoria and what she was probably doing right now—holding Johnny Boy's hand and stroking his bruised ego, doing her level best to convince him that trailer trash from the backwoods of Virginia could make just as good a wife as a blue blood with a seat on the *Mayflower*. *And she'll pull it off*, he thought, *because that's what she does best*—twist men like pretzels until they take on any shape she wants.

He stopped for a few seconds to catch his breath. He doubled over with his hands on his knees, panting and spitting and wiping his mouth with the back of his hand.

He imagined Vic's response when the authorities told her what he had done—how he had kidnapped some poor woman and tried to kill her, but had escaped at the last moment and was still at large. *She won't even bat an eyelash*, Riddick thought. *She's good at that too.* And he knew exactly what she would do then: She would deny all knowledge of his actions or intent; she would pin the whole thing on him; she would claim that it was his own insane desire to defend her or to protect her reputation—and then she would call down on him all the wrath and holy indignation of the self-righteous Bradens until she looked even better than she did before. And in a way she would be telling the truth: The whole thing *was* his fault, because she never actually asked him to do a thing. The whole thing was his idea—exactly as she intended.

Riddick shook his head—all this, just for the chance to be with her one more time. But that was the bargain Victoria always struck with men: not the promise that they *would* be with her, just the suggestion that they *might*. That was all she ever needed; that was always enough to get her whatever she desired.

He heard a sound in the trees behind him and looked up; an ugly little dog suddenly popped out of the brush and took a stand in front of him, throwing out its bony chest and yapping at the top of its lungs.

"Shut up!" he whispered, swinging at the dog with his foot—but the dog easily sidestepped the blow and continued to sound the alarm.

Now Riddick heard another sound in the woods—then another, and another. He squinted in the moonlight and saw the silhouettes of dozens of dogs rapidly moving toward him—and they didn't look friendly.

He turned and ran.

He weaved back and forth as he ran, thinking that he might out-smart the stupid dogs even if he couldn't outdistance them—but each time he glanced back he could see the dogs not far behind. They were bunched together now, traveling in a pack. They seemed to stride along easily, almost effortlessly—all except for one of them. The lead dog, somehow silently elected by its companions, would take off after Riddick at a dead sprint, barking and growling and snapping at his heels. When that dog tired he would quietly drop back into the pack and another dog would seamlessly take its place, forcing Riddick to run full out without rest while the dogs conserved their strength.

Riddick couldn't believe it—the stupid mongrels were working as a team.

At last he stumbled to a stop, exhausted, and turned to confront the approaching dogs. He bent down and picked up a broken tree limb and waved it back and forth at the pack, shouting and screaming at them in desperate rage.

"Get back! *Back!* Get away from me—go back where you came from!"

But the dogs simply formed a crude semicircle around him and began to lunge at him one at a time, each one watching for the right opportunity to move in.

Riddick picked the dog closest to him and decided to make an exam-ple of him; if he could badly injure one of the dogs, maybe the rest of them would learn the lesson and back off. He took a step forward and raised the limb high overhead—but before he could bring it down again an enormous black dog leaped forward out of the darkness and took him by the throat, sending him crashing backward onto the ground.

Riddick lay on his back staring up into the sky; the rest of the dogs quickly gathered around him and began to bark frantically just inches from his face. The black dog stood across him, gripping his throat in its massive jaws; Riddick could feel hot saliva dripping down the sides of his neck and he could hear the dog panting through its nose with great blasts of hot wet air. He felt one of the other dogs bite into his pant leg and tug, stretching him out like a man on a rack; two more dogs did the same with his other leg, and he felt a chill of primeval terror when he thought about his unprotected groin and abdomen. He tried to kick his legs free but the dogs just pulled harder; he grabbed at the black dog's snout with both hands and tried to pry it off his throat, but when he did he felt its teeth sink even deeper into his flesh.

He tried to wedge his fingers in between the dog's teeth and his throat, but once again the dog clamped down harder and he felt the flesh pop as the teeth began to puncture his skin—then he felt something else running down his neck.

The muscles of his neck began to cramp and he tried to scream, but almost nothing came out. He now realized that the dog was crushing his windpipe and he started to panic. He began to beat at the dog's head and face with both fists, but at such close range he couldn't generate any power and the dog just absorbed the harmless blows. He tried to squeeze his fingers into the dog's eyes, hoping to blind it or cause it so much pain that it would momentarily release its grip—but the effort only strengthened the dog's resolve, and it tightened its grip even more.

Riddick lay flailing in the dirt like a grounded fish, with each flop of his exhausted body a little weaker and less defiant than the one before. He slowly sank down and lay motionless, straining to draw each tortured breath through his slowly collapsing trachea. His eyes bulged out and he stared unblinking into the sky with a look of frozen astonishment on his face. His mouth gaped open and his swollen tongue jutted out between his teeth, and a final hiss of air was abruptly cut short. His oxygen-starved brain began to boil and his mind slowly faded to a single pinpoint of light—and when that light reached its zenith, it simply clicked off.

His hands dropped away from the dog's head and his arms fell limp to the ground.

The pack of dogs fell silent. They cautiously moved closer, sniffing at Riddick's inert body and pawing at his lifeless limbs.

They raised their muzzles into the air and with a single voice let out a low, long, mournful howl.

Victoria poured herself a drink from a crystal decanter; she quickly drank it down and waited for the burning liquid to steady her nerves. John knew everything now—her less-than-noble ancestry, her illegitimate beginning, even her humiliating birth name. To his credit he had said very little as she showed him the pages of the scrapbook, confessing each humbling detail of her true past. John seemed understanding enough, even sympathetic—though she wondered if it was the kind of polite and practiced sympathy he might show at a homeless shelter or a school for the "alternatively gifted."

She kept a light, matter-of-fact tone as she spoke to him, as if she were doing nothing more than briefing him on a policy issue or some detail of the campaign. It was a lesson she had learned from Eleanor Roosevelt, a particularly homely woman who lived by the motto "No one can make you feel inferior without your consent." And why should Victoria feel inferior? She had only learned these revelations herself a few days ago, and she took no responsibility for them. It wasn't about her, after all; it was about her mother and her father, whoever the irresponsible jerk was—about things done to her and not about things she had done herself. None of it changed any essential fact about her—about the woman she was or the things she had managed to accomplish all on her own. So she told John all about it in a simple, forthright manner, as if she were talking about someone else, because to be fair, she was—and she hoped that her husband would hear it that way.

She wondered if he did.

She poured another drink. For some reason she still felt that something precious had been taken from her, and the feeling made her angry and afraid. She hated that feeling—the feeling of being alone, of being the only one who was different. And she wasn't the only one, because John Henry Braden had a secret too—a secret he didn't even know about—the secret contained in the second scrapbook. Maybe he deserved to know; maybe she should tell him—at least that way she wouldn't feel like the only one standing with her dress up over her head. But Johnny was a vain and fragile man, and she wasn't sure how he would handle it. Maybe it was better if she handled it alone. It was okay; she could do it; she had enough strength for both of them.

She finished her drink and fit the crystal stopper back into the decanter with a dull clink. She needed to keep a clear head right now, because they had bigger things to worry about than who gave birth to whom. Dr. Polchak said that her mother had somehow managed to kill an FBI agent—Danny Flanagan. What was that all about? The news would have been nothing but a morbid bit of trivia, except for the fact that the old woman happened to be related to her by blood—and the whole world would soon know it.

Talk about lousy timing—how was she supposed to handle both revelations at the same time? If only the news about her ancestry could have been exposed first, giving her time to build sympathy and win public support—then after a few months the news about the murder could have followed, easily attributed to some sudden decline in the old woman's mental condition. But no, both events had to happen at once, and both stories would hit the papers simultaneously, giving the public the clear impression that Victoria Braden was the spawn of a deranged killer. How would she ever handle that—before November?

What about Chris? Polchak said that a woman had disappeared this evening: Alena Savard—the Witch of Endor. *Chris—the moron—actually did it.* If the man had enough sense to do the job right, it might actually help; but if he bungled the job, it would make things infinitely worse, because it would bring an act with criminal intent right to her doorstep. Unfortunately, Chris *was* a moron, and there was a strong possibility that he was already under suspicion—as indicated by Polchak's visit. If that was the case then her best option might be a preemptive strike—to accuse Chris of wrongdoing and distance herself as quickly as possible. Who should she call first? What was the best way to do it?

And what about the Patriot Center? The bodies discovered there were now known to be victims of murder. Would that news delay construction even further? Johnny was carrying the construction loans himself; he stood to lose a fortune. And even worse than the financial loss would be the scandal—which could grow ugly enough to turn the public against them and cost them the only thing that actually mattered: the White House.

But there were ways—there were ways to handle everything. She began to see options, angles, possibilities—but she needed time to think, and she needed to talk with Johnny. That was the answer—to take all these issues to her husband, to figure out a strategy together, because they were always closest when they were standing back-to-back, fighting off their opponents together. The news about her true ancestry would pale in comparison to these larger concerns, and as they worked them out together he would appreciate again the woman that she really was.

She felt a faint glimmer of hope as she started down the hallway toward her husband's study.

As she approached the study she saw that the door was open slightly, and she could hear John's voice speaking in a subdued tone. *He's probably on the phone*, she thought, but when she reached the door she heard a second voice: It was Brad, their chief of staff. She stopped at the door and quietly listened.

"I only get one shot at this, you know."

"I agree, John. Timing is everything."

"My question is, will we be able to recover from this? Will there be time before the election?"

"The public has a short memory."

"Not that short, Brad. Watergate, Iran-Contra, Monica Lewinsky—nobody has forgotten those."

"They don't need to forget—they just need to overlook it at the polls."

"But will they? That's the question we have to answer."

"Your wife is a very beautiful woman, John. She's intelligent; she's accomplished. Women like her; they connect with her; men would like to connect with her too, if you'll forgive the crass expression."

"I quite understand. Victoria is no ordinary woman; she's an ideal, you might say."

"Exactly. A symbol to other women of what they might become; a symbol to men of what they wish they could have. Your wife has brought you publicity and recognition that you never would have received without her. Victoria smiles and the camera clicks, and all that goodwill rubs off on you."

"But what if the ideal has become tarnished? That rubs off on me too."

"I suppose that's true."

Victoria stepped closer and strained to hear. She heard her husband say in an even lower tone of voice, "What I want to know is, are Victoria and I still a winning ticket?"

"This is your wife we're talking about. It's a moot point, isn't it?"

"Not necessarily."

"She's not just a running mate, John. You can't just replace her."

There was a long pause. "No—not yet. But I could go on alone."

Victoria stumbled back from the doorway; she felt as if someone had punched her in the gut. What did she just overhear? Is that all she was to her husband—one half of a "winning ticket"? And if he now calculated that she was more of a liability than an asset, was she about to be dropped from the ticket—or replaced by another "ideal" with a little less tarnish so that her husband might have a better chance four years from now?

She felt a series of different emotions washing over her like storm surges crashing ashore. She felt shock, then disbelief, then sorrow, then indignation—but it was anger that took the stage last, and it was anger that remained.

Who does that weasel think he is—and why in the world am I trying to pro-tect him?

She returned to her office and unlocked the top drawer with trembling fingers. She took the stack of copies from the drawer and tucked them under her arm, then charged back down the hallway to her husband's office. She reached the doorway in full stride, stiff-arming the half-open door with the butt of her hand and sending it crashing back into the wall.

The senior senator from Virginia and his chief of staff both jumped like startled deer.

"Darling," the senator fumbled. "I didn't know you were still—"

"It's a little late for a staff meeting," she said. "Funny—it wasn't on the schedule. What's on the agenda?"

"Brad and I were just discussing—"

"I know what you were discussing—I've been standing outside the door for the last five minutes. Tell me something, John. How are you planning to explain my sudden absence to the American voters? Am I supposed to just drop out for 'personal reasons'—or am I supposed to suffer a 'nervous breakdown' from the stress of the campaign—something that might win you a little more sympathy? Or do you have even bigger plans? Tell me, who do you have in mind to replace me on your 'winning ticket'? I think a wife has a right to know that, don't you? Or maybe I'm not supposed to think of myself as a wife—maybe I'm more like a campaign volunteer who just happens to share your bed."

Brad rose awkwardly from his chair. "Maybe I should—"

"Sit down, you little quisling." She tossed the copies onto the floor at her husband's feet. "I want to thank you for being so understanding this evening. I know how important good breeding is to you, and it must have been shocking for you to learn that your purebred wife has been tainted with common blood. It was so noble of you to just sit there and say nothing. Not a single insult or contemptuous laugh—not even a roll of your eyes—what self-restraint! But that's so like you, John—never looking down on anyone until after they've left the room."

"Sweetheart, I never once thought—"

"Don't bother. I understand completely—really I do. It's just not easy to be in the presence of an inferior—believe me, I know. And the idea of being *married* to one—it almost turns your stomach. I mean, what if we'd actually had children together? Can you imagine the consequences, mingling good blood with bad like that? What kind of moral or intellectual half-wits would we have produced?"

"Victoria, please."

Now she turned to the chief of staff. "I'm actually glad you're here, Brad, because my husband has raised a very important question: Is this still a winning ticket? A genetic inferior matched with a superior specimen? Can we really keep this charade going—won't the public be able to sense the difference? And even if we do win in November, doesn't this country deserve better than that?"

"Darling, I don't blame you for being offended—"

"Offended, John? I'm not offended—really I'm not. I just need to get these questions answered, that's all, because I have a career to think about here and I need to know what's going to happen when the voters find out about you."

Braden blinked. "About *me*?"

"You might want to take a look at those photocopies. I think you'll find them interesting—I know I did. Go ahead—I'll just stand here and say nothing while you read."

Braden gathered up the papers from the floor and began to look through them. "I don't understand this," he said.

"That figures—it probably has to do with your background, and no one should make fun of you for that. Maybe I can summarize it for you—bring it down to your level. I think Brad will find this interesting too."

She looked at Brad. "By now I'm sure you know all about my sordid past; the copies John is holding have to do with *his*. The copies come from a second scrapbook. My mother put it together; it must have taken years. Have you heard of my mother, Brad? Mom's a serial killer, but she's also a sweet old lady and a pretty darned good historian. The scrapbook contains a series of historical documents; some of them are more than two hundred years old. The documents are mostly genealogies and land deeds—pretty boring stuff unless you know what you're looking at. There are a couple of old diary entries in there too, and they make terrific reading. Stories about murder, intrigue, stolen fortunes, deathbed confessions about unforgivable deeds—real page-turners."

Braden stared down at the copies with his mouth gaping open. "Oh, no," he kept mumbling. "This can't be happening." His face was as white as January snow.

"I think John's starting to get it now—I knew he would eventually; it just takes him a little longer than most people. Let me sum it up for you, Brad. John's family fortune consists mostly of landholdings—thousands of acres in rural Virginia. That land has been in John's family almost since Jamestown, or so the story goes—but the documents in that scrapbook show the story isn't quite true. It seems the land didn't belong to John's family in the beginning—it was ceded to another family when Virginia first became an independent commonwealth in 1776. John's family apparently didn't like that—so, being the band of scoundrels and cutthroats they were, they stole the land—they murdered the people who legitimately owned it and claimed it for themselves. There was the problem of the land grants and deeds, of course, but they managed to work that out. They had a few lawyers in the family—wherever there are scoundrels, you find lawyers—and the lawyers had connections in the Virginia Land Office. You can guess what happened: The old deeds mysteriously vanished and new ones suddenly appeared.

"Of course, the other family wasn't going to just roll over and let their land be taken away, so one of them decided to go complain to the governor, Patrick Henry—remember him? Only he never got to Patrick Henry. Somebody in John's family ambushed him along the way—cracked him over the head with a barrel stave, according to his deathbed confession. See, that's the endearing thing about John's family: Whenever they do something immoral or illegal they always feel bad about it later.

"Now here comes the really fascinating part. Guess how John's ancestor got rid of the body. That's right—he got the clever idea to bury it in a graveyard, right on top of an existing grave. Who would ever think to look there?"

"The Patriot Center," Brad said. "The two-hundred-year-old body."

"That's very clever of you, Brad. I don't think my husband has made that connection yet, but then you always were a lot quicker on the draw. It's the result of your good breeding, I think."

"The Patriot Center," Braden whispered.

"There, he got it—I think a little lightbulb just went on in his head somewhere. That's right, John, the Patriot Center—and it wasn't just the body at the Patriot Center. Check the copies again: There were lots of victims over the years, all from that same family—the original owners of this land. Apparently they passed down the dirty little secret of what the Bradens had done to them, and every generation or two someone in the family set out to prove it. But every time they got close, someone in the Braden family made sure it didn't happen—and another body got buried in a double grave."

"May I see those copies?" Brad asked.

"Help yourself—here you go. My mom figured it all out—can you believe it? I'm very proud of her. She probably started researching Johnny's family when she first heard I was about to get married. You might say she ran her own background check, and it's a good thing she did—otherwise I might never have known what a scoundrel I was involved with. A girl can't be too careful these days—there are all kinds of poseurs out there."

"Why is this happening?" Braden moaned. "Why now?"

"Why not now?" Victoria replied. "Can you think of a better time? Don't you think America has the right to know if the descendant of thieves and murderers is in line for the highest office in the land?"

"That was centuries ago," Braden said. "This has nothing to do with me."

"I'm afraid it has everything to do with you, John. It exposes you for what you really are. Sorry—no more blue blazers with gold embroi-dered crests and no more starched pajamas—you're just old Johnny Braden now, an ordinary lump of Hokie Stone like the rest of us. John Henry Braden was born for the presidency—he was bred for it—he *deserved* it—but now you'll have to earn it like everybody else. *Like everybody else*—that thought just kills you, doesn't it? Or maybe it hasn't sunk in yet. Well, give it time—it will."

"That's not the biggest problem," Brad said, studying the documents.

"I thought you'd figure that out, Brad, since you have a law degree. Would you like to explain it to my shell-shocked husband?"

"It's the land deeds, John. There are copies of some of the originals here; apparently some of them survived, and they'll clearly prove that the ones your family holds are fraudulent. The original deeds are dated 1777—that's after Virginia broke away from the Crown and became an independent commonwealth."

"Very good, Brad," Victoria said. "You see, John, if the deeds were dated just a couple of years earlier, then the land would have been granted by King George—and then your family could have claimed that the grants were no longer valid. Unfortunately, the land was granted under American law—right, Brad?"

"I'm afraid so," Brad said, "and that opens up the possibility of legal challenge by surviving members of the original family."

"Translation: They can sue to get their land back, John—every last bit of it, including the very room where you're sitting. There goes Bradenton; there goes the Patriot Center; there goes every last penny you own."

Braden was shaking visibly. "No one has to know this. We can find the originals—we can cover this up."

"Spoken like a true Braden," Victoria said. "You're right, John—it might still be possible to cover this up. It was my mother who put the scrapbook together, and she probably knows where the original docu-ments are. But she killed an FBI agent tonight, and the FBI will want to know why. She might be tempted to tell them about *both* scrapbooks—unless I get to her first and tell her not to. She never has to mention the

second scrapbook; only the first one needs to become public knowledge—the desire to protect that little secret would be enough to explain
the murders she committed. I could go to her; I could tell her what to
say; I could handle this—but I won't."

Braden blinked in astonishment. "Why not?"

"Because I don't think this is a winning ticket anymore."

"Don't be a fool, Victoria—this would cost you everything too."

"Would it? I'm not so sure. See, I'm only in the first scrapbook, and
I can survive that. And as for the second scrapbook, who can blame me
for that? I'm just the victim of a bad marriage. How could I have known
what a degenerate you were when I married you? It's guilt by associa-
tion, that's all. Thank heaven my saintly mother was able to uncover all
this before it was too late—and it's too bad that the stress of it all drove
her to such extreme measures."

"You're out of your mind," Braden said.

"Am I? I can survive this, John—but not you. You're more of a liability
than an asset to me now. I'm better off going on alone."

"It would mean the election—the end of everything we've worked
for."

"*We?* I'm not sure I've ever heard you use that word before."

"Victoria, why are you doing this?"

"You figure it out. The election's over, John—we're out of it. You're out
of it for good; me, I'm not so sure. I just might wait for the smoke to blow
over and make a run for it myself four years from now. Who knows?"

She took the copies from Brad and looked at him. "If you're looking
for a job, let me know. I can always use a bright young man like you.
The pay would be the same—and if it's not enough, we can talk about
benefits."

By midmorning the Warren County Sheriff's Department was on the scene in force, barricading the wooded area with black-and-yellow crime scene tape while a CSI team was busy collecting forensic evidence under the supervision of the local coroner. The day was clear and hot, and the morning mist had already lifted from the ground; Nick and Alena stood beside Nathan Donovan, watching as the coroner made his initial observations.

"There's significant bruising on the throat," the coroner said. "That indicates a prolonged struggle prior to death. The hyoid bone is broken; that's a sure sign of strangulation. There are bite marks on both sides of the neck, but the punctures are small and there's relatively little blood—that indicates the wounds themselves were not the cause of death."

"Then what was?"

"I can tell you that," Alena said. "Suffocation—his windpipe was crushed. But it wasn't Phlegethon's fault. He only did what I trained him to do."

"And what exactly was that?"

"To take the intruder down by the throat and to hold him there until help arrived. Phlegethon would never kill anyone on purpose—he barely even broke the skin with his teeth—but once he has you by the throat, he won't let go no matter what."

"That's true," Nick said. "Trust me on that point."

Alena nodded. "He must have tried to get away. He shouldn't have struggled—I would have told him that but I never got the chance."

"He got as much chance as he gave you," Nick said. "He got what he deserved." Nick stepped a little closer. "You know, if we just left him here, at this temperature the blowfly and flesh fly maggots would reduce his body to a skeleton in a little over two weeks. If you look at the soft tissues around his eyes and nostrils, you can see where they've already begun to lay their eggs—it looks like grated cheese."

"Thank for sharing," Donovan said. "We can all hack up our donuts now."

"No kidding, it's an amazing thing to see."

"Sorry we have to miss that—but I think the coroner plans to take him away."

"What happens now?" Alena asked. "They won't try to take my dog away, will they?"

"I wouldn't worry about it," Donovan said. "A security dog attacks an armed intruder on private property—it was obviously self-defense. You shouldn't have any problems."

Donovan's cell phone rang and he stepped away to answer it.

"Now what?" Alena asked.

"Now the FBI starts asking all kinds of questions," Nick said, "and unfortunately some of them don't have answers. Why did Chris Riddick try to kill you? Was he doing it to protect Victoria Braden, and if so, was he acting independently or under her authority? That's the one unfortunate thing about his death—nobody can ask him. And you can bet the Bradens will deny ever knowing the guy—they'll make him out to be some whacked-out employee who just went off the deep end. We know why Agnes killed four men, including your father—but why is there a two-hundred-year-old body at the Patriot Center that was killed in the same manner? The truth is, we may never know."

"I wouldn't count on that," Donovan said, dropping his cell phone into his shirt pocket. "Two of our agents paid a visit to the Bradens early this morning—and you're right, Nick, they've denied everything. According to Victoria Braden, Riddick had become paranoid about losing his job. He was with her the day she visited Endor; they stopped at the library, and the old librarian showed them the scrapbook. Victoria says she took the news in stride but Riddick went ballistic; he thought the news about his boss's true identity would cost the Bradens the election, and that would mean his job for sure. So he decided to go after Alena—acting independently and without his employers' knowledge—to keep her from digging up any more dirt."

"Did your people actually believe her?"

"Not at first—but then she showed them the other scrapbook."

"What other scrapbook?"

"It seems the old librarian put a second scrapbook together, and this one held a lot of dirt on John Braden himself. Apparently Braden isn't the nobleman he thought he was; his ancestors stole all their landholdings from another family and murdered anyone who was able to expose them—then buried them in existing graveyards."

"The two-hundred-year-old body," Nick said. "All four victims must have been part of that family."

"Exactly. Riddick knew about the second scrapbook too, and he figured the Bradens could never survive both scandals at once—so he decided to intervene."

"And Victoria just handed this scrapbook over to you?"

"She said she had hoped to keep it a secret until after the election—but the moment she learned what Riddick had done she immediately handed it over. She said that she and her husband plan to go public with it—tell everyone all about it before it leaks into the papers anyway. They figure they'll take the ethical high ground and hope the American public is in a generous mood."

Nick frowned. "Do you buy that?"

"No—but it doesn't matter what I 'buy.' It only matters what I can prove, and I can't prove otherwise—yet."

Nick looked at Alena. "Don't you have a liar-sniffing dog somewhere?"

"Sorry—I'll get to work on that."

"I need to ask you a lot of questions," Donovan said to Nick. "Can you stick around for a couple more days?"

"Yeah—I can do that."

"I'll give you a call. Get the cell phone out of your car and put it in your pocket—you'll get better reception that way."

"Thanks for the technology update. Can we go now?"

"Yeah. Thanks, Nick, I owe you one—and sorry for all the trouble, Alena. You shouldn't have any more."

Nick and Alena started back through the woods toward the trailer. "Donovan's right," he said. "Things should get back to normal around here pretty soon. No more intrusions on your privacy. No more late-night interruptions. You won't have to worry about me climbing your fence anymore."

"Too bad," she said. "I was starting to get used to it."

They walked in silence until they reached the clearing in front of the trailer. When Alena saw the black lump still lying across the trailer door, she stopped in her tracks.

"Would you do me a favor?" she asked.

"Sure."

"Help me bury my dogs."

It took three hours to roll the dogs onto plastic tarps and drag them into the woods, then dig two shallow holes and cover them with earth. Nick knew that the burial afforded little protection to the dogs' remains; the few inches of loose topsoil offered no protection at all against the insects that were already at work reducing the bodies to bone and fur. But Nick knew equally well why burials were important, and it had nothing to do with the dead. A burial is a ceremony done by the living, for the living. A burial is a chance to say good-bye, and Alena deserved that chance.

They stood leaning on their shovels and staring at the fresh mounds of dirt.

"It's not fair," she said.

"What's not fair?"

"A dog lives only one year for every seven that a human being gets. You barely start to love them before they're gone."

"A blowfly only lives a few weeks," he said.

She frowned. "Nobody can love a fly."

"That shows what you know. My life is one long funeral."

She laughed in spite of herself.

"So what's next for you?" he asked.

"What do you mean?"

"You found your father; you got your little white towel. Now what?"

She reached into the pocket of her gown and took out her father's dirt-encrusted buckeye. She pushed it once.

CLICK clack.

"I'm a dog trainer," she said. "It's what I do. It's what I love. Tomorrow I'll make the rounds at the local animal shelters. I'll talk to the dogs. I'll find one that can do what Acheron did—one with the right gift. Then I'll bring him back here and I'll train him—one step at a time."

"Good. That's your gift."

"I guess I won't be wandering the woods at night anymore. That should free up my evenings—in case you're ever in the mood to climb a fence."

"Great—I'll bring my neck brace."

She let her shovel drop to the ground and turned to face Nick. She brushed the hair back from her face and looked up into his eyes. The morning sun rising behind him set her emerald eyes on fire.

"Thank you," she said.

"For what?"

"You came back for me. You don't know what that means. You just can't . . ." Her voice trailed away.

Nick cocked his head to one side. "You know, I've been thinking."

"About what?"

"Dogs and insects—they both detect the scent of death in very similar ways."

"So?"

"I don't think they've ever been studied together. A blowfly can pick up the scent of human remains from two miles away. Can a dog do that?"

"Not likely—but can a blowfly find a body after it's been dead for a hundred years?"

"Not a chance. You know, I wonder if we might have an opportunity here."

"An opportunity?"

"For further study. I was thinking—maybe the Department of Entomology at NC State could host a study. Dogs and insects—it would give us a chance to study them side by side—to compare their relative strengths and weaknesses."

"Are you asking me to come to Raleigh?"

"Just for a couple of days—maybe a weekend. Dogs and insects—it's never been done. I just thought—maybe—the relationship should be explored."

She smiled. "Dogs and insects. That could be interesting."

I must be out of my mind, he thought. *A woman who loves dogs and a man who loves insects—we'll never agree about fleas.*

"It really isn't fair," she whispered.

"What isn't?"

"Life. You barely begin to care about something before it goes away."

He looked at her face. It was an almost perfect face, and he began to notice features that he had never seen before: her upturned nose, her milky white skin, the faint constellation of tawny freckles arrayed across her cheeks. But there was something about her eyes—the clarity, the brilliance, the almost mystical power that seemed to grab hold of him and draw him closer.

He began, almost in spite of himself, to slowly lean toward her.

CLICK clack.

ACKNOWLEDGMENTS

I would like to thank the following individuals and agencies for their assistance in my research for this book: Morris Berkowitz, CBP Supervisor, Canine Enforcement Training Center in Front Royal, Virginia; my research assistant, Samuel Thomsen; Dr. John Strasser of Kildaire Animal Medical Center; John Smathers of Falls Church, Virginia; and all the others who took the time to respond to my e-mails, letters, and calls.

I would also like to thank my literary agent and friend, Lee Hough of Alive Communications; story editor Ed Stackler for his insights into story, pacing, and character development; copy editor Deborah Wiseman for her unerring red pen; my publisher, Allen Arnold; and my editor, Amanda Bostic of Thomas Nelson, for her helpful suggestions on the story; and the rest of the Nelson staff for their kindness and dedication to the craft of writing.